DYING TO FLY

JEROME GLADYSZ

FAWKES PRESS

PART ONE_

02 MAY 1964_
CAPE ST. JACQUES, SOUTH VIETNAM,
USNS CARD

Captain Stallworth felt uncomfortable with precautions. The Military Sea Transportation Service (MSTS) took 300 ships out of moth balls in the National Defense Reserve Fleet to bring war equipment to Vietnam. Unlike his previous trips to Saigon, this ship showed her age with the top deck jammed with H-34 helicopters.

MSTS pronounced the thirty-five miles of river from Vung Tau to Saigon as *particularly hazardous.* They sent an urgent message to Captain Stallworth detailing safety measures to be implemented immediately. From all personnel in helmets and flak jackets to sandbags around the bridge, it was more than he could stand. He crumpled the directive onto the floor of the bridge. "A pansy-ass, bunch of bullshit. How much longer to Saigon?"

Helmsman Malley responded. "Saigon Harbor Pilot Two-Five requested a steady five knots. They're boarding now."

As the Captain refocused on the river, he finished his single-malt Scotch. "On the last trip, the Harbor Pilot cruised up in his big, fancy Riverine. Look at the pile-of-shit he's floating in on now. Saigon must be crowded. I've never seen the pilot boarding area so far out. Can't even see the city lights yet."

The Captain hated an empty glass and searched nervously for

another bottle. A silenced .45 caliber pistol blew his head against the wind screen. His body pitched off his chair into the corner, on top of the crumpled message. Malley took the second shot and fell to the floor.

The boarding party of the VC 12th Sapper Battalion took control of the bridge. A small flotilla of fifteen junks disgorged the specialized units. Assassins proceeded to each deck, methodically killing every crew member found. Interpreters captured the eight helicopter instructor pilots and crew chiefs. Mechanics packaged maintenance equipment and aircraft parts. Crane operators swung twelve H-34s in their protective cocoons to the uniquely camouflaged junks below. A small demolition team attached charges to the hull in the engine room, set to explode by remote control. No sound emitted other than bodies falling on the decks.

Colonel Cuong Danh, Commander of the 12th Sapper Battalion ordered, "Abandon ship, board the junks."

Each junk motored in a different direction loaded to the water-line. They waited for Danh's scuttling charge. A muffled explosion tore a gaping hole in the US Naval Ship Card. The sappers watched it list in silence. Until it stopped.

Colonel Dahn shrieked, "Aaaah yaaaah. It must sink." All on board thought he had been mortally wounded. He shouted to the radio operator, "Junks with helicopters proceed direct to the Hon Heo depot. All others return to the Card."

Colonel Danh watched the leaning monster, stuck in the water, sneering at him. He called Sergeant Phu, "Set up a perimeter with the first fire support team. Dispatch the second team to the forklifts and dump the on-deck aircraft into the water. Hurry. The next ship is scheduled in less than two hours."

Sergeant Major Phu assigned his men. "Colonel...this was too easy. Where was the ship's security? Our advance party did not even authenticate when they boarded."

"You're right. Have the team leaders meet me on the bridge."

Colonel Danh strode across the deck while his men improvised to complete the mission. One after another, the helicopters splashed in the river. Expectant faces waited for him on the bridge. "Check all the decks. Bring anyone alive to me."

As the Sappers combed the passageways, they found a strange sight in the officers' mess. Five dead, fatigue-clad soldiers were taped to the tie-downs on the bulkhead. A sniveling little man, dressed like an officer of the ship, was discovered from a trickle of urine underneath a cabinet door.

The Colonel smiled at the shivering prisoner. "What is your name and mission?"

"I am First Mate Johansen. I am not in the US military. I'm a contractor of MSTS. The Military Sea Transport Service. Our load contains everything needed to train the South Vietnamese Army how to fly." First Mate Johansen's trembling eased; his head rose.

Colonel paused, "Did you have any problems? Was your destination Saigon?"

"Oh yeah. The new directives from MSTS were bullshit." He giggled, "We captured the elite SOG Team that came to secure the ship."

"Interesting." The Colonel looked deep into his eyes. "And how did you do that?"

Johansen laughed. "The cook poisoned them..."

Sergeant Phu reported, "First Fire Support team identified another US transport approaching. Second team has completed the aircraft removal."

"Perfect. Congratulate the teams. The National Liberation Front now has an air force." The Colonel drew his revolver. "Have all junks depart immediately. Go." Colonel Danh said to Johansen, "Thank you for your service," and nonchalantly shot him in the forehead.

━━

The next day the US Armed Forces newspaper, *The Stars and Stripes*, carried the front-page headline, "Viet Cong Sink Ship," with a picture of the listing ship next to the dock in Saigon. It read:

> *Monday, May 4, 1964 - An explosion, assumed to have been placed by Viet Cong terrorists, did not sink the USNS Card at its dock in Saigon. No one was injured. The Card, an escort carrier used as an aircraft and helicopter ferry, had arrived in Saigon on May 3, 1964.*

"DANNY, what the hell's she doing here?" Fred crushed another empty beer can.

Beau floated a smoke ring at the air vent. "This flight's chartered for the military. She's probably a stew dead-headin' it."

I laughed, "A pissed-off MP couldn't get her down the aisle, so I helped him. They even bumped two privates to give her enough space."

"No shit. Must be somebody. Kinda' cute." Fred used his church key to open another beer. Foam shot up to the luggage rack then dripped down on row 43.

"God...damn..." A snotty female voice emerged from the drip zone ahead.

"Fred. Quit shakin'em," I said, "Grow up."

"Nah, I'd never do that..." He flicked the can, like a priest blessing us with holy water.

Beau and I got some of that sacred stuff. Even a splash for the girl in 43.

She leaned over her seat back and squirted a can of soda into Fred's face. "That's how you do it, Dumbass."

He wiped his Cro-Magnon eyebrows with his sleeve. "I think she loves me."

A couple of rows each way laughed and hooted.

I smiled. "Want a beer?"

She stared at me. A peace sign in diamonds hung low in her cleavage. "Only if there's no scotch."

"Ya' know, Fred acted grown-up for the last eight months in flight school. We all did." I sat back.

Speakers blared, "This is the Captain speakin'. Tan Son Nhut is under mortar attack. We'll drill some holes in the sky until it settles down."

The cabin erupted in shouts and whistles, then petered out into an invigorated level of noisy recommendations. "Head fer Manila." "How 'bout Hawaii?" "I'll take San Fran-tits-go."

As the stew marched the drink cart down the aisle, the girl requested a double scotch. After the first sip, she looked at me again. "Are they hootin' for our delayed arrival or the attack on Tan Son Nhut?"

I said, "Yes."

A sour expression spoiled her royal smugness. "Oh?"

"These guys're scared shitless. They'll hoot for anything."

"You mean Uncle Sam's finest baby killers? Well, bless their little ol', merciless hearts."

Fred opened another can of beer. "Stupid bitch. We're goin' to war. Bet you made every one of those damn commie–pinko protests."

"As many as I could. So, what're you fighting for?"

"That Vietnam doesn't fall to the Communists. You know the domino theory."

"Actually, it is not quite proven yet."

"Oh yeah, says who?" Fred slurred with more dribble on his chin than usual.

It looked like a slaughter, I had to help. "What he means is, just remember history."

"I do. But can you understand the message of 10,000 protestors last week? In front of the Washington Monument. Do you know the polls showed voter support of Vietnam down to 47 percent?"

"Yeah, a bunch of ungrateful pussies." Fred squinted. "What a shame you didn't have a draft card to burn."

"You're goddamn right." The shrillness of her voice rose. "If they gave me one, I'd tell 'em to shove it up their ass."

"That's a bunch of crap." Fred loved his own jokes. "Which manure spreader did ya' flip off of, honey?"

"I'm not your honey." She faced him. "How did you ever get through flight school?"

I separated them before they got messy again. "When we got our wings, he was first in class, before that he graduated *Cum Laude* in engineering from Case Western Reserve and played college football." I offered my best bored, professorial sneer. "And you? What exactly are you doing here, other than checrin' up the troops?"

She toasted me with her tiny drink. "Journalism, *Magna Cum Laude*, University of Texas, now a columnist for the *Plain Dealer* in Cleveland, Ohio."

"Answer the question."

"I'm gonna prove this war is illegal and immoral."

"So, your opinion must be ours. Is that why we're fighting?"

"Not really. You're here to support the Military Industrial Complex...which dear old Ike warned us about."

Beau reared back in his seat. "Yah mean the dirty politicians, don't ya? The biggest war mongers of them all. What's your name anyway?"

"I'm Kaelyn DeHaven."

Beau smiled like a hunter seeing his first deer of the day. "Wow, hope you're not related to that ol' war-whore from Texas."

Kaelyn bared her teeth. "Kinda. He's my daddy."

Another announcement from the captain. "We got approach clearance. Buckle up. Chug those drinks. We're on final."

The Boeing 707 lurched its way down through the clouds. Torrential rain amplified a violent display of lightning and thunder so loud it stung our ears. As we landed, turbulence knocked bags and packages from the luggage rack. Soldiers fussed, cussed and deflected the stuff to the floor.

Giggling out loud, the stewardess said, "Felt like a big one."

Big one my ass. More like a belly flop. But any flop's good if you can stop.

When all wheels managed to stay straight on the runway, A grapefruit-sized chunk of fuselage blew into row 42, through two soldiers. It wasn't an explosion but an ear-punishing puncture from a large bullet ripping its way through metal, plastic, and people.

Body parts bounced across the cabin. A shoeless foot ricocheted off the overhead into Fred's lap. He screeched like it was his and pushed it into the aisle.

The plane jostled sideways. Pandemonium erupted and stayed with us at maximum volume. Disjointed groans disappeared under the thunderous roar of 140 miles per hour and rain ramming the hull. Water sprayed into the cabin, onto Kaelyn and Fred.

"This is the captain." He paused until the shouting stopped. "Get back in your seats. We'll be at the terminal soon. Emergency folks'll clear the wounded. Welcome to Tan Son Nhut." Everyone held their breath to see if this crate would stick together.

Fred held up the bloody foot and dropped it on Kaelyn. He screamed, "So you want to let those fuckin' Cong get away with this?" His eyes widened; his face glowed like only a ten-hour drunk could produce. "What cha say?" The roar from the damaged wall obliterated the response from believers in the aisle. Washed-out faces twitched and mouths gaped open.

"Talk about pissing in your pew." Beau murmured as the open holes sucked out a dense cloud of cigarette smoke. The stew's arms trembled as she covered the remnants of the men in row 42. Blood stained the white sleeves of her uniform.

Kaelyn stared at the empty seats. Bits of paper, clothing and debris littered her hair. With oil splatters on her face, she said, "They never knew what hit them. A goddamn waste. Gotta stop this carnage."

The aircraft slowed with one last, loud screech in front of the floodlights on the terminal. Emergency trucks and ambulances swarmed with red lights blinking.

I squinted through the water flowing sideways over my window. The sign on the building swayed. "What in the hell does MACV mean?"

Kaelyn spoke into the last of her scotch, "Material Assistance Command Vietnam, or more affectionately... Madmen, Assholes, Catastrophes, and Victims."

"Come on, lighten up. We didn't come here to discover a jungle paradise or to walk down a pristine shoreline. Uncle Sam taught us how to fly and now we have to pay him back. Then we go home."

She eyed the enlisted faces behind me. "These are the young and dumb. Once they know, they'll all meet me in the protest lines."

I said, "Nah, still don't get it, do ya? They'll do whatever they have to do 'cause they want to go home. Preferably conscious, not in a bag."

"Now you're the fuckin' dreamer."

"And, you're an asshole."

11 MAY 1966, 1030 HOURS_

FRED'S HANGOVER CREATED A ZOMBIE. All he could say was, "Aw shit. We can't let them get away with this. Beau and I steered him through the constant stream of humanity called Tu Do Street. People flowed by in over-loaded bicycles, motor scooters and busses. While GIs jammed the bars, shops and brothels. Clouds of blue exhaust stung my nose.

In the bubbling cauldron of Saigon, we awaited our orders from the Army to prove our manhood again. We conquered the greatest summit when we learned how to fly a helicopter. As an aerodynamically challenged aircraft, it had the flight characteristics of a bowling ball and the stealth of a cannon. Yet, it provided the unalterable joy of hovering on a treetop, landing on a wall, and flying backwards.

I loved them noisy buckets of luck.

Flying also required synchronized body movement, which alluded Fred at the moment. He mastered such extraordinary skills as patting his head and rubbing his stomach while hopping up the steps on one foot, backwards and blindfolded. Could it be that such extraordinary talent would graduate into a shit-magnet?

All I wanted to do was go home.

We stopped at a gift shop, where a poster-sized cover of *Time* magazine, hung behind the counter. Dated August 9, 1963, an attractive Vietnamese woman in a tailored red dress posed above the headline, "South Vietnam's Madame Nhu."

Beau stopped. "That's the Dragon Lady. The real power in Vietnam." He thumbed through a dog-eared copy from the rack. "She's anti-Buddhist, pro-Catholic. Claims the US assassinated President Diem, her brother-in-law, and her husband, Ngo Dinh Nhu."

International affairs never caught my attention. This baloney seemed like a soap-opera drama. "I suppose the CIA did the job?"

"They did." The shopkeeper leaned against the door frame. "Now she's more powerful than both ever were and hates our guts. And the CIA is after her too."

"Hot damn, I knew we would find a pony if we just kept on digging in this crap." Beau gushed over the possibility of an intellectual exchange on the sweaty streets of Saigon. But he was like that, a baby face where no hair ever grew, steely green eyes, fuzzy eyebrows and cherubic peach complexion. To compensate, he was a brain, a soccer jock, and one witty dude.

"Don't tell her she's crazy or they'll find you split-open in the river." This shopkeeper could pass for a lawyer or doctor with his flawless English. He had a thin neck, slicked-down hair and a high stiff collar on a cool-looking Vietnamese shirt. His refined features had never seen a day's labor in the sun.

Beau extended his hand. "I'm Beau Buncher from Texas. Where'd you come from?"

"I'm Trinh Le. Born in Saigon. Spent some time at Texas A&M."

"You're an Aggie?" Beau inspected Trinh and his store.

"Yep. It's a long story but I'm back in my homeland because my father needs me. I also interpret part-time for MACV." A note of sadness quieted his voice. "Madame Nhu inspired many with her morality efforts against abortion and brothels. Then offended everyone when she applauded the self-immolation of a Buddhist monk and called it a barbecue. It's hard to say who wants to get her more, the Buddhists, CIA, pimps, or the VC."

This guy had to be a professor or a spy.

"Where do you get all this stuff? Hollywood would give their left nut for a character like her." I shook his hand. "Danny Hellberg's my name. Did you ever make it up to Mineral Wells?"

Trinh grinned. "I learned to fly there. Flight Class 65-22. Quite a training program. I'll never forget the main heliport. Got lost a couple of times among all those helicopters."

A burly grunt with a wide-brim Aussie hat stumbled into the shop. He reeked of sweat and booze. The .45-caliber automatic dangled from his hip and clattered against the glass counter. In a gravelly bass he said, "Hey papa-san, you got good bourbon?"

Trinh's faultless American delivery switched to the vernacular, imbued with a groveling air. "You bet GI, what kind you want? Got Wild Turkey and Jack Black."

"Gimme both."

Trinh stooped his shoulders. "You got American dollar, GI?"

"I got plenty fuckin' money." The boozer swayed backward. "You ain't supposed to be asking for greenbacks."

"And you not s'posed to be packin' here." Trinh's eyes did not waver.

"Get the bottles, goddamn it."

"Put forty dollar on counter. You be very happy. This good stuff. Tax seal in place."

Boozer crumbled a wad of money out of his filthy fatigues and tossed it on the counter. "Get the fuckin' booze."

Thinh reached for the money and Boozer grabbed his wrist. "Now."

With a slow bow, Thinh stepped into the rear room and returned with two gleaming bottles. "Here you go, Big Guy."

A wide smile appeared on Boozer's face. "Now ain't that sweet," he stared at the labels.

Trinh moved toward the money and Boozer's fist shot to the side of his head. He crashed into the shelves and onto the floor in a shower of packages.

"Damn, I hate ass-kissin' gooks."

"What the hell did you do that for?" Fred stuck his big nose in and his bigger chest out. "That little fella didn't do shit to you."

Boozer rammed a fist into Fred's gut with such power that it lifted him off his feet. He doubled up in a ball. "I guess he didn't hear. I said I hate gooks." He wiggled the barrel of his gun under my nose, hammer cocked. "Did you understand me? Lieutenant."

A raspy voice commanded from outside. "Krotch, put the fuckin' gun away and let'm go."

Krotch eased the hammer down and turned to the door.

Beau muttered. "Dickhead."

Krotch spun around and jammed his gun under my jaw. He lifted me to my toes. "Listen, Boy Wonder, I can hear a fly fart at fifty feet. If you so much as breathe another word, I'll spread your red head."

This nutcase mistook me for someone who wasn't shitting in his pants.

"Krotch, goddamn it. Let's go." The command reverberated through the door.

"Yes, sir." He did a quick about-face, with two bottles in one hand and his money in the other.

With clenched teeth, I hissed at Beau. "Shut up, will ya'."

Fred lay face up. His thick football-player neck and his broad, farm-boy shoulders were limp. Blood trickled down his forehead.

I shook off my mental paralysis. "Fred. You, all right?"

"Not exactly."

Beau strained to pull Fred to a sitting position. "That's one mean son-of-a-bitch."

Boozer's odor arrived before he did. "Don't you ever learn, Wonder Boy?" The stinkin' slob jammed the damn gun under my jaw again and pulled me up like a flag. His eyes twinkled with excitement until Beau's size-twelve, cordovan boot kicked the pistol into the ceiling, and it discharged. The concussion from the muzzle blasted against my face. Hell, I had never been at the business-end of any firearm before.

The gun fell at my feet.

Krotch bent down to grab it. Right in front of me. "You smart-ass bastard."

I kneed him between the eyes. This time old-boozer flipped ass-backward and smacked his head on the floor.

My knee hurt bad, but it felt real good.

1400 HOURS_

The Officer's Club swimming pool served relaxation amid the squalor of war. As we got comfortable at the pool, two senior officers talked loudly about being "out of uniform."

Fred ignored them and stretched his sore, bruised ribs in the sun. "It's hard to believe there's a war goin' on. Only things missin' are some round-eyed beauties."

Beau chimed in. "This place is creepy as hell. All day I've been lookin' over my shoulder, thinkin' the next pair of slant eyes is gonna get me."

I said, "Relax. You haven't been here a whole day yet. Your ten-gallon imagination is runnin' away with your teacup of experience."

"Oh yeah? Fer sure our tour of Saigon was boring as hell." Beau squinted. "Savin' a local storekeeper and escapin' a drunken nutcase. Yes, siree. Enjoyed every damn minute."

"Nonetheless," Fred flipped an ice cube at me. "We sit here in apparent isolation while there are military operations less than 50 miles away. I wonder what's in store for us?"

Fred amazed me with some of his observations.

"You both got the jitters. My flight instructor told me the key to returning home. He said, 'If you don't get killed the first day in country, you're lucky. But, if you get through the first week, ya' got it made.'"

Fred opened another beer. "No shit?"

Beau held up his hands like a referee after a touchdown. "Got it figured. We entered Vietnam's airspace at 0340 hours this morning and made it to the Club by 1400. We've survived ten hours and twenty minutes of our first week."

"Hala-fuckin'-luya." Fred clapped his hands. "And only 364 days of this year-of-hell remain. Then we're either good-to-go, or we'll be gone."

━━

Hot and sticky took on a whole new meaning as the afternoon broiled on. Boredom and beer forced me to push Fred into the pool. He bellowed like a gored elephant and chased away the serene atmosphere. His splash landed near the only two other officers there.

The bald one scowled. "Com'on lieutenant. We're not here to swim."

It would have been a tragedy if water got on his plaid walking shorts, Hawaiian print shirt, and Army standard low quarters with black socks. The look of a career dork.

Fred ignored his remark. "Why the hell did ya' knock me into the pool?"

"Cause I'm not having any fun yet." I jumped in the water with my legs tucked in a classic cannonball. The slap on my back and the smack in my ears meant an enormous splash erupted.

Beau leaned over the edge and laughed at me. "You dumb shit. Your water-spout drifted right on the two perplexed, little pricks." Water dripped off their faces.

"Goddamn idiot." The bald one stood up to prove he was big, too. I lifted myself out of the pool to face an aviation sunglass case on his belt. It read: *Major Maxwell Ray*.

He said. "Very funny. What's your name?"

"Lieutenant Daniel Hellberg, sir." I straightened up. "Sorry I splashed you." My best attempt at an innocent, sheepish grin failed.

"What unit ya' with?"

"Presently unassigned. Get'n my orders tomorrow, sir."

All five big hairy fingers poked into my chest. His neck veins throbbed in disturbed unison. "Just pray we don't meet in the field. I'll make your fuckin' life miserable."

His buddy flicked water off his shirt. "Let him go, Max."

Major Ray's well-tanned, bald head beaded with water, like it was simonized. Dense peach fuzz balanced his head on both sides. Thin lips, pulled tight across his teeth, looked like razors. He tapped my forehead hard enough to shake water out of my hair. A barely audible hiss leaked from his scaly face. "Just pray Danny boy. Just pray."

"Well, fuck you very much. Sir." *No one yells in my face, much less pokes me.* "It was just a simple, goddamn mistake."

Major Ray's stance turned aggressive. His left foot forward and right one back. "You're the only fuckin' mistake here."

My chest imploded from the impact of something I never saw. It knocked me into the pool. He screamed as I went down, "Having fun yet, Lieutenant?"

I gasped for breath. My wide-open mouth sucked nasty pool water instead of air, like a fire hydrant blasting down my throat. Airless spasms turned into thrashing jerks on the rough concrete at the bottom of the pool.

FRED SCOOPED my damn-near-dead ass off the bottom. Beau pulled me out. All by myself I became a vomit comet, wrenching my guts out of my body.

Pool water never tasted as good as it looked.

Beau said, "You gotta great way of meeting freaks and influencing lethal actions. That Major didn't even watch you suffer."

Looking cool and collected failed. Some dry, hurtful heaves always followed the painful, nasty green.

Beau shook his head. "No way to fight a war. We're supposed to kick ass. Not get maimed."

I used the rest of the afternoon to recover with a shower and a shave. Fred and Beau fought another insipid wave of boredom by drinking all afternoon.

A big man, in civilian clothes joined us at the bar despite their moans. He said, "Saigon got a really cool floating restaurant called the My Canh. Lots of action, choice of whatever you want as long as it's Chinese. Not too far away."

"Sounds great. Why don't you show us the way? I'm Beau Buncher."

"Ted Bradley. Sure, let's go." Ted staggered on his feet and shook hands with all of us. He'd had a tad too much already.

We walked a couple of blocks to My Canh, a restaurant floating in the Saigon River about 25 yards offshore. Towering three and a half stories out of the water, it monopolized the shoreline.

Fred looked at the long stretch of coordinated colors. Turquoise and white covered awnings, shutters, tables and waiters. "It's packed already. Are they giving money away or something?"

"Yep, it's war time." Ted slobbered. "Even if you're not fightin', you're makin' a killing."

At 1800 hours sharp, music poured out of the aft deck as an enticement for us to explore. More than forty tables surrounded the dance floor of the grand ballroom, the wait staff scurried around in traditional loose-fitting, pajama-looking outfits. While we waited for a table, Ted took us to the highest room in the ship. A grand staircase, embellished with intricate carvings in mahogany and teak, led to the Lookout Bar.

Beau ignored the view of the harbor and focused on his paranoia. "We're sitting ducks here." His eyes scanned the crowd.

Fred pointed out the two majors hovering around a woman with her back toward us. "Look at your old buddy."

"That son of a bitch." I moved toward the stairs.

Beau held me back. "He has about thirty pounds on you, plus a hundred percent more mean. Not to mention the old oak leaf he wears. Don't screw with him."

Ted said, "Or her. Yeah, she's a bitch, with brains and balls."

"Sounds like the same broad we met on the plane."

"When she gets in your face, she'll get what you have even if you didn't know you have it. Doesn't matter if you are a slick-sleeve or a general." Ted looked serious stroking his big black mustache. "This is her second time here. I heard she'd walk on babies to get a story."

Beau got excited. "Yep, that's Kaelyn DeHaven from Row 43. Spilled soda on Fred. Gave the finger to the whole cabin."

Combed, dark hair contrasted with her crumpled fatigues.

Colorful gestures and animated body language mesmerized Major Asshole.

Ted raised his drink. "To the daughter of Senator Orville DeHaven."

With a flourish, Beau spit on the floor. "Fuck 'im and his crooked staff. Ruthless. Worst of what Texas represents in Washington."

Ted smiled. "I've been told your chances of throwing this bar across the room are better than you gettin' a piece of her. The waiting line is field grade or better. And remember this bar had an earlier life as a Montagnard canoe. One solid piece of mahogany hogged out by hand. Saved a French officer from the Viet Minh. You still can play with the bullet holes."

Beau touched the damaged contour with reverence. "It must be four feet wide. I didn't know they grew this big."

Ted signaled the bartender. "You guys ready for another round? My treat. It's good to chat. Who'd ever believe I started as a political science major at Grambling State." His black face beamed. "In the Army, I was a clerk with an intelligence specialty, but I got busted when I called the general a dumbass. So, after I got out, I took this job."

"So, what do you do?"

"Nothin' I could tell you about. How about you guys? You goin' to the First Cav?"

"How'd ya figure that out?"

"A lot of hot-shit pilots headin' there. And they'll need them 'cause their original team is rotating back home. Not to mention they have the most diverse landscape in Vietnam: rice paddies, coconut trees, triple canopy forests, beaches, and mountains."

Fred said, "With any luck, this'll be our last night here. We're gonna get hot or go home."

Beau wobbled around until he found an empty table. He twisted his beer can to about an inch high and flipped it in front of Fred. "Your turn, Sonny."

Always a competitor, Fred chugged the rest of his beer. He carefully aligned the seam in the can and shouted at the top of his lungs, "Heee yaaaa" and smashed the can on his forehead. Then he climbed on top of the bar to stomp the can flat. We whistled our applause.

A full bull Air Force type approached the highest-ranking Army officer, good ol' Major Asshole.

At the table, a mature Vietnamese waiter, with a long white beard, bowed abruptly and left. The Army officers rose to their feet for a curt conversation in which the Colonel motioned directly at us. Both majors turned with a coordinated, dirty look.

I locked eyes with Major Ray. He pointed his finger at me, squinted one eye, and squeezed the trigger of his imaginary gun. With a nod, I faked a wound and blew him a kiss.

When the Colonel left, so did Kaelyn DeHaven. The other guys in the room watched her cross the floor. Of course, anything vaguely resembling a round-eyed woman would turn horny heads here.

The little major glared at us. About five foot six, he could have passed for a drill team commander: gig line straight, shoes shined, brass polished, hair groomed, sideburns short, and clean shaven.

He paused, extended his chest, and marched up the stairs. "Good evening, gentlemen. I'm Major Gonzalo Scivetti." His twitching right cheek matched his high voice and Napoleonic air.

"Good evening, sir." Fred and I rose as Beau rested with his head down on the table. The booze had taken its toll.

Scivetti's demeanor changed. I could hear the firing squad chambering a round. "Colonel Wadsworth, Base Adjutant, complained you embarrassed the Air Force officers present. You also embarrassed me. You're just a bunch of fuckin' drunks."

"I ain't no buncha' fuckin' drunks." Beau spoke to the puddled beer on the table, and laboriously tried to stand. He lost balance, caught himself and knocked both cans of beer to the floor. One can landed flat and squirted beer straight up on Major Scivetti's pant leg.

All resemblance to humanity drained from his face. "Very. Fucking. Funny." The enunciator leaned over the table. "You are officers and gentlemen." His voice strengthened. "Not a bunch of dummies."

"I said Bun-cher was my name, goddamn it." Beau's lower lip sagged, and spittle dribbled to the table.

"If you don't shut up, I'll break a bunch of your face." The major couldn't stretch high enough to be nose to nose with the hapless drunk.

"You must be I-talian." Beau stretched the 'I' pouring more fuel on the fire. "But I don't care. You shouldn't mispronounce my name. Can you say Bun-cher?"

That ripped it. "I'll have you thrown into the stockade."

He marched down the stairs. The creases on his pant leg held up well under beer. Halfway down he halted to see who was flipping him the bird. Not a one. His stressed-out face sagged.

The sheer stupidity of the moment overcame me. I hummed in the middle key of C, "hmmm, hmmm." Both Fred and Beau stuck out their arms in a giant conductor's motion for all listeners to accompany the helicopter hymn. These boozed up baritones bellowed just when the orchestra ended its tune. Everyone heard, "Him, him...fuck him."

The words had the resonant, embarrassing sound of a bride tripping into the wedding cake.

Scivetti spun around with his fists clenched. If looks could kill, we would be dead meat on a toilet seat.

Gunshots stole the peril of the moment and the kitchen doors kicked open. Three gunmen dressed as busboys walked into the room aiming their AK-47s at the crowd. The band stopped playing. Dancers froze. Automatic weapon fire cleared the dance floor. Bodies fell.

Bedlam broke out. Everyone dove for cover. Tables overturned; glasses broke. Hysterical people jammed the exits, so Kaelyn DeHaven ran up the stairs. A line of bullets ate up the grand staircase towards Major Scivetti, who jumped over the banister. Kaelyn tripped at the top and slid into the tables.

For the Cong, it was shootin' pigs in a pen. They fired in short bursts with magazines taped together, simply turning them over as they ran out. The smallest gunner's long black hair cascaded over her shoulders onto the stock of her rifle. During a magazine change, two young officers ran along the edge of the stage and dove at the intruders. The Vietnamese clubbed them to the floor.

The Seventh Circle of Hell would be peaceful compared to this nightmare. The girl Cong tossed grenades while the others shot. Two explosions went off a split second apart with a deafening roar.

The bartender threw a whiskey bottle, knocking one of the shooters down. When the girl discovered our presence, she tossed two grenades through the smoke-filled air. I batted the first one back at her. It exploded with a bright, phosphorous flame.

I missed the second grenade, slipped on beer cans and crashed to the floor. Into a puddle of beer. On top of a body.

People covered with burning phosphorous screamed nonstop until they dropped. The flaming chemical had the adhesion of jelly on a donut. Another deeper explosion made grenades sound like cheap firecrackers, and buckled the floor, pitching the canoe high enough for light to leak in. We rolled over and over. I got thumped on the head and pounded in the nuts. With a crash, I jerked to a stop, with the body plopping on top of me.

Another explosion flipped us, wedging me where the canoe met the floor. I ended up on top, my ears ringing. The floor actively creaked, sounding like a crowd was dancing.

"Hope it's over." In utter bewilderment, my voice sounded like I talked through a pillow. I squirmed away from my wedged friend. When I opened my eyes, the sensation was darker than when they were shut.

My fingers explored the curvature of the canoe to a warm body part, possibly a thigh. I hoped it wasn't mine. They promised if we lost a limb, we wouldn't feel it. Right away.

When I reached an empty crotch, the legs came alive. An inquisitive, staccato, whisper demanded, "What in hell you doing?" Human contact could be so sweet, but it scared the squirt out of me.

I said, "Tryin' to figure out what's mine...or what."

"Or what 'what'? That's not yours so get out of it."

I jerked my hand away and hit my crazy bone. "Oooo. Who're you?"

"I'm Kaelyn DeHaven." Now he sounded like a she. "Someone fell on me. Was that you?"

"Probably. I slipped . . . this canoe saved us."

"Shhh. Listen. The rescue crew." My heart pounded out of control.

"I have a better idea." She pushed her hand against my thigh. "Why don't you get the hell off me?"

"Where do you want me to go?" In my best stuffy tone, "Mademoiselle, the restaurant closed, and the orchestra went home."

"You're a wise-ass. Where are we?"

"It's like this. The canoe is just a hair over my head. My elbows touch both sides. It's a hollowed-out log. Does that help?"

She straightened her legs. "Let's scrunch around until we're at least going the same way."

Claustrophobia smoldered in my mind as we struggled for a new position. I sweated like a hog at a barbecue. "There's only room for one of us to move at a time."

She stretched her body against mine until her breasts rested on my chest. Her breath smelled from cigarettes and scotch.

"I'm sorry. I guess I'm scared."

"Okay. No sweat."

"We're screwed." Her breathing increased. "Under the wreckage of a barge. On a river. In a foreign city. At a war no one wants."

I pushed away from her face. "What happened to Fred and Beau? And old Major Asshole? Maybe the lightning shooting out of his eyes caught his head on fire."

Her voice cracked. "But what if we can't get out of here? Will we drown? Who'll dig us out? Do you smell something burning?"

"More like stale beer and cigarette butts. I hope it's old smoke. Phosphorous couldn't start a real blaze. Could it?" I felt the surface of the canoe and the floor. "Not real hot. Just sticky." Operating in the dark was a bitch.

She gripped my shirt. "I can't stand it. I covered a building fire once and heard a fireman scream until he died. Can they hear us? Heeeellllppp." Kaelyn screamed like I was at the other end of a football field.

When she squirmed on my chest, her breasts felt much firmer. My confusion grew. Should I help her enjoy it or redirect her?

"Maybe if I bang on the canoe, they'll hear me."

I tried to pull away, but lights flashed in my brain, white flickered. Finally, the big black won.

"WAKE UP. DAMN IT."

My head hurt, inside and out. The cramp in my leg felt fantastic compared to it. "What happened?"

Kaelyn shook me. "Your head hit the wall when I elbowed you. Then the floor moved. Water started dripping."

"As long as it's not gushing."

She groaned, "Damn, quiet is spooky. I wonder if they've got enough equipment here? After the fireman's death, I did a follow-up story about the city's capabilities. Another front page, left hand column splash with picture. Watching a fire truck go by will never be the same."

I grabbed my thigh. "Oh, goddamn. . ."

"What's the matter?"

"The cramp I thought was good, isn't."

"Let me massage it." Her strength surprised me. She kneaded, wringed, rolled, hacked, and let her fingers dance.

"Wow. That's good."

"Daddy taught me. He could untie a square knot in your thigh by only working his fingers. One of his favorite sayings was, 'If you can find the right spot, you can make things happen.'"

"The Right Honorable Senator from the Great State of Texas?" I spoke in a syncopated rhythm, to sound more down-home. Her soothing pressure disappeared. The pain returned immediately. I suffered a heartless fate.

"None other. How did you know?"

"The barfly we met at the club filled us in."

"What else did he tell you?" Icicles formed from her clipped tone.

"Why're you so testy?"

"I'm sensitive."

"No shit. Actually, Beau just called your daddy an institution."

More like he wanted him convicted.

"My daddy is maligned constantly. You'd think, as a reporter, I'd get tough enough to handle it."

"And you work for the *Plain Dealer*, that's in my hometown." Her hand came back to life. The pain disappeared.

"You're kidding. Where are you from?"

"Parma. Went to John Carroll University. How did a nice girl from Texas end up in Cleveland?"

Kaelyn inhaled deeply. Her boobs moved.

I loved it.

"Daddy could have gotten me a job on any Texas paper, but I had to prove I could make it myself."

"My leg's crampin' like hell. Gotta find a different position." The canoe had barely enough room for us. Insufferable heat made her sweat like a whore in church. She turned our shimmy, squeeze, and scrunch into a slither.

"Maybe if you were on top of me." I panted.

She squirmed into position. Her hips nestled down, clamping the outside of mine. I whispered, "Nothing like a tight, hot hole, to make me scream in this suffocating nightmare."

"Have you always had it?"

"What?"

"Claustrophobia?"

"Nope. I don't. I'm just scared of small, dark places."

"I did an article on it, once, a child gone totally mad after being locked in a clothes chute. When did yours start?"

"As a little kid. We lived behind my mother's store, Lillian's Meat Market. Played in the finished part of the basement behind a coal bin, storage, and furnace. The rest of the area was walled up with only an eighteen-inch high crawl space. One day I snuck through a ventilation grill to explore with an old, dim flashlight. On my belly, I crept in the dirt across empty tin cans, glass, and nails. Every discovery excited me.Until I met the big rat, as long as my forearm. It didn't move but I did. In the wrong direction. The faster I crawled, the more dust I made, dry tasting, kind'a salty yuck. My nose stopped up, too. When my flashlight went out, darkness did funny things to me. Don't know how long I was there. My hands bled and my voice only squeaked from screaming. Through the cobwebs and dust, a light beam got me back to safety. When my brother saw me, he laughed at the little lines of mud down my face from my tears. I found splotches of black dirt in my hair and cobwebs on everything else."

She pressed her hand against my chest. "Your heart's pounding."

"Yeah. Yours isn't exactly standing still." I pulled her blouse out of her pants until I found skin. When I stroked her spine, she snuggled into my neck. Even with the dust, her head smelled like a woman should.

Faint noise stopped me. I held my breath. Voices said, "Come on, get the lead out of your ass. Move those beams!"

My eyes flung open to see nothing.

"What the—" Kaelyn bounced her head off the canoe.

"The rescue party's here," I said.

As she hollered, I yelled. We both pounded the canoe. The silence persisted. We beat the canoe even harder. I held my breath and listened. My hands swelled with pain.

Her sweat dripped onto my face. "They didn't hear us."

I said, "Can you scream?" Her screech would've broken crystal at ten paces. Of course, being less than two lips away helped.

She stopped. "Something happened. There's no sound out there." My nose accidentally touched her neck.

Her hips wiggled as if she were curling her finger, saying come on. I nosed around. She said, "What're you doing?"

"Don't you like my nose job? In gunnery school, they would have called it a target of opportunity. I just wanted to relax you. Okay, I really want to undress you."

"That won't help." She pulled away. "I don't even know your name. Which one of the three dummies are you?"

"You've been talking to the Major Asshole. I'm Danny Hellberg. On the same flight with you. Ya' called me a fuckin' dreamer."

She chuckled. "And you told me I was full of shit."

"Ta daaa." I loved her belly laugh when her knees pressured my thighs, her nipples hardened against my chest. Then her hips paddled slowly from side to side. Pressure against my stomach withdrew and pressed again. I held her belt. "Your daddy said, if ya' find the right spot, you can make things happen."

The ice monster reappeared. No longer soft and inviting, the extended nipples went flat. She said, "What're you doing?"

"What do you mean, what am I doing? What're you doing? How'd I find the 'off switch' again?"

"You brought my daddy into this."

"That's bullshit. I just repeated what the hell you said."

Her hips wiggled against mine. "Don't patronize me."

"That's the last thing I wanted to do."

"You don't know anything about me."

"Oh yes I do. First, you're nutty as a fuckin' fruit cake. Second, you'd walk on babies to get a story."

"Should I shoot 'em instead? I bet you voted for Goldwater."

"So, what if I did?"

"Well, I'm here to report on the desire of the Vietnamese people for freedom. Both South and North, the Viet Cong and the loyalists. Even our dumb draftees and those smart-enough to dodge the call. And why this puny-ass little war is costing a fortune."

"Oh yeah. That's right. So, every other war was free?"

"Okay, wise-ass. I'll find out who the crooks really are here. Is it our military-industrial complex or the Communists?"

"And your daddy's gonna let you bang around on the deck of his ship? When the largest contributor to Congress is the defense industry? Give me a break."

"Damn it, I told you." Her decibel level ratcheted up. "I'm riskin' my ass to record the right view for history. Remember what they say, if you control the past, you have power in the future."

I said, "Yes, siree. Sounds like you're Daddy's little girl to me."

12 MAY 1966, 0647 HOURS_

Kaelyn nudged me awake.

She said, "Water dripped on my neck. This goddamn thing's leakin'."

The drip smelled like a solid stream from a latrine. It splattered against my face. "Auch. Can you block it?"

"No way."

I wrapped my arms around her to find the leak.

She kicked the canoe and it resonated like a drum.

Dogs barked and howled. Debris moved above us. Each chunk had its own sound, some sharp, many muffled, some sliding away. Rescuers answered Vietnamese commands. Then in English, "You okay in there?"

I shouted, "Yeah, keep diggin'."

When they pulled the canoe away, peripheral trash and filth poured on top of us with brutal, beautiful daylight. My eyes stung with exquisite pain.

She said, "Tastes like crap, too."

"How the hell ya' doing?" Fred's gaze riveted on Kaelyn straddling my waist with my arms around her. "Wow. Hope we didn't interrupt."

"About damn time you got here." I smiled. Kaelyn peeled herself off me. More rumpled than when she started, but better looking than before.

In a class move, she fluffed her deep brown curls and looked at me. Her eyes glistened. "We lucked out." She threw me a kiss and reached for Fred. "What happened?"

He pulled her over the debris. "It was nuts. After Danny batted the grenade away, I dove for cover and landed next to Beau. The phosphorous grenade herded us toward the exit."

"What exit?" Then I noticed the big beautiful My Canh club had vanished. Only a huge pile of rubble survived, protruding out of the water like a grotesque island of garbage.

Beau reappeared with a broad smile, exposing his nicotine stained teeth. He had the scraggly beginnings of a moustache. "Actually, the exit sign glowed after the lights went out. About halfway down the shitty fire escape, an explosion blew both of us down. I mean the flat-ass, dead bottom of the stairs."

Fred said, "Couldn't get on the gangplank. People panicked. They bunched up at the doors. Knocked each other off the beam."

Beau helped Kaelyn along a tiny ramp. "Concussion from the second blast flicked us overboard like fleas off a dog. The walls fell. We treaded water in our boots, with dozens of our closest friends and body parts of others. No better than swimmin' in a septic tank. Thought you were a goner man. How da' hell did you find that canoe?"

"It found us. When I jumped for the grenade I fell on Kaelyn, and the second explosion knocked the canoe over us. Were you diggin' earlier?"

Beau's disgust showed. "We joined the first MP team to show up, once we realized you were missing, but the Vietnamese police argued about responsibilities. Our pleas got stuck in a pile of bullshit."

"More than forty people dead and about eighty injured." Fred looked dog-tired.

Kaelyn snapped into reporter mode. "What happened to Scivetti and Ray? Did they make it out?"

A small, pang of discomfort zipped through me. I had never asked why she was talking to them.

"Scivetti was standing in the middle of the stairs when the shit hit." Beau cocked his head with a grin. "He jumped over the banister right on a table of the Air Force brass. Major Ray was crawling on the floor to get away from the Cong. He dragged Scivetti off the table."

Kaelyn asked, "How'd they get out?"

"They dove into the river. Overheard the MP question both of them..." Beau paused.

A tall, well-built medic approached, dressed in starched jungle fatigues. He wore spit-shined boots that never saw a drop of blood. His heels clicked like a drill instructor as he stopped in front of us. "Miss DeHaven. Lieutenant Hellberg. I'm Master Specialist Jonas. Follow me please."

"Where the hell are we going in such a damn hurry?" I hobbled with a cramp in my leg.

The big medic led us to the waiting car with another medic behind the wheel. "To the US Navy hospital."

"What for?" Kaelyn and I sat in the rear.

"It's just a routine examination, ma'am."

"Do you have a cigarette?"

"Yes, Miss DeHaven." He handed her an unopened pack of Camels with matches.

"Thanks, my brand." Her shaking hands made the light-up longer. When she blew the smoke out the window, it was accompanied with a soul-moving sigh.

I sat back in the seat and tried to unwind, "Man, I don't think I'll take another canoe ride as long as I live."

She put her hands together by her lips. "Those poor people got killed because they were in the wrong place and the wrong time. We survived because we accidently fell into the right spot." Kaelyn rocked back and forth, her ashen face still. "I just knew we were going to die."

A disturbing silence snuck in. The noise level increased from the rough road. I said, "You mentioned you'd report on the respect for freedom, from damn near every side of the table. What's that mean? Can we get together tonight?"

Kaelyn did a doubletake. "I'll bet we can arrange something." Her smooth cheek bones, aquiline nose, and wide-set eyes accentuated an alluring smile. "I've been in Saigon for a month. Now I have to talk to real soldiers fighting the war. Gotta understand this miserable mess. And finish my commentary."

"What are the news wires picking up?"

"They want the same old stuff about war. Body counts of who's winning. Blood and guts of the young and dumb doing the fighting. But not the whole story. Nothing about the enormous task of sustaining them."

"Hasn't that always been the case? As the complexity of the weapons increased, so did the number of specialists required to keep those systems cookin'."

"What's different this time are the vast layers of bureaucracy and inefficiency."

"The standard baloney I learned in Officer's Basic was for every man in the field, it takes seven behind the lines to support him. And if he gets wounded, the figure goes up to eleven."

She leaned forward on the seat, "Yes, but this is 1966, the age of enlightenment, rockets to outer space, color television, laser beams... "

I backed off. "Nuclear bombs, the Cold War, and the domino theory." I didn't know exactly what this had to do with what she said, but it sounded good.

"Seriously, you could do this more efficiently."

"Do what more efficiently?"

"The war."

"That wasn't what they promised us. Our instructor pilots fresh from Vietnam said everything goes to shit in one flush when the shootin' starts. It's this aversion we all have to lead in the head."

"I'm not talking about that crap. In Vietnam there is new level of stupidity bordering on total incompetence indicating a vast conspiracy or deep corruption."

"It'll sell a lot of newspapers, won't it?

"You're damn right. They lose shiploads of supplies and simply write them off as a cost of war. These are ocean freighters, not merely a box car or two like the good old days.

"I can smell the newsprint and hear those presses churning."

Miss Jackal's brow furrowed. "Of course, it'll sell. People want to know. Who do you think pays the bills for me being here—Uncle Sam? He'd rather have me stay home, barefoot and pregnant, ironing clothes on a concrete floor. They would supply the American public with whatever they'd want, like this body count bullshit."

"Wow. Nothing like a jaundiced view. Didn't mean to put a burr in your bra again."

"But frankly, I think the most interesting story here is the one about the Emperor of Vietnam." She looked weird when only one cheek smiled.

"The what?"

"Emperor Bao Dai. Of the Nguyen Dynasty. Born in the Purple Forbidden City of Hue, schooled in Paris, and ascended the throne in 1949. Has at least five wives. As a figurehead for the French, he governed all of Vietnam. When Ho Chi Minh took over the North in 1954, he abdicated to Diem in the south. Now he wants to heal the wounds of the country. People are stirred up. Even the old Dragon Lady's fighting for him."

"She didn't look so old to me," I smiled.

"Did you see her on the cover of *Time* magazine?" Kaelyn stopped with her mouth open.

"I also saw her downtown, escorted by the Vietnamese and US Military Police."

Her lips scrunched into an *ooooooh* position. "When was this?"

"Yesterday afternoon."

"What was she doing there?"

"You're asking me? I wasn't exactly sure of where the hell I was.

We just escaped from that drunken, crazy killer out of some kind of special operations unit."

"Perfect, that explains everything." Her smirk didn't waiver. "What did she do?"

"She just popped out of the building and took off in her Jeep with the MPs."

"What else?"

"Wore a red dress and whipped out a shiny pistol as she left. Expected her to say, 'Hi ho Silver and away.' Commanded authority, for damn sure."

"Incredible. In France, she raised money for Bao Dai. But she was specifically prohibited from re-entering Vietnam. Are you sure they were MPs?"

"I know what an American MP looks like, and the other two were definitely Vietnamese. A hell of a lot smaller than our guys. Couldn't see clearly because they were too busy pointing their rifles around. I was too busy trying to look like a potted plant."

All of a sudden, we swerved to a stop. The rear door opened, "Miss DeHaven, please follow me. Lieutenant, report to admissions."

THE PHONY MEDICS who picked us up at the dock escorted me to a sterile smelling medical office with a desk, chairs, file cabinets, fancy body charts, and pictures of airplanes. As I sat down, an MP came in and saluted the flight surgeon. "Major, could I have a word with you outside, please?"

A slick-sleeve with no rank, branch, or name tag on his uniform replaced them. He led me to a maintenance crew room with cleaning supplies and motioned me to sit on an unopened, five gallon can of paint.

This mature looking nobody introduced himself only as a "technician." He told me to "sit." Another real charmer. With a ricochet technique, the tech checked me out something like, "Hi. How you been?"

I said, "Well, almost got blown up in this boat that sunk at the dock. Then was trapped under a canoe but got rescued. I hurt all over."

He continued to write on the form. "How ya' feeling?"

You got to just love someone who listens so carefully.

"Which part of 'hurt all over' is confusing?"

He didn't look up. "Thank you. Where do you hurt?"

"Only in every part of my body. Of course, my soul cries out, my mind is a wreck, and my love life probably will never be the same."

He still didn't look up. "Are ya' bleeding?"

"Let me expose the bullet holes in my stomach. I used corks to stop the flow. Nothing to worry about though."

His cursive in obnoxious red ink showed no clue to his identity nor the meaning of anything he wrote on the paper. "Can you stand?"

"Didn't you lead me here from the other office?"

"Count to ten, lieutenant." He showed real professional authority in his revised, guttural, two-octave-lower tone. I noticed a pistol bulge underneath his fatigue top.

"What are we trying to find out, your IQ or sperm count?" I hoped one of these precious shots would hit pay dirt. "In Polish or English?"

He looked me in the eye. "How many fingers do you see?"

"Just one." I gave him the bird.

His implacability did not waver. "Hell, you're all right, licutenant. Go back to duty."

The exam fell below zero on the standard contempt-for-incompetence scale. He passed me the clipboard with the medical form. "Sign here."

Those words barely left his lips when a non-commissioned officer materialized with the name "Pollhill" on his uniform. "Lieutenant, you ready to roll?"

I scribbled the words "John Hancock" on the form. "Well, I don't know about rolling, but I can still walk pretty well." And in my most non-threatening voice with an ingratiating smile, I said, "Gentlemen, I need a moment to say good-bye to the young lady I came in with—"

"Don't think so, Lieutenant." He spit out the words. "Gotta get back to Camp Alpha."

▭

They thought I wanted to miss the war. And the worst part was I actually did. By the end of my second year in the Reserve Officer Training Corps, I had to decide whether to continue with ROTC or take my chances with the draft. Since I worked part time at the cemetery, I sought counsel from one of the grave diggers, a real intellectual giant called Hoe. A veteran of the Polish Army.

From his perch high on the big Massey-Ferguson tractor he said, "Danny, you will make over two-forty a month as an officer. Isn't that better than eighty-seven as an enlisted? You gotta go anyway."

I said, "But there is not even a damn war to go to."

Hoe hesitated, "My friend, don't worry. Shit happens. War happens. Everyone dies. Hope you don't see it."

▭

In the midst of this unrelenting idiocy, I finally believed Pollhill. With a smile, I turned to the Sergeant, "Give me a few minutes with that slick little brunette?"

"No sir, I can't. My orders are to get you back into Camp Alpha." He had the sincerity of a state trooper writing a speeding ticket for forty-one in a forty.

"But we're going out tonight."

"I don't think you'll have to worry, Lieutenant. You're gonna be on a flight northbound in thirty minutes."

Why did this sound so bizarre to me?

"Who gave you those orders, Sarge?"

"Does it matter?"

"I spent the whole night trapped and now you're haulin' me off like I went AWOL."

"Lieutenant," the cheery bastard shouted as the Jeep stopped in front of the processing center. "You're in the fuckin' army and this is a war. Now get your goddamn orders and duffel bag, so I can take your skinny little ass to the airport. You gotta plane to catch, boy."

The bloom had definitely fallen off this rose. At the processing center, the staff had my orders ready to go. Sergeant Bandibarg directed the show. A sack of shit in starch and creases.

"Lieutenant Hellberg, we sure are pleased you could join us again. No telling how many Cong are out there, shivering in their sandals, knowing you're on your way." He handed my orders with a smile, proud of those store-bought teeth.

I scanned my instructions with the expectation of a flurry of trumpets, a slow drumroll, and a double-knee genuflection by all those present. Then they'd say in unison, "Olly, olly, oxen free."

"Lieutenant. We gonna get this show on the road or not?" Genghis Pollhill moved toward me with fighting on his mind. "This wagon train gotta roll." He put his big meat hooks on my arm.

I knocked his paws off. "Stick it up your ass. I'm getting real tired of this bullshit."

Bandibarg stepped between us. "Pollhill, there's no need to rag his ass. What's the problem?"

"My orders are to get him on the An Khe flight at zero nine hundred hours." Pollhill looked into his eyes from a three-inch height advantage.

I turned to Bandibarg. "Next time you see Miss DeHaven, could you get a number?" I grabbed my duffel and strode to the Jeep. "Sarge, are you going to get off your dead ass and get this boat in the creek? I'm tired of waitin' on ya'."

Reckless abandon paled in comparison to the way Genghis abused that Jeep through the crowded streets. Ending with a screech-your-brakes-off-stop in front of the airport hangar, the radiator spewed steam from the grill. He dismounted like an angry rodeo cowboy from a horse that wouldn't buck. "Now listen up, Lieutenant."

"What, no leg irons?" I leaned toward him.

He said, "I'm real tired of your goddamn jokes. Now, stay in this Jeep. I'll see which one of them birds you need to get on."

The temptation to test the strength of his heart was irresistible. I stepped away from the Jeep and leaned against the building. Out of sight.

Right on cue, Pollhill busted out of the building, saw the empty Jeep and released a litany of curses, vile and debased enough to make a grave digger blush. He jerked out his .45 and went into a crouch, holding the gun in two hands, searching the field in front of him. A real nutso driven by something deeper than a simple order to get me to the church on time.

"Great position, Sergeant." I stood behind him as he pivoted at me. This was like old times, as I peered down the gun barrel held by a lunatic.

"You son of a bitch."

"That's your son of a bitch, sir."

"And the last time you'll fun with me." He cocked the hammer. The barrel rested on the tip of my nose. He said, "It's not nice to fuck with Pappy Pollhill." A trace of a smile appeared as he flicked me on the side of the head with the gun. Kind of like swatting a fly with a hammer. Pain replaced my brain. It stressed the bone, alone in my dome.

I was a bone head.

A VOICE SHOUTED over the roar of the aircraft engines, "Lieutenant, how ya' feeling?"

I said, "Like shit." Vibrations from the wall shook my eyes open.

The loadmaster stood in front of me in his dirty Air Force fatigues, a headset slipped around his sweaty neck. "And you look even worse."

Flakes of sand and dried blood came off my throbbing head. I winced touching my swollen eyelid. "Where are we?"

"Along the east coast of South Vietnam, slightly over the South China Sea. About halfway between Saigon and An Khe, your new home at the First Cavalry Division."

"How'd I get here?"

"Some big-old sergeant dropped you off. Literally. Your eye puffed up from the sudden stop your face made against the cargo deck."

I remembered the pistol in my nose but then the lights went out. Now my duffel bag and I sat in the rear of the cavernous aircraft, as big as my mother's garage. "What are we flying in?"

"This is a C-123, one of our finest troop transports for you and over fifty of your closest friends." He sniffed and grinned at me. "Good party, huh?"

I hated patronizing smiles. "I wish it was." A smelly wetness covered my chest, pants, and boots. Like spilled whiskey on a bar rag. The other passengers wouldn't look at me.

Then a pair of polished boots, starched fatigues, gleaming belt buckle, and the nightmare gig line materialized next to my seat. "Lieutenant, what in the hell is the matter with you?" The voice of doom boomed.

Was it the mistake in the swimming pool, or maybe the hymn at the club? Gad, how lucky could I be?

He said, "You're such a dumb shit."

"Thanks major. I love you too."

"Change into another pair of fatigues before we land. Even in a combat zone, you look like puddle of puke."

The major asshole could have been right, but I doubted it. "Major, I don't even know what happened to me."

"Well, they drug you in here unconscious. Another casualty from a bar fight gone wrong?" His pompous face faded in and out of focus.

"That's just it. I hadn't had a drink since the My Canh club last night."

"So, what happened to you? Did your fairy godmother piss on your punkin'?"

"I don't know. When they rescued me and Kaelyn, they took us to the hospital. Then some sergeant latched on to me like I was on the ten most wanted list and hustled me out of camp."

"What do you mean, you and *Kaelyn*?" His skinny eyebrows jumped with the question.

"We were next to the bar when the whole place blew."

"How'd you get out?"

"The bar tipped over and sheltered us from the explosions. Anyway, this NCO, I can't remember his name, was a real jerk. Cold cocked me like a criminal. Next thing I knew, I woke up in this aircraft, with a swollen head and stink all over."

Scivetti's face resumed its compassionless stare. "That's bullshit." His ball bearing eyes didn't move in their crusted sockets. "If I was your C.O., I'd nail your ass to a flagpole until you shape up and fly right. Or let you die trying."

This time I bit my lip rather than tell Major Asshole where to stick it. With a little luck, he'd be another bad dream and go away. I got into a pair of clean fatigues for a noisy, achy, and I hoped, deep sleep.

Rough weather jolted me awake for the first glimpse of my new home in An Khe. Endless rows of tents and dirt roads around a giant green area laced with lines of helicopters.

A fixed-wing runway butted up to a hill in the center. Actually, it looked like a tiny mountain with a giant patch on top. The mighty horse blanket, in yellow and black, was more like a triangle with a bold black stripe and a horse's head. I said, "Cool."

"Buckle in, Lieutenant." The loadmaster stood in the aisle. "We'll be landing soon." I didn't have enough time to find my seat belt when we slammed into the PSP runway. With a sly grin he said, "The pilot slipped in with a tactical approach to minimize our time on short final. A few flights got shot up here this week."

On the ground, An Khe sat a world apart from Tan Son Nhut in Saigon. Dirt roads and dusty green tents were all dress-right-dress, evenly spaced. Only a few framed buildings with corrugated steel roofs punctuated the line of bleak, canvas monotony. A large billboard displayed the slogan, "1st Air Cavalry Division is the First Team". The image grew complicated with an M-16 crossed with a lightning bolt over aviation wings.

Everyone on the aircraft herded to the processing tent. "Welcome to Camp Radcliffe," roared the world's oldest captain. With close-cropped gray hair, ruddy face, and a voice that could make bricks move. "The 1st Calvary Division is commanded by Major General Norton, currently engaged in second phase of Operation Davy Crockett. We're sweeping Binh Dinh Province and re-entering the Bong Song Plains." He attempted to pull up his pants over his distended stomach. "You're the very first, large wave of replacements."

This felt like flight school orientation. My eyelids felt heavier than my face could hold. I woke up when the captain said, "These troopers have been together for years and they know what they're doing. You're a bunch of new guys, FNGs, so pay attention and you'll survive."

Old fatso was a real bucket of cheer.

The FNG'S listened to a long litany of assignments until, "Hellberg, Daniel, J., Second Lieutenant, 229th Assault Helicopter Battalion."

"Assault helicopters, whoa . . . shit, am I ready," I muttered. It was the first unit that sounded like it should be in a war.

The captain interrupted my reverie with, "Scivetti, Gonzalo, A., Major, 229th."

A never-ending nightmare tightened around my neck. Scivetti stood with a group of field grade officers and laughed. His self-satisfying smile found me and seemed to say, "Gotcha, boy."

Blood rushed to my face. Visions of misery danced through my head. I muttered to myself, "He couldn't give KP to an officer, could he? Are public whippings still prohibited? Didn't trials precede nailing to a flagpole?" I wasn't going to let the giant finger of fate flick me in the nuts again.

A Jeep and a driver waited for us outside the tent. Another silent ride while I pieced together all that happened since I got into country. Sergeant Bandibarg's survival plan echoed in my head, "live through the first one hundred and twenty hours and you got it made." I started counting.

We pulled up next to the Command Post and another huge sign announced: "229th Aviation Battalion. Winged Assault."

I said, "These boys love their signs."

Scivetti did not respond. He deserved another hymn. The driver went into deep minutiae, well memorized, as exciting as spit on the floor. "Yes sir. The insignia of this battalion is dominated by a light-ning bolt, indicative of the swiftness of the strike capabilities."

The Command Post was not much for pomp and circumstance.

Sergeant Major Hereford greeted us, "Welcome Major. Lieu-tenant." He saluted with a smile showing his brilliant white teeth against a well-tanned face. "We are proud to have you here."

"Major Scivetti, you've been assigned as the executive officer of A Company." Herford paused, "you lucked out Lieutenant, you're going there too. You'll be taken to their OPS tent for further instructions."

It may not have been the end of the world, but I felt the heat from the edge.

Major Scivetti stood with the malignant sneer of a frog after eating a fast, fat fly. I felt water flushing around my head, as I swirled down yet another toilet.

PART TWO_

A Company operations tent appeared even less pretentious than the Battalion Command Post if that was possible. No large painted signs but rather a six-foot-tall, blue plywood triangle leaned against the flapped entrance of a dreary, GP medium tent.

Inside, Beau Buncher beamed. "Welcome to A Company, about time you got here." He stood in front of the center table. Plastic covered maps and a scheduling board hung on the center pole behind him.

Major Scivetti ignored us and walked to the rear of the tent.

I asked, "What're you doing here?"

"Helping the operations officer. He split for a battalion meeting around 1300 hours and left me here to mind the store."

"Where's Fred?"

"Assigned to the guns of D Company. Haven't seen him since." Beau froze with a cigarette dangling from his lip.

"Lieutenant Hellberg."

I spun around to a soldier in an OD tee shirt with deep set, dark eyes twinkling in a happy glow. "I'm Lieutenant Colonel Exton Givens. A Company commander. Glad to have you here."

If my heels weren't rubber, they would have clicked when I shot off my best salute yet. He returned it and extended his hand with teeth showing around the cigar he chewed.

In my best deadpan, I looked him in the eye, "Exactly, which company do you command?"

The next few moments took forever looking over his shoulder at Beau, he said, "This guy better be good, not enough folks around here have the balls to be smart-ass with me."

Everyone except Scivetti laughed. I quietly exhaled.

"We have to be at ease here. This is real-time war. Generally, there is no saluting. No standing at attention. No nothing, just a firm handshake, a pat on the back, and a jump when called. But," he connected with each of us, "we always fly in a tight formation. There's no room for bullshit. No idle talk, a lot of listening. A whole bunch of paying attention. Transmitting only when you have to. And responding when addressed. Directly."

Wow. The guy had attitude. I hoped I remembered what in the hell he said.

He eased back into his smile, "Just call me Six."

"You betchum, Red Rider." Sometimes, the damnedest things slipped out of my mouth.

Six laughed hard enough to make his shoulders jump. "You're the first of the new gang so the old guys can rotate back to the States. You have no idea how glad they'll be to see you."

I said, "This may sound weird, but I'm glad to be here. The word is you know what you're doing."

He glanced over his shoulder at the imaginary listener. "We know the system, and how to survive it. But we do what we have to, when we have to do it."

In his mid-thirties, a little over six-foot-tall, the Colonel's solid build was like a slightly-out-of-shape linebacker. His black hairline receded unevenly and added to his innocent accountant look. Yet he created a positive force-field of authority with a strong, square face that said the body blows stopped here. Perfect for a commander of an assault helicopter company.

"What in the hell happened to your face." He inspected my eye.

"You really don't want to know, it's a long story—"

"If I didn't want to know, I wouldn't have asked." Six grabbed my arm and looked at Buncher and Scivetti. "Now I want y'all to come to the Officer's Club and let me buy you a drink...meet the rest of the company. Be there at twenty-hundred hours. In the meantime, the First Sergeant will getcha squared away."

In the mess tent, I ate every morsel left from lunch, plus a couple of things scheduled for dinner. I *ooohed* and *aaaahed* to the complete delight of the mess crew. When I finally got up, they applauded. Friends for life.

Quarters were next on the agenda. The First Platoon lived in a GP medium tent draped over a wooden frame. Bamboo matting formed a wainscot on the bottom half and a wire mesh screen completed the wall. Inside, a soft hue settled over the profusion of mosquito nets, held up by every conceivable method of suspension. It looked like we stepped back in time into those WWII movies, but dingier. The musty smell was thick enough to cut with a knife.

"You get the room with a view." A soft-spoken man came toward me. He had thinning, grayish blond hair neatly combed. "I'm L. Sidney Crenshaw, Chief Warrant Officer. Call me L. Sid. Welcome to the Continental Palace."

He gestured to the rest of the tent. "This is the fabled home of the First Platoon. In A Company, we live in the lap of luxury. Not necessarily hot and cold running hooch maids, but a generous quantity of live-in mosquitoes. Fashion-conscious netting hangs in any decorator color you want as long as it's OD. And all the bunkers you want to hide in."

We shook hands. "I'm Danny. Glad to be here."

"Bullshit. But we're glad you think you're glad. You may be the gladdest one here, but a sight for sore eyes, nonetheless. Or maybe it's your sore eyes are a sight." He squeezed my shoulder in a warm way, more like a pat. His slender hand matched his build, a comfortable academic, definitely not a jock.

"Unfortunately, your room with a view is not all it was cracked up to be. The corner bunk does provide a nice breeze unless it's raining, then it blows in on you. But it doesn't matter much because it also leaks, actually a generous reference to water flow more like a dry-gulch flood. But alas, it's the best we can do until someone gets killed or goes home. We've been back at base for less than five weeks since we got in country."

"When'd ya get here?"

"Nine months ago."

"Where'd y'all go?"

"Everywhere. The Cav thinks we ought to be no longer than twenty minutes from the grunts we support. You'll find that philosophy puts you in the middle of some god-awful, dumpy places. Keep your bag packed." L. Sid looked serious.

I threw my poncho liner and air mattress on the cot and put the rest of my stuff into a footlocker made out of an ammo box, from 7.62 mm rounds for a M60 machine gun.

"Perfect. It feels like home already."

THE OFFICER's club's fifteen tables scattered around a long bar in front of two wall murals. Dancing can-can girls, with the 229th Battalion patch in the center, formed the first mural. As one of the early works of the beer-joint school of art, it bore heavy influences of a man who hadn't seen a round-eyed woman for way too long. Oversized breasts, hips, lips, cheeks, and hair were everywhere. It was a promenade of the malformed.

The second mural captured a somber battle scene, from 16 November 1965, in the Ia Drang Valley. A dreary battlefield image of Hueys flying in A Company's most famous support role of the 1/7 Cavalry.

Officers amused themselves in the club by drinkin', dinkin', talkin', walkin', dartin' and fartin'. Mostly drinking. The open beamed tin roof above a concrete floor amplified the decibel level to the point of pain.

Lt. Colonel Exton Givens held court in the corner with a table full of his officers. He got their attention. "This is Danny Hellberg, one of the three new FNGs."

"And believe it or not," L. Sid laughed, "after seeing the Continental Palace in all its splendor and eating in the mess tent, he's still glad to be here."

The whole table raised their drinks high and gave the helicopter chant, "Him. Him. Fuck him." The Mormon Tabernacle Choir they weren't, but that's what I liked: a very tight assed, standard issue bunch of crazy Army aviators. I responded with an exaggerated single-finger salute that ended in my nose.

A classy way to break the ice.

In the loose talk that followed, I learned everyone's hometown, college, family size, marital status, and tons of forgettable bullshit. The conversation eventually got around to my hammered face, so I recapped the previous thirty-nine hours from the bombing in the club to the cold-cock on the tarmac.

The colonel's face scrunched up into a wad of wrinkles. "Interesting. I'll see if I can find those guys that ran you out of town. Frankly, it pisses me off when someone picks on anyone in my command. Officer or enlisted. They're mine. And no one can fuck with them." Exton smacked his fist on to the table hard enough to make the beer cans jiggle.

I liked this guy.

"Oh, one more thing," the colonel lowered one eyebrow and raised the other. "Do you have hair on your face?"

"You bet your ass, sir."

"I want you to grow a bush." It was only then that I realized that all of the officers around the table had moustaches. Some closely cropped, others long and flowing, even a few thin and scrawny. But everyone grew something.

"I can handle it. But I don't see any that are red. I'll add a certain element of royal dignity into this plebian mess you have."

While the table suggested other ways I could screw myself, L. Sid brought out a long tube in each of his hands. "But can you handle this?" He stood one up on its fins in front of me and the other one by Beau Buncher, who just arrived at the table.

"There is an old company tradition started back in the good old days at Fort Benning. Any FNG officer must complete the sacred rocket tube ritual."

I yawned. "It's getting' deep baby."

"No bullshit. God's truth. This ritual survived the test of time for every swinging dick here. You'll notice the gutted and somewhat cleaned out 2.75-inch rocket is filled with six cans of a cool, pale nectar of the gods. Made only of barley, malt, hops, water, and a few other toxins. But a word of caution."

The warning added a certain *je ne sais quoi* to this crapola.

L. Sid continued, "Once you put this sacred vessel to your lips, you can't remove it until all the golden liquid is gone. Every drop."

"Or what?" I looked at the three-foot tube's glistening beads of condensation.

Givens chimed in with a sardonic tone and a deadpan look. "Or get every SLJO assignment I can find for you, from now until your tour is completed."

"SL...what?"

"SLJO is the Shitty Little Jobs Officer."

"What if I don't like beer?" Beau asked innocently, green still showing on his gills.

"Tough shit. Live with it. Here's where you broaden your appreciation for the lower things of life." A steel firmness concealed the mirth in the colonel's voice.

Considering I chugged my fair share of pitchers and was thirsty enough to drink my own bath water, I needed no more prompting. "Let me have it," I stretched out my hand to L. Sid.

"Nope. Only in its proper place and time. Please stand up on your chair." We stood and L. Sid held the tube high on its neck and carefully turned the vessel toward me. He did the same for Beau.

The Colonel came in right on cue, "Raise it slowly up to your lips, L. Sid will help you."

I lifted the tube up to my lips and tried to stabilize its unwieldy weight.

"Perfect. Now down the hatch. I salute you." L. Sid took his hand away to salute as pretty as they do back in the states. Movement of his hand casually uncovered a slit about five inches from the mouth of the tube. This diabolical design shot a stream onto my neck cavity just below the Adam's apple. My open fatigue collar caught more than its share like a thirsty funnel. The beer ran right down my shirt to my belt, ballooning up the foam. I felt it race into my boot. Bingo. A beer boot bath.

If these suckers thought that I couldn't handle a chest full of beer, well, they had another thought coming. Had they used this tube of joy since they got in country? I was one of the first FNG replacements, wasn't I? Was there a surprise at the bottom? I increased the angle to let more beer spill out over my cheeks to join the rest of the river down my chest. This delighted the crowd even more. Of course, I told them to go fuck themselves, which made a really neat sound into the tube while the beer gushed.

"There. Done. I haven't had so much fun since the pigs ate my flight instructor." With all the reverence of a new altar boy, I replaced the sacred vessel on the table.

Beau was still in position when he heard what I said. He laughed during a swallow, which made him cough and choke and blow beer out of his nose. War is hell. At the final gulp, Beau peered down the barrel, squeezed it vigorously with both hands and yelled, "Come on out, you son of a bitch."

Givens rose abruptly. "Gentlemen, welcome to A Company. Glad to have you here...even if you can't hold your beer."

I STOOD next to the screened window looking into the darkness. "What's that?"

L. Sid finished his drink, ignoring the sounds in the distance. "Artillery, a little H and I to keep Charlie on his toes."

"How do you tell?"

"Listen. What you're hearin' is outgoing. Real comforting. You'll like it."

"OK, so what is it?"

"Harassment and interdiction by our 81mm mortar battery. Designed to piss off ol' Charlie while he sets up to mortar us. On the perimeter, we have forward observers who've scouted a number of likely areas for enemy activity. Like a low draw, an abandoned hut, a high piece of terrain with good visibility, an obvious trail. Something like that."

L. Sid opened another can of beer. "So, during the night he'll observe and call in the fire as necessary. Sometimes we actually get lucky and see secondary explosions. But most of the time we're just blowing the shit out of trees and weeds."

"I can see flashes of white from the artillery battery. Cool."

"Nah. Can't be. The battery's in a little depression on the other side of the airstrip."

"Oh yeah. Then what am I looking at?"

"That's the Golf Course. At night it's the darkest place in the whole camp."

"Give me a break. You don't have a golf course."

"Of course not," his eyes checked out the ceiling. "It's the Division heliport. Largest in the free world. We left most of the low vegetation on it to control the dust. From the air it looks like a golf course."

At the window, he nonchalantly peered into the blackness. "Yes, sir. When you start seeing sparks out there, baby, we're in a world of hurt--" A flash lit up his face as the sound of the explosion reached us. He did a double take and shouted to the room, "Incoming! Incoming!"

Everyone moved at the same time as the fun light went out and the back-to-business sign came on. I didn't know if they really expected the Viet Cong bomber fleet overhead.

L. Sid moved through the blackness. "Just take your drink and follow me to the bunker."

We joined the mass of bodies moving in a common direction. Almost silently, other than an occasional curse for tripping on a tent stake or sandbag. The ominous explosions neared, and their flashes occasionally lit our way.

A double row of sandbags interlaced to seven feet high with a fortified PSP roof formed the bunker. Inside, body odor, booze and tobacco smoke mixed with the moldy smell of wet sand. Only the embers from cigarettes glowed.

I followed L. Sid inside and leaned against a chunk of wall when someone came to the door. "Is Lieutenant Buncher here?"

"Yo." His response right behind my head startled me. Amazing what a little booze will do to your overall sensitivities.

The voice said, "Sir, Colonel Givens wants you to help Three." Beau pushed his way out through the crowd.

My heart pounded like a runaway mail train. Rivulets of sweat formed on my face. "Who the hell's Three, anyway?"

L. Sid grabbed my arm. "The Operations Officer."

Someone slurred in the darkness, "Maybe Charlie just wants to give us a little H and I tonight. I hope we're not the only air assault company here."

Another responded, "I don't know, Operation Davy Crockett is still wide open in Binh Dinh. And Colonel Moore's Third Brigade is operating around Bong Son. There can't be much left."

L. Sid chimed in, "If you're right, they'll be calling our number soon. Lieutenant Hellberg, are ya' ready to rock 'n roll?"

"You bet your sweet ass. Can't sing. Can't dance. Too drunk to walk. Might as well fly." It sounded good but it was a load of crap and not a volunteer offer for the next mission. I couldn't find the bunker by myself. Yet he wanted me to leave its dark, stinking discomfort for the sheer raging terror of a night flight with bad guys shooting at us?

"We'd have to be pretty hard-up to fly you before your official check-out."

The same ops messenger called through the doorway, "Y'all need to report to operations immediately. Three is putting together a small gaggle to go out with the Ready Reaction force."

All I could do is follow the pack. A steel ring through my nose with a long rope would've been appropriate. We stumbled up a slope to the tent, its sandbag bunker annex not discernable. All the lights in the area remained out except for a sliver that escaped from the flap over the entrance. Inside was smoke filled, hot and crowded with sweaty bodies. Buncher filled out the assignment board under the watchful eyes of Captain Jenkins, the Three, and Colonel, the Six.

"Is this all of them, Sergeant?" Colonel Givens looked at all the anxious faces.

"As many as I could find, Sir. The second platoon is still at the Seventh Cavalry party. It'll take some time for them to get back. Presuming, of course, they're sober enough to drive."

"OK, Gentlemen. Listen up. Company C of the 227th had ready-reaction tonight, but lost six ships right on Alpha pad by the first rounds that landed. Group wants us to get six ships airborne. ASAP."

On the board, Colonel pointed to the aircraft available, "We'll need two ships to marry up with the 227th. They'll be airborne in fifteen minutes. I'll lead the White flight. Three is figuring out what we can do with the people we have."

On cue, Captain Jenkins turned away from the board where Buncher wrote the last of the names next to the aircraft numbers. "The Yellow flight will make, if I fly with L. Sid."

"I can't spare you at this time." Colonel Givens looked at me, the crow's feet around his eyes intensified to the low glow of a smile. "Lieutenant Hellberg, how about it? You feel like a little spin in the moonlight?"

He had to be shitting me. "What moonlight?"

"Pretend."

Sometimes the worst dreams of man materialize without warning. "You bet. Why not. Gotta learn some day." I spoke with no attachment to reality.

In the last two days, I took more blows to the head than I had in my entire life. Why should I expect all its processes to function as advertised?

How could I refuse Colonel Givens in front of God, country, and every drunk from the club?

Like the man said—*pretend*.

The MP maneuvered the Jeep down a series of tight alleys as pedestrians jumped out of the way and children scattered. He turned up a tree-lined boulevard pass the Opera House, the Hotel de Ville, and entered a spacious park. Whitewashed buildings with bright shutters, tiled roofs, and cultured plants surrounded an unusually large crowd of citizens. The MP driver carefully missed street vendors and stopped at the center fountain.

Crowd noise evaporated as the lady stood up in the back of the Jeep. She spoke in Vietnamese, "Loved ones. Thank you for coming, I have longed for this moment." A murmur raced around the square about this incongruous spectacle, resplendent in a brilliant, red *ao dai*. Her contrasting white silk pants reflected on the OD green of the Jeep. The MP escorts wore their tans, with patent leather belts, holsters, hat brims, and boots.

Silence fell over the crowd.

"I ask your help to return our leader, his majesty Emperor Bao Dai, to his rightful throne." She clenched her fist. "He alone can unify our nation in peace. He will help our brothers in the north to expel the Chinese. Then we will force these Americans and their allies to withdraw from the south. And all the Vietnamese people will live in peace."

A woman in the crowd raised her hands high. "Welcome back Madame Doan Vien." Crowd noise increased.

Madame Vien stared solemnly. "Our time is now. We have arms, leadership and the will." Her striking beauty radiated truth. "Remember our great inspiration from Vietnam's history, the legendary Trieu Thi said, 'Why should I imitate others, bow my head, stoop over and be a slave?" She looked around the square, stretched her arms to form a V, "We will not be dominated by the capitalists."

A disjointed response rumbled through the crowd.

Doan shouted at the top of her voice, "Or be slaves of the communists."

More people applauded.

"China has ruled us for over 2000 years. They have taken our resources, our people, our treasure, and demean us as Annam. We are not the Pacified South. We are Vietnam." She raised her hands high.

The buildings shook with the passion of a unified vision. "Vietnam. Vietnam. Vietnam."

"We should not stoop to anyone. They should not ravage our beautiful country." Madame Vien ignited the listeners with everything they wanted to hear.

The square rocked with excitement, people outstretched their arms and called, "Doan Vien. Doan Vien." Everyone drew closer except for a lone couple leaning on a road-weary Vespa motor scooter with bulging saddle bags. Wearing sunglasses and light summer clothes, they looked like business professionals in their twenties.

With the MPs encircling the Jeep, the squad leader said, "Madame, we should leave now for the next meeting."

"Be careful," she waved her hand high like a movie star. "I will be back. I promise." She sat down, "Go down Đường Bà Triệu Street then to the old French Embassy compound."

The jeep moved slowly through the overflowing streets of Saigon. Madame Vien covered her red *ao dai* with a subdued lightweight shawl. As the headquarters of the US command, military were everywhere.

AT THE DESERTED FRENCH EMBASSY, Lanh Quang, a noted intellectual contributor to the *Saigon Daily News* waited for his interview. They wanted him to find a survivor of the My Canh attack and write a bleeding hearts story on stupid, non-directional terrorism. Lanh's notoriety increased tenfold with his exposure of the US government money deluge and corruption at every level of Vietnamese society.

The five-foot, seven-inch Lanh Quang sulked in front of the French neo-classical building, an impressive relic of the former invader. His unkempt black hair blew straight up on his head as an objection to the American slicked-down look in local business. As a member of the Committee of Concerned Asian Scholars, his articles also protested against the destruction which the US military wreaked, endless havoc of the NVA and the mindless terror of the Viet Cong. Vietnam mutated into a land of nightmares in terminal torment.

A black sedan stopped at the curb and the driver opened the rear door, a woman dressed in jungle fatigues stepped out. Lanh Quang realized this was no ordinary reporter. He said, "How did you find out that Madame Nhu was back?"

"I met a soldier who saw her yesterday in an alley behind Tu Do Street." Kaelyn looked down at him. "I bet you're Quang Lanh."

"Lanh Quang. Please." This round-eye filled a uniform with more than he'd ever seen. He loosened his multicolored tie, straightened up his white tropical suit and stymied a laugh. "I'm sorry. It is a pleasure to finally meet you. Who is your boyfriend there with the sunglasses and the gun under his coat?"

"His name is Jonas. The MP commander insisted on security since my little incident yesterday."

"What happened?" Lanh smiled at Jonas without getting too close to this giant of a man.

"I was at that floating restaurant when the attack occurred."

"The My Canh, how did you survive? Where were you when the explosions went off?" Questions spewed forth like he had only ten seconds left in his interview.

"A helicopter pilot told me about Madame Nhu while we were trapped." She saw confusion in his eyes. "In one of our previous discussions, you said if she ever returned, it would be a big story. Since this isn't my turf. I didn't have the contacts, won't put up with bullshit, and can't afford to miss her. That's why I called you."

"What do you mean turf?"

"At home, I know the right cops, the snitches, and where all the bodies are buried."

He raised his hand in a halting gesture. "Listening to you will require a translator. I got the point."

She touched his arm, "I would have preferred to make our appointment instead of being in the middle of the terrorist attack."

"So where do we start?"

"Who knows what's really happening in this city? Where can I buy the right info..." Kaelyn stared at a passing Military Police Jeep with the top up. In the back seat she saw a lady in red. "My God that's her, it has to be."

The Jeep drove with care through the strangling traffic.

"Jump in, we'll follow it." She tugged Lanh into the back seat. "Can you catch 'em Jonas?"

"Just watch, Miss DeHaven," The giant punched the black sedan into the middle of the busy rush hour.

About 30 meters behind, the two riders from the square followed at a comfortable distance.

The giant had the nerve to swerve, the stuff to bluff and the will to kill. He used every inch of whatever was under the hood to get Kaelyn close enough to smell the Jeep's exhaust.

"See if they'll pull over."

"But I don't have any authority credentials to show. I'm supposed to keep you safe." His rate of closure made the Jeep driver screech to a halt.

The giant slammed on the brakes and slid to a dead stop less than two car-lengths apart. "We're screwed. Keep still."

Two guards jumped off the back bumper to a firing position with their rifles. With guns drawn, the other two stayed inside.

Kaelyn opened the rear door and stretched her foot to the street. "We're press reporters. I want to speak to your passenger."

"One more step and I'll blow your leg off." The guard shouted. "Driver, step out slowly. Back seat, close your door."

Kaelyn closed her door while Jonas opened his. He stepped out, "I'm from the US Embassy, the woman is from the *Cleveland Plain Dealer*, the man is a local reporter."

One guard moved to the right of the sedan while the other covered the left. "Back seat on driver side, come out now."

Kaelyn came out shouting, "Aw, come on, I'd like to cut this shit out and talk to Madame Nhu."

"What do you want to ask her?" Doan Vien answered without showing her face. A red glow from her *ao dai* reflected on the back window.

"I'd ask what she is going to do when Bao Dai returns? Will she be Prime Minister or Prime Mistress?"

Lanh Quang's jaw dropped. "Don't piss her off."

Doan spoke from the rear seat. "You insolent little bitch, why provoke me? Why not ask something pertinent? Like how can Bao Dai stop this meaningless war? How can he unite the North and the South into one powerhouse."

"You got to be kidding. Bao Dai wouldn't know his ass from a sewer. The only thing he's done right was abdicate. If he could unite the North and the South, it would be more like a shithouse, not a powerhouse."

Doan Vien still did not show herself. "You only know what the CIA lets you know. What have you done to find out what the real war is? Thousands of Vietnamese die every day because of the USA and China."

Lanh Quang shouted from the rear of the car. "They grab what they want because no one cares. Our leadership abdicated their responsibility to govern. They've only led us to corruption."

"Clunk, clunk" echoed as two grenades bounced on the street and sizzled their way into the conversation. "Get down—," Jonas pushed Kaelyn to the ground. His body absorbed the concussion of the blasts then collapsed on her.

Her ears rang amid the guns firing. She pushed his dead weight aside.

From two windows over the store, the young professional man riddled the guards with an automatic weapon as the scooter woman caught the remaining MPs in a crossfire. Bodies littered the street.

Doan Vien rolled under the Jeep for cover. A steady stream of bullets raked the hood, knocked out the lights, flattened the tires, blew out the windshield, and ripped the mirrors to the pavement. She held her breath as the ruptured tank puddled gas next to her face.

Underneath the car, Kaelyn watched the shooters reload. Four more shots popped out from the right side of the sedan. Each shot reverberated against the building walls to amplify its power of finality. No ricochets. Only the sound of solid hits. The scooter driver fell from the building onto the pavement, his rifle bounced with metallic flatness. A bloody window frame held the motionless scooter woman.

Kaelyn crawled over the brass shell casings on the street. Two white shoes stepped out of the rear door. She said, "Lanh?"

"Yes, are you alright?"

The Jeep ignited in a big puddle of flame as Doan Vien ran toward the sedan. "Get in the car! Get out of here!"

"But what about your men?"

"They're all dead. Find your driver's weapon. Let's go." Doan looked up and down the street.

Kaelyn pulled the gun from the shoulder holster next to a massive wound in his chest. She wiped the bloody barrel on his shirt. "Goodbye, Jonas."

Doan's English slowed her speech. She grabbed Kaelyn's hand "Can you drive?"

"Of course, I can." Kaelyn put the pistol in her bag. "What did you do to piss off those guys?"

"Just get us out of here," said Doan. "If I knew how to drive, I would. Go!"

"OK." Kaelyn put the idling car in gear. "Where to?"

"The caretaker's house behind the French Embassy."

"Show me where to go, Goddamn it."

Lanh pointed straight ahead. "Turn right by the large flower shop, in a couple of blocks."

"Don't have time to look for landmarks, it's all I can do not to hit anybody. They must have let the zoo loose. Just tell me when to turn." Kaelyn swerved to miss a scooter bus with people hanging out the back. Her hand laid on the horn.

"Don't do that!" Doan commanded. "This car is too noticeable, drive cautiously." The traffic slowed to a crawl, she kept moving across the rear seat from window to window like a nervous tiger. "I do not feel good about this. We were not a simple a target of opportunity. Why didn't any MPs come to the scene? Normally, they're like flies on a dog. Pull over and stop. Walk to the alley. Leave the motor running."

Kaelyn exited with Lanh. They darted between the buildings smelling of old mold and hot grease. Flies infested the walk, strewn with rotted plant cuttings and human waste.

Another explosion and automatic rifle fire echoed against the buildings. Doan shook her head. "Some street urchin didn't succeed in stealing the car. They'll know they missed their mark again. Hurry." Their pace quickened, almost running.

After twenty-five minutes of zig-zagging through buildings, alleys and balconies, the trio made it to the caretaker's house. It looked vacant with piles of rubbish in front. Doan rapped on a boarded window and it opened with a slow squeak. The three sweating escapees climbed over the jagged glass into the building. As Kaelyn and Lanh landed on the floor, both were seized by guards.

"We need to talk." Doan motioned the soldiers to release them. "You stumbled into the Cong's plan to kill me. But thanks to your good shooting and driving," she bowed toward Lanh and Kaelyn, "we survived."

Doan looked at her red *au dai*, soaked in gas. "Lanh, how did you learn to shoot like that?"

Lanh smiled. "In Officer Training. But I washed out and transferred to journalism at the university."

Kaelyn looked at Doan. "Who are you?"

Lanh said. "Meet Doan Vien, the lady-in-waiting to Madame Nhu."

"If you don't mind." Doan assumed an officious air. "I am the Director General of Counterinsurgency Operations, to be exact. My responsibility is to expedite the US withdraw from the country. South Vietnam and North Vietnam are mature enough to settle their own differences."

Kaelyn stared at the diminutive Doan. "That's a pile of shit. Your people have been dumbed down by foreign domination. Your brightest have always been stolen from you."

"And you have swallowed not only the hook but the entire line of the Asian experts to justify the war." Doan wagged her finger. "You get me sick. Along with every other reporter here. You are not here to drink and get laid. You are supposed to tell your world the truth. No wonder there is no support for the war."

Kaelyn's eyes widened. For the first time in her life, she was speechless.

"Bao Dai is the only one who can save Vietnam now. The Vietnamese love their royalty. It validates them as a nation. North and South will rally around his flag." Doan placed her open palm on Kaelyn's cheek. Kaelyn unclenched her fist.

Deflecting her arm like a boxer repelling a punch, Kaelyn hissed,

"OK, if that's so, where do I get the straight skinny? Who do I talk to? How do I connect the dots?"

"Talk to the Vietnamese who make decisions and those who carry them out." Doan smiled. "Good. Let me introduce you to the right people. If you don't like them, I will get you whomever you want." She turned to Lanh Quang, "Stay with her. Keep her out of trouble."

"Are you kidding? She doesn't take instructions well, or haven't you noticed?"

BARELY FIVE MINUTES elapsed since I "volunteered" to fly. After the briefing, Captain Jenkins gave me a .38-caliber revolver and holster. L. Sid loaded me up with a helmet, carrying bag, and a chicken plate: a sweaty-smelling chest protector, like a chunk of a concrete with straps.

The Army provided little comfort to its most prized possession, the helicopter pilot. We traveled on an open, flatbed trailer designed to sober-up pilots with a gentle breeze, a solid splash of muddy water, and five minutes of straight engine exhaust from leaded gasoline.

L. Sid said, "Wear the chicken plate high on your chest, cinched up on the sides. It'll usually stop an AK-47 and an M16, and only slow down a .50."

"Usually?"

"Well, maybe most of the times." He unzipped the carrying bag and looked at my helmet. "Aw, shit."

"Now what?"

"Your helmet's white."

"So?"

"So, you'll be the only white spot on the front of the helicopter. Something for the Cong to aim at. Probably miss you and hit me."

I loved his charming concern for my welfare. "Even at night?"

"Especially at night. Sometimes the panel lights illuminate the cockpit more than we want. Kind of like a dim neon sign in the front window of a broken-down bar. You know someone's there."

"So?"

"Sergeant, stop at the next puddle." L. Sid scooped up a handful of mud to spread over my helmet and white nametag.

I shrugged off his hand. "What the hell you doing?"

"Remember, they shoot officers first." He dabbed mud on my yellow, 2nd Lieutenant's bar and Transportation Corps emblem and chuckled, "I love to fuck up real officer's clothes."

The trailer stopped in the center of the road. "L. Sid. You flying triple nickel tonight?" He held a light beam on the nose numbers, 555. "Your cherished pride and joy awaits."

A black silhouette of a UH-1D Huey against the star-lit sky stood like a giant, fifteen-foot insect ready to jump into action. The sweet smell of wet grass hung in the air and pumped up my anticipation.

"We gotta look this dumpling over real good to make sure it's still flyable. This baby's been a hangar queen all its life, so I shudder to think what it's like after a mortar attack."

Both the crew chief and the gunner inspected for signs of shrapnel penetration after discovering the crater behind our tail. L. Sid climbed to the masthead to examine for dings on the rotor linkage and holes in the blades. I stood there with a finger up my nose, intimidated by the sheer girth of the D Model on high skids. "God damn."

"You act like you've never seen one of these things," the crew chief said.

"I haven't."

"You're shitting me."

"Nah. In flight school we only had B Models, and only in the advance phase of instruction."

"Fuckin' wonderful. Just what I needed. Flying with a FNG into a hot LZ. At night. And I only got 15 days left to DEROS." The crew chief's chewing tobacco dribbled on his chin. "She-it."

"Is this thing flyable or not?" L. Sid stepped up to the cabin.

"Yes, Mr. Crenshaw."

"Then let's light the fire. 227's cranking already." He got into the left seat of the helicopter while the crew chief opened the door and slid back the seat shield on the right side for me. Talk about intimidation, I'd never even seen an armored seat before. It looked like the electric chair from prison movies.

B Model Hueys in flight school sat around twelve inches off the ground so getting in was more like sitting in a Jeep. D Models on high skids were their big brothers. They stood almost three feet to the bottom of the cabin door. I climbed around the cyclic and felt as graceful as a fat lady in the circus getting in a barrel. My chest protector and pistol belt snagged, banged, bumped, and caught on every knob in the cockpit. Why didn't they play dress up in flight school, so we'd get the feel of this queer gear for combat? Maybe it was the blackness of the night, or the looming anticipation of death, or the booze that made me the biggest klutz the world has ever seen.

"Are you going to fart around forever, or did you come to this party to dance?" L. Sid zipped through the prestart procedures then turned on the battery switches. The warm, red glow of the instrument lights instantly bathed us. "Rotor." He shouted over his shoulder.

"Clear."

"Engine start." L. Sid squeezed the trigger on my collective. A low pitch whined like a strangling pig. The big blade overhead turned slowly. Not a moon in sight. His start-up procedure was like the masterful conductor in front of a symphony orchestra. A non-stop set of fluid movements to work this fire-breathing monster into a flying beauty. He growled into the intercom, "Y'all ready?"

The immediate response from the crew was two simple, double clicks while I naively reported. "I guess I'm ready as rain, boy."

"Save the comedy. Ninety-nine percent of the time when an affirmation is expected, give it by simply clicking your microphone. That goes for both intercom and transmit. Clutter on the radio'll kill you. Understand?"

I gave him two clicks.

L. Sid transmitted, "White One, Yellow Four is up."

"Roger. Flight's up. We have departure clearance from Golf Course." Colonel Given's voice had a distinct similarity to what God would sound like. If he ever spoke when he was hoarse and kind of gravely.

When five other ships passed overhead, L. Sid lifted us backward in a ten-foot hover and kicked it left to a smooth takeoff. There was something euphoric in hovering backwards and flying like a bird.

We climbed out over the camp to the pick-up zone at Bravo. The big sliding doors of the Huey stayed open during flight and the cool evening poured in. Black covered everything outside.

"You got it." L. Sid removed both hands and feet off the controls. "Keep this distance from the ship in front of you. Go where he goes, do what he does. We'll be at the pick-up zone in a few minutes, land echelon right."

My comfortable existence as a spectator vanished. It was like old-home week.

"When'd you fly last?"

"About a month ago. I got my wings in March."

"You never touched one of these before?"

"Nope."

"No sweat GI. Your first reaction will be that it floats. A little more than the B Model because it has a bigger disc area. Other than that, it is exactly the same." L. Sid paused, "Just a little bigger... faster...longer...stronger...thirstier...you know..."

"Sure. A regular mirror image."

I SHIFTED in my seat for that honey-do feeling between me and my controls.

L. Sid's smooth voice floated in, "I might take control back on short final. This ain't the place to get a checkout. Or to learn how to fly."

"I beg your Goddamn pardon. What's this shit about learning how to fly?"

He pretended not to hear me. "They get pissed when an FNG gets killed before his official check-out by the company IP."

"But after that it's all right. Huh?"

"Wise-ass."

Invisible wings floated us in the sky as I chased the dim set of lights in front of me. This ship felt like driving a bus when I was only familiar with a ten-year old, two door coupe.

"If I'm a FNG, would you be, a FOG?"

"A what?"

"A Fuckin' Old Guy.

Two sets of double clicks followed.

On short final, he didn't take the controls but leaned forward. "If you slow it down now, you won't float past the LZ when you should be stopping next to Yellow Three."

I struggled with the eager bird all the way down, like corralling a homesick angel. On the ground, the troops crouched against the downdraft, then ran to the ship like it was the last bus to the city. It took less than fifteen seconds from landing to take off.

Chief called, "We're up."

As I tried to pass the controls back to him, L. Sid said, "OK, ya didn't kill us. Drag this mother up to a three-foot hover."

"What for?"

"To see if it'll fly. You can never tell what these grunts'll bring along when they board. Problems are easier to cure in a hover than in flight."

After I proved it would get up, L. Sid adjusted the radios. "Now, without pulling the guts out of this little darling, ya' gotta catch the rest of the flight."

My attention never wavered from the long head-start of the other ships, so I didn't notice our direction from the base. "Where are we going now?"

The big, dark nothingness reminded me of Texas.

"I don't know. On ready-reaction, we fly off the perimeter a couple of clicks to insert a blocking force. The grunts will usually hide out in the weeds 'till morning and then sweep back into camp. Sometimes they'll nail Charlie on the way out or catch him hiding."

"How do they know where to send us?"

"There is a guard tower every 50 meters on the perimeter and bunkers in between. Someone probably saw a muzzle flash. Tonight, over a hundred mortar rounds came in five minutes."

An unfamiliar voice crackled over the radio, "Serpent Six, this is Yellow One. Yellow flight will drop Alpha Team into Lima Zulu Mike. White flight will drop Bravo into Lima Zulu November. Both LZ's will be cold. Land in diamond."

"White One, wilco."

"Why the hell we're using a diamond at night. It's hard enough in the daylight." L. Sid gestured to close-up.

"What . . . What did they say?" It was damn near impossible to listen, talk, and stay in formation at the same time.

What a bitch. This was pat-your-head-and-rub-your-ass times two.

"I don't know where we are. We'll just have to follow." L. Sid paused. "Bad news is we approach without lights or cover."

"What do you mean?"

"No suppressive fire on the way in to keep Charlie's head down. Nope. We stroll in fat, dumb, and happy and deposit our fine, fair-haired boys in the middle of the killing zone. Not to mention our exposure on this slow-moving kite."

I couldn't keep up with the ten quarts of jargon he poured into my two-teaspoon brain.

"Man, it's always spooky to assault cold. Absolutely nuts at night. Especially after we just got pounded." L. Sid slunk lower in his seat. "And I always had bad luck with the 227."

I fought to keep the aircraft in the pit of the diamond.

He asked, "Where are the Tigers?"

"Tigers?"

"Gunships."

"White One, this is Yellow One. Advise your ETA."

Microphones clicked.

"Yellow, White One. One minute, fifteen seconds to touch down. Over."

"Roger. Add about 30 seconds to that so we can both domino at the same time? Out." Yellow One nosed his aircraft over to widen our separation from White.

"Now stay with him," L. Sid said, "Get closer than hemorrhoid cream. That's why these guys get shot up. They fly loose because their leaders are spastic. Our air speed just increased by thirty knots. That's bullshit."

A diamond formation was the only one we never practiced in

flight school. I watched the aircraft on both sides at the same time - a peripheral hell. Between the spastic in front and his whip-saw wing men on both sides, I felt like a cockroach on the bellows of an accordion.

"OK, Yellow One started final approach." L. Sid slouched further in his seat. "Where are the Tigers?"

"We only have one," a voice from the back answered.

"Shit. Simultaneous landings. Cold. One gun. Fuck'n A. This'll get you killed. Keep your eyes on Yellow Three."

Keeping a constant distance from another aircraft in pitch black of the night, strained my entire body. At two discs away, his position lights on dim were as hard to see as fly shit in pepper.

My breath came in gulps. Was I driving the bus to a school picnic or over the cliff? No time to think. Just do what L. Sid wanted.

I brought the ship all the way to the ground. Old *terra firma* never felt so good. My muscles were as tight as banjo strings, sweat dripped off my nose.

"We're up," the crew chief said.

"Pull pitch." L. Sid grunted.

Old triple nickel gave as much as she could but still couldn't keep up. The rest of the flight banked away into the dark sky.

"Hellberg. You kept up with a spastic and once again didn't kill us. Without lights. Not bad."

"It felt pretty good." Of course, I didn't know how little I knew, or how lucky I was.

The return flight was a piece of cake. In contrast to the sweat pot that got us to the LZ, a balmy softness in the air knocked the edge off my nerves. Our base at Camp Radcliff now blazed with lights: a flaming jewel in my hope to survive.

THE CIRCLE of perimeter lights was a jewel in the middle of the forlorn darkness.

I said, "It's lit up like a ballpark, isn't it?"

L. Sid laughed. "Just keeps the Cong from over-running us. Makes them sharpen their mortar skills."

"Yellow flight, this is Yellow One. Go trail."

This time I kept a decent interval from the ship in front of me. The deafening roar of the turbine, three feet behind my head, obliterated all sound, making the pick-up zone surreal. Troops waited like silent shadows in the night. They pounced into our ship as we landed. We took off 14 seconds later.

"Yellow. Go back to diamond formation."

L. Sid slapped the glare shield and faced me. "Why the hell are they risking our asses in a night assault with not even a gunship escort? In a formation where we can't protect ourselves?"

"Yellow flight, this is Yellow One. Stomper One-Six is in position on Tango. Look for a light signal. Come up on their fox mike."

"That dumb shit." L. Sid leaned forward and yelled at the panel. "He just compromised the operation. Duh."

"Roger, identify flash." Yellow One descended in a much steeper approach than before. He dropped out of sight in front of me. I bottomed the pitch and beeped down my RPM to descend faster.

"Strike three. The dumb ass never got an acknowledgement. And the sign is a light not a flashbulb." L. Sid shouted as he peered out of the chin bubble and the side door window.

I tried to stay in formation but the three ships in front of me spread out. The one rotor width separation stretched beyond two. But I followed them anyway down into their black hole.

He said, "I think they're flaring, slow down. Slow down!"

I stood triple nickel on its tail, but it wouldn't stop. Nothing would slow my descent. The two-inch, RPM warning lit up with the blinding ferocity of a flame thrower. A brain-ripping *beeeeep* accompanied the caution. Both meant we were gonna crash.

To top it off, the ship started rotating. I added pedal to get control, but nothing happened. "Awww. Shit."

"I got it." L. Sid jumped on the controls just as we slammed into the ground, more than 90 degrees from our original flight path. He yelled, "Dumb shit, ya' forgot to beep it back to full RPM."

What the hell could I say? It was true.

A solid ribbon of a red tracers broke my remorse as they streamed over my head. They chewed out the front windshield in chunks, like a garden hose eating a bank of foam. Then my map light blew out of the window.

A ricochet off my helmet knocked me forward. Stunned into a semi-crouched position, I waited for the next bullet.

The gunner shouted, "Can't fire. Other ship's in the way . . . Grunts all dead. Blown right out. Get out. Get—" He stopped transmitting.

L. Sid brought in full power until bullets destroyed the chin bubble and knocked his hand off the cyclic. A bloody piece of his pants stuck on my chicken plate.

He shouted, "Fly this son of a bitch. I'm hit."

I hopped on the controls. The whole flight was down on my right, where I should have been.

Now it was our graveyard. Yellow One laid upside down, its main rotor stuck in the earth, dead still. Flames from Yellow Two's engine cast an eerie light against the Cong walking toward it firing with automatic rifles. An explosion in front of Yellow Three blew off the radio compartment door, flexing the main rotor to sever his tail boom. It started a death spin. Bodies fell out of both sides of the cargo area.

L. Sid pointed left with his bloody hand. "Fuck it. Just fly. We're the only ones left."

The helicopter shuddered but I got it off the ground. Hard to believe. With a flood of red, the ugly old RPM warning popped back to life. Its glare over the remnants of the cockpit made it more gruesome, while the buzzer screamed.

"Hold that cyclic steady. I mean dead-nuts still." L. Sid spoke calmly into the microphone, "The less it moves, the more we fly."

More bullets pounded my seat. Each one of them like sliding down the stairs on your back. *Halla-damn-lujah for armor plate.*

I aimed our busted old bird at the blackness. Explosions behind me flashed against the trees in front. Frozen images stayed in my eyes as red shadows. The skids scooped leaves and branches into the cockpit.

L. Sid shouted, "Reynolds, you all right?

"Yep."

"Garcia, you OK?"

Reynolds shouted over the wind noise, "He's dead."

My eyes watered from wind through the shot-out windshield. A new sensation. I had no clue where I was. Or where I was going. Maybe those were real tears.

A solid twang impacted the helicopter, much louder than anything before. My cyclic transmitted the new one-to-one vibration to my hand, a rotor blade now whistled.

L. Sid shouted, "Nice noise. Glad it's still attached and turning."

Tracers finally killed that damn old warning light and buzzer. Debris stung my face. I banked hard to escape the pinging, whacking, and thudding of bullets on the helicopter.

Another cluster of bullets made it through the floor into my seat. My ass got kicked in more ways than one.

L. Sid shouted, "Get him chief. The sumbitch's eatin' our lunch."

Reynolds attached another belt of ammunition. "Make a hard left."

I whipped the ship on its side. Reynolds fired straight down, non-stop. Almost immediately, I went past ninety degrees and feared getting sucked into the dirt, upside down. Just like they told us in flight school.

Two machine guns answered our fire in short bursts. Tracers crossing each other were beautiful in a morbid way.

Reynolds stopped firing. He held his light on what used to be our instrument panel.

L. Sid shouted, "Ya got 'em. But we lost our Intercom." In the dim light, L. Sid banked his hand away from the action, then flipped them the bird and pointed straight ahead.

I yelled, "Yea. I agree. Fuck it. Let's get out of here."

I yelled to L. Sid, "Where do I go? Point, if you have a clue." I didn't know my altitude, airspeed, or power.

He shrugged and flipped me the bird.

"OK. So, you're confused, and I'm screwed. I'll get us some altitude. Maybe find the perimeter lights." My instruments were wrecked. The rate-of-climb indicator dangled out of the panel like it gave up.

"Reynolds. Can you hear me?"

"Yes, sir."

"See anything?"

"Not a damn thing."

"Can ya' do anything with these instruments?"

He paused for a second. "I'm not the late JC. All I got's my flashlight."

"That'll work. I'll try to call White."

"Lieutenant. Ya' got no radio."

No wonder I hadn't heard a peep since the ambush.

The crew chief checked off the instruments with his light. "RPM, no. Engine stack, no. Fuel, no. Best I can tell, only the standby compass and the turn-and-bank work."

"I gotta talk to L. Sid. How long'll this crate fly? Do something with the intercom."

"How? I don't know why it's still cooking. Looks like Charlie took a hammer to it."

"Then change helmets. Get the talk switch into his good hand."

After the exchange, L. Sid's calm voice soothed me, "Good move. Keep climbing. We were never more than a couple of clicks off the perimeter, even on the second lift."

From the corner of my eye, a lightning bolt slid through the sky.

L. Sid leaned behind a chunk of Plexiglas, the last remnant of his windshield. "No wonder we're lost. A thunder bumper rolled in between us and the base. We don't have enough helicopter to get around it."

Lightning lit up the clouds. It let me see the ugly remains of the once-beautiful cockpit. Big blobs of rain splattered against the glare shield. Cold spray flicked my eyes.

"Goddamn wonderful." L. Sid wiped his face. "Does our landing light work?"

"Nope."

"Position lights?"

"Not a one."

From a drop to a flood, rain streamed into the cockpit. I tucked my head down a little so I could see something straight ahead. Nothing there. My collar scooped water down my back.

"We got to plant this bird," L. Sid's voice sounded garbled with water battering his mike. "Take it down a little."

I eased the front of the helicopter up, but the water flow didn't slacken. Strange vibrations through the controls intensified as the airspeed decreased. Rain pelted my face and ran up my nose.

If I shivered any harder, my body would self-destruct.

Wind over L. Sid's microphone made him shout. "Don't lose the horizon!"

"What horizon? It feels like I'm hoverin' in a fuckin' well: Damn dark, awful slow, and nowhere to go."

He crouched behind his chunk of Plexiglas to deflect the battering rain. "Trees! I see trees! Get some airspeed. Keep it flying."

That little flicker of ground put my survival hopes just above suicidal. Flight school told us panic would kill a pilot quicker than anything...with the possible exception of a speeding bullet. I needed another lightning bolt. My breath came in sloppy, wet slurps.

The crew chief tapped my arm and bellowed, "Lights. Lights!"

L. Sid pointed. "Turn left."

When that solitary light came into focus, it moved in a continuous circle, then up and down and side to side.

"They're signaling us." I slowed to a hover.

L. Sid squirmed, "Yeah. But why?" There's nothing around it."

"It's got to be one of ours. It's—"

A muzzle flash popped like a little blowtorch. Impact was a lot quicker. I nosed it over to escape.

"Return fire."

Reynolds's gun jammed. We took hit after hit while he struggled to make it work. Like a quail on the opening day of hunting season, it amazed me to fly with so much lead in my ass.

But a brutal sound like a hammer slamming against the transmission made me ask, "Chief, what hit?"

After no answer, L. Sid turned in his seat. "Oh God..."

I looked, and then cringed at the headless torso of Reynolds with his hands still on the machine gun.

"God damn. A great kid. Always the straight skinny. Started as a slick-sleeve. Made Spec Four in country." L. Sid deflated to a mumble.

I pointed. "Yea. Yea. But you gotta let go. Looks like we're comin' across some camp and vehicle lights. Where we at?"

"15th Maintenance Battalion! I landed here yesterday. Make your approach to their green lights."

Triple nickel shuddered again, he looked around the cabin. "No flames. No smoke. Keep flying!"

The cyclic vibrations doubled in their intensity. Couldn't hold the stick steady. Green never looked so good as the landing pad got closer.

My descent was smooth until damn-near the ground when I couldn't drop any farther. "Can't get the nose down! It wants to fly, but I wanna land. What the hell's the matter?"

"Watch out!" L. Sid used body-language on his imaginary controls while my skids punched through the top of two tents and my down-draft flattened a couple others.

L. Sid said, "With all the beatin' we took, somethin' got knocked off the ship. Our CG's way off. Get more altitude. Swirling debris will tear us up as bad as bullets. "

I climbed as high as the clouds would let me.

"Just aim straight ahead."

"Into the black area?"

"Keep this altitude and speed."

"I wish. Where's the goddamn runway?" I didn't like this fly-by-Braille crap.

L. Sid pointed above the panel, "Kinda sorta, dat-a-away."

"Quit fuckin' around."

"Okay. Okay. Only two problems to worry about. One's a fire and the other's a spin out."

"What?"

"Our skids landing on a steel plank runway cause sparks. It's only a problem if we are leaking fuel from the belly."

"If we're not leaking, it will be a goddamn miracle."

"Fuck it. Grease it on and let the sparks fly. In most cases, helicopters are slow burners."

"Most cases?"

L. Sid spoke in his dispassionate, teacher-tone. "No sweat. Concentrate on a gentle reduction of power after touch down...keep it straight. If you go off the runway, you'll roll this crate. Then we'll burn like a sparkler. So, let it slide for a long time. It'll make a hell of a noise. Don't let it spook ya."

And there it was. The runway. My pucker factor climbed high enough for my butt to chew up the seat covers.

L. Sid turned to me. "Been a hell of a night."

"No shit."

"You got one more. You can do it."

When the skids touched the PSP, I slammed in so hard one of the cargo doors fell off and blew by us, down the runway. The noise of the grinding metal astounded me. Sparks flew everywhere. A white glare flooded inside.

"We're burnin'! We're burnin'!"

"Where?"

"Probably under the fuel cell."

Out of habit, I held the controls, but they couldn't do anything. The crown of the runway pulled us to the edge. On my side, the squealing skid slipped off and became a silent earth anchor. We lunged sideways in our seats and snapped around. Mud and grass sprayed up into the air, as the helicopter stopped dead in its tracks.

Why we didn't roll, I'll never know.

"Switch it off. Unass this mother." L. Sid changed to his old drill sergeant voice. The engine spooled down as the main rotor clanked around.

He yanked with his good hand but couldn't release his shoulder harness. The fire spread to the bottom of the missing cargo door. I jerked open his buckle and pulled him out of his seat.

The fire tripled itself like it had plenty of fuel. A heat wave on my face reminded me to get the hell out.

"Don't stop now." He swung his feet to the runway and collapsed on the ground. I dragged him by his collar away from the ship until I slipped on the PSP. Cold steel against my head and back felt good. My arms stretched wide. I breathed like a runner who just stole home.

The turbine's whine and the swishing of the blades overhead had the aura of a broken carousel. An enormous belch of orange flame blazed down the side of the helicopter from the engine. The machine gun ammunition cooked off with a vengeance.

"Get us the hell away from the ship. Or we'll be toast." I grabbed his collar and pulled him off the PSP.

L. Sid moaned when I dumped him in the mud. He said, "No wonder you couldn't stop this heap."

"Why?"

"Ya landed down wind."

I SLEPT IN THE UNRELENTING, dreamless world of the total exhaustion.

A voice, neither recognized nor welcomed, boomed, "Hellberg. Wake up." The intruder galloped through the dark corridor of sleep and approached my turnstile of consciousness. I found myself on top of my bunk, still wearing my armor from last night. A thick goo covered my tongue.

"Welcome to the land of the living," the voice persisted.

I countered with "Aargh." Who was this bozo? I slurred with my septic tongue, "Go 'way."

"Ah, sweet mystery of youth. I don't know how to break this to you gently," his voice turned into a loudspeaker. "The whole goddamn company is waiting for your dead ass to get out of bed."

Both eyes ripped opened and the dreams of daylight's sweet dawn died. "How exactly can I help you?" I looked into the face of a senior captain, with clear black eyes, wide open as a tunnel. A wrinkleless face full of determination. Yuk.

"I know it's hard to believe but there is a war going on."

Focus returned to my eyes, strength to my lips, and a renewed vacuum in my brain. I wobbled to a standing position. "Well, fuck a duck. And I was afraid that I was gonna miss it."

"All hell's broken loose since ya' dragged in last night. We need you to fly. They got the First of the Ninth scouting the area." This guy thought I knew what he talked about.

"Wasn't that how we got into all that shit in the first place?" This guy looked like a real soldier. More than six feet. One hundred ninety pounds plus. Trim. Athletic. Alert.

"I guess you and L. Sid had a big ol' time. Sorry that you couldn't wait for me." He extended his big clam shell mitt toward me, "I'm Ben Mishkov. Your platoon leader and IP until L. Sid gets back."

His hand felt like a foot. "Hi. I'm glad to be here." I made my first full body move and found an insidious exhaustion down to the bone. Like playing four quarters of football without the pads. Things hurt. Movement ached. "How's L. Sid?"

"He lost a lot of blood, probably be back in a couple of days, and flying in a week or so."

"What about the other guys in the flight and Colonel Givens?"

"Six's flight didn't hit the same kind of crap you did. Their gunship took care of it immediately."

"What happened to our escort?"

"Tiger Two got shot out of the sky when you first came under attack. They found the wreckage of his helicopter just short of the LZ."

"What happened to the rest of our flight?"

"Nobody made it out. Except you and L. Sid."

"No shit."

Mishkov looked straight in my eyes. "In the nine months that the Cav's been in Vietnam, we've never been hit so bad, with so much stuff, so close to home."

Explosions, tracers and the dead grunts flashed in my mind. What a lousy welcome party.

"When our guys finally knocked out the machine guns, they found additional cases of our ammunition, solid tracers like we use in the helicopters. Even the dead gooks on the guns were wearing our brand-new jungle fatigues. "

"Sounds like they got a direct source to the stuff we can't get." I stretched.

"Yeah, and they showed you last night. I have never seen a ship so mutilated and still flying under its own power. Over seventy-five separate holes, not to mention those parts of the ship blown away completely. Our ox got gored."

"Ox my ass, they got the whole herd."

"Ya' know, as the last survivor, you're now the Ox. Let's go. Babe"

"Where?"

Mishkov said, "It's zero eight hundred and we're gonna get you ready for the war." The good captain equipped me into the company. Everything from my very own .38 special pistol with only two small notches on the grip to a chicken plate with bloody straps. I painted my helmet black because they ran out of green paint. And I became a full fledge member of A Company, 229th Assault Helicopter Battalion.

In the operations tent, I met Captain Jenkins again. This time he was less vexed. He said, "Operations controls the company's helicopters and the people who fly them. This is the first place you'll come in the morning and the last place you'll check at night. We'll tell you what you need to know, when you need to know it."

Captain Jenkins's sallow face had the wide-eyed look of a bird of prey. His eyes bulged with lids stretched to produce a haggard look of a worried man. Months of too little sleep and too many anxious moments had taken its toll. "Lieutenant Buncher is my assistant. He has the organizational skills to keep this madhouse hopping. Besides, he was the only management major I could find."

Beau turned from the board. "While you were rooting around in the dark last night, you stumbled into a major movement of VC. "

"No shit."

As he explained the bigger picture to me, Captain Jenkins

received a call on the land line. He covered the mouthpiece and asked Beau, "How many ships are up?"

"Thirteen, including the four running log."

"How many crews?"

"Eliminating sick call, we have eleven."

"Who's not flying?"

"Givens, Scivetti, Mishkov and Hellberg."

"On total availability requests, we have to include everybody. Unless Six or Five specifically exclude themself." Jenkins resumed his call, "Understand three colors to LZ Kilo by thirteen forty-five. Yes, sir."

Beau erased the assignment board. "Specialist Bensen will round up the troops and I'll configure the board."

Captain Jenkins hesitated, "Hellberg will fly with Mishkov on the log run."

"What's a log run?" I asked.

"It's logistics: supplies, ammunition, food. Whatever the guys we just landed need."

When I got back to the Continental Palace, I recapped the situation to a reclining Captain Mishkov.

"Bullshit. I ain't running log. I can check you out on a combat assault just like you can, playing pickup." He leapt out of his cot, "Get your shit together and meet me at the OPS tent."

Again, off to the races I went.

1300 HOURS_

MISHKOV NEGOTIATED our way out of the dreaded log assignment into a combat assault. Within minutes, we were bouncing on the trailer to the aircraft.

The Golf Course looked different from the night before. Rows of helicopters, lined up in relative military precision, looked far more sinister in the daylight. These endless groups of green, petrified, giant man-eaters begged to spring into action.

He pointed to the first ship in the row. "That's Serpent Six's aircraft." A fierce snake, with fangs exposed and tongue extended, coiled through the company's bright blue triangle on both front doors. "It gives the gooks something to shoot at." He didn't crack a smile.

Closer inspection of the helicopter yielded the brutal picture of combat reality. Bullet hole patches were repainted with what could be scrounged up. From Army green tape to tin cans in a variety of greens and yellows to produce an olive drab acne, on what was once the skin of a beautiful aircraft.

"When's L. Sid is coming back?"

"Don't know for sure." Mishkov frowned. "That's the downside of this war. No matter what happens to any of us, it'll just keeps eatin' us up. They ain't going to stop until we're out."

"Or we wipe them out."

"Yeah, right. In the meantime, we got to play the game. Remember, CAs are always more fun than ash and trash." Did he say fun? Where the hell was he last night? Maybe a sick mind came with tenure?

Like a little puppy, I followed him through the walk-around inspection, pre-flight and start-up. This time I was in better shape to comprehend and even participate a little bit. Amazing what a little daylight and sobriety would do.

I hovered backwards out of the revetment to the middle of the lane. Departure clearance was perfunctory, so I caught up to the company formation on the way to the PZ, Pick-Up Zone Kilo.

Mishkov said, "This is gonna be a standard combat assault with twelve ships. Givens is leading this parade in the Yellow flight. The second is White and we got the third as Red. And they are already airborne, let's go."

"What's happening on the ground?"

"The First Brigade had over-watch responsibility for a newly built CIDG camp in Vinh Thanh Valley. Nothing but a jungle bowl ringed by mountains. They made contact at noon today. Brigade decided to commit one of the rifle companies from the An Khe defense to develop the situation."

"What kind of camp?"

"Civilian Irregular Defense Group. Usually not worth a shit. We're dumping a whole company on a mountain ridge in a blocking position."

One color at a time landed on PZ Kilo for the first pick up. After Mishkov checked the loading, he said, "These guys don't fart around their squads divided up per aircraft, waiting for us."

As they boarded, some of the eager faces of the troops didn't match their uniform markings. One big baby face had 'All the Way' written on his helmet. Another one, looking barely fifteen, had a skull and cross bones. Only brush stuck in the helmet of a bored corporal.

"Should I do a hover check?"

"Nah. The flight's up." Mishkov waved me forward.

I eased the helicopter right into flight.

He said, "Establish an even rate of climb. Remember, you have three other ships trying to duplicate whatever you do. When you scratch your balls and wiggle the cyclic, thirty people behind you'll get air sick. Now, give me about fifteen seconds separation from the boys in front."

What a difference from last night. I'm learning by doing, with coaching. And maybe not as many bullets along the way. I said, "It's a lot easier to be a flight leader. You don't have to worry about any spastic in front of you."

"Actually, to lead is a lot tougher. Besides flying, you gotta coordinate with the grunts, artillery, guns and Air Force. Even as a color leader you have your hands full. Make smooth shallow turns, slow even descents, and moderate climbs. Most of all, be predictable."

"Red One, this is Yellow One." The voice of god was back on the air.

"This is Red One, over." Mishkov sat high in his seat and looked forward.

"Do you have the Ox with you?"

Click. Click.

"Roger. Try not to wear his young ass out. Remember, he's pretty tough on the flight crew and his ship."

Click. Click. Mishkov actually smiled. "You must have scored big with the old man last night."

"It was a long night. Was it the beer drinking he liked, or the way I crashed?"

"Probably both. I've flown with him for two years and this was the first time he broke radio silence. That might neutralize the way you shit in your mess kit with Scivetti."

"Yellow One, Tiger Two Eight and Two Niner are up."

"This is it." He put his sun visor down and pointed. "Look ahead of Yellow One. See the smoke and explosions in front of him on the ridge?"

"Got it".

"That's our LZ. The combat assault in the Cav is now a lot different than flight school."

"We didn't spend a lot of time on it." I squirmed in my seat because the .38 on my hip.

Mishkov laughed. "Lay that pistol between your legs. It'll give you more room in your seat and protect your balls."

I shifted my artillery to protect my big gun.

"Our combat assault starts from about 1500 feet above ground level instead of treetop. At five minutes out, the artillery or Air Force tactical bombing preps the area. They want to wipe out Charlie or keep his head down."

The two flights in front of us stair-stepped like lily pads in a stream: each flight a tight echelon right.

"As Yellow approaches the LZ, watch our gunships lay a blanket of fire. We'll land between smoldering artillery craters."

The Tiger ships flew like a pirouette of hummingbirds churning around a cauldron of death. Their machine guns trailed smoke, as they shot up all suspected targets.

White flight slipped in as soon as Yellow departed. The grunts, standing on the skids, jumped as the helicopters neared the ground. Loaded with huge back packs, many soldiers fell backwards, then did a fast low-crawl to take cover.

I slowed our closure rate to give White more time to unload. Both gunships escorted Yellow flight out of the LZ and circled back to cover White.

"Keep it going. Keep it going." Mishkov animated his directions.

"I don't want to land on their ass."

"Look at 'em. White One's picking up. White Four's hovering. They're about to pull."

The afternoon sun was like lava flowing through the windshield, sweat poured off me. Wet ran past my elbows into my flight gloves, down my nose to my chin.

White One finally got out of my way and I brought Red Flight in within five seconds. I knew it was too damn close when I could count the rivets on their tail booms.

The moment I landed the crew chief shouted, "They're out. Flight's up."

Mishkov gave me the *get out of Dodge* gesture. I felt relieved but not relaxed. For an instant near the ground I remembered last night. Tracers ricocheting through the cockpit and the Plexiglas shattering. The headless torso of Reynolds gripping his machine gun.

"Flick down your sun visor in a CA. It's good protection against flying crap in the cockpit." He got on the controls, "Okay, let me have it."

I leaned back. "Ya' know, I needed that."

Mishkov nodded. "It's a mirror every pilot's seen before. That's why you had to fly today. We double cleansed that wound by catching a little-bitty CA in the bargain."

"Thanks." I looked back at the ridge. "I still can't tell bird shit from wild honey, but something didn't feel right about that LZ."

"I hope you're wrong. Let's go back to the club and just drink about it."

"Red One, this is Yellow One. Go back to Bushwhacker for their log."

"Shit. There goes our early tee time." Mishkov transmitted, "Red One wilco. Out."

He turned our flight out of the company formation. "Now switch us to Bushwhacker net." Their requirements were simple enough. Each LZ had a specified list of ammunition, food and water. Our job was to get it there.

Mishkov dispatched Red Three and Four to the primary LZ for the biggest loads. "Rank does have its privilege, howsoever miniscule. That's why we're still running log while the old man heads to the unairconditioned comfort of the officer's club."

The topography was breathtaking. I wondered what it looked without all the pockmarks from artillery explosions.

"Besides, you'll get to take the sling load, and I'll check out your technique."

"Man, I got plenty of technique. They gave me two extra scoops in flight school."

"Shiiit. They just gave you a license to get killed. This is your real education. In a couple of hundred hours you'll know how to fly...or die."

At PZ Kilo, a Black Hat signaled me and Red Two down for our respective piles of cargo.

Mishkov said, "How much sling-load practice do they give you in flight school these days?"

I said, "Only one afternoon. I picked up one 55 gallon drum and moved it down the road."

He shook his head. "At max gross weight, this one'll be a little bit different. We have a searchlight, a DC generator with extra cans of fuel. Do a hover check."

When I tried to lift the load, it was like pulling a nail out of wood with only my fingers.

"If you're smooth, you can do it. Wanna try again?"

The nightmare of flying at the edge of destruction kept reappearing in my mind. "I'm ready for the joy of mushy controls and the opportunity to crash and burn."

Mishkov outstretched his gloved hands. "Only if you fuck up. This load dangles about fifteen feet below the helicopter, your total height is like a three- story building. So, go over small trees."

I scanned the trees for the lowest one, "Okay, I see a lane."

"Just hover forward until it flies. If you lose too much RPM, we'll die."

The cynical shit loved to drop incendiaries on my tender ass to see if I'd jump. Hovering took forever as the blades grasped for a little thing called lift. Meanwhile, my pucker factor skyrocketed enough to suck bolts out of the skids.

In a reassuring voice just above a whisper Mishkov said, "If I can see the stick move, you're over-controlling."

I squeezed the cyclic. "More smooth" simply meant more squeeze. Bullets wouldn't budge it.

Mishkov laughed at my tight gloves. "Crushing the control won't make it move less but breathing helps a hell of a lot."

Relaxing my grip helped, but I still dragged the load through the palms to make the big bird fly, like dragging the generator up the stairs. When we reached a safe cruising altitude, Red Two joined us.

"Why didn't they go ahead to the camp? We could do more if we didn't wait around so much."

"Unfortunately, single ship missions are more likely to get shot down around here. Last month one of our ships went ten minutes outside the perimeter and never returned. And we still haven't found 'em. That's why you'll go as a pair, everywhere."

"Oh."

"Besides, there's a bounty on your head. Don't know if they can retire off it, but it's a tidy sum. That's how the VC get more part-time warriors."

Our slower airspeed gave me a good look at the country. "Man, this is an endless sea of green."

"And deadly. You're screwed if you lose an engine, so always give yourself a place to land." Mishkov aligned his map with the direction of flight. "The straight route to Vinh Thanh takes us over some very dense, triple canopy stuff. Since these sling loads make us an easy target, we're gonna follow the roads even though it's out of the way."

The little beige ribbon of a road twisted over the mountain pass, amid the lifeless hulks of aircraft. "Is this a junk yard? There is some of everything down there: Hueys, Chinooks, Beavers, L-19s, even an A1E."

"That's called takin' your chance and losing. Each of those guys tried to shoot the gap in this mountain and didn't make it."

"What'd ya' mean?"

Mishkov pointed straight ahead. "There's a strange weather pattern here. We're at 2500 feet. On the other side of the pass, it drops off to sea level. Pilots try to sneak through the pass on low overcast days. The wind currents are volatile. They can change a clear-shot to zero-zero in a heartbeat."

"Red One, this is Bushwhacker One Six. What's your ETA?"

"Estimate one zero minutes."

"Roger, be advised Tigers reported ground fire."

Mishkov moved like he had a hot potato and switched to Tiger radio.

Bushwhacker came back with, "Roger, we took several rounds over the village of Dinh Quang. Keep your altitude as long as possible. Over."

After ten minutes, Mishkov transmitted, "Bushwhacker, pop smoke." Like a single daisy on a lawn, the color stood out. He responded, "Identify yellow," and pretended his hand was flying. "A shallow, flight school approach will get our ass shot off. Come in steep. Try not to splatter us on the bottom."

Some would have called my approach vertical, since I couldn't see the LZ through my windshield. I watched it over my toes through the chin bubble and out my side of the aircraft. The chief leaned outside to clear me to the ground, and I released the load.

"Let's go." Mishkov signaled upward. I brought in power to get out as steep as I came in.

"Red One this is One Six. We got eight POWs that ya gotta take back to base."

A bullet punched a small, ugly hole in my windshield immediately after, like they were listening. It scared the shit out of me. I climbed to 900 feet while Red Two placed his load.

"Roger, One Six. Wilco on the POWs. We're receiving fire from the ridge line southeast of your position. Where are your friendlies?" Mishkov slouched low in his seat.

"No friendlies there."

At nearly 1000 feet, the peaks surrounding us made our gunner aim high with his suppressive fire. The sound multiplied in the cockpit.

"Red Two, when you drop off your sling, get a load of POWs. I'll pick up what's left. Out."

"This is Tiger Two-Eight, identify fire from the ridge line." The gunship appeared to stop in midair as it punched off a pair of rockets. A hundred yards in front of the helicopter, the rockets' natural arc changed when they brushed against each other and each took a new direction, obliquely over the ridge.

"Oops." Tiger fired another pair and came in with his four M-60 machine guns blazing.

"Red Two is out with a full boat. We've saved the best for last."

Mishkov signaled me to turn inbound with a suspicious look. On the LZ, I landed where the POWs were kneeling.

Bushwhacker One-Six, a first lieutenant, stepped on the front skid to reach the door window. With camouflage paint on his face, a burnt cigar stub in his teeth, he shouted, "These are from the Communist National Liberation Front. They operated a hospital in a tunnel network under the village. The one with the bad arm is Colonel Brong of the 2nd VC Regiment. Take 'em all to the G-2."

"We'll get 'em there." Mishkov took the controls.

I felt like a giant in the cockpit next to him, with his seat full down and all the way back. I said, "That's two of you that fly in that odd position, compared to what they taught us."

"Have you ever noticed how few bullets come at you in flight school? If you wanted to shoot down a helicopter, where would you aim?"

I hated rhetorical questions.

"You'd want a real target. Right? So, all I'm trying to do is to reduce the sight-picture. Make it tougher on those little pricks."

I adjusted my seat. Seeing out the front windshield became more challenging, but I liked it. Messing with my seat under the penetrating glare of the motley group behind me made me uncomfortable.

"These POWs are disappointing: An officer, women, kid, and a gray beard.

"Don't let them fool you. The most innocent looking can be the most deadly."

"Do they all stink like this?"

The crew chief interrupted, "The grunt said the Colonel's arm is rotting off."

Scars and discolorations on the Colonel's face spoke of much conflict. His eyes glared under widespread, bushy eyebrows, on a thin, worn-down body. The right sleeve of his black shirt dripped through its tatters. Remnants of his upper arm bone protruded between the slivers of cloth, his forearm hung lifelessly in the wind. Blood caked on the gray-blue puffy shell of dead skin. Hate boiled in his glazed eye, the other remained swollen shut.

Both the crew chief and the gunner leaned downwind of their machine guns and threw up from the stench of the putrefying flesh. The odor attacked my nose and pulled at my guts.

I said, "Try kicking it out of trim to blow the smell out."

"I'll give it a try." Mishkov pressed the pedals deep to let wind rush through the cabin with the fury of a gale. The small girl screamed as she tipped backward toward the open cargo doors. Wind pushed her into the gunner's machine gun pod. While he struggled to grab her small arms, the colonel took the .38 pistol out of the gunner's holster and shot him beneath his chest protector.

With no motion wasted, Colonel Brong shot the crew chief in the middle of his back. He stretched across the cabin and placed the gun against Mishkov's cheek. His one inky eye had everything but fire shooting out of it.

With a wry smile, he shouted, "We're free."

PART THREE_

MISHKOV STOMPED the switch and snarled, "Kick it out of trim, my ass. Now what?"

"Nothing," I said, "Until he removes that gun from your neck."

A raw edge of splinters from rotting bone poked through the tatters of his wet sleeve. He yelled at me over the cockpit noise, "No talk." Beads of sweat covered his face. "Not look at me."

"Red One, this is Two." The radio blurted at us.

Mishkov never moved his lips or looked at me. "You talk. His good eye's on my side."

I mashed the transmit switch, "This is One. A Cong's holding a gun to Mishkov's head. Gunner and crew chief dead. Stay out of sight. Advise Tiger."

"Roger. We know. You've been transmitting. Wilco. Out."

Since my visor was down, I could watch him and not move. The Colonel looked out the cockpit window, turning his head back and forth. Confusion reigned supreme. Was this his first helicopter ride? Had he ever seen a God's eye view of the battlefield? I bet he would like to know where the hell he was.

My oversized chest protector concealed the pistol between my legs. Some turbulence jostled the helicopter enough to make old Rotten-Arm stagger.

I said, "He's just standing there. Not holding on."

"Yesiree. The dumb bastard."

Colonel Brong hammered Mishkov on top of his helmet with the pistol butt. "Silence. Silence!"

Mishkov recoiled but his hands never moved. He hissed, "Thanks for another fuckin' brainy tip. What are the other gooks doing?"

I checked their reflections on the glass face of my instruments. "They look like they're untied."

Mishkov started a descent. "I don't think I can knock him down. I'll try settling with power. It'll make the whole ship jump. You gotta distract him."

How do you make conversation with a beat-up, half-crazed, guerilla-fighter about to die from blood poisoning? I turned to the colonel. "Hey stinky, where you want to go?"

Translating those words made him squirm. His head eased toward me like a cat smelling a mouse. He strained to see through his swollen, blood-caked eyelids. "What?"

"Where go?" Time to simplify.

The other POWs pushed our dead crew overboard. What a sad way to go. No burial, just dissolved into the jungle. Or eaten by some animal. The old, white-haired man clenched the gunner's M16 in his bony hands. He destroyed my image of a kindly, picture postcard, Asian grandfather.

"Keep straight." The Colonel wiggled his gun forward.

I wanted to shout through my closed teeth—"Get him while he's pointing. Knock him on his ass."

When the colonel stuck the pistol behind my jaw, I nearly crapped. He said, "Where other ship?"

"What ship?" I turned my head only to face his gun barrel. It looked as big as a Howitzer. Old gramps didn't care, he leaned against the back wall with his eyes closed. The M16 pointed at the floor.

"Two ships at Vinh Thanh. Where other one?" Not only did his rotting body stink, but he had breath to match. Each time he screamed, his teeth, broken and bloody, glistened in the sunlight. His fat lip looked like a fresh break. I heard things like that happen during those G2 debriefings.

As the helicopter lost altitude and speed, the exterior wind noise decreased.

Colonel Brong's good eye looked around the cockpit, from Mishkov to me and back to Mishkov. The cold steel of the pistol dug deeper against my neck, like a cattle prod searching for action.

"Where other one?"

I shouted, "Don't know! Should we slow down?"

Something clicked in his brain about the flexibility of a helicopter. He nodded with enthusiasm. "Slow. Slow."

I made an exaggerated gesture to Mishkov, while I keyed the intercom with my foot, "Shit head wants us to slow down."

Mishkov nodded his head dramatically, killed the rest of the airspeed and brought the helicopter to a dead stop...a hover at two thousand feet.

Inflated with pride, the Colonel shouted to his comrades in Vietnamese. They yelled back excitedly.

Mishkov interpreted. "Shit. Bastard's gonna shoot down Red Two. Use our guns to shoot our guys. We'll be the first goddamn VC gunship. This better work." He stabilized the ship to disguise our descent, which was now like a falling rock.

The gauges showed he used all our power. We continued to fall, shuddering instead of the free whipping action I expected. But it still knocked the colonel out of balance until he caught his bad armpit on the back of my seat.

The clammy, stench-ridden forearm, snapped from the tendons and fell between my legs, like a hideous, bloated fish with the same slimy feel and color. Goo splattered up my chest protector to my visor and dripped down on my chin.

With all of the will power I could muster, I grabbed the big stinker and tossed it out the window. It hit the goddamn side-shield and bounced back in, like it had a mind of its own.

Like a two-bit operetta, old Snaggletooth draped over my seat, screamed louder than the turbine behind me and pointed the gun straight at Mishkov. What the shit was I doing here?

I tossed my cookies on his sandals and threw his old forearm away. It was gone except for the stinky goo over my hands and lap with its menacing, pearl essence.

GETTING my pistol out of the holster was harder than it looked, especially when the slime turned to glue. I didn't want my tombstone to read, "he couldn't blow the gook away to save the day because his gun got stuck in the muck. What a dumb fuck."

Colonel Brong never altered his deadly bead on the captain's head. He looked like he knew the captain had done something, but he wasn't sure what.

"Go slow. Go slow." He glared at me with the one nasty, bloodshot eye.

My left arm motioned for Mishkov to stop while I stepped on the mike button. "You got another chance."

The blood from Mishkov's cheek ran into his collar. "I'll make this son of a bitch spin like a top."

"What happened?"

He said, "Maybe not enough power. Maybe too much."

"Go high. More high." The colonel banged the back of my seat with the butt of his gun.

"Advise Two, he's been sighted." Mishkov didn't move a muscle when he spoke.

I continued the charade for the colonel with a thumbs-up signal. "Red Two. They're actin' like they spotted you."

"Red One, this is Tiger Two Eight. You're covered. I sent Red Two back to base."

A gunship on my tail felt good. Even if we bought the farm, he could shoot the survivors.

Brong stuck his barrel to Mishkov's cheek. "Go high. Go high."

I suspected that there was no love lost between the two.

"Tiger. We'll shake 'em loose this time."

"It ain't going to work," Tiger responded, "The Huey doesn't whip like the older ships did. Try it with a faster vertical descent at damn near full power."

"Slower. Slower." Colonel Brong pounded Mishkov's helmet with his pistol and it went off—the only casualties, the door post, land my nerves.

Mishkov put us in a flat descent, the ship pitched to the side and threw Colonel Brong into the ceiling. His good arm came down around the captain's neck with the pistol pointed at me. Mishkov released both controls and grabbed the colonel's arm to break the choke hold. The gun fired again shattered my eardrums and the window behind me. I grabbed the controls.

Mishkov arched his back as he wrestled for Brong's pistol. This time it shot the corner post in front of me. A bullet-proof face would have been nice.

I let the helicopter spin while I fought the stuck gun. When I wiggled it loose, the colonel's face turned as mean as a plateful of burning snakes. He dumped Mishkov back in his seat as he lunged at me with his mouth wide open in an ear-punishing shriek.

He fired two more times, then paused as if to say, "Great training, lieutenant."

That ripped it. I shot him in the swollen eye. Blood splattered against the cabin ceiling.

Centrifugal force pinned me against the seat. I reduced power to get the aircraft under control, but the spin continued. "Get off the goddamn pedal," I shouted.

Mishkov's leg did not move. I slammed my fist into his thigh and knocked it free. The helicopter shuddered but it flew again. My G-forced jowls turned back into cute rosy cheeks.

His eyes opened slowly like a drunk scared to consciousness.

"Fly this son of a bitch." I peered over the back of my seat like a kid at a sideshow watching the lovely Fatima dance. Our gyrations swept the woman and the little girl out of the helicopter. Brong's body lay behind Mishkov's seat. The old man sat with a seat belt buckled awkwardly around his chest and hair fluttering in the wind. Like a nightmare, he chambered a fresh round into the M16, smiled, and shot me point blank.

As close as he was, the blast from his muzzle blew by me but the bullets did not.

The first shot hit the back of my seat, like an atta' boy slap. Hooray for armor-plate. My helmet deflected the second bullet. It flicked my head like a rag doll and shattered the green Plexiglass above me. Chunks of it flew back at old gray beard. As he shielded his face, I reached around the seat and fired twice.

Recovering from Brong's attack, Mishkov made sure we could fly until we died. He said, "Did you get him?"

"Beats the shit out of me. I needed a rearview mirror to tell." But I peeked around the seat anyway.

Gramps dropped the M16 to the floor and raised his good arm. When a nine-pound club falls to the floor of flying tin can, it reverberates to the soles of your feet. Mishkov jumped in his seat.

I said. "One bullet hit the old fart in the shoulder and the other killed the sight glass for the hydraulics system. And it's smoking."

"Don't shoot him." Mishkov turned to the old man. "He may have valuable information."

The radio volume must have been kicked up in the fight, it screamed at us. "Red One. Tiger Two Eight. What's happening?"

"Tiger, we kicked their ass. We're going direct to base. Over."

"Yeah. All sorts of shit hit the fan at LZ Horse. We gotta relump, rearm and return. Over."

"Got one wounded gook for the G2 in An Khe. Stick close baby. We're on the low fuel light."

"Roger. Wilco."

Mishkov sounded tired. He rubbed his bloody neck with his free hand. "Can ya' tie the son of a bitch up?"

I attached Gramps to the web seat in the cargo space with good ol' Army green tape. His arm bleeding profusely, I covered it with tape too.

A powerful rapping, like hitting a pipe with a hammer, vibrated through the helicopter, sending a shiver up my sweaty spine.

"Goddamn, no hydraulic pressure." Mishkov turned the switch off and on several times. "When that warning stays on, it's like a red light in a whore house," he switched it again, "and we are gonna get fucked unless we find a runway."

"How long do we have?" I climbed back into my seat.

"Around 10 minutes." His hands vibrated in sync with the rapping. He transmitted, "Two Eight, our hydraulics failed. I'll be making a runway landing. Over."

"Roger. We'll stay with you until you're on the ground. Good luck. Out."

Mishkov called the Golf Course, declared an emergency and requested a run-on landing with special instructions, "be advised that we have a Papa Whiskey on board. Notify S-2. Over."

"Say again. Over." The tower operator sounded confused.

"Golf Course. We have a goddamn prisoner on board. Call the MP's. Call our OPS officer. Call Division Intelligence. Over."

"Roger. Wilco."

"Get on the controls. Spell me a second." Mishkov shook out his arms.

Our controls moved like a pipe stuck in concrete. This beautiful flying machine I controlled with two fingers turned into a lead sled.

"She-it. The pedals are like trying to budge a tomb stone."

"Rotten analogy," he said. "It's stiffer 'cause you got more aircraft to control. What's your biggest problem?"

"They're all big. At least we don't have to worry about over-controlling."

"Bullshit. That's the major problem. If our moves are too big, it may be impossible to correct."

Mishkov got back on the controls. "Stay on the controls with me. Sometimes a team effort works, sometimes not. Let's go for one-eight-zero degrees."

The giant heliport's small runway crept into alignment with the front of the aircraft. We applied too much pressure and watched 180 zip by.

I groaned. "Why don't we each grab a control?"

"Okay. Try it."

We corrected the 30 degrees of over-shot heading, maintained a thousand feet, and aligned with the runway.

I said, "They'd probably shit if they saw us in flight school."

"Fuck flight school. We'll tell 'em about it if we walk away from this landing."

Flying in the daylight had its advantages—I actually saw the runway. I've seen wider streets.

"We need to slow down this mother." Mishkov nearly stood on the control to get it down while I busted my gut to dissipate the speed. The resulting flare nearly stopped the helicopter cold, which would have crashed our ass.

"You got it Ox." Mishkov picked both hands and feet off the controls as I tried to hover 200 feet over the edge of the perimeter.

The lead sled, in all her stubborn glory, was mine alone. "Thanks a bunch."

"Good training, Lieutenant"

If I heard that saying again, I would punch someone out.

"Serpent, this is Golf Course. All appropriate personnel have been notified. Emergency crews are standing by. Any further requests?"

"How about a hamburger, beer, and French fries to go, served by a love-starved, donut dolly?"

"What color hair on the dolly?"

"It doesn't matter, just make the snatch match."

I regained forward flight. My right arm ached from the stiff controls. Sweat activated the splattered putrefying flesh and dried puke all over me. The holes in the windshield framed my warped perspective of my third day in Vietnam.

Mishkov leaned forward. "Don't flair. Just drive it to the ground. The runway'll stop you."

Raw steel of the runway met the cleats on the skids and showered sparks everywhere. It wasn't half as intimidating as the night before. Our speed amplified the sound level of ripping, shearing and the clatter like a freight train.

"Hold what you got. Reduce power." Mishkov's direction made a big difference as I tried to take the wind out of the sails of this runaway boat.

We still ate up the landing strip like we had space to waste. Normally helicopter pilots didn't worry about those things but when this runway stopped, it was the end of the world.

"Stuff it all the way down," he grunted as we both pushed the power to off. The helicopter started to turn. Wind rushed through my door. At 90 degrees to our slide path, I looked over my shoulder to see where the hell I was gonna crash.

"With luck, it'll stop before we roll. But I'll shut off what's still on to keep down the flames."

And it didn't tip over. Those big, one-foot-nine-inch-wide blades lumbered past us in a slow crawl.

"Safe." Mishkov spread both hands out like an umpire.

I sat back. "Can't remember when I had such a good time." I turned to check on the old Cong in the back seat. "Aw shit."

Mishkov look at me, startled. "What?"
"Gramps is gone."

"WHAT DO you mean he's gone? How?"

"Beats the hell out of me. My focus wasn't exactly behind us."

"I'll check with the tower. You get the runway."

I ripped off my helmet, harness and climbed to the cargo deck. Two hours in that seat caught up to me, my legs felt like logs. A crouching figure in black with a long shock of white hair headed away to the drainage ditch.

The cumbersome chest protector slowed me down but there was no time to take it off. I shouted, "Hey. Stop."

Gramps froze in his tracks and spun around with his M16 leveled at me. He squeezed a short burst into the weeds.

I stood there like a dummy not comprehending that he was about to nail my ass. He shot five single shots in quick succession. Two spun me to the ground. The impact stung, but I wasn't wounded. A numb warmth followed like a hit with a strap. Dumb, yes. Dead, no.

I waited for the bastard to run out of bullets. The chest protector probably was a washboard in its earlier life, it didn't know how to roll. *Plop, Kerplop, Kerplop* was me rolling away.

The mixed staccato of multiple machine guns roared overhead. A gunship hovered on the other side of the ditch. Gramps dropped the rifle and raised his good arm high in the sky. That cat had more than nine lives.

Tiger Two-Eight kept him at bay.

In a minute Mishkov caught up to me. "You all right?"

"Yeah. Where'd they come from?"

"After you tore off, I called the tower. Tiger monitored and offered their help. Glad they popped right over."

"You're glad? The bastard shot me again. Why don't they just shoot the little prick?"

Mishkov helped me up. "G2 wants him."

A loud MP siren penetrated the roar of the gunship. The 545th Military Police Company sent two burly PFCs with weapons drawn to take charge of the prisoner.

"Ain't that beautiful?" The smile drained off my face when another jeep arrived with my old bosom buddies on board, The Major Assholes, Gonzalo Scivetti and Maxwell Ray, were glued to the MP's actions. They ignored our disabled ship in the middle of the runway, and the company's two prized pilots just snatched from the jaws of a wreck.

While the MPs handcuffed Gramps, Scivetti turned to us, "While you two guys were fuckin' around on a log run, the entire company has been busting their asses in support of the 227th. We need you on the line..."

Mishkov's face turned six shades of red, about a nose length away from Scivetti. "Wait a second. Do you realize on that simple log mission, our prisoners killed our crew chief and gunner, then held us at gunpoint until we knocked them off the ship? Hellberg blew the shit out of a gook choking me. He landed the helicopter after a complete hydraulics failure. Other than that, we were just fuckin' around. How about you, Major, what have you done all afternoon?"

The velocity of the outburst blew Scivetti's eyebrows into his hairline. "Well...it's good training for the lieutenant. Isn't it, Captain?"

"Fuck training." Mishkov looked down into Scivetti's face. "This guy's ready to rock and roll. *Sir.*"

"That will be all Captain. It's now 1600 hours, you and Hellberg get some chow. We may need you this afternoon." Scivetti's hard-ass expression didn't change.

Mishkov spun away and muttered, "Goddamn strap-hanger." The mess tent made more sense for him. Someone was about to get their ass kicked and it wasn't Mishkov.

On the other hand, the idea of finding something edible at the mess intrigued me. L. Sid joined us at the table. I put another sandwich on my plate.

He said, "The bastards wouldn't keep me with the nurses or send me home, obviously ignorant of the true psychic damage done by our tight fight in the night. They even hauled me up to G2 to retell the story." He grimaced at the smell of our nasty clothes. "I heard you guys were on the shit list, but this is ridiculous."

"There's something I don't like about Scivetti." Mishkov explained the afternoon's adventure to a wide eyed L. Sid, punctuated by jargon and Vietnamese terms that I didn't recognize.

"Let me tell you what I heard about Ray." L. Sid glanced around the mess tent. "Very senior. Been in maintenance forever. Passed over because of gambling, booze, and women."

Mishkov drank some coffee, "What's the skinny on Horse?"

"Evidently, the Cong are gonna attack in honor of Ho Chi Minh's birthday next week. But the Cav is spread as thin as cheap salami. Hanging around Division all afternoon was an eye opener. Our new division commander, Major General Norton, has his hands full."

L. Sid said, "And the weather isn't gonna help us out either."

Beau Buncher parted the door flaps to the tent. "Captain Mishkov. You and Ox have a log mission. Earlier this afternoon, the shit-hooks brought in a partial firebase kit into LZ Hereford. But the fighting at LZ Horse forced them to relocate the base. A platoon is now on the way to secure Hereford and equipment. Y'all have to report to OPS tent ASAP."

Mishkov asked, "What's happened?"

"Captain Jenkins said something about re-supply. He was still talking when I left."

We headed to the operations tent. The company grounds, with its maze of tents, felt different in the day light.

"I can't stand my fatigues any longer. They stink." Mishkov looked at me, "And I smell like a picnic compared to you."

"The only thing I have left is a pair of jungle fatigues with no insignia, nor rank."

"Who gives a shit? You can worry about that when you get back."

I checked my pistol. "How about more shells?"

"Only five to a customer." L. Sid smiled and offered a box. "Take a hand full. They're tracers."

Mishkov moved toward the tent opening. "This time, don't shoot the goddamn helicopter."

"Obviously, you can't take a joke." I trudged along behind him.

At the OPS tent, Buncher had my name already on the board. "Ox, baby," he looked at me with a cigarette dangling from his lip. "You've been having such a good time, Captain Jenkins had to let you try another sling load again. At the rate you're going, you'll have every ship in the company down by the weekend."

"Why, fuck you very much. Anything else you want me to do?"

Beau stood there with an empathetic grin that understood my haggard look.

Scivetti stood next to the assignments board and practiced his endearment lessons. "Captain Mishkov. You took your sweet old time in getting here after I summoned you."

Mishkov gritted his teeth. "Summoned?" He hissed, "We're summoned to court. Or summoned to see the king. You don't summon."

I didn't want him to go off the deep end. "Major, I delayed us in the Continental Palace." I pulled the ammunition out of my pocket. "Had to bum these off of L. Sid."

"Well goddamn it. Lieutenant, our pilots are in deep shit out there while you play fart-around down here."

"Yes, sir." I smiled at him.

"And where in the hell did you get those fatigues?"

"This was all I had left. Got pretty badly soiled."

"Soiled?" Scivetti's diminutive uniform was still spit-shined and starched. He looked up at me, close enough to smell his peppermint breath.

Mishkov pulled me aside so he could tower above the little twerp. "More like dried puke, putrefying flesh, and a full day of bad sweat gave him a giant case of nasty odor. He farted around because he smelled like shit."

"Captain, I'm sick of your big mouth. You better straighten up and fly right. Or I'm gonna bust your balls. Is that understood?"

The silence was deadly.

Beau broke in. "Major. We gotta get the show on the road. Let me explain the mission so you can pre-flight while we find a wingman."

"We don't need to wait for a wingman. The objective is clear enough. We got a battle waging out there with no time to fiddle-fuck around looking for another ship." Scivetti turned to Captain Jenkins.

Jenkins' eyes grew wider. "You have more than an hour and a half of daylight left, and it is only a short hop."

"Isn't it company policy to never send out a single ship mission?" Beau's smile said, *gotcha* all over it.

"Depends on the gravity of the situation," Jenkins squirmed away.

"What bullshit." Mishkov changed the flow. "This is a log mission into a hot LZ with a bucket of bad weather on the way. And you want me to run in by myself? You're full of shit."

"I choose to ignore your insolence Captain, but not for long." Scivetti puckered his miniature face. "If I order you to fly, you had better sprout wings or get ready to be court martialed."

"What if..." L. Sid stood by the tent flap, "...we got ARA to come along? Good old Spark-Gap. They're bored as hell on perimeter defense anyway. And they love to shoot them rockets."

Jenkins immediately called battalion operations.

Scivetti kept his lock on Mishkov. "If I were you Captain, I'd get on that aircraft and fly, fly, fly."

"Well you ain't me, Major. But I will tell you this...*sir*, I don't give a flying fuck."

Spark Gap One-Eight married up with us on departure. Our sling load mission to LZ Hereford decompressed Mishkov, as a therapy of sorts. When we were almost there, he broke a self-imposed sentence of silence. "Scivetti's a prick. But there's something else wrong."

"Yeah, he's an asshole too." I told him about my first encounter with both of the Majors.

"Interesting...so, he and Ray were in Saigon together? He claimed not to know anyone here."

The ground commander called on his frequency.

Mishkov responded, "Cutter Six, this is Serpent Six-Six-Three. We're one-five out. What's your weather like?"

A raspy static filled the cockpit, "Lousy. It's gonna come unwrapped any second now. Yellow flight's diverted to LZ Horse. Out."

"Break, Serpent, this is Charger Six." Another new, clear, and booming voice. The battalion commander reminded me of a ham radio operator, calling from his lonely basement.

Mishkov keyed immediately, "Go ahead."

"Make your drop at Hereford then evacuate special personnel back to Golf Course. Over."

"Wilco. Out."

"Is this de ja vu or what?" The scary weather rolled in like a bull running at a red shirt.

The captain asked Hereford to mark the LZ with smoke. A wall of rain poured from a bulbous cloud in the center of the valley. Its gray-blue obscurity approached us at gallop.

"Roger, gotta red one." Mishkov had eyes like an eagle. The smoke streamed like a ribbon off the top of the rock. Our sling load cut through the air with little effect on the flight.

LZ Hereford turned out to be a simple, bare spot on the ridge line, punctuated by large rocks and errant patches of elephant grass among destroyed trees. Grunts huddled around under ponchos. Empty 81mm canisters cluttered the area.

"My approach is steeper than usual, so I don't blow those guys away. Downdraft can make their ponchos lethal for us. You sorry you're not a grunt officer?"

I wrinkled my face at the squalid encampment, no tents or foxholes. "No thanks. I'd rather get wet in the Continental Palace and die in the sky."

Mishkov brought the helicopter to a hover following directions of the crew chief. He released the load of mortar rounds smoothly. When will I be able to fly like that? Probably in another thousand hours or next week, which ever came sooner.

The smaller trees were the easier departure path, so Mishkov flew down into the valley to pick up some airspeed. Dense, dark overcast rushed to settle on top of the ridge. We had to look for another hole to escape the box canyon.

"Spark Gap, this is Charger Six. Yellow flight took heavy ground fire at Horse. Slicks got out. Gunship's down. Need your help right now."

"Roger. What's the status of the gun?"

"Yellow One is pulling out their personnel. A squad's in place to secure or torch the bird."

"Spark Gap switchin' to Tiger net. You roger, Serpent? I'll see if ops have any more in the barn."

On the intercom, Mishkov said, "Did ya' notice Spark Gap's first question was on the downed helicopter? That's the way to think. We bust our ass to pick up those guys. One day, it might be us."

"Serpent, Charger Six. How's the special personnel? Over."

Mishkov's unhappiness showed but his response was straight up. "We're inbound for pickup." He banked hard back to the landing zone.

"Serpent," Charger Six's clear voice turned rough. "Report when you get 'em. Out."

"Ox. Switch me to Cutter net."

"Forget your load?" One-Six giggled.

Mishkov said, "It's hell to be mortal. Pop smoke."

"Better have an extra oar. It's rainin' like the dike broke." The dark cloud dumped its guts over the LZ and tried to blow us into the trees. Smoke from the grenade flowed down the hill, like milk spilling off the table.

Visibility deteriorated to the width of a murky football field. Little clumps of ragged clouds floated where the rain wasn't. In the five minutes since our departure, everything fell apart.

"How do you see?"

"You don't. Just look out the door or chin bubble."

With arms wide, the Cutter radio operator directed us to the spot for the pick-up.

Two figures wearing clean ponchos ran forward. The radio operator darted off his perch to push them out of the blade path of the helicopter. All three slipped in the mud.

Mishkov gave off a big belly laugh. "What a shame. A decapitation would really piss off old Charger. Might'a had to go home." He turned to the chief. "Strap their asses in. We lost our departure path. How does it look behind us?"

"Like shit. Clouds are chasin' us—a small clear spot just opened up."

"That might get us out of here." Mishkov took off using his door and chin bubble to see. He said, "Need some help. Can't see much."

Swirling rain in the powerful downdraft of the rotor system created a vortex of water designs. The helicopter struggled up the mountain side, scattering grunts below our flight path, only to discover our route disappeared again. We gained airspeed but no altitude. The ceiling hung much lower than expected. A nightmare cave with no way out.

"Fifties. Fifties." The crew chief shouted.

Mishkov's head nearly jerked off of his spine. "Where?"

"Down behind the tail."

"Down?" He made a steep bank with nowhere to go.

Cutter busted in over his static, "Did you find the fifty?"

"Negative. Where are your guys?"

"Mostly on the LZ."

Balls of flame blew by my window. I didn't see where they came from, but they were big enough to bring down this ship.

Mishkov turned to the ridgeline, pulling all power available. "We got no place to hide. I'm goin' shoot the gap."

I remembered the story of the An Khe pass we flew over earlier. Carcasses of the aircraft strewn around. Guys had gambled and lost.

The ship jolted like we smashed into something big. Our controls jumped in sync with the blades. I shouted, "What the hell'd we hit?"

Chief said, "No, we got hit. Blew out a compartment door. Grazed the rotor and left a glowing ember in the blade."

Mishkov shouted, "They got the engine. Losing power. Turning back." I held my breath through the power surges. Caution lights lit up the panel.

Daylight faded to a surreal twilight. About five hundred feet below us, the faint image of LZ Hereford materialized between the torrent of rain and angry clouds.

Mishkov spoke in a flat, nasal monotone. "We've screwed the pooch." He switched the radio to guard. "Mayday, Mayday. Mayday.

Serpent Six-Six-Three. Engine failure. Plugged up with nasty bullets. We're tryin' for LZ Hereford. Out"

Silence, normally out of place in flight, gave way to airstream noises, splatter of rain and the shriek of rotor blades with bullet holes.

"Tell our passengers to hold tight." Mishkov shook his head at Hereford. "Cutter, I'm coming down with my engine out. Clear the LZ. NOW."

Cutter yelled, "The chopper's gonna crash. Get the hell out."

Three hundred feet at fifty knots to a dead stop should have taken about ten seconds. At one hundred feet, he dissipated airspeed. I couldn't see where we were going.

At fifty feet, I saw grunts in a landing zone. Only the outer edge was open. We had a chance with the wind still in our face.

At forty feet, enemy fire hit the belly of the aircraft. I felt every one of them in the quiet, powerless ship.

An explosion on the LZ blew debris at us. "I'm committed," Mishkov shouted. A second explosion on the flat rock wiped out the grunts, who just got out of our way. The lifeless body of a GI under a poncho liner tumbled down the hill.

At 25-feet, Mishkov flared and dropped to the clear edge of the hill. He cushioned our landing like he had full power.

"Yeah. Yeah. Babe." I laughed.

"No sweat GI." He smiled with vigorous thumbs up.

A third explosion ripped off the left skid and windshield. The blast destroyed the chin bubble, door, and Mishkov's left leg and arm. Concussion rocked the ship back on its heel. Our main rotor blade ripped through the green glass overhead, severing the left front of the cabin, pulverizing Mishkov. The console and panel shielded me from the explosion, but not from the mud and grass.

With half of the cabin gone, the empennage tilted downhill. The helicopter slid off the crest. I sat like a potted plant, not knowing if I should jump clear or stay and scream.

No real choice. The ragged strut stuck into the ground and spun the helicopter down the hill. If anyone screamed, I didn't hear it. I swirled too much. My eyes stayed open all the way down, seeing everything in our way.

The slide stopped with the sickening crunch of metal ripping against the immovable hardness of a twenty-inch tree limb. It impaled the helicopter through the right front door. My door pinned me to the seat. If I had been three inches closer, I'd be dead.

Remnants of the magnetic compass and the clock popped out of its mounting in front of me. We pointed due north at 1828 hours.

Stunned silence followed our catastrophic spin down the hill. No wind. No static. Yet despite being speared-to-a-stop at midway, I was still alive. My gray, wet world stood still with fragments of grass stuck to my face and rain dripping on me.

The crew chief spoke in a hoarse whisper, "You guys OK?"

I whispered, "Mishkov's dead. I'm pinned in."

Pulling himself up, the crew chief reached the cockpit panel. "Got it. We're stuck on a goddamn limb like an apple on a stick."

"I'll stand guard away from the ship as security," Gunner coughed the words.

On my left, I couldn't see past the body of Mishkov. The gray mist obscured the rest of the hill. Rain mixed with the mud and blood on his face. His right eye stayed open when he greeted that last moment of truth.

From the back, a pissed-off female voice whined like a lost puppy. She threw her seatbelt against the floor. It banged louder than a drum. "Goddamn, I gotta get to Qui Nhon. I gotta deadline to meet."

The gunner slammed the butt of his rifle into the deck. It made the seatbelt fall sound cheap. "Shut the fuck up. What do you think we're doing here, waiting for a bus? Get your ass out of the helicopter. You're a smaller target out there."

It's easy to admire a diplomat.

I took Mishkov's dog tags, unit call signs, revolver, wallet, wedding ring and scrambled through the hole in the front windshield. The helicopter settled against the tree with the loud moan of wrinkling metal. Both scared the hell out of me.

Rain dumped on us. I stood in mud up to my ankles in the blackness of the hillside.

Chief said, "Let's get up to the LZ, Lieutenant,"

"And mistake us for gooks? Let me try the radio." I crawled back into the cockpit, but my helmet was now pinned under the limb.

"Don't mess with it. Get the Captain's." The crew chief pulled branches away.

As I pulled his helmet up, Mishkov's head flopped forward on his chest. Attached only by the skin of his neck, the helmet was still warm when I put it on my head. I remembered Six's words, "Do what you gotta do.'

When I flicked the battery switch, the instrument panel, anti-collision and position lights lit up. A Christmas tree in the middle of a black hole. The dumbest move I could've made.

In the second it took to shut off the switches, a machine gun opened up on us from across the valley. The rate of fire was slow like that from an old .30-caliber. But the impact sounded twice as big.

"Don't fire back." I mashed the transmit switch, "Clanger Six... Cobbler...no," I couldn't remember the call sign.

"Would you believe Cutter Six?"

"I'll believe anything. This is Serpent. We slid down the hill and got stuck on a tree. Under fire."

"Can you make it up here? Do you have the special personnel?"

"We lost a pilot, everyone else is all right."

The machine gun across the valley probed again. Bullets struck the rotor head with a clang and tree stump with a deep thud. Gunfire sounded more personal without the roar of the engine.

I ducked but had nothing to hide behind. "Need to advise our location to Ops Over."

"Roger. Call me when you start. Good luck. Out."

I switched frequencies. "Yellow One, this is Six-Six-Three. Over."

Nothing. Why was the silence so clear when no one was home?

"Serpent, this is Spark Gap One-Eight. Over. "

"Roger, I'm next to LZ Hereford. We'll try to climb up to Cutter. Advise Serpent. Over."

"Roger, wilco. Standby." I'm in the bullseye and he wants me to stick around?

A dense cloud bank cut visibility from little to nothing at all.

"Serpent, this is Spark Gap. Serpent reported in route to base with wounded Tiger personnel and low fuel. He'll send a rescue. Can you hold in your location? Over."

Across the valley they opened fire again. Tracers arched and burned out in the black void in front of us. "Hold? Hell no. We're going to Cutter. Advise Serpent Six." I turned the radio selector back to Cutter. "We're coming up. Keep your boys awake. Out."

The rain pounded heavier and louder than before. Ponchos obscured the passengers leaning on the nose of the helicopter.

I said, "Chances of a rescue tonight are slim. We gotta climb the hill. Best I can figure it's about a hundred yards of steep grass."

"You can't leave him here," she whined.

"We sure as shit can't take him up that hill. We'll be lucky to climb it ourselves."

"Can't we wait here until another chopper? Didn't you just call?"

She irritated me more than the ringing in my ears.

"There's no moon, no stars, no nothing. How do you think that they'll find us? There's enemy across the valley. What we don't know is how many of their buddies are coming for us. A downed helicopter means lots of goodies. And a bounty's paid for everything, especially prisoners, dead or alive."

"Oh." She sounded deflated.

"This is bullshit, Lieutenant." The gunner spoke from the weeds. "Let's get up the hill before Charlie shoots our ass."

Love them diplomats.

"Just wait a damn minute. Who is going to take my bag of equipment?"

The pain in my ass kept on coming. "If you want it Honey, you better bring it. The bellman's out tonight."

"It's all my clothes, notes, and records."

"Nah. It's either your equipment, or your ass." I turned up the hill, "Gunner, take the point."

"Yes, sir." He crouched ahead low to the ground in the elephant grass. "We gotta stick to the slide path. If there were any booby traps, they would have blown up on the way down. Stay close. The chief and the Lieutenant will come last. Above all, this fog doesn't make us bulletproof, so zip it up."

I discovered the sloppy uncertainty of sticky mud. For every step up, I made one and a half sideward slips, a perpetual diagonal drag away from where I wanted to go. Our special people kept falling and bitching. Progress was slow.

The gunner said, "Elephant grass is our friend. Stems are coarse and hairy. Don't pull the leaves, they're razor sharp."

Automatic rifle fire blasted out of the LZ. I don't know what scared me more, the muzzle flash or the damn noise.

The gunner gasped for breath. "How they gonna know we're the good guys?"

I said, "Just talk nice to 'em."

The gunner called out, "Hey dumb shit. Stop firing."

"Hey, fuck you." A voice from New Jersey sounded close enough to smell his breath.

"We're the chopper crew."

"So? Can't remember the password, can ya'?"

I jumped in with a wild-ass guess. "Serpent."

The New Jersey accent checked with somebody. "Close enough. Come to the light, one at a time." A red light flashed.

In minutes, all of us had climbed behind the listening post but still had a long way to the LZ. Rain filled up my boots and made a sucking noise with each step. My legs burned from fighting the steep and the deep.

At the top, I found a lean-to next to the ammunition crates. A sergeant led me to the command bunker in a corrugated metal culvert, butted against a large rock. An exhausted first lieutenant sat next to the radio with a flashlight. I said, "Cutter Six?"

He searched my uniform for rank. "Serpent?"

I shook his hand. "Second Lieutenant Danny Hellberg."

"Joe Sanchez." He smiled. "Glad you made it. Where are the VIP's?"

"Outside. Probably bitching under the lean-to. That was a hell of a climb."

"Bring 'em in sergeant."

Sanchez took his helmet off. "The Shithooks brought these culverts in this afternoon. How many survived the crash?" Small talk wasn't his bag.

"My crew chief and gunner, plus those two people. Mishkov's dead. His body is in the front seat."

"Hell, we thought you bought the farm. We were gonna look for you but then they chewed us up before we could launch. Lost six guys."

"What about LZ Horse?"

"They are up to their ass in alligators, too. Lot of wounded. No way to get them out. Nothing's flying."

The flap opened by a poncho-covered figure, who sat heavy against wall. "Hello Joe. Sorry to be back so soon." He pulled the hood away revealing a man in his early forties, salt and pepper hair. The twinkle in his eye was like an alcoholic who just found a bottle.

"Hi, Frank. You're getting more of a story than you bargained for. Where's your little buddy?"

"I never saw her before this afternoon. She just bummed a ride out here like I did. This was supposed to be a secure fire base."

I chuckled. "Surprise."

"Surprise, my ass. I'm too old for this crap. So, I get shot at, blown up, slid down the hill, then some mountain-goat lieutenant ran my ass up a cliff. That's the part that nearly killed me."

"If you stayed there, you'd be dead for sure."

He looked at me. "Who're you?"

"The mountain goat." I extended my hand.

With a flushed face, he took my hand in both of his. "I'm Frank Lastrand, *Time* magazine. I appreciate the great job you did. Sorry you lost your buddy. What was his name?" Frank stuck a floppy straw hat on his head and wrote in his notebook. "Is this still the 13th?"

"Captain Ben Mishkov." I spelled our names, "And yea, it's Friday."

"The Cong got everything on their side. What's more powerful, weather or superstition?"

Another dripping figure sloshed in, tripped on her poncho and did a face-plant in the mud.

I rolled her over. Mud made human features almost indistinguishable, "Should've known...Kaelyn DeHaven...enjoy your trip?"

MUD OOZED FROM HER NOSE. She gagged.

"Nice move." I said, "The good news is you landed in mud. Too bad it doesn't taste as good as it did when you were a kid." I pulled the hood back to see her curly black hair stuck with mud.

She grimaced when she looked at me. "Oh, God."

"Aww. You said that would be our secret."

"I see that you know each other," Frank guided her to the wall next to him.

Sanchez checked his platoons on the radio, "It's way too quiet out there." He turned to us, "Third platoon secured your helicopter. Perimeter's set."

Kaelyn's brain clicked in. "Don't tell me you were the pilot?"

I blinked and smiled. "One of them."

"I wish you would have called in another helicopter."

Sanchez broke the tender moment. "Brigade discovered a major Viet Cong force on the eastern rim of the Kim Song Valley. That's right where we are. As soon as this weather turned to crap, they came out of the woodwork."

Frank chuckled, "Like catching a Tiger in quicksand."

"I really need to get out of here," Kaelyn grabbed Cutter Six by the arm. "Could you have a squad take me to Horse?"

The radio blasted again, "Cutter, this is Charger Six."

Sanchez almost broke his arm grabbing for the microphone. "This is Cutter Six."

"Send a romeo papa north to Hill 784 and report."

"What did he say?" Frank asked.

"Battalion commander wants a recon patrol."

"Right now?"

"We do this every time we set up for the night. And tonight, I sent one to secure your aircraft."

"So why the hell did we have to climb back up here? Couldn't we have just waited for them?"

"Because you're valuable civilians, inadequately armed, poorly trained, and under fire."

"This is nuts. It's as black as a witch's heart out there yet you want to send 'em to look around? For what? A bullet in the head?" Even in the dim light. Frank glowed.

"Listen. You think we know what's happening out there—we don't." Sanchez looked at Frank like he was four years old. "I need a clue."

"At night? This is fuckin' ridiculous..."

"And you're an asshole. I'm tired of your shit. Now back off and keep out of my way." The honeymoon was over.

Kaelyn looked into a small mirror and wiped mud off her cheek. "There has to be a way for me to leave."

Sanchez exhaled in obvious exasperation, "One-Six, report to charlie papa, ASAP."

Kaelyn smiled. "Who's Charlie Papa?"

Another dripping soldier entered, "What's up, Joe." He squatted on his helmet. Obvious delight streaked across his face when he saw Kaelyn.

"Send a squad to reconnoiter the ridge line. Keep close contact with 'em."

"How far up?"

"Get to Hill 784 to see both sides of the ridge." Sanchez flattened out a map. "There's enemy activity across the valley on Hill 975." The muddy lieutenant winked at Kaelyn. "We always have room for tag-a-long friend."

Kaelyn smiled to Sanchez. "Can I go with him, Lieutenant?"

He contorted his face like a hot coal fell into his jock. "Noooo."

"Goddamn it, lieutenant. What is your problem?"

"You're my problem. I am just a stick-in-the-mud grunt, who wants to keep his guys alive. Their chances right now are 50/50. With you along, they hit five percent. I could give a shit l if you take a bullet, because you're an inconsiderate, pain in the ass," Sanchez spoke slowly, "But if you got shot, on an ill-considered mission, no matter how much you hampered its success, I would get screwed, blued, and tattooed. And that is not my career path."

"You are an impertinent prick."

"And you are a stupid bitch. Just stay in this bunker, it'll be the safest place. Now I gotta see what's cooking." Sanchez rearranged his poncho, checked his ammunition and left.

The never-ending rain swelled the small stream in the center of the culvert. Frank stirred it and mumbled, "Misguided shits. Tell me what good they can do out there. Stumbling around in the darkness. This kind of Army bullshit chews up these young kids."

I put my hand up to slow him down. "There are lots of bad guys out there."

"When that fifty tore your helicopter apart, I knew that's not the problem."

"Then what is?"

Kaelyn preempted, "Is the information received worth the risk of lives? Have you ever considered how stupid this whole war really is?"

"No. It's freedom and democracy against enslavement and communism."

Kaelyn twirled her pencil. "Actually, that's an artful fabrication. War is an opiate for the great American middle class, who pay for all of this waste. With their blood and money." This woman talked like a flaming eyed beatnik out of California. She couldn't be from Texas.

"Serpent, this is One-Six." The hushed tones made the radio shrink in the corner. "Tell Six, romeo papa deployed."

Frank chirped, "Let me tell Sanchez. I wanna see what's happening outside with that recon patrol anyway." He rose with his camera in hand. "Maybe I'll get some good tracer pictures."

Kaelyn stood up. "We have politics and big business combining to pillage and plunder." The shrill call of an inbound mortar dislocated Kaelyn from her soap box. Our culvert took a direct hit which sucked the door covers up and let our light pour outside. I switched the flashlight off and pulled Kaelyn down.

A few meters outside the door another shell landed. Concussion tore at our ears and chunks of the hill ripped the sandbag flap to shreds. An orange ghost of the explosion hung in my eyes. Round after round exploded and mushy earth fell in clumps and splatters. Screams blended with commands and formed a grotesque terror in the night.

I laid as flat as I could next to a Kaelyn. Her squirming body movements and rapid breathing matched her shaking hands. Machine guns and small arms fire erupted and careened off everything.

"Cutter Six. Patrol's pinned down below a steep, fortified ridgeline. Without air, they're history. Over."

As quickly as the attack started, it finished. Ten minutes of carnage and bedlam ended so completely, the silence that followed was off-key. But the rain didn't stop.

Simple sounds turned brutal. Medic shouts during roll call turned into a body count. Kaelyn's breathing slowed as she listened to the damage.

Every time I heard heavy machine gunfire; I remembered our ambush. On the ground, the 50 dug foot-long furrows in the dirt, chewed limbs off trees and turned logs into splinters.

A raspy, excited voice blurted over the static. "Cutter Six. This is One-Six. We're getting' wiped out. Get us Spark Gap."

Quick bursts of the high-pitched M16 contrasted the steady drone of the slower, louder .30-caliber.

A shaky young voice transmitted, "One-Six is dead. This is Davidson. I pulled the Lieutenant to cover, but he's gone. We all gone."

"Easy, Brian. Easy." Sanchez came back with authority, "What's happening now?"

"Got the men behind cover. Set up a M60. Went from rock to tree to hole." Davidson's voice rose, his words ran together. "No room to run. Got us in a goddamn crossfire."

"Brian. We've got some choppers. They're coming. Hold on."

Kaelyn stared at the radio and yelled at it. "You're a fuckin' liar."

"CHARGER SIX, I'm relaying for Cutter. At Hereford. We're..." I didn't know how to tell him in Army talk we're getting creamed.

"This is Charger. Say again."

"Hey. We're gettin' our ass kicked. Need Spark Gap to deliver some shit on these gooks."

"Roger, Serpent. Spark Gap Two-One's on a night training mission. I'll divert now."

The cold finger of fear brushed me when I heard the sound of sloshing through the mud. Kaelyn pulled me back against the culvert wall. The footsteps got closer. I cocked the hammer of the .38 and aimed at the opening.

"Hey Hellberg. You in there?" Frank peered through the door flap.

"Jesus." Kaelyn exhaled.

"No. Just Frank, your friendly correspondent."

"What happened?"

"The third platoon's trying to rescue those boys on the hill." He collapsed against the culvert. "Did you get any help?"

"Yep. Spark Gap's on the way."

Frank wiped his face. "Sanchez also pulled some men out of the second platoon. He shrunk the perimeter and our protection."

Heavy gunfire erupted on the hill. Loud enough for us to feel it. I switched frequencies and heard Cutter Six shouting over the gunfire. "Goddamn it. Gimme your coordinates."

"I don't know where the fuck I am. Just shoot it up the hill."

A dull thud with a residual ring like a cheap glass marked the 81mm mortar tubes going off only ten yards away. "Adjust what you see, and I'll send more."

"I didn't see anything. Put it on the goddamn ridge line in front of us. Where are the choppers?"

The mortar tubes fired. Cutter said, "You'll see this."

At a count of five, Davidson screamed. "Yeah. White phosphorous. Move it north."

Our choir of mortars played a mournful tune. Fifteen shells fired in as many seconds. It sounded automatic until the first explosions occurred on our LZ.

With unerring precision, the Cong walked their shells down the LZ. Both of our tubes were taken out by the first explosions. They blew into the air and bounced like empty trash cans off the curb. A pause replaced the shrill voices of command with an agonized wail of pain. And the rain kept increasing.

Heavier machine gun fire raked the LZ, but now the darkness of the night made the tracers look like neon lights. Hereford changed to a shooting gallery with one major difference. We were the target.

"Serpent. This is Gap Two-One. We're on station. We think. Mark the target."

"Are you shitting me? I don't even know where I am." I fingered the mike for a second, "Spark Gap wait one. Break. Cutter, give them something to shoot at."

"Roger. This is Davidson. Hang on." He keyed the mike while he searched. "I got one willy peter."

"Get it close. Then tell me what direction to drop the load."

"Okay, hang on."

Spark Gap's voice had an irritating New York accent. He said, "Cutter, what's your ceiling?"

"What ya' mean?"

"I mean how high are the clouds?"

"How in the fuck am I supposed to know? Not much."

"All root, babe. Not much is better than nothing."

All root? Only one person would answer like that. "Hey, Fred. What in the hell are you doing?"

"Who's this?"

"Danny. Playing grunt."

"You've been playing hard for a couple of days. They're calling you Ox in battalion."

I smiled. "What're you doing in Spark Gap?"

"They're running short. They thanked me by giving me this shit detail."

"Thanks. I resemble that remark. Can you find the trigger?"

"No sweat. I justa flippa da switch, and squeeza da stick. And pop goes da sparkler."

"Serpent, this is the real Spark Gap Two-One." A humorless voice intruded. "Quit fuckin' around. We have limited time on station."

"Spark Gap, this is Three-Six. Davidson tossed it near the gooks. That's the spot, dump it on their ass."

Spark Gap banked out of the very tight holding pattern directly to the hill. Ragged clouds sat on the ridge. Rotor blades flapped and popped as the helicopter approached. It slowed to a hover over the culvert. Our shredded sandbags fluttered from the downdraft.

JP4 exhaust flooded our bunker. Spark Gap proceeded up the hillside like a giant bird of prey looking for its quarry. Each rocket left its tube with a burst of flame that profiled the helicopter against the cloud layer overhead. Tube after tube lit up and streamed out.

"Love those rockets," Frank stood outside with his camera. "Finally. Some action."

"Get down before you get your ass shot off."

Ignoring me, he moved from one position to another. "Only war has this kind of drama. A modern knight sparring with the fierce dragon of the mountain, lashing out with its fiery tongue. Love it. Love it."

Spark Gap disappeared over the hill. The thunderous roar of rotors and the rockets' red glare evaporated from sight. "Forty-eight's all we had. We shot our wad. And our fuel light's on."

Big, fat, juicy balls of fire pawed at the offending death bird. On the ground, tiny piss-ant responses of M16 shot at the source of every tracer.

"We stopped them. We stopped them." Three-Six shouted.

"Can you pull your men back to our position?" Cutter asked through thick static.

"Roger. Wilco. What about our dead?"

"Gotta leave them." Desperation reeked from Sanchez. "Go back in the morning."

"All that bravado crap," Frank's disgust reduced his voice to a bitter whisper. "This is a crock o' shit."

"Everything that happens out there is either the probe to find the enemy, the joy of killing the son of a bitch, or the terror of protecting yourself. Anyone who thinks it's something else is pissing up a rope." I eyeballed Lastrand.

"Serpent, this is Gap."

"Go ahead."

"You and your buddies ready for pick up?"

"You bet your ass."

"Mark your spot."

I couldn't find anything to mark until Kaelyn put the flashlight beam directly in my eyes. "How about this?"

"Brilliant," I shut off the light.

"Serpent," The unfriendly one growled again. "We can't standby forever. Gimme a visual or we're gone."

"I can hear them out there, but I can't see them." Lastrand looked out the opening, his white straw hat drooped from the rain. The brim was at least five inches wide with one side pinned up in Australian style.

"Do you want to get out of here Frank?"

The question got his attention. "I don't know. It smells like home and I love the decor."

I grabbed his hat and poked my finger through the crown.

"God damn it, what the hell ya doing--"

Spark Gap transmitted, "Serpent, I can't see you."

I stuck the flashlight inside of the hat to form a primitive reflector. Outside of the culvert, I moved it from left to right.

The sound of the helicopter blades changed from the "just-drilling-holes-in-the-sky" to my favorite, "I'm-coming-to-get-you babe."

"Ya' ready to make a mad dash?" I looked at Lastrand and Kaelyn. "He'll be here in less than thirty seconds."

I leaned my arm against the culvert roof. Gunfire shattered the peace. A single bullet tore Frank's hat from my hand. Somehow, I held on to the light. More gunfire raked our roof. Rock fragments knocked my hand away, numbing it. Chunks of skin stood up like a plowed field. "Damn." Blood appeared but did not drip.

We took a direct hit to the side of the culvert that made our space hum.

I called, "Spark Gap. They got our number. Your ass is grass if you land." Another mortar drowned out the transmission and blew debris inside.

"Ox. You still there? What'd you do to piss them off?"

"Told 'em your name. Don't land."

"Nah. I got your sweet little, flat spot in sight. Just get your ass out here when we land."

I loved his confidence.

The bombardment turned into a barrage. Every second a mortar round exploded with a strobe light effect to paralyze clumps of mud in mid-air, or soldiers running, or tracers glowing. A bad dream gone nuts.

"We're getting' pounded. Don't land," I yelled over the explosions.

Charlie's guns had the scent of the warbird. Bullets chased the fuselage and sounded soft when they hit the wide underbelly and hard as they ricocheted off the skids. Those that hit the rotors disintegrated into the boney, lonely whistle of a holey rotor.

On top of the maddening ferocity of bombardment, an eruption cast a massive, orange-yellow bubble of flame into the sky.

"That's gotta be my helicopter. Holy mackerel."

"Nah, just a couple more gooks entering the promised rice paddy," Frank aimed his camera to catch the panorama of a fire ball behind the approaching helicopter. "What did they pack in that sucker anyway?"

Guns all over the LZ responded to the enemy fire. Tracers chased tracers.

Spark Gap turned back to the valley. "Gotta go. Out of ammo and fuel. Good luck. Ox."

Kaelyn lunged at the radio, "You can't leave. Land. Land!"

I pulled the mike from her hand. "Negative. Do not land."

She threw a handful of mud at me. "You son of a bitch. You..."

Her fire, and our hope, dissolved in the silence left by the retreating copter.

PART FOUR_

KAELYN and I watched the giant, orange flame die after the helicopter exploded.

Lastrand put down his camera and said, "Ox, are you from a big city?"

"Cleveland, Ohio. How about you?"

"Thibodaux, Louisiana."

"Where's that?"

"About 55 miles from New Orleans. A beautiful little town with some of the darkest nights you'll never see."

"I thought everyone from the south had an accent?"

"Not if you spend twenty years running all over the world for *Time* magazine. My native tongue's worn away just like my enthusiasm, replaced by a dab of Yankee. Or is it a damn Yankee?"

"Well when will you hang it up?"

"My last assignment was two weeks ago. That was until I split with *Time* about the strategy here."

Kaelyn couldn't bear the sidelines any longer. "What do you mean?"

"The real issue here is the First Cavalry Division. They've proven the Airmobile concept works. Now they want to take it to the north and finish this war once and for all. How would the grunts react to such a strategy?"

"They'd say, why not?" She answered in the same inquisitive tone the Queen must have used on Columbus.

"Wouldn't it be cool to interview one in a foxhole?"

I interjected. "Hold on. If you go crawling around out there, you'll get your ass shot off."

Kaelyn tugged on my arm, puckered her lips, and oozed sweetness. "Call Sanchez, would you?"

On the radio, Cutter Six exuded his normal charm. "I want this bullshit off the air. We got a real situation here."

I loved it when he called about-to-be-overrun-by-the-Cong, a real situation. "If we see dawn's early light, then we talk about it. Other than that, keep the goddamn channel clear."

His ominous reference to the probability of tomorrow resonated more in the blackness. I laid down the microphone. "Press relations wasn't a course he stayed awake for."

"Let's hope night fighting was...especially without airpower, and out of the reach of his artillery." Frank had been around this game before. I gave him Mishkov's pistol.

The bunker served us well, surviving at least two direct hits. Our guard didn't like the arrangements as he pulled a couple sandbags off the top of the rear wall to see if there was an exit. He found only a small crawlspace so he disguised the front entry with sandbags and branches.

Kaelyn leaned against the wall. "There's a bigger story here."

"What's that?"

"The black market."

Frank said, "Nah, come on. When the commercial infrastructure doesn't work, the black market does. They're in every war zone. No big deal."

"In Saigon, the brass said it's bigger than anything yet."

Frank sighed. "Modern technology. New thinking. More money. They speed up everything. So what?"

. . .

Kaelyn bounced the light beam on him. "This is different. It's controlled by two major players. First is the Vietnamese mafia, the Binh Xuyen."

"Can't the MPs handle it?"

"That's the curious thing. They ignore it. Or they're allied with the forces seeking to return Bao Dai as the Emperor."

Frank looked up. "Wow, I thought you said 'the Emperor,' now *that* would make this situation hemorrhage."

"I did."

His mouth gaped open. "Where's he? What's he doing? This is a front cover story. I love it."

"Wait, it gets better." Kaelyn's excitement showed. "Bao Dai lives in Paris. They want him to unify the South and the North so they can rule forever. And throw out the American capitalists and the Chinese communists."

I asked, "Why the Binh Xuyen?"

"They're the only ones who can make things happen. Their graft and corruption pull the strings in both governments. They'll inherit the wind if Bao Dai's ship will land with the people."

Frank said, "Can't believe the MPs won't shut 'em down."

"They're in it up to their ass." I described Sergeant Polhill running me out of Saigon.

Kaelyn leaned in to us, complete with flapping eyelids. "Actually, the power of Binh Xuyen is what lured me here."

"Did you get what you expected?"

She said with glee, "This valley's the entry point from the South China Sea to the central highlands. It's isolated with a controllable boundary."

The dawn broke in my mind. "Ah ha."

Frank inflated like he solved the mystery. "Exactly. The perfect staging point for the Binh Xuyen."

Kaelyn said, "Well it was until General Norton took over and every crook in the province came here to hide. This was Binh Xuyen's safe haven. He forced the crooks to join the Cong."

Frank erupted, "It still doesn't matter, and they're one and the same."

"Not really. The Binh Xuyen works both sides of the street. And they don't care who wins."

A grave digger smile crept up on Frank. "So, who are we fighting, Charlie or the Crooks?"

"Yes." Kaelyn turned the flashlight off. "And don't forget the NVA. The North Vietnam Army advisors are here to get their part time warriors out of the box that we put them in. Like a cat cornered, they turn ferocious. "

The radio blared again with Sanchez preparing his platoon leaders. "Don't let your men fire unless they have a definite target. As soon as this stops they'll come with everything they have. Break. Serpent see if you can get battalion again. Tell him the situation's in the toilet."

Before I replied, a whistle blew three times. The slow clatter of an old machine gun punctuated the regularity of the mortar shells landing. Across the LZ, eight figures walked in a loose formation, firing their weapons at everything, except us. Our guys responded with a grenade launcher and took out a bunch of the first line. But they continued to walk.

I fiddled with the radio but couldn't find battalion. Rifle fire tore up the dirt in front of the culvert and ricocheted off the walls. Flat on the ground, I drew my pistol. A helmeted figure walked toward us, firing his AK-47 in bursts from side to side. Between the leaves of the bush, I aimed and jerked the trigger. The flash from the gun barrel obliterated the silhouette. My ears rang from this echo chamber.

"Shit. I can't see him." I pulled the hammer back. "Kaelyn. Frank. Did I hit him? "

"Yeah. He's down. Why the hell did you shoot? He would have passed us." Frank whispered like a foghorn.

"Serpent, this is Charger"

I struggled with the clumsy microphone. "This is Serpent, we're getting overrun. Send some fucking help."

The mortar rounds came back in waves, the concussion made our culvert feel like a bass drum. A phosphorous explosion spread its burning tentacles of fire. Smoke hung over us with a salty, chemical odor of sulfur.

Vietnamese voices yelled over the roar; explosions illuminated their conical straw hats. A second line of Cong advanced in a crouch, more systematic than haphazard.

"Shit." I grabbed my pistol with both hands, "Okay, I won't shoot unless they see us."

Mortar explosions provided the flash of reality. A Cong stopped directly in front of the opening, firing laterally across our position.

"Serpent, this is Charger Six." The damn radio boomed back into life. I lunged to shut it off but only increased the volume. "Serpent—" I beat the damn thing to silence in the mud.

The Cong caught the sound while he reloaded his rifle and shouted in Vietnamese. Two more hats flicked our way. They raised their rifles to the middle of their chests and marched in an evasive pattern at us.

"Frank, baby, this is it. Shoot straight." The element of surprise had to count for something. I aimed for the inquisitive one and this time squeezed the trigger. Twenty yards wasn't the toughest distance I'd ever shot, so the first Cong grabbed his stomach with a scream. Not bad for shooting at his head. I swung to the next man and squeezed again. Bingo. Two down, eight to go.

Frank pushed the bush to the side of the opening. His gun erupted, and the third and fourth Cong dropped.

My next two shots found their marks before I ran out of shells. Talk about timing. I had nothing left but to hug the ground and disguise myself as dirt.

Frank made every shot, until his hammer clicked. Two more Viet Cong fired back. Bullets ricocheted off the walls. The flash from their barrels looked like cannons.

Scared to death, I laid face-first on the ground and wished the chest protector covered my ass. And I wished I were any place but here.

The whistle sounded four times. An artillery flare showed the line of khaki uniforms and helmets disappearing into the blackness.

I said, "They've gone. Are you guys all right?"

Kaelyn gathered herself. "What if they come back? Can you get me a gun?"

"I don't even have bullets for mine. Hey Frank. Nice shooting. "

No response. "Frank. You okay?"

He seemed to be resting against the wall, head down.

"Frank?"

A mortar flare lit up the sky and drifted at the edge of the clouds. I touched his shoulder and he fell backwards. Blood dripped off the wall. His eyes were closed.

Kaelyn came forward. "How is he?"

I felt for a pulse. "Dead."

Kaelyn emitted a moan like her soul was kicked. "Just when he had a front cover story. What a waste." She moved to the opening, pushed away the bushes and shouted into the void. "Ho Chi Minh's an asshole."

Frank's body lay in the ditch between us. Kaelyn stared at him. "He was such a sweet man. What a terrible waste. I gotta get out of here. Did you reach anyone?"

I dug in the mud for the mike and tried battalion first. "Charger Six. This is Serpent. Over." It was a normal Army procedure: when I couldn't talk, they called; when I desperately need them, nobody answers.

Kaelyn shined the flashlight on the radio, the squelch and volume knobs were bent. I skipped through the frequencies until I heard Sanchez. At first, static blared, then he said, "South perimeter is lost. We're the last ones standing. In the boulders and elephant grass. Got one M79 HE and a willie peter. I'll signal when I hear—" Rifle fire wiped out the rest of his transmission.

"We're shit out of luck if he thinks we're gone," I said.

"Roger, Cutter. We are about twelve minutes out. What's your ceiling?" The voice wasn't recognizable, but he was a pilot with a two-blade helicopter vibrato.

I heard the shot and felt the impact of the .50-caliber again. A powerful rhythm. If I could hear anything hit, I was way too close.

A new replacement flight from battalion reported from the beginning of the valley. Cutter shouted, "Preacher, they're chewing us up. You can't get in."

Preacher paused. "Let me find you, then we'll worry about Charlie."

"'The Cong are coming again, aren't they?" Kaelyn checked the empty cylinder in Frank's pistol, "What do we do if they find us?"

"Depends if we have something to protect ourselves with- I'm gonna check out the gooks we shot".

"You can't. Don't..."

"You wanna do it?"

"No,"

"He had something when I shot him. I have no choice."

Once outside, a new sound enveloped me, different from the tunnel sensation of the bunker. I laid still for a moment to listen for the helicopters. Nothing penetrated the continuous exchange of gunfire and explosions up the hill, nothing except my heavy breathing.

In my low crawl, I couldn't see much. The Cong's feet were the first body part I touched; his small sandals were made from a tire. I grasped the AK-47 and his hand grabbed my wrist like a zombie coming out of the grave.

Another flare lit up the LZ with a flat light against his hideous face. The conical hat tilted backward to expose the bloody remnants of his missing chin. Teeth from his upper jaw protruded and an ugly noise emitted from his throat. Great. At least he couldn't bite me.

If looks could kill, I'd be a center-cut roast already. His eyes flashed hate. His fingernails dug into my skin. If I could make him laugh, maybe he would choke? Can you laugh without a jaw?

With one hand, I swung the AK-47 around into his unsuspecting forehead with all the power I could muster. Which wasn't much. The stock crashed through the bridge of his nose and sounded like smashing a melon. His grip slipped loose.

I gasped at the damage. It's one thing to shoot someone, but beating their brains out is the limit.

Movement caught the corner of my eye. I froze. Another flare silhouetted more conical hats. I laid my face on the ground, released the rifle and withdrew my hand.

A new set of voices came through. Women's voices. Some crying, others talking. One shouted commands in the high pitch, melodic tones of Vietnamese. I didn't understand it, but I knew she meant business. She screamed the name of Bao Dai several times. They talked until they were next to me, at least two on each side. Someone kicked dirt on me. I didn't move.

Next, I got a kick in the ribs followed by one to the butt and then two feet stood on the center of my back. This child or woman did a jig. All jabbered at once—some laughed. A bug landed on my cheek and crawled into my ear.

My superhuman effort to remain motionless crumbled when the little jigger reached between my legs and grabbed my balls. The end of the world was a twitch away. Should I buck her off? They probably discussed the relative merits of cutting off a souvenir, when the command lady discovered their jawless soldier still had a pulse. Fortunately, she ordered everyone to drag old broken nose away.

The *whop-whop* of approaching helicopters excited their babble. The command lady now screamed orders until they faded in the distance. Weapon fire dwindled to nothing while everyone waited to see what the birds of the night had in store.

I jumped at the soft sound of a solitary M79 grenade launcher, *Caachonk*. White phosphorus exploded about ten meters away. My snake-eye peek of the slow-moving streaks of flame showed the sizzling beauty, both majestic and terrifying. Fire splattered on a retreating Cong, he screamed and rolled in the mud with the torment of fire, eating his flesh to the bone.

One of those smoldering tentacles stretched towards me, I twisted my hips away and the molten fire splattered with an ugly crackle. I ran toward the culvert and knocked over the radio.

In the darkness Kaelyn said, "You're on fire. Your feet."

My left toe and right heel burned. It illuminated her contorted face. I scraped off the flames against a rock.

Kaelyn said, "Those were just villagers. With straw hats and black, baggy pajamas. They didn't even have weapons except for the leader. And she was frail as a child."

I caught my breath. "One more move, and their souvenir hunt would have launched me to the stars."

"How could you stand it out here?" She actually looked at me with compassion.

A synchronized beat of the approaching helicopters overcame the old, slow sound of Charlie's .50-caliber. Six rockets in a row punched off to stop its big tracers that streaked across the sky.

"Listen to that." I looked into the sky. "Did you hear anything else?"

I found the frequency of the assault team and listened. Someone screamed, "...it's no good, can't see the LZ."

"That was our last marker. Try something else." Sanchez couldn't hide the desperation in his voice.

"Okay, Cutter, Yellow Three has a dead bead on you. We'll back off and let the Tiger stay close."

The rain stopped.

"Cutter, this is Yellow Three, inbound. Over."

I said, "Clouds are down to the treetops. How in the hell is he gonna land in this stuff?"

Kaelyn looked in the direction of the valley. "I hear him." The chatter of helicopter blades echoed off the mountain.

"Yellow Three, this is Cutter. Can't see—you don't sound right."

"Negative. I got it lined up."

"No. You stupid son of a bitch. Ya' don't . . ."

The Huey's rate of closure slowed down to a deadly crawl. Several abrupt power changes altered the pounding of the blades.

"No. Let 'er down." Yellow-Three transmitted, "Turn on the landing..."

They lit up the LZ with a searing intensity that showed nothing but white. "It's zero-zero."

"You're turning. Pull." More power changes made blades sound like a swimmer thrashing in the water.

With a throaty echo, the .50-caliber opened fire on this ripe target. Endless bullets ripped through the illuminated, thin skin of the helicopter. Like a mighty bull, speared to death a thousand times by an angry matador.

One bullet ripped the landing light apart, leaving a burning ember at the spot. The helicopter crashed into the mountain above us. So low it blew sediment in. In the downdraft, the smell of JP4 exhaust was bitter.

I choked up when the sickening sound of the rotor blade broke off into the earth; the aluminum frame crunched, and the Plexiglass shattered with a pop.

Kaelyn covered her ears while I looked uphill. No explosion. No flames. Only the red anti-collision light turning at the pace of death. The .50-caliber continued to devour the carcass, like a lightning bolt, that kept striking and striking.

Other automatic weapons opened fire from all around the LZ. My soul screamed at this killing frenzy.

I touched Kaelyn's shoulder. "Move back. As soon as the Cong get their jollies off, they'll come. This bunker is too close."

She stretched out her arms with empty palms. "We don't even have a gun."

"We gotta disappear." I herded her to the back and stumbled into Frank. "That's it."

"What?"

"Help me with Frank."

"Do you want to take him with us?"

"No. A diversion. Anything to keep the Charlie from looking too deep. Let's get him to the opening."

We leaned Frank against the wall. Moving the stiff was no fun.

"Cutter, this is Tiger Three-Five. I got the 50 in sight. We're rolling hot." The powerful sound of rockets firing out of their pods meshed with the rotor blades and turbine roar, then disappeared in the explosions. "We nailed the bastard. We got him." The helicopter turned back to the valley.

Loud voices startled me back to the reality. Vietnamese voices. A bunch of them. Getting close. Checking out the crash.

The radio sounded like a cackling goose. "I gotta shut that damn thing off."

Kaelyn peered over Frank to see what she could. "Moon glow. First time tonight. What's that..." She hushed when a hat bobbed up into the picture. The soldier stopped next to his slain comrades and turned to the sound of gun fire up the LZ.

We moved farther back into the cave. Kaelyn pushed aside the top sandbags of the wall and crawled in. "Get in here."

"What?" I could barely make out what she did, but I slithered through the opening. Too bad it was only about ten feet from where Frank leaned, manning his lonely post. I replaced the sandbags.

Time to hold our breath. Kaelyn positioned herself against the wall and I leaned against her with my back, toboggan style. Her rapid breath cooled my neck, her breasts heaved against my back. Water seeped down the wall while I watched through a wedged opening.

The Cong's flashlight slowly turned back in our direction, he noticed Frank for the first time. He fired his rifle. Frank's head snapped back, and his body fell into the mud. The Cong shouted jubilantly to his fellow soldiers. They must have cautioned him because he went into a guarded squat, pulled the pin from a grenade, and tossed it into the cave.

I heard the sizzle for a fraction of a second. It hit the metal of the radio and kicked it into operation. "Okay, Cutter, we're coming in hot. Anything live on that LZ ain't friendly..."

Then it exploded.

THE GRENADE DISLODGED from under the Cong and the explosion surprised us. Increased concussion strength widened our view holes between the bags. Everything hit us harder than before. Our ringing ears locked out all hopes of sensitive sound.

Bitter fumes hung low at our vantage point in the fourth row from the bottom of sandbag wall. Three more Viet Cong with helmets and backpacks pulled bodies out of the way and set up another machine gun. Within seconds they opened fire next to the gnarled remains of the damaged fifty.

Kaelyn whispered, "These Cong are good."

"Yeah. Every trigger squeeze has a target."

"So, what do we do?"

I looked through my hole. "Rifle's still leaning against the wall."

She said, "Without the magazine it's useless."

"I don't give a shit. It'll be a great eight-pound club. Our only chance. Help me over the wall."

Reflected light from the machine gun's muzzle flash made it not quite as pitch black as before. "Step into my hands...I'll get you up." Kaelyn connected her fingers and pushed me up with surprising ease.

Like a cat, I balanced on top then lowered to the mud. Trying to attack three armed, guerilla fighters with bare hands wasn't exactly a stroke of genius.

A stream of bullets chewed the top of the sandbag next to the Cong guarding with the rifle, the splatter made him flinch. I held my breath and didn't move. He cursed. Damnations translated in all languages.

I found the AK-47 shorter than the M-14. My opportunity arrived when ricochets jolted him away from the incoming fire. I smashed his skull with the butt of the rifle and knocked him into the mud. From this awkward position, I swung the rifle straight across into the ammo bearer's ear. He crumpled on top of the ammunition belt. The machine gunner deflected my next lunge with his helmet and grabbed my rifle.

His helmet slipped off and long hair fell to his shoulders. Her shoulders. He was a she.

Her hand was as big as a foot—especially when squeezing my throat. Towering over me, she plowed forward. With her knife, she jabbed at my head. I ducked left and she sliced beneath my rifle; a searing pain radiated up my side. Her shoulders rammed me into the wall andmy head bounced off the steel. Mucous sprayed out of my nose. As I slid down the wall, I kicked her knee as hard as I could. She growled.

I poked at her with the rifle. She knocked it away and kicked me against the wall again, knocking my breath away.

The giant smiled in anticipation of the kill.

From above the sandbag wall, Kaelyn screamed in Vietnamese. *"Dung lai dinky dau"*. The giant turned toward the scream. *"Bok-bok...Du...."*

With all my strength, I lunged into her. Like trying to move a fire hydrant. She tittered into the split barrel fragments of the fifty. The ragged splinters of steel punctured her neck on both sides, framing her face in agony. Desperate hands reached at me for the kill she was denied.

I collapsed to all fours, struggling to pick up the rifle. It felt like a sledgehammer. A rocket exploded in front of the bunker, deflected by the sandbags, snapping me back to the present. With all the ringing in my ears and my heart beating its way out of my chest, I tuned out the outside battle while I fought the monster Cong.

Kaelyn shouted over the noise, "Danny, get in here."

I found the loaded magazine in the mud and picked up a small machete. "This time I'm prepared." Every step I took hurt. My head throbbed. The fire in my side sapped my will to go on. Dead bodies littered the bunker. I smiled at my luck.

Kaelyn helped me up that mountain of sandbags. Behind the wall, I leaned against the dampness and it felt good, down deep to the soles of my boots good. No mistakes this time, I slammed the magazine into the rifle, propped it up in the corner then stuck the machete under my belt.

"What did you yell at her?"

"I thought it was, 'Stop you crazy...'"

"And what'd she say?"

"Something like fight or fuck off."

The rumble of the helicopters shook the culvert. Sweat dripped off my face, "Come on, baby. Land it already." Three separate times helicopters tried to land. Their downdraft blew leaves, bark, and branches on us but no rescue.

Kaelyn touched me. "You all right?"

"My ribs only hurt when I breathe...or move. Yeah. I'm fucking great." Blood trickled down my hip.

Outside, the gunfire filled in where the explosions left off. A high-pitched New York accent shouted into the bunker, "Okay, I'll call 'em out Sarge. CHIEU HO."

Kaelyn tried to see over the wall. "That's our amnesty program."

Pain streaked in my chest as I pulled her away from the bags. "No sudden moves. Everyone out there has a gun. All safeties are off. And they're damn good shootin' things that peek at 'em."

I whistled as loud as I could and yelled, "Hey, did you forget how to speak English? We're here."

He answered, "Who's we?"

"Lieutenant Danny Hellberg, Huey pilot, A Company, 229, and Kaelyn DeHaven, newspaper reporter."

He yelled. "Sergeant Woffard, We found them."

A red beam of light searched around the cave. The new voice spoke lower and louder, "Holy shit, what a mess. Where are you?"

"We're behind the wall. I'll get some sandbags out of the way." Kaelyn pushed them out and helped me over the top.

"There're supposed to be three of you. Where's the third?"

"Dead. In front of the bunker."

We chugged some of the sergeant's water and we told him what happened. He said, "We're at An Khe base to rest up from three weeks in the bush. This was our first night combat assault. What a bitch. First flight got shot up pretty bad. Crashed before the landing zone. A squad is extracting them now."

This buck sergeant couldn't have been more than nineteen years old. He presented a formidable sight with camouflage face paint, full pack, and bulging web gear. I asked, "How about Cutter Six?"

"He and Two-Six consolidated what was left of their men up the hill. My squad objective was the immediate sector."

A skinny, slick-sleeve showed up with a back full of radios and a first aid kit on his hip. The sergeant radioed battalion with our status and turned to us. "Serpent Five's in route to evacuate you guys and our wounded. Estimate arrival eight minutes." He looked around. "You're a lucky shit, Lieutenant. You too, ma'am."

Thunder trumped all other noises in the LZ and the rain poured again.

Kaelyn taped a wide bandage to my side. "Who's Serpent Five?"

"Major Gonzalo Scivetti. Our new XO. You met him at the My Canh."

"Old hot pants. He and his buddy propositioned me in more ways, in less time, than I had ever experienced."

"Let's get back into the bunker." Paranoia made me yearn for the security of our palatial pipe. I put on my chest protector and slid the machete inside a strap. "Operations must be desperate. I didn't think an XO flew much, especially not a single ship mission, at night, to a hot LZ."

"That's it. That's where I heard about the Viet Crooks." Kaelyn's face lit up. "If the mafia are the ants, the Viet Crooks are the elephant. Scivetti tried to lure me into his room to see files on them."

"Files?"

"I never saw them because shortly after he floated the bait, the other guy came to the table."

"Who?"

"The old Vietnamese waiter. He looked so ridiculous in that white uniform, with his Fu Man Chu beard, placid smile, and perfect teeth. But they changed when Major Ray mentioned Hon Heo.

Turned into three snakes, hissing at each other in a Vietnamese dialect that I couldn't understand."

"Both understood Vietnamese?"

"I think so. But they shriveled up when the Air Force colonel complained about you helicopter pilots. Then the old man disappeared."

A radio transmission came before I heard the helicopter. "Runner Six, this is Serpent Five for landing instructions, Over."

Sergeant Woffard snatched the microphone. "Roger, proceed up the valley. We'll mark our location. Please identify." He removed the red lens from his flashlight and swung it in a circle toward the sound.

"Roger. Got circle. We're turning final."

I asked. "Why didn't he request enemy activity?"

"He might be too hot or too dumb." The sergeant circled his flashlight faster. "It sure is quiet here all of a sudden. No sniping, no whistles, no nothing."

Kaelyn stood up, "The last time it got this quiet, they overran us."

The Huey on final approach got everyone's attention. The solitary *whop, whop* of the rotor, without a chorus of gunfire, sounded naked. It landed next to the bunker in complete darkness, no landing or running lights. Dirt and grass blew with the JP4 exhaust. "Damn it, I love that messy, noisy, smelly, old bucket of bolts."

The helicopter never settled but kept light on its skids. I helped Kaelyn on board. Major Maxwell Ray sat in the right seat, Major Scivetti in the left. I gave a smiling thumbs-up over the console. "Boy, am I glad to see you."

Scivetti turned. "Sit down and buckle up. We gotta go. Is DeHaven with you?"

His cheerful demeanor infected me as usual. "Sure is."

The helicopter immediately rose to a hover, I tapped his shoulder. "Aren't you gonna wait for the other wounded? And our crew chief and gunner?"

"Nope. They cleared me to take off. Sit down. And shut up."

Once airborne, I scrambled for a seat and dug for a safety belt.

Kaelyn motioned me close. "The old waiter," she nodded over her shoulder.

My old bosom buddy from the village, Gramps the Cong, grinned at me. "I'll be damned." His arm dangled in a sling. An about-to-throw-up look replaced his smile, while his jaw distended to a scowl.

It's not easy to talk in the back of a Huey, with doors open, flying at eighty knots. I shouted at her, "That old bastard tried to kill me three times. Last time I saw him, the MPs were taking him away."

Kaelyn's eyebrows went up like a kid at Christmas. "I want to talk to him. This is exactly what I need, a prisoner of war, a real Viet Cong."

"Well, he is as real as you can get. Get up and ask. Scivetti is on the left. You stand a hell of a better chance to get something than I do."

She removed her seat belt, unfastened the first two buttons of her shirt, and leaned over the console. Kaelyn distracted Scivetti enough that he almost stuck his helmet mounted boom microphone in her cleavage.

She yelled anyway. "Can I talk to the prisoner?"

He recoiled. "What for?"

"I want to interview him for my paper."

"About what?"

"About what was happening? You know—the war, the Viet Cong, the US presence."

Scivetti turned. "Nah. Just sit down. We're landing soon. You can talk to him then." Old Gramps revived enough to stare at Kaelyn for a long time.

Blood seeped through the bandage onto my pants. The big momma Cong didn't cut me too deep, but it stung like she did it with salt on her blade.

The helicopter climbed through low scud obscuring the valley and leveled off above the clouds to a clear night.

Why were we going south? We're going the wrong way to An Khe or Qui Nhon. Was hot pants lost?

After the storm, the air felt extra clean, extra crisp, but I got woozy anyway. The ringing in my ears increased, the pain in my side throbbed. *How much blood had I lost?* I needed a lift. Even C-rations would taste good.

I reached around the corner to where the gunner normally rat-holed a case or two of that great, government-issued grub. To my utter amazement, there was nothing. No grub, no gunner. I scooted to the other side. No crew chief there either, just sick old Gramps laying down. Their guns were loaded and ready to go, their helmets dangled on a hook.

Suddenly the spectacle of Gramps, only strapped into the seat, was scary. I remember him in action before, he changed from a sweet looking old man to a surreal killer.

Kaelyn sat down grumpy. "That son of a bitch is an asshole."

By reflex, I unclogged my ears from the descent and motioned silence to Kaelyn. "Reach around Gramps and get the helmet. I'll get the gunner's. We'll listen." The helmet had a strange odor. As I adjusted the mike boom, I found blood on my hand.

Scivetti talked in Vietnamese to a ground station, then to Major Ray. "Max, I can't find the double campfire they promised. Is this the right valley?"

"I don't know. I didn't understand him either. Was that the Second Viet Cong Regiment?" Max turned the panel lights lower.

"No. This is the Binh Xuyen. The meeting you missed. Our ticket to the big time. All we have to do is get this guy back and we'll be in the loop. He's promised to buy all the goods we can supply him plus sell us all the dope we need."

"Why would they go to all this trouble for a chief from some rinky-dink hamlet."

He turned to Ray, "Because he's not just a province chief."

"Well, what the hell is he?"

Scivetti's pompous attitude reeked in his condescending tone, "He's Ho Chi Minh's brother."

SCIVETTI LAUGHED at Ray's surprise. "Can you believe it? That old fart is Ho Chi Minh's brother. He runs the whole black market operation in the south. Every GI who pays for a piece is helping the Viet Cong. And they try to kill every GI they see. Beautiful, isn't it?"

Scivetti, the scum ball.

"What're ya' gonna do with Hellberg and DeHaven?" Major Ray fidgeted in his seat like his hemorrhoids were on fire.

"They're going to be wiped out by the same VC attack that killed our crew chief and gunner. That's the beauty of war: so many casualties, so few inquiries."

Scivetti said, "There's the valley. I don't see the signal fires."

"And some asshole is shooting at us." Ray choked with the excitement of one who was never the center of a bullseye.

"They were warned not to shoot. I'll call their commander again." Scivetti transmitted an excited burst of Vietnamese. The response echoed in equally animated tones.

The machine gunner on the ridge didn't stop firing. Tracers arced over the helicopter and disappeared. Then they arced right and farther left. Then dead center. Nothing scarier than being shot at past the tracer burnout range. Damage is assured, but the destination is to be determined.

Scivetti banked hard enough to get out of range.

Gramps did not take well to flying. He convulsed. And puked on the rear wall.

Kaelyn pulled away. "Goddamn that stinks." And she threw up.

That was the moment. Both pilots distracted by gunfire. Gramps on the verge of closing his shop. I shifted out of my seat belt and crushed a straight right jab to the side of Gramp's cheek. Leftover vomit spattered on me. His head knocked against the machine gun. My fist radiated pain. I've hit softer walls.

Gramps crumpled toward the open outside until I grabbed him by the collar. I slammed his head against the floor for good measure. Neither Ray nor Scivetti noticed what happened. Sometimes preoccupation with probing gunfire was a blessing.

The machete handle fit my hand, I leaned to Kaelyn. "This is our only chance. We gotta get 'em now." She looked as bad as the helicopter smelled.

Across the valley, a second machine gun opened fire. Bullets danced off the top of the rotor and Scivetti rotated in his seat. "God damn gooks."

Ray flinched at green tracer fire under us. "Keep climbing."

Any distraction was a good one, so I jumped to the back of Scivetti's seat and put the blade against his throat. His whole body quivered. "What the hell?"

"Gonzalo, you're dead if you move." I looked at Ray, "Take the controls and level us out." The lights of the instrument panel showed his teeth baring. "Now!" I shouted loud enough to be heard without the intercom.

He grabbed the cyclic. "I'm not a pilot. Don't know how to fly."

I repeated 'shit' a thousand times in my brain. No aviation wings on his uniform. A dumb-ass assumption for every officer in the company to be Huey qualified. Machine guns fired at us from two directions. No time to rethink my assault. More like an impulse than a plan.

"Pull the cyclic back to climb. Put your feet on the pedals."

He stared at me.

"Do it."

Scivetti grabbed at my face with a pistol in his other hand. I felt the muzzle blast of his gun, the bullet twisted the helmet off my head, dragged the mike boom over my nose and the ear pad across my eye. My head flicked back from the concussion. I pulled the blade hard against Ray's throat to catch myself. It stopped at his spine. Blood spurted on the panel and side of his seat. His body shook while his right leg knocked the helicopter into a radical yaw.

I pointed at Ray's feet. "Make the pedals even."

Slowly he corrected them to level flight.

"Listen!" I touched the big blade to Ray's neck. Some of Scivetti's blood dripped on his arm. "Hold everything still. Or I'll cut your goddamn head off." He froze on the controls.

Kaelyn didn't flinch when I handed her the machete. "Kill him if he moves." She laid the blade on his shoulder.

I crouched to pull Scivetti out of his seat. The pain in my chest was like fire. His body fell to the cabin floor, head twisted at an obtuse angle.

Maneuvering into Scivetti's seat made crawling up a rope ladder look easy. Blood loss from my side weakened me. I squeezed the intercom switch, "Get off the controls. Hands on the glare shield. Feet flat on the floor. Don't move."

Pings, thuds and *cachonks* told me the machine gunners finally found their range. The louder the bang, the more to worry about. All vital instruments checked out and no warning lights were on.

My concentration broke with movement behind the pedestal. Old-man-wonder straddled Kaelyn on the floor. His pajama clad legs twisted around her waist. One of his hands had a death grip on the gun I forgot to remove from Scivetti. Another dumbass move.

The cold steel of Ray's .45-caliber automatic poked my cheek.

"Turn around and fly. Let him have his fun." His eyes sparkled like the cat that just caught the mouse.

"You can't shoot me. How you gonna get Ho Chi Minh's brother back?"

"You stupid shit. I don't have wings, but I can have more bootleg time than you have total. I've been wanting to do you for a long time." He pulled the hammer back.

I shouted, "What about the gold?"

My seat jolted from the fight behind me.

"Gold. That's bullshit." Major Ray pulled the gun from my face and the machete blade cut through his arm at the elbow. When the gun launched from his severed arm, it hit the panel and fired. The bullet struck my armored seat and splattered ceramic pieces all over me. I couldn't catch the the gun and slammed the main fuel off instead.

The dreaded sound of the engine spooling down overpowered the moment. We were about to crash.

I SNATCHED Major Ray's pistol as he screamed in pain. His forearm dangled from his elbow. "If I die, you're coming with me." The Major jammed a pedal to the chin bubble and wagged his stump. He sprayed blood on the panel, windshield, and me.

With the engine out, I aimed to maintain the rotor RPM and the airspeed to land safely. He wouldn't let me. I pointed the gun at him. "Get off the pedals."

"Fuck you." Ray made the helicopter's nose go higher and its speed slower. The RPM warning light came on with the familiar beep but sounded three times louder than before.

I pulled the trigger. The shot startled me in the quiet cockpit. My muzzle flash captured the image of Ray's contorted face. Two more times I squeezed the trigger, nothing happened.

He shrieked at me, "You can't do anything right. You and that goddamn, dumb bitch are gonna die."

Kaelyn screamed, "Not from you, asshole." She plunged the machete up into his arm pit and he looked surprised. His head arched back as his hand dropped and feet fell off the pedals.

I reclaimed the aircraft and over-controlled it from a stall to a dive and almost a barrel roll. Somehow, I got back into a flyable attitude.

Kaelyn caught her breath behind Ray's seat. Gramps lay motionless on the cargo deck. She withdrew the machete. "Now what? How can you see where we're going? What happened to the engine?"

"I can't see anything. We've lost about two thousand feet so far. Read off the altitude and keep reading." I tapped the altimeter.

She figured out the gauge then said, "Three thousand one hundred feet. What the hell are you doin'?"

L. Sid's advice echoed in my mind. "Fly it, if it's still flying."

I said, "An engine restart should take about sixty seconds. We're falling at twenty-two hundred feet per minute." I went through the five-step emergency procedure so fast it sounded like six.

She said, "Two thousand eight hundred and fifty feet."

After I began the restart, nothing happened for the longest four seconds ever recorded. "If I knew where the ground was, I'd feel better. With luck, we'll find a deep valley-."

Then the most beautiful *pop* that I'd ever heard signaled engine ignition. "Seventeen hundred and fifty feet." Kaelyn shouted like a cheerleader.

I increased the power as fast as it would go. My guts tightened in a solid ball. Couldn't see a damn thing outside.

"One thousand and fifty feet," the quaver in her voice sent a shiver to my brain.

She choked up. "Five hundred . . . and fifty feet."

We were falling into a horizon-less, black void. At least the machine gun fire stopped.

At 350 feet, I nearly had flyable RPM, I turned on the landing light to a windshield full of palm trees less than fifty feet below. They artificially washed out from the blinding light, almost to a sandy gray.

"Holy shit!" I banked to miss the first tree but glanced off the one next to it. Branches whipped the ship on the right side, coconuts fractured the chin bubble. Parts of palm leaves scattered in the cabin. Kaelyn screamed loud enough to peel paint.

"Hold on," I racked the ship to miss a big tree and dragged my skids through its top palms.

She screamed again. So did I. It felt good. The blades kept digging for lift and we flew.

Kaelyn hung by her armpit on the back of Ray's chair.

"Get in his seat."

She strained but pulled Ray out. Her petite body looked small in his seat, he filled it so completely. She wiped the blood off the helmet microphone with her hand. I pointed to the mike button on the floor, "What did you do to Gramps?"

"When he was on top, I poked him in the eye, then kneed him in the nuts. The aircraft movement slammed his head into the back of your seat. He never got up. When Ray pointed his gun at you, I tried to knock it away. He moved. I missed. Where're we going?"

"To the sea. I'll climb to 10,000 feet and fly east. Then look for lights."

The black nothingness could have been peaceful, if I wasn't for my pain, bleeding, and being scared shitless.

At 9370 feet, a giant cluster of lights appeared to the south. My excitement interfered with finding the Guard channel. "Mayday, Mayday, Mayday, this is Army helicopter..." I didn't even know the tail number of this thing. "This is Serpent OX."

A voice responded, "Say again all after Serpent."

I had the urge to shout but used my best phonetic alphabet instead, "Oscar-Xray."

"Roger Serpent, this is Qui Nhon Tower, state your emergency and position."

"I don't know where the hell I am, other than at ninety-three hundred feet on a heading of zero-niner-zero, in a UH1D . . ."

Kaelyn found the floor switch. "Don't mess up my storyline and tell him too much. Okay?"

"Aw, fuck it. Hey, we're lost, wounded, short of fuel and the aircraft's been shot to shit."

"Roger Serpent, we have you. Turn to a heading of one-two-zero and maintain your altitude. Do you have any aircraft issues? Over."

"Only two: the noises you hear are bullets holes in the main rotor.

And we have 185 pounds of fuel, the 20-minute warning just came on."

His serious tone differed from the glib, authoritative responses earlier. "Serpent, you have another problem. You're 35 minutes out, with a headwind of forty knots. We're in a mortar attack, they've penetrated the perimeter and they're on the active runway. No choppers to escort you at this time."

"Qui Nhon…I don't know how to conserve juice in this fuel-guzzling monster, so I will be 15 minutes short. Give me an alternate location and directions. I have no map."

"Serpent, stand by. How long you been in country?" I heard the disdain in his voice.

"Almost three days. Hard to keep up, I've had so much fun."

"Serpent, call Zulu on three-three point six. They're standing by." My hope faded in ten seconds of silence and three repeat calls. I asked Qui Nhon to relay.

After fifteen long seconds, Tower came back agitated. "Serpent. Start an immediate standard-rate turn. Switch your position lights to bright for five seconds then off for five. Repeat until you reach 4000 feet. Over."

"Roger."

I pointed to the light switch for Kaelyn. For the next five minutes, my beautiful turn of thirty degrees cut through the evening air in an effortless glide. Not a word broke our focus on the outside world. We were desperate for some sign of life.

Why the fuel gauge moved a lot faster near the bottom of the barrel, I never understood.

"Qui Nhon, where am I going and how long will it take? I now have less than 145 pounds, 12 minutes of flight time left."

"Serpent, with any luck you will be on the ground with 50 pounds to spare."

"What happens 'without any luck'?"

"Then kiss your ass good-bye. But now, switch to forty-three point five and try again."

I keyed the frequency. "Zulu, this is Serpent."

"Serpent, where you at big boy?"

"Just dropped through four thousand feet."

"Shit. Stop your descent and come this way a little bit."

"Which way is that?"

No answer. I leveled off at 3900 feet. "Break, Qui Nhon, can you vector me?"

Zulu interrupted. "Fuck Qui Nhon. Turn north and maintain your altitude until I tell you to dump it. Scud's moving in and you are too damn close to that mountain."

"Roger."

Kaelyn kept looking for lights. She scanned every bit of our windows we had plus the chin bubble and door.

"Serpent, this is Zulu, start your descent NOW! Do your best tactical approach."

"What you mean, tactical?"

"What are you, an FNG? That means don't go slow and low, come in fast or lose your ass."

"Where the hell are you?"

Another pause. "Right underneath you. We have a cross. Identify."

Kaelyn moaned. "What in the hell is he talking about?"

I dropped out of the sky at 1500 feet per minute. Like jumping down a deep, black well with no rope and someone saying, "Trust me."

Wind blew palm leaves around the cabin—the aircraft was out of trim. "Keep looking." The altimeter went through 3100 feet.

"Zulu, this is Serpent. What's your elevation?"

"About three hundred and twenty-eight feet. Give or take a little. When you drop through four hundred, check with me. We'll try to keep 'em busy until you shut down. Land on the spot. Inside our perimeter. Unass quickly."

Flying through 1800 feet, I said, "Got you in sight, I see red."

"Roger, Serpent. A layer is coming in, tighten your loop."

When we blew through the scud, the altimeter read 1000 feet. Our relentless drop to the dirt raced the fuel gauge.

At 400 feet I switched on the landing lights. "Serpent on final."

Zulu screamed, "Goddamn it, shut 'em off. Turn right. Get out."

I climbed away from the tentacles of the day-glow monster dead ahead. Tracers hit between the Plexiglas over my head and the rotor.

My escape turn wasn't enough. They still hit me with the motherlode of shit-out-of-luck. The instrument panel lit up more lights than I could read.

"Zulu, this baby just died. Where do I dump it?"

"Serpent, you're downwind. Make an immediate 180 to the right. We'll be in your chin bubble."

I stood the helicopter on its side and turned on the landing light. Kaelyn looked out her door. She said, "Wow. We're low."

Zulu said, "Down. Bring it down,"

The cross went by. "Shit, there goes home." To see down from a Huey floating in a 45-degree flare, means looking out the side window. I searched for a landing spot anyway.

Sure as hell, two little shacks appeared next to a church steeple. I killed too much of my speed and my fifty-eight foot, five-thousand-pound, lead-sled dropped.

What a lousy feeling to realize that the only thing left was a double shit landing. We hit something that cracked and broke. It wasn't the aircraft in torment. It sounded more like...wood?

Dust erupted. After we stopped, I didn't know what happened. Talk about feeling stupid. I shut down as many switches as I could, except the radio. Only the rotor blades kept turning.

The clock read 0410 hours. A new sound, guttural in its ominous depth, eradicated every other noise. Explosions erupted first 30 yards out, then 20, then 10 at two seconds apart. The hellacious pyrotechnic display fascinated me, as I sat with my head up my ass, fiddling with Kaelyn's harness.

The first blast nudged the helicopter forward, the second one launched us down into darkness and a big, knock-the-shit-out-of-you, landing. Chunks of the chin bubble shattered at me and the roof crashed over my head.

What I didn't have was always the same...silence instead of reply...low fuel instead of full...lost instead of found...hit instead of shot at...crash instead of land.

But through it all, I wondered, could I still fly instead of die?

Sixty yards from the crashed helicopter, Zulu returned the microphone to his radio operator. "Poor bastards, the Cong had a lock on them. Request an extraction. Have the gun bunnies bring down some serious shit on that northern bluff. Krotch, direct the fire."

"Yes, sir. Saw where the gooks were shooting from. I'll drop it on their soon-to-be-dead asses."

"Good. I'll check out the chopper," SOG Team Commander Smith looked like a camouflaged arsenal, with a Swedish K submachine gun hanging from his rucksack, a Browning high-power pistol in a shoulder holster and frag grenades everywhere. The six men weaved toward the remnants of the church.

Sappers shot at them from outside the perimeter. Half of the team laid down covering fire so the others could get to the church. Krotch silenced the sniper with his grenade launcher.

In the belfry of the church, they found the bunker collapsed from the Cong's bombardment. Multiple explosions dropped the helicopter into the first pew, its tail rotor protruded through the roof. JP4 puddled under its nose. One of the main rotors leaned on the altar. A long lamp swung from the remaining beam of the ceiling.

Z saw movement but couldn't believe anything survived in the cockpit, "Serpent?"

Kaelyn said, "Not exactly."

"How's Serpent?"

"Unconscious. I can't tell how bad, 'cause I am stuck in this God damned seat."

A solitary artillery shell whistled into the mountain and two more adjusted on the Viet Cong targets. Then the entire battery opened up and Z smiled at the secondary explosions.

His men approached the helicopter with weapons drawn, Kaelyn struggled with the harness on her seat. "Come on boys, get me a hand." A team member slit the harness to free her shoulders and waist.

"What happened to Serpent?"

She shook her head at the damage of the church. "The last explosion knocked us down, the rotor blade chopped open the helicopter and glanced off his helmet."

Another team member laid Danny on the church floor. Z felt for a pulse, "He's still ticking. See if Krotch has the extraction coming."

Kaelyn stepped to the ground. "So who are you guys anyway?" She buttoned up her jungle fatigue shirt.

Z followed her movements. "The real question is who are you? You crashed my party, so you're first, sweetheart."

"Okay, but I'm not your sweetheart. I'm Kaelyn DeHaven, a columnist for the *Cleveland Plain Dealer*." She reached for Danny's helmet strap. "Will he be okay?"

"Get your hands off him, don't touch his helmet, it may be holding his brains in. You sound like a reporter, three questions and no way to answer—"

"So, you're Zulu? What does the name mean?" She eased into a stoic pose in a classic, investigative style.

"We're MACV SOG TEAM 2 Alpha, a Special Operations Group in II Corps." Zmith bit his lip. The interview style of this little dolly plainly distracted him. "Our current LRRP mission means a

Long Range Reconnaissance Patrol. I am Zulu, which is an acronym for my name. Phu Cat is your location right now."

"Are you monitoring Bao Dai's alliance with the black market?" She eyed his mismatched fatigues, irregular Army weapons, unmilitary sideburns, and a sweaty headband with a Communist Red Star.

He had no reaction to her question. "Say again your name. And what do you know about him?"

"I'm Kaelyn DeHaven. Bao Dai will return as the next emperor of Vietnam. He lives in a luxurious apartment in Paris. His followers are making life difficult for the North and the Americans."

"Your name sounds familiar. Are you a national columnist?"

Her eyes twinkled. "Just recently. Are you into politics?"

"Yea. That's where I know know it from. Orville DeHaven, Senator from Texas. You related?"

"He's my daddy."

"Really? He gave our commencement address at West Point."

"Oh?"

"Yep, I introduced him to the assembly."

The radio crackled, "Zulu . . . echo, two-five. Kilo, out."

"Kilo, get here ASAP. Leave the squad intact."

She put her hands on her hips. "What in the world did he say?"

Z's smile vaporized. "And you're getting on my nerves already. There's helicopters in route, with an ETA of less than twenty-five minutes."

"I'd call it good news."

"We have three serious problems: a disabled helicopter's here, the words 'special personnel' made the airwaves and the Cong heard it. The bad guys get serious money for each one of them."

"So, what's the problem?"

"Look up. Do you see any stars, moon or visible horizon?"

"Well, no. So what?"

"It means we're in deep shit. With two monsoon storms coming, the helicopters may not be able to reach us. They can't extract what they can't find."

She mumbled a quiet, "Oh."

"And with an unconscious guy, we can't just go slipping off into the weeds."

"Okay already. So, what are you gonna do?"

"I need to figure out how to get all of us out…at one time."

Doc, the team medic, approached. "Two Army majors in the helicopter. Both dead. One messed up POW, secured only with a seat belt. Considering his clothes, fair complexion, smooth hands, and groomed hair, he's pretty senior."

"How serious are the wounds?"

"Probably broken ribs, one arm in a sling. Barely conscious. He's on the other side of helicopter. I'll bring him here."

Kaelyn said, "Oh my god. Danny called him Ho Chi Bro. He's important in the black market."

Doc hurried behind the helicopter, in its near-vertical position. He dragged Ho Chi Bro out to the ground with a vengeance.

Kaelyn said, "That son of a bitch has more lives than a herd of cats."

"Don't kill the bastard, he is our only trading asset." Z taped Ho's hands together behind his back at the edge of the pew. "Get him conscious. I need to talk to him NOW."

Doc poured a thin stream of water into Ho's mouth and nose. Ho convulsed, coughed, spit, and tried to sit up.

Ho looked up, "What do you want? I am a humble farmer."

Doc gave him another river cocktail.

The choking and slobbering seemed endless. Ho mumbled, "Stop this."

Z pushed his knee on Ho's chest and listened to him scream. "Who are you?" No emotion showed in Z's face, no glint of enjoyment. "I have time to break every bone in your rib cage then gouge out your eyes."

Ho's entire body shook. Perspiration exuded from his impressive brow. His long, white goatee and mustache glistened with water off his golden skin. "I am Nguyen Danh, Province Chief for the National Liberation Front of South Vietnam."

"What province?" Z thumped Ho's sling.

"Binh Dinh, Binh Dinh." Pain contorted his face.

Z tightened his grip on Ho's neck. "Why are you here?"

"Meeting." Blood dribbled from Ho's mouth.

Kaelyn shouted, "What deal did you make with Scivetti and Ray?"

"Who are they?" Ho's eyes shifted side to side looking for the voice.

With the power of a cedar hacker, she swung her machete into the back of the pew, inches above his head. The sound reverberated all over the church and showered Z with wood chips. Kaelyn got nose to nose with Ho. "Bullshit. You knew 'em in Saigon. You had a drug deal."

Z kicked the pew. "Listen, I'm gonna let her have you with the machete if you don't come up with some straight answers."

Ho wheezed, his words obscured. "They were, how do you say it, daffodils?"

Kaelyn said, "You mean pansies."

"Pansies, yes, yes. Gullible pawns. I helped my brother source some products in demand." He gasped for air.

"What is your brother's name?"

"Cuong Danh. General. Central Command..." Ho inhaled in shallow, painful gulps.

Feet shuffled in the sanctuary. All eyes turned, rounds were chambered. Krotch came in the door, perspiration soaked his clothes. "Lots of movement out there. Gotta get the hell out. Everyone's repositioned. Who's the gook talking about?"

"General Cuong Danh. Sound familiar?"

"Damn right. That's the prick who led the raid on the CARD. I lost my whole team there." Krotch curled his top lip, scrunched up his flattened nose. "My whole fuckin' team." He lifted Ho by his shirt. "Where is he?"

"I don't know."

Dispassionately, Krotch poked his finger through one of the broken bones in Ho's chest.

Ho screamed until he couldn't scream anymore. His face reddened and looked like it would explode.

"But if you did know, where would he be?" Krotch's hand moved to Ho's chest.

Ho tried to squirm away. "At his mountain headquarters."

"Which mountain?"

"Hon Heo. Hon Heo."

Krotch looked at Z. "That's the highest peak on this mountain group east of our position."

Rotor blades penetrated the night air. The radio lit up. "Zulu, this is Serpent Two Six, Over."

"This is Zulu, go."

"Identify."

Krotch moved into the open and circled his light toward the sound.

Z said, "Roger Serpent, we got a light on for you."

The pause took forever. "Got zero in sight."

"How many can you take?"

"Give me six."

"How many birds?"

"Got two."

Z looked at Kaelyn. "I'm glad he's cautious. Let's hope the other's not a gunship. But under any circumstance we're screwed. We have ten bodies on the ground...and we've been compromised."

PART FIVE_

Z REMEMBERED his reconnaissance of the Phu Cat valley. Hon Heo on the east, a ring of mountains from the north to the west and Qui Nhon in the south. He looked out the cargo door. "Where in the fuck is Bravo?"

Two-Six pointed to the airspeed. "They went IFR back there when I dropped all that altitude and speed. Rather than coming down into our rotor blades, they climbed straight ahead on a south heading."

"So now what?"

"He'll keep climbing until he gets on top of this stuff. Ideally, we'll stay in contact and go in the same general direction."

"Ideally?"

"Yeah. A lot of things can go wrong. He's in the clouds and we're not. If he can't climb out fast enough to the east, the mountain'll get him. His ship's over-grossed with a lot of junk hanging off."

Kaelyn shouted, "What the hell did you mean? Talk English will you."

Two-Six looked at her. "His chopper won't fly very high because its overloaded. He'll be safe if he gets over the storm layer."

Z looked straight down to palm trees whipping in the wind. "He doesn't know where he is and neither do we."

Two-Six turned to Z. "Yep. We're two single ships now. Each trying to survive. We wanna be near enough to the other, in case one of us run into a load of double-deep shit."

A giant palm tree suddenly appeared in front of the windshield. The pilot collided with it on the right side, destroying the chin bubble. Metal-against-coconut impacted the ship like an unexpected slap in the face. Plexiglas, palm leaves and water burst into the cabin.

Two-Six grabbed the controls. He swerved through the never-ending grove of coconut trees, hitting more that he missed. The clouds lingered at tree-top level and sometimes even lower. He motioned to the pilot. "Can't move these pedals."

Henry pulled palm leaves off his chest and helmet. "Yes, sir. A coconut's stuck between them."

From his left seat position, Two-Six couldn't see the problem. "Get it out."

"I can't. My chest protector's blocking me."

"Take the goddamn thing off. I need my pedals. Z, help him."

Henry unstrapped his chicken plate and squeezed like a snake to reach the coconut.

Wind and rain gushed into the cargo area each time he would make a turn or change power. The helicopter slid sideways through the air instead of cutting a path in control. "Goddamn it. I need the pedals."

Z checked it with his light. "Why don't you shoot it out?"

"What if I hit the pedal?"

"Don't miss. Or better yet, let me shoot it." Z reached for his pistol.

"Go ahead." Two-Six stiffened his legs.

Z stretched low and shot, the blast startling everyone. The coconut debris blew around the cockpit. Milk splattered over Henry. "How's that?" He laughed.

"Bravo One this is Two-Six. We're damn-near hovering. Heading is two-zero-zero. Over."

"We're struggling at 7000 feet. Climbing at a miserable 150 feet per minute. Heading one-eight-zero. Qui Nhon is not answering. Don't know where we gotta go to beat the storm."

Two-Six moved his eyes constantly from the panel to the outside. "Okay. I'll keep this heading until we cross the pass to the highlands."

"Serpent, you don't have to worry about the Cong. The mountain's bad enough. Hey. We just broke out on top. Morning light's beautiful. 7,300 feet indicated. Over."

"Bravo, you're a lucky bastard. We've been in and out of it since you split. Now we're zero-zero. Turning to a shallow climb. Going IFR."

"Go fast as you can to clear those mountains. We'll be waiting for you. I am putting every light I have on. How is your fuel?"

"I have about 40-50 minutes." Two-Six recoiled as a stream of red flew by. "Holy shit. I thought you said there're no Cong here. They're firing down at us."

Tracers in the clouds scared Kaelyn because she couldn't see them coming. They just appeared and disappeared. Only a blur of color. She gritted her teeth for the next hit.

Bravo said, "They're shooting at the noise. Don't return fire."

Two-Six perspired while his eyes ran in a constant cross-check of his instruments.

Z said, "Let my guys get a crack at 'em . They have flash suppressors and no tracers in their weapons. Even if we don't kill them, we'll screw with their heads."

"All right, all right," Two-Six showed annoyance.

A strong wind rushed into the cargo door and blew Kaelyn's hair into her face. Z noticed the ship was seriously out of trim, in a steep bank and a near vertical climb. "You can't get to heaven in a spin."

"What in the hell are you talking about?" Two-Six shook his head and bolted back from the panel. "Goddamn, I'm fucked up, you got it. Take it. Take it."

Henry grabbed the controls like it was the last hot dog on the stand. "Got it." He corrected both the steep climb and turn. The angle of the aircraft changed so quickly that everyone's stomach jumped.

Two-Six slid the armor shield back and stuck his head out in the wind. He gulped the air like a dog in a car window. Back inside he said, "I don't know what happened. Couldn't tell up from down. Thought I was straight and level."

Kaelyn pointed. "Tracers."

Z shouted at his men in the door. "Return that fire, croak the bastard." He turned to Henry. "We're too close to the mountain. Get the hell outta here. "

"I'm pulling her guts out now. We're overloaded. Missing chin bubble acts like a brake." The cabin lit up when a monster burst of tracer went underneath the skids. "Damn, was that a rocket?"

"No, up close it just looks like one. It's a fifty. Let's try this." Z pulled the pin from a white phosphorous grenade and tossed it out of the door. "If they're scoping, it will fry their eyes. Or maybe they'll think we crashed. All we need is a little time." The explosion was like a fuzzy bolt of lightning, breathtaking by itself but magnified in the cloud layer.

Henry said, "The head wind blew us back into that mountain. We're heading right into the eye of this storm. This old pig isn't climbing worth a shit."

Two-Six came back to life. "Then don't climb, go straight and level. Get distance from the mountain until we can see through the pass."

Kaelyn stood up. "Why should we go back to the mountains? This is crazy. The storm might be out of Qui Nhon by now."

Z said, "Where'd ya come up with all this stuff. He motioned to Two-Six. "Check with Qui Nhon."

Two-Six switched to tower radio.

Kaelyn said, "If we can get to Hon Heo today, you could break a big one." She blinked her eyes at ol' Z. "The Cong must be on the ropes after that barrage on the mountain, the big mess at the church, and this storm. And I want to go in there with you."

"You want to what?"

"You heard me—I'm going with you."

Z looked down into her eyes. "You are out of your fucking mind. This'll be heavy-duty recon, high-level assassination. This won't be a typical combat assault where you fly in, hang around base camp, take pictures, and get my men all horny. You'll face physical demand beyond your capability."

"Not even if we help you find the right people and the right place?"

"We? What place?"

Two-Six interrupted. "Z. The tower says the storm's simmered down. Mortar attack stopped." He dialed another frequency. "Bravo, this is Two-Six. Qui Nhon has a hundred-foot ceiling with clearing from the sea. We're gonna land there. Over."

"What happened to An Khe? That little bunch of tracers scare you away?"

"No, the fifty did. What's it like on top?"

"This storm's moving inland in a hurry. I can't handle any more change of direction. We'll be on the fuel warning light in six minutes. Heading now due east. Out."

Two-Six shouted to all aboard, "We gonna climb at five hundred feet per minute. On an East heading. Let's hope we get above the storm."

Z asked Kaelyn. "What do you know about Hon Heo? And who is *we*?"

She knew he swallowed the hook. "Lanh Quanh is my Vietnamese partner and a reporter for the *Saigon Daily News*. Part of an old-money family in Vietnam. They had a summer home on Hon Heo. As a child, he played in the rocky jungle of the mountain. He knows the network of caves, hidden fissures, and ravine trails."

Z licked his lips. "Okay, maybe. Can we trust him?"

"He's a real bright guy and hates the Cong. They killed his father and torched most of his net worth. His columns regularly riled them. But, if you use him, I'm part of the deal." She knew if he could get face-to-face with Lanh, he would trick her out of the ride.

"Where do I find him?"

"Lanh should be in Qui Nhon, his girlfriend was a stringer for the paper. They live in an apartment above the *Saigon Daily News*."

"Hallelujah," Henry shouted, "we got a break in the clouds. And a piece of sunshine. It's almost Caaa Fabb."

Z changed the frequency to SOG operations. "We need two slicks and a gunship to insert Two Alpha teams. We'll take off later this morning after you find a local in Qui Nhon, by the name of Lanh Quang." He gave full instructions.

The helicopter hit turbulence and rocked Z into Danny on the floor. Danny awoke to this body on his arm. "Who are you?"

Z rolled away. "You called me Zulu earlier. I am Captain Duane Zmith, leader of SOG Team 2 Alpha. My men call me 'Z'. And you're Serpent. What do you remember last?"

"I remember artillery fire..." Danny's face contorted.

"We fell from the church tower," Kaelyn broke in. "We landed one pew short of the altar." She smiled. "How do you feel?"

Danny sat up. "Just about Ca Fab. Then what happened?"

"One of the rotor blades hit you in the head. By the way, what does Ca Fab mean?"

Z interrupted. "Since then the bad guys tried to capture us, your POW tried to kill us, the overloaded helicopter tried to crash us, the Cong at the pass tried to shoot us, and the monsoon is still trying to finish us off. CAFB means Clear As a Fucking Bell."

The radio operator handed the headset to Z. "Ops said if this team is flyable when you return, you have to use them. There is one other slick, but a pilot's missing. Partying someplace."

"Two-Six. Will you and Bravo One be flyable when we land?"

"I can't rightly speak for him, but in general it depends on how hard we land. And where exactly we are when we do."

"No shit." Z explained the new mission. "Any new problems flying without the chin bubble over water?"

"Yeah, it won't float. Hon Heo's only 40 clicks out. It will be noisy, windy, and wet. What will you do for the missing pilot?"

"Talk about good luck. I got one here." Z turned to Hellberg. "Ox, how about it?"

Danny looked at Kaelyn, then back to Z. "Like they said in flight school, it beats walking."

"Qui Nhon. This is Serpent Two-Six. Inbound from the west, at 2000 feet. Landing at hospital. Over." With only one beacon and radio operational, the airfield cleared him to land. Two-Six searched the airspace. "Bravo what is your position? Over."

"Broke out over Qui Nhon. Got you in sight."

Two-Six pointed to the gunship and everyone on board cheered.

Both ships landed in the parking lot of the hospital. The helicopter blocking the pad had the familiar blue triangle on the front door. Four corpsmen in fatigues and T-shirts ran out with two gurneys. From the other side of the lot, three SOG team members disembarked from a Jeep with weapons drawn. The helicopter shut down and the SOG team handcuffed Ho Chi Bro to the gurney and escorted him into the hospital.

Z turned to Hellberg. "Why don't you get checked out." Danny tried to ignore the two corpsmen who let him collapse on their gurney. His eyes closed as soon as he laid his head back.

The remaining member of the new arrivals, Sierra Six, stood next to the cargo door. All of the SOG team stopped what they were doing when he arrived. He looked at Z. "We couldn't field a retrieval squad for Lanh Quang. Pick four of your team and let's find 'em."

Z turned to Serpent. "Call the gunship and have Krotch join us. Be ready to launch when we return."

"You need me to identify Lanh," Kaelyn's eyes drilled a hole in Z.

He turned to Sierra Six. "Kaelyn DeHaven is one of the special personnel from the helicopter. She and Lanh Quang interviewed Doan Vien. He knows the Hon Heo mountain because his family's summer home was there."

Six extended his hand to Kaelyn. "Pleased to meet you. How's your dad these days? I'm Colonel Jack Bobson. Last May, I met him at the White House." Bobson stood a little over six feet tall with short brown hair, bushy eyebrows, and a big mustache on an angular face. He carried a small backpack, plus a pistol and hand grenades. "We have stayed in touch."

He turned to Z. "We have two Jeeps; there's room for her. The *Saigon Daily News* office is at the intersection of Le Loi and Tang Bat Ho. We'll approach tactically, advise the rest of the team to report when they're in position."

Kaelyn settled down for a quiet ride down the main road from the Air Force Base. Colonel Bobson and Zmith were antsy as a cat on a stove. They looked from side to side, front to back and top to bottom at everything along the way. The Colonel radioed the MP detachment with a heads-up.

Kaelyn poked Bobson's shoulder. "Why are we approaching this like an attack? He is just a nice local reporter."

Colonel Bobson stopped the Jeep to wait for Krotch. "I checked with the Cav and MACV. Lanh shows up in the active files for both. He's a true, crusading believer for a unified Vietnam. After the Diem's assassination, Lahn crossed over to help reestablish Bao Dai as Emperor."

Kaelyn said, "You'd expect that from a scholar of history. He'll tell you how Vietnam suffered the invasions by China, Thailand, Burma, France and Japan. And he's wound up in the Vietnamese, as masters of the art of the shadow government to control the people. That's why Bao Dai has reemerged."

"All that's wonderful but irrelevant." Bobson faced her, "He doesn't trust anyone and . . ."

"He's a conscientious reporter. No need to come in shooting." Kaelyn crossed her arms.

"But he's killed before. Lot of folks out there that would like to see him roast on a stick."

The radio blurted. "Zulu. Something's happening inside Lanh's—"

Z heard muffled shots. "Do what you have to, don't let anyone leave. Where are you?"

"Next to the front door. The back is covered."

The Colonel glided out of the Jeep. "Kaelyn, stay here, we'll call for you." He moved with Z down the desolate street.

No one could keep her from the action, but she needed protection. The Jeep's rusty, mud-covered tire iron would have to do. The stealth parade walked down the sidewalk with their guns drawn. Colonel held a pistol with long magazine. Z gripped a stubby rifle with a silencer.

Kaelyn had to follow, not wanting to miss a thing. The gentle rain continued to erase the sour smells of the street and puddle on the sidewalk. A simple, illuminated sign hung above the door: *Saigon Daily News.*

They scanned the roof line of the buildings.

She stopped.

They looked around the corner, up the intersecting street, and exchanged hand signals.

She smelled sweet tobacco smoke, strangely out of place in the fresh morning air. A door closed. She froze. The lit cigarette got stomped out by a black, pajama-clad leg.

The pajamas turned into a body with a long rifle aimed at the Colonel. She didn't know what to do. Reflexively her right hand windmilled to pitch the tire iron straight at pajamas, like she did for the Texas Fast Pitch Softball league. Then it was velocity over control, now she just hoped to hit the sucker. The iron struck low on his tail bone and forced his chest forward. Both arms dropped low. His gun and the iron bounced on the concrete.

Z spun around and shot two muffled bursts into the intruder. Pajamas slammed against the building and crumpled to the ground.

The Colonel pointed his gun at pajamas while he felt for a pulse. He pulled the body back into the doorway. Sternly he said, "Thanks. Now stand back."

He handed her a grenade. "If anybody comes after us, just pull this ring out, release the handle, count to three and throw it. It'll explode in two seconds. A killing radius of five yards. Just get it close. Now lay low but pay attention." He slung pajama's rifle over his shoulder.

She always admired a no-bullshit guy.

Kaelyn watched the Colonel and Z enter the branch office of the *Saigon Daily News*. She followed them upstairs in the dim morning light.

Inside the doorway, Krotch stood over a man with his face blown away. Another body tied to a chair dripped blood from a soaked, white shirt and a battered head. In front, a woman and a man were bound and gagged in a kneeling position.

Holding his silenced M16, Krotch continued his report to Z, "I have no idea who's who, except the faceless one tried to kill me. He failed. The two on the floor are scared shitless. I left 'em 'til the girl gets here."

"I'm here," Kaelyn shouted from the stairway. A large cat sat stoically on a stair, unmoved by the chaos around him.

Z shook his head and turned from her. "Krotch, reposition your guys on all sides for security. Has anything been touched in here?"

"Yes, to redeploy. No, to touch. This place gives me a bad feeling." Krotch's heavy boots made the building rattle while he charged down the stairs. The cat scurried away with a guttural yowl.

Kaelyn looked inside. "My god, that's Lanh. Why did you shoot him?" She reached toward the woman on the floor.

"Stop," the Colonel pulled her back.

She shrugged off his hands. "Ask these people what happened."

"Don't move a goddamn muscle." The Colonel's eyes darted around. "This is what the Cong does to intimidate the unconverted. They're both booby-trapped."

To the woman bent over on the floor, he said, "Speak English?"

A cone-shaped, straw hat obscured her face. She wore dirty black work clothes; her hands were taped underneath her ankles in a supplicant position. Her forehead was near the floor. The woman creaked, "Aaaa ha."

"Don't move." The Colonel got down on his knees. "Does the man speak English?"

A low growl emerged. The Colonel laid his cheek flat on the floor, shined a light underneath the hats of both people. "Holy shit. Both are pressing a long flat piece of wood with their head. Connected to small switches. Like the trigger of a Claymore. If one moves, the other goes off. Ingenious."

"Aaaa ha." The woman got louder.

Bobson said, "Don't move. Look for wires." The Colonel's light swept the room.

Kaelyn stood still as a statue.

The Colonel pointed behind the woman. "The line from her switch is jammed between the floorboards."

Z's light followed the slit. "Bingo. Wire's taped up the back of the desk to the box on top."

Kaelyn's eyes moved from face to face. "I can't see it."

Z pointed. "Move slowly back through the door. Don't touch anything, you didn't touch before."

Kaelyn took one step, tripped on the threshold, and fell hard into the hall. She lay motionless, gasping for breath, her heart tried to melt down.

Z cut through the stunned quiet. "Enjoy your trip?" With great care, he rolled the edge of the carpet. "It's traveling to the hall..."

She whispered, "I can't see crap. It's too dark."

He said, "Can you catch?"

"Shit. I pitched for three years in high school. We won state twice." The Colonel's impatience bubbled over. "Just get the light to her and cut this shit."

"Here," Z tossed the lit flashlight.

A short burst of automatic fire rang out from the street. Bullets chewed up the windowsill and blew out the bottom pane.

Kaelyn flinched when glass sprayed her. The flashlight bounced off her hands, against the door molding, to the desk and onto the floor. The lens popped out.

Silence ruled. All waited for the end of their lives. Nothing happened except a sigh of relief.

Kaelyn said, "Son of a bitch."

"Forget it. What's in the hall?"

She remained on her back and inserted the lens. "The wire is covered by mud and goes to another box near the top of the stairs. In the pile of trash."

The cat stood next to the box, rubbed its head on the lid and smoothly nosed it off. "Oh my gosh. The wires go to a curved container with the words: FRONT TOWARDS ENEMY."

"Which way are they facing?"

She swallowed hard. "Down the steps."

"Great, I can work with it. Unless the goddamn cat changes our mind." Z detached the wire to the desk. The lid slipped to the cat, which jumped to the man bending over. "Meow" the cat complained.

The man growled in surprise but did not move a muscle.

Z disconnected the wires to the Claymore. "Both of these mines are fresh out of the box. You can smell the packing, like acid on metal. Did he install anything else here?"

"Naaa na." She sagged to the floor in relief.

Z cut the tape from her wrists, ankles, and mouth. He said, "Who are you?"

"Kieu Quang." She stood erect with the bearing of one unafraid of confrontation. Her delicate features obscured by a swollen lip, dried blood under her nose and a puffy eye. The signs of trauma glistened.

Kaelyn spoke from the darkened hall, "Nah, I don't think so. Lanh Quang called you Doan Vien the last time I saw you. Were you his woman?"

Doan Vien said, "No, he was my brother." No tears came to her eyes, but her voice choked. She stared at his dead body for a few moments. "My name is Kieu Quang..." The top of her black shirt exposed the stiff collar of the red *ao dai*. "I assumed a *nom de plume* while working for Madame Nhu to protect my family and not jeopardize Bao Dai's return to power. It didn't work."

The man on the floor grumbled. "Aaa ha, aaa ha."

Z pulled the tape from his hands and mouth. Another smooth skinned, thin-necked professional with trimmed hair and refined features.

The kneeler said, "Thank you. My name is Trinh le Dung. No relation to the famous General in the North." He spoke with a mild accent and assured delivery.

"So, what are you doing here?" The Colonel saw the starched collar of a dress shirt under the black top and his manicured fingers holding the hat.

"I came to Qui Nhon for my part-time job. With MACV. I am a translator."

The Colonel said, "Okay, Okay. But what are you *doing* here?"

Trinh looked at the Colonel. "I was in the city when the monsoon blew in. Took refuge in a bar. Saw Lanh, who I knew forever. He introduced me to Doan Vien, who I knew as a child called Kieu Quang. We chatted through most of the storm, and they invited me back here since I did not make hotel arrangements."

Trinh's tailored summer clothes spoke volumes. He said, "Lanh bought these black peasant clothes for our disguise. Several attempts on his life were made since his stories about the Binh Xuyen criminals. The last one occurred in Saigon, right in the middle of the day. They killed eight people."

Kaelyn put her hands to her lips and nodded. "I was there to interview Doan."

Z rubbed his jaw slowly. "What was the name of the bar?"

Trinh lost his smile. "The Bat Bar. It's a good luck symbol meaning long life." He spoke in a hushed voice. "Lanh discovered the Binh Xuyen had moved their headquarters out of the Rung Sat jungle to the Hon Heo mountain. After the Americans moved into Saigon."

Doan Vien brightened up. "Our family's summer home was there. We played everywhere on that mountain since we were children. It wasn't a big mountain, but it was ours."

The Colonel said, "So how did he get shot?"

Trinh continued, "We were in deep conversation as we came up the steps. The hallway was dark. When we opened the door, this man stepped from behind the *Shoji* screen with his gun drawn. Lanh immediately rushed him but got pistol whipped. Two more men appeared and taped us up. Doan was the first one they slapped around but she didn't give them anything. They tied Lanh to the chair, beat him and threatened to shoot him if he didn't talk. He didn't. They did. But they knew someone was coming here tonight."

"What do you mean?"

Trinh said, "After the other guys left, only this faceless one remained. As he put the detonator under our foreheads, he called it a special message to MACV. He laughed saying, 'Claymore' in English. Then the door got kicked open and I heard three shots. I felt something warm splatter on me. Blood and brains."

Two short whistles pierced the air.

THE COLONEL MOVED KAELYN, Doan, and Trinh into the hall. "Wait here 'til I call." He ran down to the ground level entry.

Kaelyn peeked through the blinds covering the window to the intersection below. Krotch hid behind a planter across the street for cover. Z positioned himself on the stair landing. He looked lonesome.

Down the block, an innocuous grey sedan stopped near the building. The windows rolled down in unison and three rifles came out slowly. With a long blast from his M16, Krotch shattered the windshield and killed the driver. Three VC rolled out to the pavement firing their automatic rifles. From the stairs, Z surprised the shooters with three bursts and stopped the attack. Leaving only the sad sound of a hubcap spinning in the street.

Krotch signaled all clear. The Colonel ran with his three passengers and hoped the Jeep was still on the street.

Z stayed in position when a US Army deuce and a half with a white star on the door, lumbered around the corner. Canvas covered the cabin and cargo bed. Its unique sound echoed down the street. Once clear of the intersection, the rear cargo gate dropped to expose a 106 mm recoilless rifle inside. It shot a spotting tracer at the *Saigon Daily News*. Z took off running. A rocket exploded right behind him to remove most of the second floor. Its concussion flung him down to the ground. The city magnified the sound of the explosion, debris bounced off buildings and broke windows. Everything echoed. Its flash illuminated Krotch flattened against the curb loading his M79.

None of the stores on the street were open yet. When the Colonel heard the explosions, he kicked in the front door of a butcher shop. He and his passengers ducked between the cutting blocks.

Z fired at the launch vehicle. The 106 responded with a tracer round to the other side of the street. A flaming blast followed and demolished the shop next to the Jeep. The explosion tore off the canvas roof and tipped the Jeep on its side.

Krotch fired his M79 into the bed of the deuce and a half. The double explosion blew out the sides from its cabin. The 106 barrel bounced on the street like a chapel bell.

Colonel and three passengers ran from their cover and pushed the Jeep back on all four wheels. He tried to start the engine which only coughed and backfired. Z fired the machine gun from its mount at muzzle flashes and movement from the buildings. He destroyed window moldings, doors, and scarred the handsome facades. Shattered glass, bricks, and roof tiles fell to the sidewalks.

A minute felt like an hour when the engine finally started. They jumped on board and accelerated down the street. Kaelyn said, "I can't believe we made it. This would make every newspaper in the country."

Z shouted, "We're not out of it yet. My machine gun jammed."

Bullets ripped through the hood and rear tire. A ricochet hit Trinh in the shoulder. He lurched backward in his seat and blood splattered on Doan. "Damn, ouch." Trinh grabbed his shoulder.

Doan wiped off the blood from her face.

More gunfire strafed the hood and the windshield disappeared. Bobson swerved the Jeep down the road. The rear wheel rode on its rim. Sparks showered the street.

Kaelyn hugged the sobbing Doan. "Help the Colonel find the

Binh Xuyen bastards and make them pay. And help me tell this story to the world."

Doan wiped the tears away. "If I could only tell you the whole story."

The Jeep limped through the gates of the air base. Colonel Bobson advised the MP unit of the encounter and drove to the hospital. Waiting medics carried Thinh Le inside.

With his cigar lit, Bobson parked on the helipad next to the chopper. "Too much fun. Now tell me your plan again."

Z exhaled a sigh of relief. "It's simple. A double feint. Use three helicopters. One diverts attention to a high probability LZ. Two inserts the drop team. Three's a gun ship, hanging loose enough to kick ass when needed."

"And where are you going to land?" Doan studied the helicopter.

Z said, "An area adjacent to the valley on the west side of the mountain."

"That pasture is not flat. Steep cliffs on the north peak capture the swirling winds. I'm no pilot, but we could not even fly our kites there."

"Then where do you suggest?"

Doan rubbed her bruised wrists. "The Binh Xuyen must have their headquarters at the high end of the valley. Our home was there. The high cliffs formed a natural defense, like the inside of a castle. Of course, my family had a security force stationed there."

'The Colonel said, "I'm confused. Where do we deploy our teams?"

Z rubbed the stubble on his chin. "Which side had the least guards?"

Doan paused for a moment, "The cliffs probably. A couple hundred feet above the beach. A tough climb, even if you know the way."

"So, if we came through the Thanh Ha village," Z shrugged. "Where would the guards be?"

She said, "Waiting for you in the little houses on the cliff."

"That doesn't make sense," the Colonel jumped in. "If I was Binh Xuyen I'd have that village wired as a listening post. The only way to it is from the sea or along the beach."

Z got excited. "That's it. We'll come directly at that village from the sea. In the big storm front. Low level, about ten to fifteen seconds apart, in a line. Think of it as a long stick poking at you. What do you concentrate on?"

Doan said, "The tip."

"And what don't you see?"

"What's behind it." Kaelyn nodded.

The Colonel laughed. "A team will be a half-mile offshore. With a power assist to the raft, it should make paddling distance within six minutes."

Colonel slowed down the irrational enthusiasm. "We should go through the proper channels."

"Fuck the channels." Z shouted, "At Phu Cat, they waited for the helicopter to land. And laid for us at the pass. And knew about Qui Nhon. I don't believe in coincidence."

Bobson said, "So what are you saying?"

Z twirled his knife. "We have a mole."

"How is that possible? This whole situation developed on the run. The helicopter pilots didn't know they were going to land at Phu Cat, they were running out of fuel. They didn't know the pass was socked in; it just was. I didn't know we were walking into a trap here."

Bobson blew a smoke ring in the air. "So what? A mole is a problem, I agree. But what does that have to do with this mission, and its questionable strategic importance?"

Z pounded his fist. "The POW we brought in is the Province Chief for Binh Dinh in the National Liberation Front. His brother is the General of Central Command. Connected with the insurgency of Bao Dai. Allied with Binh Xuyen, who has major political influence over the Cong, Bao Dai, and the current Saigon government. The prick that led the raid on the USNS CARD, where I lost my team. Hon Heo is his mountain headquarters. They should be in disarray after the beating they took at Phu Cat last night. Now if we wanted to wipe them out, we could just call in an Arc Lite. But, we have more to gain by capturing the three leaders."

The Colonel pulled back. "Overly ambitious. Not enough assets. Probably only enough to create havoc. Just get me any one of those three guys."

"I beg your pardon, when was the last time that we created havoc?"

"When was the last time you went out?"

"So, when do we go?" Kaelyn chirped.

Z said, "What's this *we* crap?"

"You agreed I was a part of this deal if I led you to for someone who knew the players and the mountain. Doan fills the bill."

"This ain't no tag-along adventure."

Kaelyn fumed, "Tag-along? Bullshit. I've been through more this week than others would in a lifetime."

Silence thundered in the Jeep. Z said, "I really don't give a rat's ass what you experienced. You were a passive player and lucky to be alive."

"There is no such thing. Either you are passive, or you are participating. It's a contradiction in terms," Kaelyn gently pissed on his point.

Z continued without missing a beat, "Right, you were as active as wallpaper. Now, if you didn't take up valuable space and weighed absolutely nothing, it would be a different story. But that is not the case. Your weight will displace the amount of fuel I need to my destination. Your ass, cute as it is, will take up room for the equipment. I appreciate you connecting me with Doan. She'll be invaluable. But there is no room in the inn for you. I'll give you an exclusive when I return."

"Talking about it afterwards is no substitute for living it," said Kaelyn. "Unless, of course, I expose how fucked up this war really is. How unjust it is to the Vietnamese people. How many cowboy stunts our military do for the sake of adventure. And how many of our young boys are dying because of the fuck-ups."

Z stuck his nose in her face. "You little bitch, you know that shit ain't true."

Kaelyn smiled. "Maybe it is, maybe it isn't. But I will guarantee you this: I've never penned a story yet where I didn't sound like an expert. It's a talent."

"You bitch."

Colonel put up his hands in surrender. "There's no winner here. Let's think on this. One: We have a strategic opportunity." He looked at Kaelyn. "Two: You probably have enough balls to keep up with the team without crumpling. Three: If you get killed, I'd have to answer to your father. And he'll have my ass. Four: If you don't go, you'll have my ass."

With open palms, Kaelyn suggested, 'What if you have plausible deniability? You and Z didn't know I snuck on, disguised as a guard for Doan. You only found out when it was too late."

Z said, "Who's gonna believe that shit? It's not like we'll make that drop from a C-130. In a Huey, a seven-man team is a crowd."

The Colonel stepped out of the Jeep. "Figure out a way. You have two hours before this front will pass. Make it work. Any questions?"

Z WALKED to the front desk of the hospital. "Where are the pilots from the ship on your pad?"

The attendant behind the counter looked up at a bandana-head, with full camouflage face paint, scruffy uniform with a Red Army insignia on a flak jacket. He lowered his head and continued to write. "Well, I'll be damned. John Wayne's here for a visit."

Behind the desk, an MP guard straightened his starched uniform and stepped forward with a stern look. He cleared his throat with authority.

Z laid his Stoner on the counter. "Sergeant, forgive me for being so rude. I'm Captain Zmith, MACV SOG Team 2 Alpha. We're about to launch a top-secret mission. I need both of those pilots."

The obese sergeant scowled in his wrinkled hospital greens. He watched the Stoner's butt plate drag the paper away from his pencil. "And I sorry I didn't tell you this is a hospital. You hot shits ain't supposed to bring your shootin' irons in here. *Partner.*"

Z lowered his barrel. The acrid smell of a freshly fired weapon floated across the admission desk. "We just shot some fuckin' gooks because they really pissed me off." He jabbed the sergeant's massive stomach with the muzzle. "And I would hate to get upset again. All we need to make this mission work are some fuckin' pilots." Z watched the assholes behind the counter pucker up. "Now, where are they?"

The sergeant and the MP matched their manufactured smiles, which grew wide across their faces. "I'll show you. But there's a problem."

"What?"

"As soon as the first helicopter landed, both pilots went to the Officer's Club."

"So...I know where the Club is."

"They dragged back a little while ago and passed out upstairs."

"Any other pilots here?"

Sergeant scratched his bad comb-over. "Yep. Two admissions earlier. One ambulatory and the other on a stretcher."

"Which unit?"

"First Cavalry or something like it. They probably traded in their horses...haw, haw." His knee-slapper didn't go anywhere.

No smile appeared on Z's face. "I'll look at all of them. Where are they?"

"Two passed out in the lounge. Two admitted to recovery."

Z turned to Krotch. "Go to the lounge and see if they're flyable. I'll check the others."

On the second floor, Krotch followed the MP. They opened the door to an overwhelming stench and found a young Warrant officer face down on a table.

"He's one of them." The MP pulled the face out of the vomit puddle to verify the identity. "And the one on the floor's his buddy."

Krotch asked, "How about the other jocks. Are they able to fly?"

The MP returned to the hall. "Each admitted separately. Got patched up, slammed down some food, and crashed."

"Okay, wake them up and have them report to their aircraft."

They met Z at the elevator. "Hang on Krotch, Got their charts here. Both from the same company."

Sergeant said, "You'll need Major Bromo, the Flight Surgeon, to sign them out. I'll see what his schedule looks like."

"Fuck his schedule."

"But he really gets pissed when..."

"Where is he?"

"His office is next to the lounge."

They walked into the Flight Surgeon's office, which smelled like a bar. On the floor, two naked bodies entwined their limbs in love on a tiger skin rug. A bra dangled unceremoniously on the lamp. Men's shorts laid next to the waste basket with an empty bottle of Dewar's. Panties flapped around his forehead.

"Excuse me, Major Bromo. We need to chat." Z stood on one side of the Major, Krotch on the other. Both bounced the butts of their weapons on the floor in time with the love birds' stroke.

The Major slowed down but made no attempt to exit. "Yep... What ya' need?" She moved her legs to a more comfortable position, crossed on his back.

Z bent low to see the woman's face. Her eyes were closed. A grin parted her lips. Perspiration beaded to a healthy glow on her forehead.

"I need two more pilots for an important mission, now. Can Crenshaw and Hellberg fly?"

After each stroke, Bromo gave a breathless analysis. "Most of the time...but they need a helicopter...got lot of bruises...and broken bones...but their heads...are on straight...can work...most of the controls." She gripped handfuls of flesh on his back. Her breasts moved with her gasps.

"Sign these," Z laid two forms next to the Major with a pencil.

"Is Chunky...here?"

"Yes sir."

"You know...the drill."

Chunky struggled to bend down but only reached his calves.

Bromo kept his beat and grabbed the two sheets. Then held them up. "See you...later."

Chunky snatched the forms. "Love is beautiful." His eyes twinkled as moans turned to laughter.

Bromo shouted, "Shut the door."

Circadian rhythms are one thing, total exhaustion another. Combine 'em and it's lights out, baby.

I could have slept through a turbine engine test but not through the bellow of a whiskey-baritone. "Lieutenant, get the fuck up, we gotta go."

Despite the earthquake-like intrusion into my sleep cycle, the voice sounded familiar. I opened one eye. "Aw, shit."

He stuck his face right next to mine. "Where is my fucking forty-five?"

I recognized the nut-job from the store in Saigon. "I returned it to your goddamn holster. What happened sweetheart, did ya' lose it again?" The contorted face in full camouflage was even worse than I remembered.

"You wise ass." He grabbed my t-shirt with two hands, pulled my head off the pillow and swung his leg over my cot.

Pure reflexes drove my knee hard up into his balls. He pulled his hands off me for an unbalanced fall into the wall. *Thunk.* His head sounded like a dropped pumpkin. I pushed hard so old nut-job fell to the floor, flat on his back. *Thunk.* That ole' pumpkin bounced again. My hand found the edge of my bed and I struggled to my elbows.

"Hold it, Ox."

I didn't recognize the face.

He said, "I'm Zulu, let him be." Z looked at Krotch on the floor. "I don't know if I've ever seen him knocked out before. It ain't pretty."

"The son-of-a-bitch yelled in my face."

"Yeah, I saw it from the door. Figured out the rest of the story. You're the FNG who knocked him down and got his pistol."

"Well not exactly, but close." I grinned.

"I don't give a shit what happened. But I need him with me and you to fly. We go in thirty minutes."

"Okay. Who do I fly with?"

"There's is another pilot in the next room."

I wobbled up, staggered around the corner, looked at the camouflage poncho liner over a body. A pillow rested on his head.

Z read the chart. "Warrant Officer Crenshaw. Wake up. You got a mission."

"L. Sid? You gotta be shitting me. My instructor pilot." I yanked the covers off and jerked away the pillow. "Good morning sunshine. You ready to fly?"

He moved slowly. His head first, then his shoulders. "Ain't supposed to. I'm on R and R."

"Need your help on this mission." Z offered his hand, "I'm Duane Zmith, Captain, SOG Team 2 Alpha. We're fresh out of pilots. The two we counted on are dead drunk. You volunteered."

L. Sid said, "Normally, it doesn't take me long to look at a hot horseshoe. I'll meet you at the helicopter. Who else is on the mission?" The blanket fell away from his bandaged hand and splinted fingers.

Z said, "Serpent Two-Six is Captain Ed Barkwart, flying with a warrant named Henry. The gunship is Bravo. We're trying to sneak a team in."

"Yeaaa, right. Me and my silent helicopter." L. Sid never looked up from trying to tie his boots with one and a half hands.

Within five minutes we were all at the helicopter: Six pilots, six crew and two SOG Teams. Serpent Two-Six identified his ship as Yellow One, L. Sid and I were White One. He continued, "After you deploy Team Alpha, your goal is to circle above the foothills of Hon Heo."

L. Sid said, "This ship is a pig. Can't lift much. Too slow. And uses too much fuel. Pretend I'm a B52 and give me lots of time to climb. Otherwise, I'll get my ass shot off. If we can crawl out of small arms range, we'll still divert their attention."

Colonel Bobson flicked the ash from his cigar. "But your clear objective is to bring back some high value prizes."

Two-Six hesitated to figure it out. "What if shit happens?"

"Depends if you're the shit-or or the shit-ee." Z patted the flat raft next to him. "We make it up as we go along. Stay tuned."

"Make up what?" Doan's voice turned more than one head.

"It means we'll find a way."

"And protect our high-value targets?"

"Our prime objective is to snatch and extract. We can also escape and evade. So, if there are no more questions, let's go."

"You didn't answer my question." Doan demanded.

Z looked at his watch. "We can smoke their ass."

"One last request." Bobson stood up. "Transmissions were monitored both at Phu Cat and at the pass. So, we'll run a little misdirection play."

Two-Six said, "Like what?"

Z inserted several magazines into the carrier on his belt. "About fifteen minutes out. Broadcast a change of plans where the main force lands at Chang My. We want the Cong to move off the cliffs."

"Gentlemen, gotta go." All crews and teams moved to their ships.

L. Sid climbed into the left seat with difficulty because he couldn't use his right hand. He mashed the floor button. "What was the flight surgeon thinking when he let me go?"

"He was coming to a new appreciation of a lot of things." I chuckled when I buckled into my seat. The crew chief slammed my armor plate forward. Another sound I loved to hear. Yellow One's anti-collision light started rotating.

When I turned to the crew chief, I looked square into the face of Kaelyn and Z. Her camouflage face paint and hair bunched into her helmet didn't do much for her. "Holy shit, what're you doing here?"

She smiled, "I'm along for the ride." Wink. Wink.

Z shrugged. "Whaaat? What? Just fly."

I squeezed the intercom switch, "Did ya' see who's on board?"

"Nope. We're supposed to have one Vietnamese scout and a bunch of SOG Team super-hot-shits."

"What the hell . . ."

L. Sid moved like everything hurt. His stick-finger pointed up, his voice caustic. "Just get ready for take-off. Sometimes exhaustion plays tricks on you."

I coaxed the bird into a hover and laughed. "How 'bout that?"

"Follow Yellow One." L. Sid cleared in all directions and made an upward sweep with his hand...as if it could fly.

L. Sɪᴅ ᴘᴏɪɴᴛᴇᴅ ʜɪs ᴄʟᴜᴍᴘ. "Catch him."

I made old Nickel-Dime whine and caught up to Yellow One. He gave us a convincing dose of misinformation, complete with specifics about the new LZ and time.

Bravo acknowledged the mission change and descended. Yellow One dropped out of sight and I scrambled to follow suit. "Holy shit, flying trail formation in the clouds is a bitch."

L. Sid laughed. "We're trying to out-fox the fox."

Our ceiling deteriorated when big, ugly chunks of gray clouds forced themselves to our dance floor. Bravo descended to about 50 feet above the water.

L. Sid leaned forward. "What the hell's he doing? This low-level approach is like flying up a witch's ass."

"That shitty, huh?"

"Funny. You really don't want to go there."

Bravo rolled out on a new heading straight to Thanh Ha. "Bravo's out."

This abbreviated radio stuff was total bullshit.

L. Sid said, "Chief, tell Z we're three minutes out from his drop zone." He looked directly at me. "When they jump off the skids, this old girl will want to get up and go. Keep it steady and low."

We bobbed and weaved with Yellow One through the front edge of the weather. From clouds to clear. Not quite as much fun as the bug-eating contest but close.

Crew chief yelled. "Damn, the Team got on the skids when I just mentioned it. But she won't move."

"Mine won't either," echoed the gunner.

"Those damn broads. Don't fuck around. Throw 'em off."

Our trail formation whip-sawed me. I almost passed Yellow twice. When it settled down to a dim daisy chain, the only thing I could see ahead was Yellow's tail. He screamed, "I got a bogey ahead."

"What the hell's a bogey?" L. Sid shouted at the windscreen without the intercom.

"That's Air Force for enemy fighters. If there's a goddamn bogey here...it's operating on Braille."

All of a sudden, Yellow One filled my windscreen and I yanked Nickel-Dime into a quick stop. "Oh shit." The attitude of the ship went past a sixty-degree angle as I floated forward.

Sid put his arm to the door frame as if it would help us stop. A sure sign he was not engaged. "Whoa. Don't let them jump, yet."

Our big turd of a bird came to a shuddering hover about forty feet above the drink. The controls went limp and mushy, even at full power. Nickel-Dime slipped backward into the gray abyss below. In my overhead glass, the bottom of Yellow One came close enough to count the bolts in his skid. "Son-of-a-bitch. I'm losing it."

L. Sid spoke like a pissed-off parent. "Get out of his down wash, dumb ass. Keep it flying."

Wind noise obliterated most of the chief's words. "...at fifteen feet."

My turn and bank indicator pegged to the right. I corrected the attitude, but the ship continued to fall.

"Five feet. Whoa. Stop. We gonna--" The splash drowned out chief's voice.

Hitting the drink had more impact than I expected. Like a slap when you didn't watch. Salty water jumped above my cabin window and blew back in my face.

L. Sid transmitted, "White's out."

WHEN THE TEAM jumped off the skids, the reduction of weight made Nickel-Dime pop up. What a great feeling. Lift never felt so good.

"Easy does it. Just fly it." L. Sid was back in control. "Stay low until you get some speed. Chief, did our little honeys get out?"

Yellow broke in, "Bravo, we got a bogey here. I'm climbing out."

Through the haze, I saw it. Three lines of tracers chased his helicopter. A monster of a sea-going freighter sat broadside in front of me. Made of steel like a big Navy ship. Its cargo crowded the shore with giant crates, barrels, boxes, and sloppy piles. Row boats and junks waited at the dock. Soldiers ran for cover like we came to spoil their party.

"Holy shit." L. Sid pointed. "Turn left, pull up."

I slammed us over into a 90-degree bank and bumped the switch for the landing light. A really bad move. It illuminated our position in the haze. The world could now shoot us easier in this gloomy morning.

L. Sid switched off the landing light, rotating beacon, and the position lights. But the first tracers came from beneath us. He said,

"Yellow this is White. We're taking fire from the junks. Can we respond?"

"At your altitude, you better."

Even with the load gone, ole' Nickel-Dime continued her piggish ways. Okay, a pig that could swim and fly wasn't all that bad.

The cloud cover came with an intense haze, punctuated with lively orange tracers from the junks. The shooter held his machine gun stationary ahead of us and we flew right through it, like a kid running through a hose spray. Instead of a splash, we took four hits. My seat felt that familiar whack-in-the-ass. I said, "Chief, did you see him?"

L. Sid cross-checked everything. "It's still cooking, keep flying. Don't get too far from the beach. A long morning swim with a chicken plate is not all it's cracked up to be."

Another burst of orange came at us. Longer this time. "I see him."

The gunner tore off a long series of bursts from his machine gun while I corrected our flight path to the south. He hung a new box of ammo. "Make another circle back, I'd like to get that sum' bitch."

L. Sid shook his head. "Bullshit, is there something you like about being a slow-moving target? We'll keep climbing."

An enormous mushroom ball of red vaporized the junk and the haze around it. "Halafuckinluja," the gunner shouted.

"Serpent Yellow One, this is Hog, over." A new, crystal clear, voice entered.

"Go ahead."

"Alpha Team sent me a vector to the bogey. I'll stay inside your corridor. Anticipate strike in twenty seconds."

"Roger, our flight'll go bright on all lights."

L. Sid gave a safe thumbs-up signal. "Make a quick one eighty to the left, I want to watch this."

I rolled east and the sun broke through a tiny crack in the clouds. A vintage aircraft followed the rays toward us, close enough to see numbers on the engine cowling and tail, plus an Air Force Star on the fuselage. Underneath the straight, low wings hung rocket pods, big bombs, and other things I didn't recognize. I said, "Did they run out of jets?"

"That's the A1E. Been around since World War II. Stubby and prop driven. You're going to love 'em. Carries a lot of ordinance. Stays on-station a long time."

To prove the Air Force had no immunity from the Cong, the freighter fired at Hog with the familiar 30 caliber tracer stream. Hog boomed, "Nasty, nasty. Mommy said not to play rough." Then he fired four pair of rockets toward the ship, followed by 20 mm cannon fire from four visible mounts.

Firing from the ship did not stop, even though the rockets and the 20 mm found their mark with bright flashes. At the end of the run, the A1E dropped a bomb. It landed on the dock with an enormous explosion. A line of secondary blasts silhouetted the ship against the mountain. Hog climbed into the sky followed by non-stop tracers from the ship as well two more machine guns from the Thanh Ha cliff. These were the big ones. Their rate of fire was slower, but the bright balls of death were larger. Baseball size.

I said, "They're gonna cream old Hog. We gotta do something."

"Yep, but all end up with us dead. We ain't got shit to fight with. Our mission is to stand by for Team 2 Alpha." L. Sid waved his hands in exasperation.

"Bravo has lots of stuff to distract the cliffs with..." Sometimes my brilliance amazed me.

L. Sid nodded.

"Bravo, this is White. Why don't you pick off those cliff dwellers for old Hog?"

"What? And spoil all his fun. I'd love to. Break...how about it Hog? I'm inbound from 4000 feet." Bravo had an irrepressible need to contribute.

"You betcha red-rider, rain some death on 'em."

L. Sid sat back in his seat for the first time. "Make another loop and keep climbing. This show is about to get better."

I leveled off at 1000 feet. Quite an accomplishment for old

Nickel-Dime.

Hog's second run came right at the ship with the sun on his back. The freighter was impervious to the beating it just took and all three machine guns opened up much earlier this time. Hog responded with a steady barrage of 20mm, punctuated every five seconds with a pair of rockets.

The fifties on the cliff opened up and their monster flame balls streamed over the harbor. Bravo saw the opportunity as he dove through 2000 feet and carefully walked several pair of rockets, accompanied by quad machine guns, across the ridge line. He put six shots from his 40mm down through the control center of the freighter's bridge.

In Hog's third run, he released the second big bomb under his wing. A mix of fog and smoke cast a creepy ruddiness on its casing and fins gliding through the air, at a majestically slow speed. The moment that dark blob touched the ship, an explosion consumed the top deck. Even from our vantage point, I was closer than I needed to be. Big chunks of ship were flung in the air.

Hog sang as he did an aileron roll, "Yahoo. That old gray ship, oh, it ain't what it used to be."

Kaelyn shouted. "Aaaaah, shit-fire. I'm out of film." She stood with a camera in one hand. Our eyes connected. "Can you go around again? It will take me just about 30 seconds to put in more film. Blink. Blink."

"I can't believe it. She's still onboard."

Her voice got stronger. "How about it?"

L. Sid gave me the non-splintered finger then circled his clump.

"Fuck it. One more time." I nodded.

"Yellow. Yellow. This is Bravo. Got chewed up by the fifty. Engine's on fire. I'm try for the beach."

"Shit, that's what Hog just bombed." Sid craned his neck to find a hole through the solid cloud cover below us.

Getting Bravo to distract the cliff was not as brilliant as I first thought.

We slipped out of the clouds again and the FM blared, "We got you in sight Bravo. This is Zulu. Can you make it to the outcrop?"

Bravo said, "Can't find it. Wind's tricky over these cliffs. Stand by."

"Look at his trail of smoke, shiii-it." L. Sid did a corkscrew maneuver with his hand toward the shore.

Without his engine, Bravo glided over the water, back toward the tiny beach in the cove. Tracers from the village punished him all the way down. He flared almost vertical at the bottom to dissipate forward airspeed. It stopped suddenly as a ball into a catcher's mitt. He landed hard on the beach right next to the outcrop.

Bravo transmitted. "We made it."

"Wow, nailed it." L. Sid and I cheered. Until we heard the loathsome sound of bullets killing Bravo, gouging holes in the ship, and the screaming of the crew.

Two openings in the cliff, about 50 feet above the water, kept firing at them.

Team 2 clung to the rocks and returned fire without effect. The Cong tossed grenades down the cliff to keep the team pinned down.

Ol' pumkin-head Krotch and his trusty M79 stopped the madness. With two precise shots, he plugged up the horrid streams of death.

"White this is Zulu. Mission aborted. Bravo's crew are dead. When can you extract?"

L. Sid pointed me to the beach. "We are on the way." He switched radios. "Hog, can you work over Thanh Ha."

"Roger, stay low. I'll go pole to pole."

This time I only saw the blurred belly of the A1E. His four 20mm cannons stopped all the guns from the little village.

I used the outcrop to shield my final approach. The burning helicopter violated the pristine white sands of the beach, in the middle of the cove. Very little cove. "Zulu this is White. No beach left to play on. How deep's the water? Over."

"Very deep. Six feet off the sand is six feet down. Land on the big rock"

"You mean the outcrop? Roger." The ragged bunch of rocks had hardly any flat. Flames from the burning hulk on the beach engulfed the co-pilot and gunner, still in the sitting positions. Bullet holes covered the windscreen, rotor blades and door. The smoldering body of Bravo hung in his seat harness, inches over the water.

"You got to make it. The shit from the village is about to erupt on us again. We have one chance to get these guys off." L. Sid squirmed in his seat. "Just put the toes of the skids in the middle of the rock. And hold enough power to keep 'em in place."

I wondered if he really thought I was daydreaming since nothing was happening here. Except, of course, the bad guys down the beach, all pissed off because we sank their ship and destroyed their village. Then the cliff dwellers, or their next-of-kin, probably didn't score us five-out-of-five on the big-smile meter.

My approach to the rock was dead on, except for actual touchdown. More like bounce-on, or a smash-it-to-a-stop. Exhausted, overloaded, wet grunts grappled through the down draft to climb into the helicopter. They threw everything carried on the floor, making enough noise to drown out the engine.

Expecting the ship to wobble like a turkey, it stood dead still.

During my cross check of the instruments, the rotor whistled from new bullet holes. I felt a thumping feedback in my controls.

L. Sid yelled to Z, "Don't fire up at the cliffs. You'll shoot our goddamn blades off."

Krotch ran in front of the ship and took cover behind the rocks. His movements were like a machine. Two quick shots with his M79 sealed the caves forever.

L. Sid slapped the glare shield. "Fly, baby, fly."

Without any warning, the A1E came over so low that we felt the buffet from its wing tip. But it was the bomb he dropped that frosted this cake of chaos. We swayed from the concussion and felt the heat from the explosion. I have no idea how I stayed on the rock.

"We're up. Go. Go." The crew chief shouted from the rear.

I added power. Nothing happened. Added more power. Wouldn't budge. Felt like the skids were welded to the damn rock. Finally understood why I didn't wobble during loading: It couldn't fly.

L. Sid pointed the clump down the beach and flinched when bullets ricocheted off the rock. "Either die flying or die trying."

PART SIX_

I PULLED in power like I meant it, but it made me a liar. "Come on baby." If I could get off the rock, I'd have instant altitude. All of forty feet to make it fly or hit the water.

It flew, kind of. Actually, it flopped more down than anything. A strong sea breeze saved me at the bottom. I leveled out and bounced the belly of the helicopter off the water. Twice. We picked up speed and lift. Like an albatross trying to fly. Not very high, and not very fast.

No one cheered. They were too busy shooting at the village. That probably made the difference, we shed all that weight.

"White, this is Yellow. Nice job, babe."

"White, this is Hog. You done fucking around? And you didn't die. Good."

I breathed again.

"Hog, this Sierra Six. Destroy that helicopter on the beach and then the freighter. Over."

"This is Hog, wilco. Out."

"AFTER ALL THAT BITCHIN', moanin' and connivin'? What in the hell ya' mean, you changed your mind?" Z stood nose-to-nose with Kaelyn and poked her shoulder.

Kaelyn deflected his hand with a smooth movement. "Don't ever touch me again or I'll have your ass on a fuckin' pole." She turned away and spoke out loud. "I was too close to get it right." An unusual quiet fell over the pilot's lounge, the temporary operation center for the SOG Team.

"Get what right?" Colonel Bobson looked up from the map.

Kaelyn said, "During the mission briefing, Doan Vien questioned the *alternate response plan,* and your ability to protect the *high value targets.* She recoiled when you said you'd *smoke their ass.*"

Bobson scanned the wet camouflaged bodies sitting around the room. "Where is she? Did we get a nose count?"

Krotch shook his head. "She made it out of the water, on to my raft."

"I saw her." The radio operator held up his arm. "When the helicopter took fire from the cliffs. She had to duck and weave in the rocks. Then disappeared."

"Anyone else?"

L. Sid stood next to Danny asleep at the door. "If she was on board, we wouldn't have made it back."

Z persisted. "So, what happened to her?"

Like a teacher losing patience with a slow child, she said, "...probably bowed out to see her daddy."

The Colonel said, "She what?"

Kaelyn paused until the murmuring stopped. "Doan Vien's concern about the *high value targets* bothered me. Until I remembered the Binh Xuyen's leader is a guy named Le Van Vien."

Bobson erased the chalk board and wrote in large numbers, 10,000. "Intelligence called him a skilled politician. He supplied the Japanese during the war with a security force. Later, the French let him run Saigon. He grew the Binh Xuyen into a well-armed, well-disciplined force of more than 10,000."

Kaelyn cleared her throat. "By the time Ngo Dinh Diem became premier, Le Van Vien was the richest man in Saigon. A real Robin Hood character. Attractive, powerful, a riveting motivator, yet illiterate."

"Okay, Okay. So what?" Z had the patience of a cricket on a fry pan. "He was a ruthless river pirate with a fortune in opium and prostitution."

"She's his daughter. Her facial similarity to Le Van Vien is as remarkable as her ability to motivate a crowd. It may be just the power of the princess, but Doan has it. In spades."

"Bullshit. They all look the same. And the power of the princess is more the desperate journalist using half-ass assumptions to get headlines." Disgust crept through Z's camouflage painted face. "I'm embarrassed I bought her story."

Colonel Bobson threw his map down. "Cool it, goddamn it. These high-level men are essential, not Doan. In North Vietnam's war effort, Bao Dai replaces the current government leaders of the North and the South. The Binh Xuyen will provide finance and control. Doan's as important as a dimple on a frog's ass."

Z showed his pearly whites. "But she knows our plans. Ah, for the joy of an Arc Light in the night. That'll finish this fuckin' mess."

"And you called my observations bullshit. Your patented dumb-ass approach won't do anything except thin out the forest." Kaelyn smiled. "And fuck up the beach."

Bobson said, "I've personally reconnoitered that whole area, low and slow. And didn't see diddly shit. I tried not to buy into the ghost stories that scared everybody away."

"The Cong are masters of disguise." Z stood up. "I bet that place is loaded with caves. If Bao Dai and Le Van Vien were there, you could picnic in the pasture and nothing would happen. I'd bet guns followed you from the moment you popped into the valley."

"My pilot said it was quiet as a graveyard. He was nervous."

L. Sid came alive again. "Who was he?"

"From Serpent, a big old boy, senior captain, black eyes, black hair. Name sounded Russian."

"Mishkov?"

"Yep. Nice guy."

L. Sid tilted his head back. "He was one of the best we had. He survived a dead-stick landing. In a ship that was on fire. To an LZ that was being overrun. And he was nervous?"

"Was?"

"He bought the farm at LZ Hereford. Danny and Kaelyn were on board."

Bobson grimaced. "That after-action report drove deployment of Team 2 Alpha at Phu Cat."

Z turned around. "The Cong expect us to follow up the bogie in the bay trick."

"But policy says we can't." Bobson glanced around the room. "We gotta go through the proper channels. One freelance mission is OK. Two's a grade-buster."

"Bullshit. This isn't something new. We're finishing what we started. We caught 'em with their pants down and kicked 'em in the balls."

L. Sid laughed. "Only because we took away their free pass. Who would ever think we'd attack in unflyable, monsoon weather?"

Bobson signaled for quiet. "Since officially I'm not here, do whatever the hell you want. I can beg forgiveness later. It makes sense. Lots of Cong wouldn't guard 'em if the high value personnel and big-time supplies weren't there."

Kaelyn spoke from the corner of the room. "All those troops are commanded by General Cuong Danh, previous commander of the 1st Sapper Battalion. Responsible for our largest personnel and supply loss of the war. That was never reported. In their Hon Heo base, the Cong are right under the nose of Air Force squadron in Qui Nhon. So close to the South China Sea, the Navy could probably smell them if the wind was right. And on the doorstep of the First Cav Division, the biggest, most advanced unit in country. How can this be?"

"It can't. There is a big fish somewhere and it's smellin' up the pond. There's nothing we can do right now, but this evening is another story. Half of you guys are zombies and the others are asleep. Report back here at 1700 hours. There'll be a mess set up downstairs. You're excused."

An affirmative grunt arose from the room as all boots hit the floor. All except the Danny, the deep sleeper next to the door.

L. Sid closed the blinds over the window. "And more monsoon rains are on the way."

THE DAWN of a new day shone someplace, but not here. L. Sid dragged his smelly clump under my nose at least twelve hours before he should've. Its toxic odor was like doing a face plant in a honey bucket. "Come on Ox, get your lazy ass up."

I said, "Is it decaying flesh or bad breath?"

"Quickest way to your brain is through your nose. But I forgot no one was home."

"Yeah, but mine was occupied more recently than yours."

"Wise-ass."

"Dumb-fuck."

"We gotta pop-in on the Colonel in fifteen minutes."

"Shit, there goes din-din." Lucky me. Didn't have to dress, 'cause I never shed the stinking clothes.

Kaelyn slept on the floor across the lounge. Her good looks survived the facial camouflage of black, green, and gray. A camera hung around her neck and a writing pad rested in her lap. I kicked the sole of her boot. "Hey, wanna eat?"

Only one eyelid moved, then her beautiful mouth opened. "Two eggs over easy, s.o.s. in the corner, dry toast, jelly on the side." She licked her lips.

"You're dreaming. But there's food on the way to the meeting, I can smell it."

"What meeting?" Both eyes banged open. Puzzled wrinkles magically appeared in the grease paint on her brow.

The grouchy L. Sid frowned. "Actually, you weren't invited. But you haven't been invited to so many things, one more wouldn't matter. Neither were you, Ox."

"Well, fuck 'em if they can't take a joke."

Kaelyn mumbled. "I love to...not take a joke." A hint of her smile appeared. "When's the meeting? Is the food hot?"

L. Sid pointed to the chalk board. "Meeting's here in twelve minutes, food's downstairs."

"Done. Let's go Danny."

Something reignited in my core. Would I take food instead of sex? Probably not. Kaelyn flittered down the hall to the delightful aroma of bacon and eggs. Bad or good, it was food. And following her was an appetizer for sure.

Kaelyn paused next to one of the insulated serving containers. "So, what's happening?"

"We gonna plan what we gonna do." I smiled.

"No shit."

"If you're askin' what the plan is, don't know. Fell asleep before it came up." I scooped some eggs, s.o.s. and a couple pieces of toast. My tray runneth over. Hallelujah.

Kaelyn talked between bites. Her knife and fork banged on the steel tray. "I'll bet it's an assassination, pure and simple. Followed by a B-52 strike to destroy the supplies and clean up the evidence."

"Why?" The fog hadn't cleared from my pea brain.

"Because the high-value assets represent a powerful threat to the stability of the Saigon government. It's what these SOG guys do. Sneak in, shoot, and scoot. You can't expect anything else. My daddy used to say, 'If a man has only an axe, every problem looks like a tree.'"

She pushed open the meeting room door with her lovely butt to a room with all ten of the SOG Team members. "Morning boys." She purred with an inflection in her voice.

The noise in the room stopped. Most of the ragtag assembly glanced at the Colonel. He acknowledged her with a bad attempt of sincerity. "Good afternoon Miss DeHaven. We're here to discuss our mission. Would you excuse us, please?"

"You mean how ya' gonna kill them, or who's gonna do it?" She added an extra helping of twinkle and grin.

His expressionless face reared back. "Why Miss DeHaven. Down deep, you know we stand here with the purest of intentions. Only to make substantive contact and communicate our issues, clearly." He could have been a used car salesman.

"Of course, I'll portray it exactly to the hordes of waiting media around the world." Her slight bow forward and a miniscule hunch of shoulders indicated fake servitude. "Now, may I slog this grub down, oh my commander?"

"Only if you let me review the final draft. We have agents to protect. Strategy to disguise."

"Sure. Review it all you want. As long as you don't change a fuckin' word." She excelled at the art of never conceding defeat.

"How lucky can I be?" He locked eyes with me and in the frosty tone of an exasperated drill instructor said, "Ox, glad you're here, have a seat."

A scary stillness enveloped the room. Bobson continued. "Gentlemen. Saigon provided new intelligence. The value players are dividing up the country. They've unified in a triumvirate to support the North Vietnamese campaign. Its objective is to defeat the First Calvary Division."

Z grinned maniacally. "A strike here would be like wiping out a NATO summit. Get our boots and guns on the ground and we'll find 'em. His boys smiled at him. Only teeth sparkled through the camo paint. A low growl arose.

Bobson said, "Too much is at stake for these enormous egos. Boa Dai thinks God gave it to him. Le Van Vien stole everything he has, and General Cuong Danh prefers killing rather than a strategy. All were independent before we upped the ante. The real question is, what is the best way to get you in place?"

Barkwart's eyes opened wide in an epiphany. "They're looking and listening outbound, let's drop our guys inside their perimeter."

The Colonel said, "Trouble is, we've no place to land. Ask yourself, 'Can I hear a helicopter a klick away?' In this circle of mountains, you're damn right."

L. Sid leaned back in his chair. "And there is nothing silent in the Cav's inventory. Except people."

The Colonel did a double-take. "What?"

"A couple years ago, at Fort Benning, I saw the Golden Knights, the US Army Parachute Team. Really cool. They jumped from an altitude so high, we couldn't hear or see the aircraft. Their chutes didn't open 'til they landed in front of us. Never expected it."

Z puffed up like a cat about to pounce. "Yep, the HALO concept. It'll be a cake walk."

"If we only knew where the cake was. What did we learn from the prisoner?"

Krotch spit tobacco into the wastebasket. "He's cooperating. The meadow is the only open area in the center of the mountain. If the guns on the canyon walls don't get us, the wind currents will."

"What options do we have?"

"Another place is the north ridge of the cliffs. At the ruins of the temple."

L. Sid stared at Krotch. "You want to land on the heavy gun emplacement that shot down Bravo this morning? Brilliant, fucking brilliant."

Krotch moved with a speed defying his girth. L. Sid ducked him, and Z intervened. A loud knock on the door stopped movement. "Military Police with prisoner, sir."

Z nodded to Doc. "Check 'em out."

He verified the MP guard, who brought in Ho Chi Bro with his hands tied behind his back. Army green tape joined his legs together at the ankles. He wobbled more than he walked. Mucus and dried blood soiled his long white beard. Wet with perspiration, he bowed to the Colonel. "Sir, I am Nhat Danh, Province Chief for the National Liberation Front, brother of General Cuong Danh, Central Command."

His fluency in English shocked me. Three times he had tried to kill me. He escaped death enough to embarrass a cat. But in the smoke-filled lounge, Ho stood like a statesman. "Perhaps I can help you. I seek asylum and your assistance in return for my cooperation."

The Colonel studied him for a moment. "If you help us and we succeed, you'll receive asylum. If we don't, you won't need it."

"Fair enough. What do you want?"

"Tell me about the Cliffs of Hang Thy and the gun emplacements." The Colonel chewed his cigar in anticipation.

Ho Chi Bro raised his chin. "One of the most beautiful spots on the Vietnam coast. The bay's intense blue water, pure white beaches, and the quaint Phu Ly Bridge."

The damn guy sounded like a chamber of commerce president making a pitch for a convention. Will this lucky bastard never falter?

"What troops are on Phu Cat mountain?"

"Actually, it is called Hon Heo."

"Okay, Hon Heo."

"The 18th NVA Regiment."

"How many soldiers?"

"Many."

"Give me a number."

"With your overpowering air and artillery, large formal units with specific troop levels are rarely available. Instead, they are constructed on an *ad hoc* basis."

Krotch snarled, "What the hell is *ad hoc*?"

"It's Latin, meaning crafted with whatever force is available to accomplish the mission. Sometimes cannons, other times hooch maids. Both the hardware and people vary widely. All are expendable."

He spoke better than some of my college professors.

"I don't give a shit about the view, describe the top of that goddamn hill." Colonel's voice rose a hair, amplified by his fist rapping the desk.

"Not to be argumentative, but the ability to see is central to my response. The location is much revered by the villagers. When they cooperated with the Korean forces, the NVA destroyed the temple in reprisal. In the rubble is a large caliber, anti-aircraft gun emplacement, with a crew of five."

"So, what about the fuckin' view?"

"The view is important. You can see and be seen by the observation point on the highest peak of Hon Heo."

"So?"

"A 51-caliber machine gun is in a bunker, between the two, big boulders on the peak."

L. Sid came alive. "The big boys, who fly the big toys called it Little Titty Top. The Air Force use it as an IP, an Identification Point, for landing at Qui Nhon runway one-eight."

"Back to the question." Kaelyn had the persistence of a mess hall cat. "And I know that you don't know, but if you did, how many troops are on that mountain? Where are they?"

Colonel radiated irritation. "The question's been covered already. We're in a whole new area. *Miss DeHaven.*"

"But we didn't get a usable answer. *Colonel.*"

He didn't move a muscle. "How many are there?"

"The number I have heard is two hundred."

Kaelyn's face paled. "And you're takin' only *ten* guys?"

"You're right. Didn't spot them enough. We'll only take five."

KAELYN COCKED her head in disbelief, "How did you figure that?"

"About a month ago, one of the Hon Heo cadre got drunk in a nearby village. He talked too much."

"And the second part of the question?"

Ho Chi Bro shrugged. "Which was what?"

"Come on." Bobson's legendary patience eroded. "Where are they?"

"The soldier was not that drunk."

She asked, "OK, where are the soldiers normally?"

"I would guess half on the outside, half in the caverns."

Another face of Ho Chi Bro materialized as the sincere helper. He uncoiled like a snake and said, "But sir, you did not ask me about the help that I need."

"I addressed the issue of asylum."

"You did. However, I asked for asylum *and* help." Bro straightened his posture, "my miserable, skinny, little ass isn't worth much, but the help I need is life or death for my village."

Another big sigh from Bobson. "OK, what is it?"

"At the southeast edge of the meadow of Chang My is the mouth of an enormous cave. It holds over 150 people from the Hung Lac

Hamlet. They work as slaves, making munitions, and cleaning the hospital.

I learned my free-thinking, Saigon-educated daughter is among them. She had not converted to the ideology of Ho Chi Minh. Does not even use our family name. For over 20 months, she has been missing."

Z said, "Where's that in relation to the main house?"

Bro lowered his head. "It was destroyed."

"Where do the big guys meet?"

"In a cave."

"With the prisoners?"

"No. Many natural caves in the mountain have been improved. That's what slaves do. They dig."

"So where is the big meeting?"

"About twenty meters up the meadow from the worker cavern."

The Colonel rose. "So, the question is how can we accomplish our mission and not kill the prisoners?"

Z addressed the room, "I think that we should—"

"Hold that thought Z," Colonel Bobson stuck out a familiar 'halt' gesture and turned to Ho Chi Bro. "I appreciate your assistance. Radio, take him into the hall."

As Ho waddled toward the door, he said, "Remember: every cave must have an escape tunnel. They feed the mother tunnel, which leads to the sea. Inside the cavern many explosives are made. Their inventory contains more than 250 satchel charges and over 140 grenades." With a cryptic nod, Ho exited.

The Colonel modified his halt gesture into a *shhhhh* with one finger to his lips.

Another rap came against the door. The Colonel snapped, "Yes."

"One final item from Ho."

"For pity's sake."

Ho's ingratiating smile made the interruption palatable. "The cave complex also contains a regimental-size hospital. Large enough to accommodate 75 patients. Plus, two acres of munitions and weapons storage." He bowed and departed.

All in the room sat in silence until Bobson gave the 'OK' sign.

Z spoke first because it never took him long to make a point. "My plan is still good: first, we get Hog to work-over the cliffs and the meeting cave. Second, we'll HALO jump in with both teams. Romeo will split between the Hang Thy and Little Titty Top to silence both gun emplacements. Third, Team 2 Alpha will land at the caves for the value assets. Fourth, Navy Swift boats will patrol the bay at the Thanh Ha village to plug their escape routes."

Bobson spoke, "OK, so what do you do with the prisoners?"

"Team Two Alpha would turn the prisoners loose and disappear into the trees for an extraction. Romeo will escape north down the cliffs to the sea for pick up on the beach."

L. Sid asked, "And how do we find you?"

"Hog will make a pick-up zone for you with a 500 pounder. As long as you're in a Huey."

Bobson inhaled the cigarette. "If you land around 1830 hours, you'll have an hour and a half to get it done. Sunset is at 2006 hours. But those prisoners are dead meat. They'll be hunted down like dogs by the Cong."

Barkwart said, "Why not have Hog scorch a path through the least vegetated, most direct line off the hill. His four 20mm cannons and napalms will open up the canopy and scare the bad guys away."

"Sure, why not. But how in the hell do we communicate with the prisoners?"

"How about a native?" Kaelyn's strong, confident voice cut through the meeting like a sharp knife through cotton, "Doan Vien with be with them. She would help motivate and direct the prisoners."

Z said, "And if she didn't survive? Krotch and I both know enough Vietnamese to get us through. There is a lot to do. Got to be in the air by 1800 hours."

Colonel's voice had a hint of enthusiasm. "I'll handle the Navy for the boats, Air Force for ol' HOG, and the First Cav for artillery support."

I asked, "How high do we climb for your jump?"

Z paced the floor. "What was your altitude when you first established contact with us at Phu Cat?"

"Don't remember exactly. Around 9000 feet when we connected with Air Force base."

"It'll be enough, considering how noisy the A1E can be."

I pointed at L. Sid, "How long will it take us to get that high…"

Krotch actually laughed. "Depends on what you're smoking."

"And how much crap the boys bring to the party." L. Sid connected with Z. "Give me a body count and weight before we fly."

"How 'bout leavin' your crew chief and gunner." Z smiled.

L. Sid didn't hesitate. "Fuck off."

Z nodded, "That's not a nice to say to the guy that might save your ass."

ASSHOLES AND ELBOWS MOVED in a flurry after the meeting broke up. No one questioned the mission or their part in it. Thirty-nine minutes to prep. An hour and a half to get it done.

No pressure.

I followed L. Sid out to our venerable Nickel-Dime and wondered what surprises we had in store. The crew chief and gunner were both aboard and sleeping.

L. Sid started the preflight inspection, "Chief, we're pulling pitch no later than 1800 hours. That's thirty-five minutes from now. Fix this skid so we're not luggin' mud or draggin' wind. Leave the ammo. Remove all extra bullshit including c-rations and souvenirs."

While I inspected the main rotor, L. Sid checked the sight gauges. "I gotta tell you L. Sid, I just don't trust the old gook."

"Neither do I." Kaelyn materialized in front of the helicopter. "His story had everything going for it...lowly village prisoners, underground factory making explosives, hospital with seventy-five beds, and the pathos of a misguided daughter caught up on the wrong side of the philosophical tracks. He's bettin' we're gonna get wiped out."

"Nah, you guys are terminally cynical. He wouldn't knowingly feed the blood lust of this insane team of killers. What little faith you have in your fellow man." L. Sid found the light.

I smiled at Kaelyn. "Yeah, verily sister, another bag of bullshit."

"They may be a bunch of killers, but damn few soldiers aren't. My daddy said bloodshed is a building block in the career of a lifer. It makes 'em do dumb-shit stuff." Kaelyn leaned against the avionics door, the top buttons on her shirt laid open.

I enjoyed the view.

"Hey L. Sid." Perspiration dripped off Barkwart from his run to our helicopter. "Crank 'em up, crank 'em up. Need to pick up our teams at 1740 hours by the control tower. Time is now 1726."

"What's the deal?" L. Sid motioned the chief to remove the blade tie-downs.

Barkwart said. "When Bobson called Air Force for the A1E, he learned of an Arc Light scheduled at 1830. It'll hit the mountain directly west of Phu Cat. So, our teams should land at 1830. The head winds at altitude are increasing. Let's go."

I hovered Nickel-Dime to the tower as instructed. L. Sid focused straight ahead instead of his usual, all-direction search. I nudged him, "What's the matter?"

He slid his seat back and down. "This jump-through-your-ass routine is for the birds. Quick is wrong, especially for a complex plan. Who knows, maybe the Arc Light is the best subterfuge yet. You're in for quite a show. Unless it kills us."

I loved reassuring thoughts. "Com' on L. Sid, quit shittin' me."

"No lie, bud. This bombing will strike right across the valley from our drop zone. The B52s release their loads from 25,000 feet or better. We're too close. If the bombardier so much as scratches his ass, he could wipe us out."

The front door of the control tower slammed open and both SOG teams rushed out. Team 2 Alpha boarded our ship with a daunting load of combat equipment, ammo, plus a parachute and a reserve. It doubled the girth of each man.

L. Sid said, "No sense asking what they weigh now. See if we can fly."

The radio blared, "Yellow One's off."

I grabbed an armpit of power. But the helicopter wouldn't get off the ground.

L. Sid slapped the glare shield. "You should know better. Instead of lifting up, drag us forward until we get some speed. And hope we fly."

I coaxed it forward, ignoring the obscene scraping noise of skids fighting the concrete. Two bump-to-fly-tries later, Nickel-Dime stayed off the ground and everybody applauded.

Yellow One circled over the bay. When I caught up, I broke radio silence with, "Ta daaa." For the next twenty-seven minutes, we climbed to a much cooler 9000 feet. Vietnam's pure white beach sands bordering the crystal blue water of the South China Sea were easy to follow.

L. Sid shouted to Z, "Arc Light straight ahead."

At 9000 feet, our 80-knot airspeed seemed like hovering. So, I watched the placid mountain top explode in front of me. With no apparent separation between blasts, the top of ridge line vaporized into a rolling cloud of deadly dust. I couldn't tell how long it was, but it extended across half the width of my windshield. We were at least ten klicks away.

Screams, whistles, and cheers erupted from the rear. Z shouted an unintelligible command and they started to jump. My altitude increased as each one left the ship. When the last soldier leaped, we were climbing like a shot out of hell.

A dark shadow skirted across my overhead Plexiglas with aircraft-shaking roar. Any noise louder than our ear-deafening, thunder-box meant it was too damn close.

I twisted my neck and watched the bottom of the A1E blow by in a chandelle. "Hog, you goddamn dumbass."

L. Sid shook his head. "Not exactly how you want to break mandated radio silence. Especially to a nut armed to the teeth."

Hog's voice, tinged with amusement, came in with the clarity of god in a recording studio. "Ya' changed from a blimp to a rocket. But I dare not dally when duty demands." He flew away.

The turtle-like crawl to 9000 feet in 30 minutes deadened my mind and bored me out of fears. When ol' L. Sid motioned for an aggressive bank; I gave him a turn in a heartbeat. Cranking it deep any time was fun, but it became absolute liberation when I bent the mother over 90 degrees. A shout from the rear scared the hell out of me.

"Goddamn, what the hell?"

I discovered Colonel Bobson, looking like death had cornered him, barely holding on to his cargo seat. "Sheee-it. What're you doing here?"

He said, "Not many folks alive ever call me 'shee-it'."

L. Sid slapped his knee. "No wonder we couldn't get this bucket in the air."

"Had to. No C'nC ship available. You'll have to stick around 'til we see how the plan is working. Advise Barkwart."

L. Sid transmitted, "Six wants us to stay on station. See ya' at the ranch."

"Did I miss something?"

"Naw. He's on-board."

"We'll wait up for you."

The team radio squawked, "Alpha, this is Romeo One. Chute open...looks quiet on Little Titty...What the fu...Taking fire... Crawling out everywhere." Static flooded the cockpit until he reported from the ground. His voice cracked, "All fucked up. Cut down everyone. In the air. They're coming." Gun shots, static, and screaming raised the hair on my neck, "*CACA DAU, CACA DAU.*"

I said, "What's that?"

Bobson stomped the floor so hard it sounded like we hit a sea gull. "They're yelling 'I'll kill you.' Has Romeo Two opened?"

L. Sid said, "There's 600 feet difference in elevation. We added twelve seconds."

"I can't see shit. Too high." Bobson put down his spotting scope. "Descend to 6,000 feet."

At 3000 feet per minute, I got there as the radio blared, "Hog, this is Romeo Two. Help out Little Titty Top. Team is overrun."

"Roger, I'm just north of it, rollin' in hot."

Hog sent a steady stream of 20mm plus four brace of rockets into the top of Hon Heo. "Yahoo, got the bastards celebrating..."

From a hardened position, three streams of machine gun fire lead him too much then stopped but kept shooting. Hog flew right through it and his wing exploded. The fuselage spun in a blazing barrel row, heading straight down.

Bobson put up his monster scope. "He bailed out...chute's open."

The Colonel redirected Barkwart to pick him up. We watched the sickening sight of the wingless A1E careen into cliffs of Thanh Ha, on top of the battery that brought it down.

Ya' gotta love poetic justice.

GIANT CHUNKS of aircraft led the fiery wave of a massive explosion, disintegrating Hog's A1E.

"Alpha, on the ground." The radio screamed out like there was no limit on the volume knob.

The Colonel dispassionately transmitted, "Roger. Hog is down."

At 6000 feet, I drilled holes in the sky. Our fuel emptied by the bucket while he had to watch his men.

Z's voice blurted from the radio, "Three's in the bag. Little resistance. Lots of prisoners. Found Doan Vien. She doesn't know where the assets are. Get the big guns cookin'. We're goin' for the meeting."

L. Sid tapped the fuel gauge. "Time to head back to the ranch. Unless ya'll wanna walk. Falling out of the sky here gives us a shitty choice of the devil or the deep blue sea."

Bobson's erupted through the noise. "Goddamn it, I gotta to stay here. If we extract these guys, every minute counts."

I said, "Let's put you on Yellow One. He should be refueling now."

"Change ships? Can't take the time. Z'll be dead by the time we get back."

L. Sid had a worrisome 50-mile stare. His transmission squeaked out. "One, this is Two over."

Not even a peep in return.

What a time not to connect. My heartbeat accelerated by a multiple of two.

I tapped L. Sid on the shoulder. Spoke in a slow rhythm, "Check Qui Nhon tower. See if they've arrived."

He moved like he had a problem. Fumbling while he switched frequencies. Pausing between entries on the radio. Looking around at nothing.

Qui Nhon found Yellow One just as I flew over our burning wreckage in the Thanh Ha village. Debris from the bombing and the destroyed freighter cluttered their dock.

The Colonel peered out the door. "Plenty of little islands to make the switch. Get down there so we can inspect them."

"That's a bad idea, Colonel." L. Sid revived. "Each one of those little pieces of shit are full of the amateur bad guys, protecting their harbor."

"Roger." The Colonel's tone changed. "I arranged for a Navy Swift boats to patrol the area. It's their bag." He switched to the Navy frequency and outlined the plan of exchange to Sealord Two-Six, the boat commander.

With a gangbuster, Boston accent, Sealord said, "Six you are in luck, man. I'm two klicks south...right near a reef. Probably big enough for your helicopter...Come take a look, why don't ya."

I hated it when commanders said "probably."

"Sealord, we'll see what ya' got. Over." L. Sid sounded downright suspicious.

In the cargo area, the Colonel moved like a caged cat. "I have 'ta check with Z before we lose contact. If you can land, do it."

The ugly clump directed me into a turn. "Dump it low and circle the ship. Just don't block Sealord's line of fire to the beach."

"Gotcha," I plunged straight down, zipping past 3,000 feet per minute. A dead-nuts dive to swoop and poop on the Navy. Like a sonic seagull.

L. Sid twirled the clump. "Now make a tight circle around that ship."

I flared big-time to kill my speed from 80 knots to 20 and didn't see a thing. "Where?"

Stomping on the transmit button, L. Sid roared, "Sealord, where's that fuckin' rock? As in landing spot?"

"Never did promise *land*. I said piece of *coral*. I believe that the reef is big enough for you to set down on..."

"It ain't the size of the reef, it's the depth of the water. This ain't a goddamn boat."

"How well does your man do in water? Over."

"Strong enough to swim up a waterfall. But not with the pack he's carryin'. Can't go quick or far."

"It should be only foot or two. I'll put a man on it to guide you in."

"Good idea." L. Sid motioned me for another go-around.

"Yellow Two. You havin' fun down there boy? Over."

I answered, "Big time jollies. Where you at?"

"About a thousand feet indicated. Enjoyin' the view."

Sealord pulled his impressive Swift boat over the spot and let a sailor out. That one foot of water made him look deceptively like a double amputee as he sank to his chest. "Oops. It's looks more like three or four feet, don't ya' know. Can you still land there?"

The Colonel jabbed his finger toward the water like he was stickin' a pig.

"We'll hover and drown a skid or two. Six will be on the right side. Make sure your man leaves enough reef for him. Over."

L. Sid brought Yellow One up on the latest, while I watched the Swift Boat cut circles in the water. My turn was less severe, so I had a chance to look toward shore. That's when I saw the muzzle flash.

TRACERS in the twilight weren't half as bad as at night. But still way more than I wanted to see.

L. Sid switched my radio and didn't look outside the aircraft. "Bring it around to hover in front of the man."

"Did ya' see those tracers?"

"Yep, and so did Sealord. He'll engage the target. Goddamn it, just get us to the old boy in the water. Advise Yellow One. I gotta talk to the Colonel and the chief."

Without Sealord circling, the sailor in the water was hard to see. I asked Sealord, "Where's your man? Have him pop smoke again. Over."

"You can't see him because he got hit with the opening burst of fire. Blew off his hat and chicken-plate. Saw him go under."

L. Sid leaned forward to see better, "Gunner, crew chief, look for the guy in the water... Danny, land at the dark spot."

"Light spot, dark spot, no spot, give me a break. Finding fly shit in pepper would be easier."

"Just pick a spot. If it ain't right, hover 'til ya' find something. But be careful when your skids are in the water. You'll whip up more mist than you can stand."

The low fuel light went on in all its radiant beauty.

As I prepared to land, Sealord said, "Yellow Two, go around. When we find that reef again, we'll float a bottle for you."

I flew in a large circle as Sealord looked for the reef. His big 50-caliber fired steady bursts at the shoreline. I got up to about 50 feet above the Swift when the water exploded in a huge geyser. "Now what?"

"Whatever it is, the observer is pretty damn good. Watch the next one come closer." The clump estimated the flight path to the sea and another spout erupted right where L. Sid pointed. Kind of spooky.

Turning with a big wake, the Swift boat veered off. Behind him several big bottles floated in the water.

I dropped onto the promised, shallow spot in the sea. Still couldn't find it. Maybe Navy eyes were different than Army eyes. Water still looked a hell of a lot like water. When my skids went under, the Colonel stepped off. The weight of his back pulled him over. He vanished.

"As soon as he stands up, we'll pull out." L. Sid watched the Colonel flail in the water. Like wrestling an alligator. First the boot showed, then a hand, and finally his helmet. He stood, spit and gestured, "Get the fuck out."

Mist whipped up to form a small, churning fog bank around me. A giant explosion erupted at the edge of my non artillery-proof, hiding place and blew what felt like a ton of water on top of the helicopter. The concussion came with a wall of wind and a blizzard of wet followed by deafening thunder. Then a sucking-in and blowing out sensation drove the sea through by side window. On me.

"Get out of here." L. Sid pointed his dripping clump in the opposite direction as we wobbled like a duck. He reached for the fish with his good hand. It slipped out and flipped between my legs.

I prayed it wasn't a man eater.

The slippery monster jumped as if it landed on hot charcoal. It flopped on top of the glare shield next to the windscreen.

L. Sid shot me the finger with a twist to point the way front. "Fuck it, fly."

I took off to the left. Another explosion came safe enough to enjoy the mist. "Did the Colonel make it?"

"No, I can't see him," said the crew chief, "I mean, yes. There's his helmet and his head comin' out of the water. Still attached."

L. Sid called for an ascending right turn to see Yellow One landing for the Colonel. Their crew struggled to get him on board. Strands of seaweed draped off his back.

I headed south to refuel. Our crew chief shouted through the wind noise, "The Colonel's dangling from a seat leg. Their holdin' him by his flak jacket."

L. Sid laughed as he transmitted, "Yellow One, a simply elegant departure."

"Yeah, at least we're not in the drink. I'm a lousy swimmer."

Our chief broke in, "They got him. Crew chief, gunner, and somcone else pulled his ass in. The Swift got hit...Knocked a tire from the side of the boat. Skipped across the water like a flat rock. "No. No. The boat's moving. Firing toward the shore."

"Yellow Two, this is One. You'll have to extract. Get back as soon as you can. Out."

L. Sid hung his head low. "Man, what I wouldn't do for another ship." He switched frequencies, "Sealord, this is Two, thanks. Can ya' make it back?"

"Is a whale's ass wet? Bye-bye fly-boy."

"Danny, we're losin' daylight. Mountain ain't any fun in the dark." L. Sid switched to the patrol frequency again. Static chewed up our reception leaving only, "...we're pinned down...separated... only me and Krotch. Geronimo. Killer Junior. Geronimo."

I looked to L. Sid. "What'd he say?"

"He's asking for artillery. Right on his position. Killer Junior's an air-burst barrage. Z's overrun." L. Sid mashed his floor transmit button. "Yellow One. Zulu's out of range, let us know what happens."

"Roger, out."

An uneasy stillness followed despite the helicopter' roar. At balls-to-the-wall speed, cargo doors open, in a direct crosswind.

The radio crackled again, "Yellow Two. On the way wait...splash."

"What in the hell is he saying now?"

"The barrage for Z just landed."

No one talked on the journey back.

L. Sid called Qui Nhon for a fuel truck to stand by our landing pad, so we didn't shut down to refuel.

Between sea water and sweat, I was drenched. My legs cramped from all the time I had on the stick. During refueling, the gunner offered a can of beans from C rations. I chugged it. My feet tingled. Circulation was great. Tingle was bad.

Starting at the bottom of the radio dial, L. Sid searched battalion frequency for assistance. He shook his head in despair. "Battalion is fully committed. First of the Ninth is up to their ass in a fire fight. We gotta do whatever we gotta do if we want it done. You're doin' great. Haven't crashed us in the last hour and a half. Maybe you're a real helicopter pilot after all." He grinned, struggled with his helmet, and moved the clump finger in a circular motion for full flight RPM.

To make up for the silence coming in, no one talked on the way out. About five clicks from Hang Thy, we picked up the static-laden transmission by the Colonel, "...and advise your location."

Gunfire broke up the voices in response, "...at Delta Charlie Seven, in one-zero minutes, over." Z spoke in an exhausted voice. Gone was the command bravado.

Yellow One cruised high off the west side of the mountain. "Yellow One, Two is back on station. Over."

"Roger Two, stand by." The air went dead for at least a minute. "Yellow Two, we've located the Echo Zulu. We'll reconnoiter and land if possible."

I shook my head. "Didn't he see where the prep hit?"

L. Sid motioned, "This is triple canopy, man. Even if you watched it, you wouldn't be able to tell exactly where it hit after the strike. And they called for seven Daisy Cutters. Artillery doesn't make good extraction zones, the Air Force does. These are piddly-ass in comparison. He'll be lucky if he can get in."

"Yellow Two, it's skinny as a piss-tube." Tension distorted Barkwart's voice.

Z cut through, "Lookin' good, man. Bring it down."

I circled the valley and L. Sid leaned forward. "Gunner, watch for any movement. If they shoot at ya' from anywhere except that hole, return it." He pointed in the direction of the EZ. "Fly directly over their position, I gotta see this."

My altitude above ground level disappeared as I flew up the mountain side, to about three hundred feet above the entrance.

How Yellow One got into that small hole in the trees, I'll never know.

Barkwart's screamed, "...watch the clearance from my tail...any more room...talk to me." He held the transmit button down to broadcast the mixed sounds of a helicopter in torment: low RPM buzzer, shouts abruptly stopped, a blunt thud leaving a single, scratchy note of static.

I flew over the hole, an authentically ugly sight. The helicopter laid on its side with its blades frozen still. The dirty skids and naked belly of the aircraft lay exposed. Separated from the body, the tail pointed up hill.

"Peel down into the valley and get more altitude." L. Sid switched radios, "Zulu, this is Two, over."

"This is Doan..."

"Where's Z?"

"Pulling people out of the helicopter. He said not to come. It's burning. He'll call you back." Smoke poured out of the hole. Flames spouted from the engine compartment and the cargo doors.

A seamless canopy covered the steep side of the mountain with solid green treetops. No breaks, no undulations. Only one hole let smoke across the orange sun, hanging low in the sky.

"Yellow Two, this is Zulu." Static sounds. "Passengers are out. None of the crew." His voice grew hushed again. "Gotta move to Delta Charlie."

"Where's that?"

Good old L. Sid. I had no idea which side was up.

"The Daisy Cutter opened six spots west of the crash. We'll pop smoke when we get there."

"Roger, wilco." L. Sid gestured to climb.

All my instruments read what they were supposed to, the crew chief aligned them all to point in the same direction. It helped my cross-check, but not my feet. I stomped the floor. "Chief, I'm numb again."

"The tail rotor probably got dinged from the big blast in the water."

"Great. Nothing to worry about there. Who needs a goddamn tail rotor anyway? I'll just fly until it falls off.

L. Sid stretched. "When ya' lose a tail rotor blade...ya' crash your ass."

The gunner saw it first. "Red smoke at four o'clock."

L. Sid transmitted, "We see Christmas in the trees."

Z's voice sounded winded, "You read it right. We got a load of five."

"Shed all your non-essential shit, we're comin' in."

L. Sid pointed so fast I thought he threw something. "Dump it baby. We got only one chance."

Through the chin bubble, I didn't believe the chute we had to enter. Could've swore my rotor wouldn't fit.

Poor old Nickel-Dime shuttered at the edge of the opening. Darkness hid the floor on the inside. On the outside, treetops descended straight down to the creek below. Above it, the trees ascended at forty-five degrees. Great choices.

Inside the hole was like a silo. An epiphany of sorts blossomed: they couldn't describe anything like this in flight school. I had to land this lead-sled. Or at least not burn to a crisp in mangled metal.

"Looks like the rock is the only place to put it." L. Sid searched the pulverized trees at the bottom of the crater. Some still smoldered.

And so, it was, the promised rock appeared to me. And it was not underwater. Hallelujah.

At the bottom I bounced on the toes of my skids. Not landing but a stabilizing hover to pin the helicopter against the rock. The main rotor blade swung low to the ground. Crew chief jumped out to direct our passengers. Z stood at the farthest edge of the clearing. His Stoner M63 in both hands. Krotch chose the center, close to the path of my blades.

Colonel Bobson limped out of the bush, dragging one foot. Without his sidearm or radio. A slow-moving Doan followed in her black peasant clothes, assisting another. Each thrashed through the remnants of the Daisy Cutter debris. All were thoroughly disheveled. I fought to steady the helicopter as they boarded.

Z lowered his M63 and headed to the ship, when two Viet Cong leapt out of underbrush. One blind-sided Krotch and knocked him down. The other slipped a garrote around Z's neck. He dropped his Stoner and grappled to find his attacker. When his hands fell limp to his sides, Z collapsed to the ground.

The first Cong triumphantly put a foot on the back of Krotch and pointed his AK-47 at me. A stand-off. Both of the gooks yelled and motioned with their guns.

All I could do was keep the helicopter dead still.

Krotch pulled his face out of the mud to see a boot next to his nose and feel the other on his back. He moved like the snap of a bear trap and threw a single jab straight up into the Cong's balls. The gook fell on Krotch and hit him with a butt stroke from his rifle. The Cong stood up and pounded his chest.

On intercom I said, "I'm gonna try to distract the little-shit over Krotch. When I do, get the other one." A gentle nudge of the cyclic sent the steel tip of the rotating blade downward into the top of the Cong's head. The impact reverberated back to my hand. A red mist of blood and brains splattered along the rotor path. Like a priest blessing the congregation.

I said, "Oops."

Some of the spray splashed the other Cong. He fired a wild burst across the crater. Bullets hit Krotch in the side and face, his fatigues flapped with each impact. With his rifle leveled at me, the Cong moved away from Z and screamed over and over.

Couldn't he see I only drove the bus and didn't play with guns?

Z shook his head to clear the fall, then tackled the Cong. Both rolled into the crater. They wrestled below the water until the Cong surfaced gasping for air. Z's legs flailed in the air.

Behind my seat the crew chief shot his pistol. The Cong grabbed his neck in torment and slid under. My ears rang.

Chief jumped out to the freshly exploded dirt lining the crater. Z swayed in the center of this bloody sink hole gagging from the water. They struggled for every step on the climb out.

Krotch leaned against the gunner for help into the helicopter.

L. Sid continued his endless search of everything around us. He motioned me to fly. I discovered a solid canopy of trees overhanging the helicopter. My way out was skinny as a piss-tube at about a 60-degree angle. "Chief, can I turn around?"

"No, sir."

L. Sid peered out the window. "Just fly the goddamn thing. It's getting dark and there're more Cong where these came from. Chief, gunner. Hang your head out and watch the rotors."

I brought in all the power I had but couldn't get off the rock. All of the pearls of wisdom about taking-off overloaded rolled through my pea-brain. But nothing applied.

L. Sid twisted to face the chief. "I told you to dump those goddamn water cans and C rations."

With movement and noise, both of which I did not need, the chief and gunner threw six, five-gallon cans and two cases off the ship. Z shot 'em as they hit the ground. At over 40 pounds each, it was like throwing a body overboard. My skids rocked, wanting to fly. Actually, it was more of a hover to the rear and fly up slowly, rather than a take-off.

Flying backwards, overloaded, and unable to see, is the ultimate test of faith in your team. All directions were given to me by two yoyos hanging out the sides of the aircraft.

One would say, "Stop drifting left," or "quit moving right" or "don't go up so fast" or "we need more backward." Every correction bled off power and demanded either wait for it to build, or don't—and die. I did this for 95 feet.

The best part came when I got to the top and L. Sid clapped. "Ya' made it, Ox. I bet the tail rotor is rejoicing in uncluttered breeze."

As soon as I saw the dim sky above me and no trees on either side, I did a pedal turn and dropped the nose almost vertical down into the valley. Instant speed returned with enough RPM for forward flight. I laughed out loud. The wind in the cabin soothed me.

Sunset behind the mountain and dusk rushed in along with tracers from the lone peak ahead of us. Brighter than the daylight versions and not as brilliant as the night critters, but still scary as hell. The shooter used the tracer-burnout path to correct his aim and swayed the gun, back and forth.

Viet Cong instructions must have read, "why aim and lead, when you can spray all over?" S

"Turn left and climb." L. Sid let the clump show me the way in case I forgot. Our machine gun looked even better in solid tracers. Z made a beautiful sound with his Stoner, more throaty than the gunner's M60.

The valley turned us back toward the center of Hon Heo. Into a box canyon. "I can't climb any faster. Won't make it over that ridge line." As if I needed more reasons, the ridge line opened up on us from at least four positions.

"HOLY SHIT, it's like a firing squad. Turn around, return fire," L. Sid commanded. 7Both guns of the helicopter engaged. "Damn…"

"What?"

"Krotch is a bloody mess. His pants are blown open at the hip. It looks like he's holdin' his guts. The gaping hole in his cheek is big enough to see his teeth. And one of his eyes is swollen shut. But he's sittin' up with his grenade launcher. He's pissed."

L. Sid caught me turning and shook his head. "Don't. Keep your eyes on what you're doing." He tapped the RPM, "You're pulling the stuffin' out this son of a bitch, ease back. If ya can't climb, then dive to get more speed."

Flying at the tree top level was something I enjoyed but not in the bottom of this damn valley of no-return. Dusk slipped out while night galloped in with flaming fire balls. Like a bride and groom running from the wedding hall through a shower of tossed rice. And like every good wedding, someone's gonna get screwed.

Shooting proverbial fish in the barrel did not come close to this. Tracers crisscrossed in front of me. I couldn't do anything but grit my teeth and fly over the trees, down the glens to the barely visible river bottom.

One wise ass laid a line of machine gun fire across the river at our level. I was too close to do much more than pull the front of the cabin above the bullet stream. The sickening *ka-thonk* sound of bullets punching holes in aluminum returned. No warning lights lit up. We were still flying.

"Yellow Two, this is Henry." A throaty whisper from the team radio sounded like a voice from the grave.

"This is Two, go." L. Sid's clump redirected me to fly lower.

I banked the aircraft at the river. High trees crowded both sides. It was narrower than my 46-foot rotor needed, so I clipped skinny branches and blew leaves against my windshield. Things hit the main rotor, each one sounded like a rifle shot. We hoped no stringers greeted us in the twilight.

Night flight demanded a steady search in all directions, including the instrument panel. My cross-check shrunk badly. Only flames erupting from a gauge would be noticed.

Ahead of me a small spark above the water preceded a blinding explosion stretching to the trees on each bank. Since I flew too fast and way too low, I had no place to go. In a millisecond the yellow flame turned into a puff of white, like from the bowels of hell to a cloud in the sky. The giant burst ate up my night vision and left an overwhelming stench of bad garlic.

"White phosphorous! Don't slow down now. For god's sake, don't slow down." L. Sid inspected the aircraft though his front windscreen, side window, chin bubble and overhead glass, "It doesn't look like any of it stuck, except for the pitot tube."

There is nothing like a flame plugging your airspeed indicator. I said, "Chief. Anything else burning?"

"...not yet."

"Yellow Two...come on...this is Henry."

The chip detector light on the panel erupted: big, bold and bug ugly. My heart sank to my boot tips, "Shit. They must've hit the transmission. We gotta land. Where do I go?"

"As long as you keep goin', I don't care. We're in the middle of a tub of shit: bad guys everywhere. As a single ship, no one knows where the hell we are. Night's falling, with a cargo bay full of fucked up guys. What chance do we stand? Fly it until it drops." L. Sid made expansive gestures; you'd think he could fly.

"Yellow Two...come on...I hear ya'."

"Henry, where you at?"

"Made it to the river. Near the bank. This radio is on a rock."

"Can you signal?"

"I got a .38 with tracer rounds."

"Bad idea. Anything else?"

Henry's voice strained and slurred. "No...nothing."

"How deep is the water?"

"Man, I don't know...it's moving. You're getting close."

L. Sid turned to Z, "He has to signal. Get ready to pull him in."

L. Sid directed me to slow up. "Henry, okay for two pops straight up. Only when we're close enough to stop. Flip me the bird when you see me."

Two tracers went up in a different shade of red. "Slow down, I'll on turn the position lights."

Even on bright, I could barely see, but it was better than nothing.

We got the finger from a hand out of a bush.

"Get next to him."

I lowered my skids into the water. Again. I felt like a riverboat captain.

With his helmet on, the gunner stood on the skids. "OK, move to the right. Some bush here. You'll probably chop 'em down. It'll sound like we're hit."

I moved slowly to the right, hit the brush, saw leaves and twigs spattered all over. Fresh, chopped-up green cleansed the air.

The gunner shouted into the cabin. "Perfect. I got his hand... shit...he only has one. Help me pull him in."

While the helicopter swayed, tilted, and dipped from the weight of the rescuers, I swung into bush again. A big weight jolted on the cargo deck and nearly swamped me.

"We got him, we got him." Gasping for breath, the gunner said, "Thank you, ladies."

With wild swings, L. Sid pointed forward. "Get out of here."

Even with another body on board, it wasn't as bad as it could be. Old Nickel-Dime climbed into the dark and foreboding valley.

"What the hell ya' doin', tryin' to kill us?" He had a way with words, "Climb fast. Aim for the sky. Don't hit the fuckin' mountain."

Then it dawned on me. "Ladies? Did you say 'ladies'? Another Vietnamese woman?"

"There are two of them. And they both helped."

L. Sid slumped back in his seat. "Forget that shit. They're on board and we're flying. Watch outside, inside, panel, rotor path and listen to every sound."

This intense concentration wore out my little ass.

I checked the panel and except for low fuel, it looked normal. My feet no longer felt numb. That I could not understand. Nor were we screaming into the wild-dark yonder.

L. Sid said, "Can we get enough altitude to escape this canyon? It's our only chance."

I shrugged. "Beats the shit out of me." The black ridge grew larger and larger. An unexpected, explosive crash of a treetop against the belly of the aircraft whipped the skid and broke branches. Scared me half to death.

"Go toward the lower part of the ridge. On the left there."

Once again, the something from the dark slammed into our helicopter, far more severe than the last. It lurched both of us against our seat harnesses. Initially a loud single, solid, jolting wham followed by a short, tearing, shearing screech. More debris danced around the cabin.

"God damn it. Ya gotta get higher. What'd we hit?"

The chief said, "I think a tree. It won. We lost our skids. I can't see any on the left."

"None on the right either," the gunner yelled through the wind noise as he looked down.

"You sure are hard on these helicopters, boy." L. Sid chuckled.

"Well, fuck you very much. You did say fly it until it dropped. Just doin' it one piece at a time."

The Chip Detector light went out and our rate of climb improved. Old Nickel-Dime was no home-sick angel, but it did gain some separation from mother earth and the dark side of the mountain.

Things improved until Little Titty Top came back to life. The 50-caliber reported as destroyed, was not. At least three times I watched the bullet stream across my overhead glass. Had no place to go but straight ahead. Couldn't go any faster or higher even if I wanted to. Going lower didn't make any sense since I was all out of skids.

"Gunner, do not open fire at the fifty." L. Sid leaned to the edge of his seat.

"Z told me to go fuck myself. He's laying on the floor, loadin' his piece."

The gunner must have been a dog in an earlier life. He did not know how to transmit unless his face was in the wind.

L. Sid turned around, "They're shootin' at sound. If you fire, they'll find us."

"I can knock out that son of a bitch." Z cocked the M63.

"Which part of a death wish don't you understand?"

No response.

Two more times tracers probed for us and I brushed only one more tree before we got to the other side. Over the ridge didn't give me a 'get out of jail free' card like I hoped. But I got some valuable airspeed.

"Turn West and make this mother climb." L. Sid changed frequencies. "Qui Nhon, this is Serpent Yellow Two, Over."

Another voice-of-god fill-in said, "This is Qui Nhon, go ahead Two."

"Roger, we're airborne out of Hon Heo Mountain, east of Phu Cat turning south to your location. Got two gravely wounded on board. And a helicopter with some serious mechanical issues, includin' missing skids. Request medical personnel and mechanics to meet us. Wherever you have us land. Probable ETA, one-six minutes."

"This is Qui Nhon, wilco. Keep at least two clicks west from Highway One. An Arc Light is scheduled in four-zero minutes for Hon Heo."

"This is Yellow Two, just happy to be leaving. Out."

Once I cleared the adjacent mountains, I turned south to Qui Nhon, "How are we gonna land this mother?"

This time L. Sid's face glowed from the light of the instrument panel. "Carefully, very carefully."

PART SEVEN_

Z CALLED OUT, barely above a whisper, "I'm here, ol' buddy." Loud shouting and wild cheers persisted from the NVAs in front of the helicopter. In a raspy voice he said, "Krotch, ya' loaded?"

Sitting rigid against the transmission wall, Krotch held his M79 grenade launcher and uttered "...hess." Swelling closed his damaged eye and chunks of bloody, busted, teeth kept open the hole in his cheek.

Z said, "Can you takeout the guys on the right?"

Krotch struggled with his mutilated mouth. "hree hots, hree hots."

A single NVA stood in front of the helicopter and guarded us. He relaxed with his rifle at hip level. With childlike amazement, his head explored every aspect of the aircraft.

I tried to unlock my seat harness without being noticed. When the buckle jammed, my fingers explored every inch of it. I whispered, "I'm fuckin' stuck. Arc Light's scheduled in six minutes."

"Where'd ya hear that?"

"Qui Nhon told L. Sid after he filed his medical request for you all. Anyone else alive back there?"

More shouts outside, "...*Bao Dai...Ga mug...Lai Dai...*" Over twenty soldiers cheered Doan, like they just received a weekend pass.

Z said, "They're praising Bao Dai and want him to come back. The girl and Bobson were injured when we brought them on board. Got clubbed like I did. They're still out. When the bitch slammed her helmet on the cabin floor, I woke up."

"So, what we gonna do?"

"How much time left?"

"About four minutes."

"Okay, we'll wait until the whistling stops. At the first explosion, I'll pull the trigger. Krotch'll get three shots off, I'll clear the rest of the area. Then we unass this chopper to the ditch down the hill. You carry the girl and the pilot, I'll grab Bobson and Krotch. Can you get out of your seat?"

"No. Still stuck."

Z pulled himself up on the back of my seat. "Now this ain't gonna hurt a bit. My Ka-Bar has always wanted to cut a fancy aviation belt."

A light tug later, the harness fell from my shoulders. Time passed —not in minutes but eternities. The Arc Light Program had a great reputation but dropping anything from 25,000 feet in the dark was dicey. If it hit the wrong spot, I would have been endlessly disap-pointed.

Screaming soldiers only 25 feet away made it a strain to listen for the whistlin'. Their backs hid Doan from my view.

"If the gooks turn on us, I'll pull the trigger."

I said, "What kind of whistle will the bombs make?"

"A goddamn whistle's a whistle. The shrill sound starts quietly and gets louder." Z moved into a better firing position. "The louder it gets, the deeper shit you're in. A couple of weeks ago, they dropped the first Arc Light just north of Saigon. The surviving gooks called it the Whispering Death."

A faint, high-pitched whistle sounded like a children's choir holding the high C. It blended into the lower, vulgar tone of a thun-derous blast; many times greater than any explosion I'd ever heard.

Detonations struck in a line on the other side of the valley. Like a zipper opening the mountain. The flash brought back daylight at noon. It captured the celebrating soldiers in midair. Each successive blast inched their way forward.

Z needed no other reason to unleash his stream of death. In a flash the soldiers changed from joy to agony. They could not hear, but only feel his wrath. And only a second too late.

Krotch's Thumper sounded innocent until Doan exploded. The center of her body disappeared, clearing out the heart of the crowd. His next two shots knocked down a bunch of soldiers each time.

This slaughter wrestled me back to action. I had to escape being the only clear target in the front row. Scrambling out, I knocked the compass into the chin bubble, then my head almost got impaled on a switch for the position lights.

This rolling cataclysm of death stopped as quickly as it began. All the soldiers and Doan were motionless on the ground. A sweet smell of cordite hung in the air.

Z switched ammo boxes, "Go to the ditch." He dragged the unconscious Bobson by his collar out of the helicopter and down the hill like a log.

I untangled myself enough to shoulder the girl and head out. Her floppy crew hat fell off to expose Kaelyn, with camo paint on her face and blood crusted in her hair line. With my night vision cooked, the hill became more treacherous. She didn't wake when I left her in the ditch next to Bobson.

On that pile of pallets, the helicopter glowed like a stop signal on a deserted road. I ran up the hill and passed Z with Krotch against his shoulder. He said, "Where ya' going?"

"To shut off them damn lights."

"Good."

I jumped into the helicopter. Rifle fire drowned out the faint whistling sound. My panting from the run uphill stopped when the left door window shattered. I hugged the floor next to Henry.

The whistling in the sky turned into a high-pitched ear-buster. A muzzle flash from the bush sounded louder since it was so close. Bullets riddled the pilot's seat, L. Sid's body jolted from every shot. Shards of Plexiglas and ceramic flew around the cabin.

My pistol hung up on the holster strap.

Someone rushed out of the bush and tripped over the lights. A male voice shouted in a southern accent, "We-ll gauddamn." He slammed another magazine in his rifle.

My damn pistol felt like it was sewn in place. As the shooter reached the cargo door, I broke the gun loose and pulled the trigger. The flash blinded me. His body fell.

Whispering death turned into a full-fledged screamer. I ran like hell. Explosions followed the ridge toward our position between the second and third bombs. At a hundred times louder, the blast wave knocked me off my feet. Concussion popped my ears and slapped my face into the gravel. I shielded myself from the shower of rocks, clumps and branches. Like being a practice dummy for a bulldozer.

The clamor ended before the debris finished falling. A spinning NVA helmet landed in front of me next to a burning red epaulet and crumpled yellow star.

I felt lucky.

I HEARD RINGING. My face-plant punished my skin. Unidentified, noxious odors smelled like we blew up a shithouse and half fell on me. I didn't know which body parts still worked.

A cool hand touched the side of my neck. I jolted like a lightning bolt struck me. Words in Vietnamese followed in a soft, female voice.

Response from a male came as an unmistakable command, "...dinky dau...Dung Lai... bookoo."

The female turned me over, "...soldier...GI..." then louder, "you okay?"

"Maybe." Only one of my eyes opened.

The Vietnamese woman flicked dirt off my face and hair. She cocked her head. "What is maybe?"

"It means I don't know." I smiled. "Who are you?"

"I am Anh." She bowed her head slightly. "And this is Minh."

"What're you doing here?"

"Prisoners."

My other eye helped me focus on this woman, dressed in a tattered, dirty *ao dai*. "How long?"

"About twenty months..." She lowered her voice.

Z's head emerged from the pile of debris like an alligator in the swamp. "And we better pay attention, or they'll have to make room for us." He spoke in Vietnamese to Anh and leveled his M63 at Minh standing behind me.

She helped me stand. "Can you walk?"

"I think so." I still had my pistol in my hand.

Z rose out of the rubble. "Pilot...what's your name anyway?"

"Danny Hellberg. Oh, shit, I just remembered."

"What, your name?"

"Nah, the pilot we rescued out of the river is still in the chopper."

Several lights around the landing area survived the bombing and glowed with a spooky blush. The blast shoved ol' Nickel-Dime directly backward until its tail laid on the mud and its nose pointed to the sky. Both rotors were covered with dirt. Even the poncho liner still clung on the mast.

Henry leaned against the transmission wall. Blood soaked the gauze over his shoulder and down his uniform. The first aid kit lay beneath the body of the crew chief, the last thing he did before Doan shot him. And Henry still had a pulse.

Hal-le-damn-lujah.

L. Sid's clump dangled from the front seat, blood crusted on his fingertips and dried on the floor. I don't know how long I stood there. He taught me what flight school didn't. But I needed more. Like when I saw my father in his casket. Didn't really know him either. I was four when he died. He and my mother separated but I liked him anyway. I missed having a father.

Henry cleared his throat and jostled me out of my daze. Underneath the layer of blown-in-dirt, his face twisted in pain.

"Glad you're still with us. I'm Danny Hellberg. I'll take you where the others are. How ya feel?"

"Like...shit," he slurred. "So, you're Ox. What happened?"

"Later. We gotta get out of this ship after I check the radios." My inspection showed a bright indicator light and good static. So, we left.

Henry wobbled like a 6-foot bag of bowling balls. He carried an odor of dried blood—musty and metallic. His legs buckled after three steps. I caught him before he hit the ground.

He said, "Man-o-man, I'm sorry." His hold on my neck kept slipping. Steep and uncertain footing doubled his strain and pain. But muzzle flashes from a gunshot about twenty yards in front of me, turned his squeeze into a headlock. I stopped and watched the silhouette of a man with a rifle in one hand and a flashlight in the other. He said with a southern draw, "If ya' move, you're dead."

Whispering into Henry's ear, "I'll put ya' down here and..." His weight unbalanced me. I slipped on loose rocks. He tumbled ass over teakettle and groaned.

I peeled him off me. "Be quiet."

Z and the two Vietnamese stood in the direct flashlight beam. Krotch, Bobson, and Kaelyn were motionless on the ground covered with debris. The shooter talked quieter than I could understand.

I tried to sneak closer but slipped on loose rock and skidded through the rubbish. Yet the shooter never flinched. Anh did. Her quick stare made him turn in my direction. He dropped the light and shot from the hip. I rolled down the hill.

Z drew his .45 and shot three times.

The shooter reeled backward and fell.

I hugged the dirt for a moment then trudged back up the hill. Henry slurred something indiscernible. His eyes told me he was on another planet. I grabbed him by the collar, and he didn't seem to mind. I dumped him next to Kaelyn. "This one's still alive, L. Sid's gone. The radio works."

Z said, "Get his rifle, ammunition and ID. I'll arm everyone here with something in case this shooting draws the Cong. Which radio is operative?"

"Both."

"Good. Go broadcast where we are to anyone who will listen."

"But I don't know where we are."

"Lieutenant, you shittin' me? You're in the middle of the third Arc Light in country. You think someone will have a problem finding us? Give me a fucking break. There're probably scheduling a BDA right now."

"A what?" *It was hard enough to understand regular stuff, much less garbled acronyms.*

"Bomb Damage Assessment team will count bodies, drag out the wounded, collect weapons and anything else that will help pay the bills."

What was left of the shooter looked like someone took a chain saw to his neck. I slung his M14 and ammo belt on my shoulder. Then collected his ID, flashlight, radio security list, and a wad of funny money. When I brushed the mud and blood off, I recognized good ol' Ted Bradley from the Officer's Club in Saigon.

He had to be China Jade. That prick. Why he didn't stay down after I shot 'em, I'll never know.

Climbing back to the ship was harder than I figured. Fortunately, the military guard frequency was easy to find. I transmitted, "To any aircraft hearing me, this is Serpent Yellow Two. I'm in deep shit on top of this mountain over." A red light went on in the brush, each time I keyed the mike.

No response. I repeated the entire transmission. Then I threw my head back. "Aw shit."

Two taps on my helmet made me jump out of my skin. Z motioned to remove my helmet. "What is the problem?"

"No response. What's happening in the ditch?"

"Everyone's conscious. Bobson and Kaelyn got pounded from debris so I'm looking for the medical kit."

"How's Krotch?"

"Don't know how he survived. Need somethin' to ease his pain. Keep trying to make contact." Z took both aid kits and left.

None of the frequencies on Ted's list responded, except the damn red light up the hill. I had to see what was there.

Reloading the M-14 magazine and chambering a round made me feel better. Never thought I'd have to use one of these damn things.

Each step I took was harder than the last. The blinkin' bush turned out to be a bitchin' bunker built into the side of the hill. Sandbag walls and roof reinforced by PSP was precise. Like an idiot, I walked around a long blast wall in front of the opening. A steel pry bar leaned next to the bunker entrance. The red light ran from the door over the wall.

With the flashlight, I peeked into the room. Against the side wall stood a US Army field table, in front of a gigantic US Aeronautical Chart. Same as the one in the helicopter, complete with symbols indicating First Cav unit locations. The bad guys matched every spot of ours with at least two of theirs.

A big door and another table with a stacks of radios lay along the other wall. This hoard was more than we had in our ops tent, by at least three or four big piles. Whatever it was, they had a lot of it.

The red light lit up again with its fiery beauty. I found the volume control and overheard, "...assuming that damage occurred at China Jade's location. We need to get there as soon as possible. Just re-secure or eliminate the prisoners. Then reseal all cave entrances to prepare for the Cav's bomb damage assessment team, scheduled tomorrow at 0700 hours. We'll brief our helicopter team in three zero minutes."

"Can we get the BDA rescheduled?"

"This was a First Cav mission. We don't have effective sources there yet."

"Roger, wilco, out."

Holy mackerel. American voices. Those fuckin' commies.

I gasped like running a mile in combat boots. The map folded into my fatigue shirt. That wooden door, with big hinges bolted into a thick wooden frame kept calling my name. Pushing and pulling the well-worn handle didn't help. Slamming a wooden beam into it didn't either. All I got was a hand full of slivers.

The Cong wouldn't use this bunker for communications alone, they had to be doing something elsewhere. Then I remembered the pry bar and ran to the entrance. As I turned past the blast wall an explosion erupted. A piece of the disintegrated door hit the double row of sandbags behind me. Hugging the ground felt like a good idea, so I did. Flames shot out of the entrance. Dust and smoke bellowed like slow death. Cordite's toxic stench burned my lungs.

Stuck into the blast wall, a small chunk the door smoldered. One step slower and that could've been me.

THE CONCUSSION from the disintegration of the big door came in first on my list of what to avoid. Of course, being smashed into the sandbag wall probably helped.

War was nothing but a noisy, dirty way to get killed. Way-too glorified.

After the dust cleared, my coughing stopped. A massive, smoking hole replaced the heavy wooden door. I found another blast wall protecting OD colored, 55-gallon drums, stenciled on the sides with 'JP-4'. Wow. It would have made a hell of an explosion. Barrels stacked ten wide and six deep. A large coil of black hose, attached to a pump engine, gathered dust in one corner.

It never took me long to look at a hot poker. I put the red lens on the flashlight and made my way down the hill. The break of a lifetime stayed with me until I reached the ditch.

Tension hung thick as the first wave of Cordite. Krotch starred at me in silence. His blood-soaked gauze leaked onto his pants.

Bobson's tattered shirt revealed a bandaged stomach. One arm hung limply, the other with a .45 ready. He scanned downhill.

Kaelyn leaned against a tree stump with her eyes closed, a

carbine in her lap. Even with facial camo, hair messed, dirty fatigues, bandages everywhere, she still looked pretty good.

I touched her gently, "How ya' doing?"

Her eye lids flickered. "Doin'?"

"Can you move?"

"Yep."

As Z replaced gauze over Henry's empty shoulder socket, I said, "How's it hangin', partner?"

"Been better."

"Can ya' help me fly?"

Henry's eyes popped open. "Bet your ass I can." He coughed and blood oozed down his chin.

I squatted next to Z. "Listen to me." I gave him the map from the bunker, relayed the bad guys conversation. Described the storage facility. "We can get the hell out of here. But only if we can refuel the helicopter..."

Z scratched his head. "Will it crank?"

"Got lots of battery. Concussion from the blast tilted it backward. Still on the pallets. Should rock forward. We got 40 minutes."

"Sounds like a wild-ass dream. These guys won't make it any other way." He grabbed his M63.

"What'll you do with the prisoners?" Kaelyn swayed as she stood. "You can't just leave 'em to be massacred by the Cong."

Bobson cleared his throat. "Can't take 'em but we'll help 'em. Anh and Minh will fill in."

They emerged from the deep shadows. "What can we do?"

"Go to the NVA bodies. Anh, collect all their weapons, explosives, ammunition. Search 'em for papers. Minh, pick villagers who know how to use the weapons. We'll figure out something. The NVA will be back." Bobson's hand shook when he gestured, but his command presence thrived.

Minh said, "Anh will get the weapons. I'll talk to our people." They both disappeared into the night.

Z picked up another ammunition box. "Let's get to the chopper."

Kaelyn slung the carbine on her shoulder. "I can help."

"Yay, but can ya' climb the hill?"

"Just watch." Kaelyn wouldn't accept my help and struggled to the top. She stopped several times to catch her breath.

During my pre-flight inspection, dents and debris marred every flat surface. One blade had a couple of ugly holes large enough to fit my finger. Both shots missed the leading edge of the rotor by a hair.

"We need to get it level." I lifted the tail boom onto Z's shoulder. He grunted. I moved around him closer to the cabin and took the tail onto my shoulder. Movement reseated the ship on the pile. With a loud creaking sound, the mast dipped down. My world slid on its last few inches to the edge of the pallets. Just like my heart, it stopped.

Unaffected by the near disaster, Z asked, "Ya' hear anything comin'?"

There we were, three deafened survivors of 500-pound bomb explosion, close enough to feel its heat, trying to hear approaching helicopters. Give me a break.

"Let's get this ship refueled before it slides the rest of the way down the hill."

The pump, hose, and drums were the same kind used to refuel our ships. I'd never touched one before. Fortunately, Z had, and hooked it up.

I said, "Four drums is minimum, five is better. That'll give us 30 minutes flying time. You handle the drums; Kaelyn can hold the nozzle. I'll get the bodies out of the aircraft."

"Then ya' gotta go balls to the wall and get our guys up here. The clock is tickin'."

Talk about a gut-wrenching task, try pulling three stiffs out of a helicopter. All with head wounds. Revulsion swept over me with each body I pulled to the ground. Dust caked L. Sid's open eyes. Blood encrusted the gunner's peach fuzz on what was left of his face.

Then I ran down the hill to the ditch. Bobson's position had not changed. He leaned against an impressive pile of weapons. Several

AK-47s lay on top of carbines, pistols and grenades. I said, "Anh was busy, where is she now?"

"Still collecting. Get Henry and Krotch up the hill. I'll wait for Minh." Bobson's voice was fading.

Getting Henry up the hill was like dancing with a log. Much of the time his heels drug on the ground. He said, "I know why they call ya' Ox. Sorry I can't help more."

I deposited his body in the right seat. That proved harder than getting him out of the damn ditch. Kind of like putting spaghetti in a shot glass.

Then there was Krotch, who easily weighed 40 pounds more than I did. After I busted my gut to get him off the ground, he surprised me by powering some of his own weight to the edge of the cabin floor, where he simply collapsed. I scooted his legs in and propped him up against the back wall. His hand still clutched the 79.

I asked, "Is it loaded?"

If his swollen face could've smiled, it would have been then. "Aarg." His eye kinda twinkled when I spread out some ammo next to him.

At the fuel bunker, Z had four empty barrels on their sides. "Do I have time for one more?"

"Squeeze it in. I still have to get Bobson."

"Take her to help. We gotta go."

Kaelyn didn't exactly demonstrate lightning speed nor stability. I said, "How's your head?"

"Like a fuckin hangover." She wobbled. Her footing slipped on loose stones, formerly big rocks. I tried to catch her. We skidded to a stop in my arms.

She said, "Thanks."

"Any time."

"Good. I need your help again."

We both stood. I said, "For what?"

"I want to be with the prisoners. And see what's really happening inside the caves."

I couldn't believe her. "You mean stay here?"

"This is really big." Her perky self returned.

The hill got steeper at the high edge of the ditch. I couldn't see anyone, "Colonel, how ya' doing?"

Anh responded, "He dead."

I shouldered my rifle. "Where ya' at?"

Kaelyn gasped when her flashlight beam found Anh rising from behind a bush with an AK-47 in her hands.

"Want'a put the rifle down?"

She laid it on the ground. "Sorry. I was scared when I heard you coming. I tried to hide."

"Did you find anything?"

She handed me a small stack of papers.

"What happened to Bobson?"

"The Colonel's breathing was bad. He say, 'If we block tunnels, we delay NVA.' Told Minh to blow up entrance ways. Only few of surviving villagers have experience. US Army will come. Then he die."

"What do you mean surviving villagers? How many were there?" Kaelyn always had questions.

"Twenty months ago, we had 157 people. Entire village of Hung Lac. Many died trying to escape. Now maybe fifty-six."

Ahn tried to pull her hair into a bun on top of her head. The worn-out *ao dai* she wore had simple long sleeves with buttons on the front. Bare feet gave the look of a skinny twelve-year-old.

Kaelyn focused. "Where is your home?"

Anh backed away. "Qui Nhon."

"What is your family name?

"Danh. I am Anh Danh."

Dots connected in my brain. She was Ho Chi Bro's daughter.

I got her attention, "Hey, we gotta go."

"To do what?"

"Our only chance of saving them is to get the word to the Cav."

"What chance do you have?" Kaelyn understood reality.

"Okay, it's a long shot. I don't know if old Nickel-Dime'll start, much less fly."

She reached for Ahn. "I'm going to stay with her. If they capture me, daddy and the paper will pay 'em handsomely. And they'll get famous."

"Ain't that simple. Everything goes to hell in a bucket when bullets start flying."

"My chances are the same as yours. Probably better. If I make it, I'll have a hell of a story." She stuck out her bottom lip in a playful pout. "Now get out of here. I really do hear helicopters, and they don't sound like yours." Then she turned to Ahn. "May I come with you?"

Ahn looked at me as if to say: Is she nuts? Then she bowed to Kaelyn, "We have little, but we are honored."

"You really are out of your mind...be careful."

She mouthed, "You too," with a little smile.

I hoofed it up to the helicopter and plopped in the left seat, the aircraft commander position. I nudged Henry, "Hey. How you feel?"

"This shit didn't improve any." His head drooped.

"Can't find the damn start-up check list, you gotta help."

"Okay." He slid back in the seat. His deep breathing left drool on his chin.

When I turned on the battery, all 52 of the panel gauges glowed red. But the immensity of the panel, pedestal and overhead console unnerved me.

In flight school, I was blown away by the 28 steps in the Starting Procedure. So, I fumbled on with what I remembered, Henry pointed at a couple and I guessed at the rest. When I squeezed the start-engine trigger, I held my breath.

The ringing in my ears didn't let me hear the sound of the start. But I felt the turbine spooling up. When the rotors turned, debris pelted the cabin and windshield. It sounded like bullets landing.

Z said, "Okay, when can we go?"

"I'm cranking it as fast as I can without the fuckin' music." I reached for L. Sid's bloody helmet. The bullet that ended his life left a hole behind the right ear. I had to put it on. It stunk. Like holding a stinky relic. Or being held by one.

I turned the radios and intercom on for everyone and focused on getting out. The more power applied the more rubbish swirled around us. Vibrations from the cyclic shook my hand. Holes in the blades whistled. Feedback from the tail rotor made my boots dance on the pedals.

When Nickel-Dime finally broke ground, only the nose rose. The more power I added, the higher it got. "Shit. Something's wrong." I lowered the nose. "We're stuck. What's holding us?"

Z stepped out with his flashlight. "a piece of the strut's rammed through a couple of pallets. Ya need it?"

"Don't think so. Got no skids anyway." A long blast from his M63 made me jump.

"Ain't stuck now. But I wrinkled the skin a 'bit."

"Is it dripping?"

"Naaah... just fly da som'bitch."

Old Nickel-Dime shuttered and rose a little bit, then forward and up. Ahhh. Fan-fuckin'-tastic. Still I couldn't see in front of me. I would've used my landing light only if I wanted every gook and their dog to get a piece of me.

In that instant, a giant tree loomed in front of me like a boogie man. I took a glancing blow that knocked the avionics door off its hinges, up on the windshield, into the rotor, back down on to the cabin roof, then away into the night.

Bat a ba. bat a boom.

Emblazoned with the 229th Aviation Battalion shield and the number 510, it would make a fine trophy next to some braggin' Cong's firepot.

I said, "Well shit. They don't make 'em like they used to." The attempt at humor fell on deaf ears. But that avionics compartment carried my radios and intercom.

Lucky me.

As the helicopter faded away, Kaelyn knew her fate was sealed. "Did you hear the shot?"

Anh looked down the hill. "It could come from air vent. Main entrance collapsed during bombing."

Loose rock, blown debris and the steep fall line slowed their pace. They stopped dead-still at the edge of the opening. Muffled sounds emerged through the small, wooden grate, camouflaged with greens and bamboo.

Anh slid the cover aside. "Vent narrow and steep for meters. I hated every bit I had to dig." She rubbed the calluses on her hands.

More gunshots. Shouting. Anh moved down the vent like she could see in the dark. Kaelyn kept close with her pistol. Her breathing quickened.

The crawl space widened to a high ledge in the cavern. Rows of worktables on the large floor were illuminated by a few dim lights hanging from a power line.

An odor of oily, metal shavings overwhelmed the space, like a factory Kaelyn once investigated. She said, "What do you do here?"

"We make bombs." Anh climbed down a ladder to the floor.

Nothing stirred. No soldiers or prisoners. Only the generator purring in the corner.

Kaelyn followed across the work area, past eight lines of tables with piles of material in place. "What is all this stuff?"

"Suitcase charges. And grenadiers."

"What? You mean satchel charges and grenades."

Anh blushed. "In English class those words were never used." She crossed over the graveled floor. Desks, chairs and a blackboard made it look like a commercial operation. Except for three bodies in a pool of blood. Two were clad in blood-stained NVA uniforms. One was in a scruffy shirt and the black pants of a villager. A rifle mounted bayonet stuck through his back into the ground. He twitched painfully. His agonized moan surfaced like pus from a wound.

From a distance, Anh addressed him in Vietnamese with a caring tone. The tenor of his response forced her backward. He spoke between sobs. She said, "These soldiers tortured and impaled him. They put an explosive device under him in case he moved. Minh shot both soldiers, took their weapons and went off to find someone to defuse him."

"He's a booby trap? Oh, god." Kaelyn put her hand over her mouth.

Anh spoke in a stern whisper. "Not touch him. Both shoulders broken. He paralyzed. Minh look for help. Or put out of misery."

A new voice startled Kaelyn and Anh. "Lay down rifle. Put hands behind head." Approaching with his pistol drawn, the short soldier had red stars decorating his collar, epaulettes, and pith helmet. In a high, child-like voice he continued, "Kneel. Pig."

Kaelyn looked at Anh and laid her carbine down as they knelt. The villager's sobs grew more hysterical as he grabbed the soldier's ankle. Frozen in his tracks, the soldier crouched while he peed in his pants. Nothing happened. Embarrassed, he stood up, straightened his shirt and fired one shot from the hip, missing the prisoner's head.

More embarrassed, he squatted lower, held the pistol with two hands and shot three times. The sobs stopped.

The little soldier attempted a guttural command in Vietnamese. Kaelyn didn't understand all the words but knew as a round-eyed prisoner, the soldier wanted the reward. Anh slowly moved out of his way.

The soldier sneered with his blackened teeth showing. His neck swam in a shirt too large for him. Big pleats, cinched together with a heavy belt, hid the excess width of the wet pants. His helmet slid over his ears for a moronic look. He grabbed Kaelyn's hair and forced her head back.

Anh said, "*Sin loi, minoi.*"

His jaw dropped as he turned. Anh fired her pistol twice. One bullet knocked his helmet off and the other caught him below the eye. Blood splattered on Kaelyn's arm. The little soldier slammed backward on top of the dead villager. Everyone hit to the dirt.

With shaking hands, Anh put the gun under her *ao dai*. Tears ran down her cheeks. "He was a child. But children kill. Many new tunnels and ancient caves honeycomb this mountain. NVA stragglers are everywhere."

Kaelyn said, "What did you say?"

"*Sin loi, minoi* means, 'too bad, honey'." Anh grinned.

A thunderous sound shook the ground. Dust clouds bellowed from the tunnel. Noise from the commotion of running feet echoed in the cavern. Minh suddenly appeared out of the dust with sweat glistening on his face. He spoke rapidly to Anh until he saw Kaelyn. "And why are *you* here?"

Kaelyn relaxed her rifle. "Our bridge club cancelled its game today. so I thought I'd pop in for some tea." Minh's blank stare under a furrowed brow signaled her sarcasm was lost. She said, "I want to understand what the people of Vietnam are going through in their fight for freedom."

Minh's eyes drilled into her. He gestured for silence from the villagers, some with rifles strapped on their backs. "We have sealed off the entrance from the sea. The first two explosions collapsed much of the tunnel. These last two plugged it completely."

"How could you tell?"

"The draft stopped. Before, the breeze cooled me as I walked. After the last explosions, the breeze stopped." He gestured at the dust still lingering.

Kaelyn looked at the motley group of about 20 villagers. A mix of both men and women, young and old. They moved with the slow trot of prisoners in a daze, held too long in confinement. "Is this all of the people that will fight?"

"No." Minh raised his voice, "This is all that is left. A similar group defends at the tunnel blockade. Most have weapons they know how to use."

A man with short gray hair divided the group among the tables. Anh watched, "They will prepare grenades for the defenders. Some will fix food. Those with weapons will clear the trapped NVA from the tunnels. Only two ventilation shafts remain, they will be guarded."

Kaelyn watched the armed group saunter away. "How much time do we have before the NVA get here?"

"Four to five hours. They won't attempt it at night. The cliff is too dangerous."

A young girl ran out of the main cave. Sweat streaked the dust on her face. She shouted in Vietnamese, over and over again. Minh wrapped his arms around her.

Kaelyn turned. "Did she say a tank?"

The color had drained from Anh's face. "On the other side of the blockade."

"WE WILL MAKE those blood-sucking Americans pay for this." General Cuong Danh leaned against the side panel of the Soviet-built T54 tank, the only survivor of the attack on the freighter. His stomach churned every time he thought of the other three tanks lying at the bottom of the harbor. Thick, blue smoke poured out of the 12-cylinder engine. He said, "The sound and smell of diesel in the breeze rejuvenates me."

The adjutant wiped oil off his hands. "The blade is attached, sir."

"How much of the tunnel has collapsed?"

"Twenty meters maybe twenty-five. It is hard to tell exactly, until we remove the debris."

"Did you make contact with the guard in the west cavern yet?"

"No sir. Could not connect."

The General's agitation grew when he thought of the time it would take the guards to climb up the mountain and track down the prisoners. Even though behind schedule, Hon Heo sparkled among his career achievements and the reason for his second star. These mysterious, haunted natural caverns had become the distribution center for the National Liberation Front in South Vietnam.

General Danh ran his fingers along the track of the T54. He said,

"You remember our meeting with the Central Office? I promised to mire the Americans in the mountains, confound them in the jungles, destroy them in their bases. They called Vietnam a cesspool. I will drown them in its toxic waste from the last 1000 years of occupation, oppression, and misery."

The unit commander stood on the rear of the tank. "General, your orders?"

Danh said, "Use the tank blade to drag out the collapsed tunnel. The villagers from Thanh Ha will form an extraction line here."

"Yes, sir."

The general studied the tank's turret. "When will our helicopters arrive?"

A young captain joined the group. His regulation shirt stuck to his body from his run up the hill. "Sir, there is a problem."

Without facing the captain, Danh said, "Damn helicopters spend 10 hours in maintenance for every hour they fly. Unlike my beautiful tanks that work for 10 hours with only a half hour of care. He propped his hands on his hips, "So, what is it?"

"They've crashed, sir." The captain braced himself.

Danh looked like he saw into hell. A soured expression froze on his face. "What happened?"

"They found a target of opportunity, an unescorted American helicopter, so they tried to capture it."

"Capture it!" The General pounded the armor. "Then what?"

"They got shot down."

"By whom?" Danh's rage echoed against the walls.

"The target of opportunity."

"You said 'they' before?"

"Our helicopters fly in teams of two, the second team joined in the fight."

"And got shot down?"

"Yes, sir." The captain lowered his eyes.

"I ordered the pilots not to engage any US helicopter. Ever! To do everything possible to disappear. Just because they trained in Texas, they think they're cowboys. Have the flight leader see me."

"Ahaaa...We do not exactly know where he is."

"Not exactly?" Danh's back arched, his face radiated pain. "Our radar on Hon Heo had to see this great dog fight unfold. What'd did they say?"

"Lost sight of them after they went below the west ridge."

"Did the south outpost see anything?"

"Yes sir. "Our two helicopters chased a single Huey flying south-south east, without lights and landing gear."

"How could they tell?"

"Our ship illuminated it."

"Then what?"

"They flew into a blind spot on the back ridge. Only the Huey left."

Danh's impenetrable demeanor crumbled as he shouted, "*DU MI AMI*. They did not follow instructions and one catastrophe bred two more, like rats in the garbage." He motioned to his radio operator. "Contact our agent at MACV office, scramble the transmission."

The General faced the lieutenant. "Did their brains rot into cow shit?"

"Our men were caught off guard when the US soldiers parachuted on them and then the top of the mountain exploded. They had to avenge somehow."

"Never avenge." The General strained. "Always keep in control. Plan your response. Fight when you can win. The Americans are not invincible...powerful, yes... invulnerable, no. We dishearten them with every victory. Think more, fight less."

He put his arm on the lieutenant's back, "Lin, I want you to rendezvous with Sergeant Chien Phu and his patrol tomorrow. You must reclaim the cavern workshops. Be sure you punish the renegade leaders. Make it bloody but leave witnesses. Your fame will spread, and fright will deepen your mark. In the meantime, you're in charge of the tunnel excavation."

Lin bowed his head. "Thank you, Father."

General Cuong Danh hurried to the radio and transformed to an in-control, leader of the resistance. "MIHN OI, how are you?"

A syrupy female voice responded, "I am fine. What is the emergency?"

"Tell the MACV commander, a captured US ARMY Huey is in route to Qui Nhon with nerve gas. Enough to wipe out the entire base. This is a statement to the world. A show of the power by the National Liberation Front. In fifteen minutes, this ship will reach town. The helicopter is flying in an east-southeast direction. A diversionary attack on Qui Nhon will coincide with the helicopter's arrival. Tell them this message was intercepted by one of your operatives."

"Yes, dear."

"Questions?"

"Yes. When will you be home next? Your daughter cries for you every day. She is so proud of what you and Lin do."

"And you in my thoughts every day. Hug her for me. Tell her of my love. *GA MUG.*" He paused with the microphone in his hand. "Now call the commander of the First Sapper Battalion."

In radio contact, the General said, "*DI WEE,* launch an attack on Qui Nhon. Use your 51-caliber machine gun and mortars on the hospital. Then hit the officer's club and hangars. No longer than one minute on each. Americans can't respond fast enough. After the third attack, have the sappers disappear. Even their empty shells. Start immediately."

"Yes, sir. Out."

General Danh smiled. "About time. We will see the *DU MI AMI* shot down by their own jets."

Lieutenant Lin strut around with pride in his first, real command. He spoke to his men, "Herd the villagers of Thanh Ha to the tunnel. One armed guard for every three volunteer households. If they refuse or delay, kill them."

Shovels and rakes were minimal, so the weary "volunteers" filled the containers by hand. Villagers packed work tubs, ammunition boxes and burlap bags. When rocks got in the way, they strapped them onto long wooden poles for dragging. The soldiers made no provision for rest, food, or water.

"Water, please, sir. Water." The workers pleaded again and again to the soldiers, who looked to Lin for guidance. His eyes steeled with contempt for their ignorance.

He shouted over the noise of the tank. "You lazy bastards. There is no time to waste. We need your backs for Vietnam, your sweat will assure victory. You can't stop now."

When the T54's mighty diesel engine wound down to silence, villagers paused. The young driver stuck his head out of the hatch. "Out of diesel," he shouted.

Everyone remained silent until two women broke into a high-pitched giggle then into a loud guffaw. Lin gritted his straight, white teeth and knew these stupid peasants were mocking him. "Silence." His voice broke higher as it got louder, more women laughed. He fired at the first two. They fell to the ground, screaming. He approached them with caution and shot them again.

The traumatized villagers stared at the lieutenant. He pointed with his pistol. "Now, lay down your containers. Follow my men to the dock. Bring the barrels of diesel stacked at water's edge. All of them." He said to his sergeant, "*TRUNG WEE*, if anyone gives you a problem, shoot them. And get rid of these bodies."

The husband of the number one laughing lady stood grief-stricken and tears streamed down his face as soldiers dragged his wife feet-first while her face scraped the rocks. Their child would have been born in four months. His stare promised a slow and painful death for the pompous, little-shit of an officer.

THE WHACK JOB from the trees did it.

Without my instruments, I couldn't tell which direction I flew, or how high, or how fast, or how much longer. And it was too dark to see landmarks.

Without radios I couldn't talk to anyone. I couldn't tell them who or where I was.

Without electrical, no one else could see me. The gooks shooting were troublesome but not as much as other aircraft flying into me.

Without my helmet, noise came from everywhere. With cargo doors open, Henry's chin bubble gone, bullet holes in the rotor blades and the avionics door missing. Everything that could possibly catch air, caught it. This diabolical combination could make a real pilot deaf. Or a dumbass pilot proud.

Proud of this piece of shit 'cause it kept on flying. But I had to keep this mother in the air until it died. Or I did. I burned up too much fuel in my quasi dogfight.

And what could I do without landing gear? Of course, it would only be important if I had a controlled landing to a friendly lighted area. Instead of a dead-stick auto-rotation into black nothingness.

I leaned close to the only two instruments working. A spot of light danced on the panel from Krotch's new-found joy, a flashlight. He followed my pointing finger to the good ol' magnetic compass, which read 90 degrees. No wonder I couldn't see anything but black, the color of mountains at night. I turned south for Qui Nhon.

My head swiveled like a windsock in a storm, looking for anyplace with lights. Until I felt a double-thump on my seat. Krotch's beam locked on the windshield and city lights in the distance. It had to be Qui Nhon. My heart flip-flopped in excitement.

This rosy picture changed when ground explosions flashed, and a hanging flare popped over the base perimeter. What a wonderful time to drag home—in the middle of a fire fight. I checked my don't-give-a-shit-meter which said, "fuck it".

Then my worst nightmare appeared. A pair of fast movers dove at me from three o'clock high.

The light reappeared on my panel. I turned around and shouted, "Turn off that goddamn..." until l realized he had the only thing to communicate with those aircraft. I shouted, "Ya' know Morse Code?"

He put the light under his swollen, blood-caked face and nodded twice. Immediately after, two jets buzzed us about four seconds apart. They flew so close I thought they were in my cabin. I felt their wing vortex, smelled jet exhaust, and shook from the enormous roar.

When they materialized again on my right side, they cruised up much slower. I yelled at the top of my lungs, "Tap out 'SOS'. Twice."

The jet responded with its landing light in three long flashes and a long-short-long for 'Okay'. My fastest speed couldn't keep up with the first jet flying. So, the second ship lit our cockpit like center stage. His lights blinked four letters, "r u ok." It took me a while to figure it out their response and by then he was gone. Tears welled up in my eyes...and streamed into my ear.

An agonizing, slow return to Qui Nhon, the city grew more distinct like a thread pattern on a burlap sack. The Air Force base occupied part of the peninsula. Swimming at this time of night did not appeal to me but neither did a firefight on the west side.

A beacon flashed from the control tower. Damn most gorgeous

light I'd seen as it changed colors. Green. White. White. The Cong loved it too. Their tracers knocked out the lights before it rotated a second time. The bastards then killed the light at the end of the runway.

Our Air Force jocks must have witnessed the whole thing. I howled with joy as the big old jets kicked into a firing run. A stream of pink fifties followed by rockets. Secondary explosions proved they were on target.

The jets returned to circle around us until the dreaded silence began. My turbine spooled down to a stop. What a pisser to be out of juice and ideas at the same time.

Wind noises blended into the new gushing silence of dead-stick air, which every pilot hated to hear. Dark oblivion swallowed my descent, until the earth got bright again from the jet. My glide path led to dead center of the rockiest stretch of shoreline. With the smallest chunk of beach. It glowed like a tiny fingernail.

About eight seconds above the ground, I tried to squeeze it to the beach. Old Nickel-Dime shuddered when I pulled the nose up to dump all my forward airspeed. We dropped straight down. And the light went out. Again. Sheeiit.

Only the ghostly image of the lighted beach lingered. As I pulled final pitch, we hit the beach hard. A split-second later, my yank for maximum power kicked in to take the full 5000 pounds of the Huey high into the air again. Literally it bounced like a ball, only this time there was no way to cushion the second landing. Its wildly flexing rotor blade cut through the right front of the cabin, deep enough to sever Henry's head and slam it out of the cargo door.

Old Nickel Dime didn't roll. It stuck into the beach.

It didn't burn, because it had no fuel.

Everything stopped. No engine noise. No wind noise. No gun shots or explosions. No damn tracers.

Only the sound of water beating against the rocks.

PART EIGHT_

MY HANDS SHOOK as I held the 63. I couldn't erase the image of the gook with his face on fire. His scream penetrated my soul. The ringing in my ears blended into a different kind of sound. A higher pitch, tandem rotor helicopter like they once demoed in flight school.

More gunfire erupted. Bullets tore apart Nickel-Dime's cockpit. Ricochets played off the rotor like a bad piano. Chunks of Plexiglas splashed to the water.

Muzzle flashes outlined the rowboat, its lantern swung as waves licked the bow. A Cong screamed out, *"Dung lai"* and the other Vietnamese stopped. The shooters stood in the boat with their weapons aiming at the helicopter.

Nervous as a snake on a stove, I hid from their view behind Nickel-Dime. The monster hog 63 was my only hope. Their spotlight found Krotch sitting motionless. All I had to do was pull the trigger. Yep, a real case of shit or get off the pot.

Shooting from chest level, my first blast chewed up the nose of old Nickel-Dime. The second shattered the dingy lantern, the third smashed the spotlight, and the fourth blew two shooters out of the boat. Then the gun jammed.

They always instructed us to clear a jam by pulling the receiver back. I tried and the whole damn gun slipped into the water. Drowning my weapon gave time for the Cong to fire back. Geysers popped up around me. More screwed than usual, I belly-flopped into the sea.

I landed on the beach instead of the water and knocked my breath out. From the helicopter, Krotch took out all three of the shooters at once. A halledamnlujah explosion.

Our first real hope of rescue sounded when a Huey gunship crossed high above the beach with its familiar *whop, whop, whop*. I climbed into Nickel-Dime with my pistol. Krotch still sat where I left him. He popped open the breach of the 79 and slipped another round into it. His focus was on the boat, "...shoooot."

One of the gooks resurrected from the water and aimed at us with a pistol. He fired two rounds so quickly, the muzzle flash looked like a continuous flame. Both shots hit to my left. His gun clicked empty.

I squeezed two out of my .45 to kill the beach and knock the gook down. Shooting from inside the helicopter acted like a megaphone, making my pistol sound like a cannon.

Krotch closed the 79 and patted the two large gouges in his chicken plate. He said, "...good."

The Huey crossed our position at low level. Its machine guns blazed, and rockets exploded into the hill. Empty casings rained on us. A Chinook followed closely, flared to a high hover with a louder, whiny, whirly sound and 80 mile per hour downdraft.

I laid on the floor and held the bench supports as the maelstrom enveloped us. Sand stung me right through my wet clothes. Our left front door ripped off its hinges and blew down the beach like an empty bag. Up close the Chinook with its rear door down, looked like a flyin' single-wide.

A strange bunch of soldiers disgorged, many without helmets, shirts, or back packs. They were not the normal ready-reaction force, but they dispersed to form the defensive perimeter. An NCO came at a dead run. He had a cigar in his mouth, *LAI DAI* (come to me) written on the front of his helmet. With sleeves rolled up and shirt unbuttoned, he stopped like he saw a ghost. "What the fuck you doing here?"

I said, "Just waiting for the next bus home."

He was not amused. He sneered. "Sure do love a smart ass."

"No, you don't either. And I'll shoot ya dead if you fuck with me again Pollhill." I pointed my pistol at his bare chest and cocked the hammer.

Krotch closed the 79's breach with a loud snap.

I said, "Get us out of here."

"Are you Ox?"

"Yep."

A strange look came across his face. "No shit. The gunship reported a firefight on the beach. What happened?"

"I took fire from the hill. Krotch took them out with his 79. Then the rowboat came with five shooters. I got a couple. He got the rest."

A straight-faced Pollhill signaled the medic and the radio operator. The back of his helmet had *DU MI AMI* (mother fucker) printed as a warning of his disposition. In less than two minutes the CH-47 was back. They carried Z on a litter. I helped Krotch. Henry made the load in a body bag. The back door closed and the Shithook flew offshore to wait.

I asked the medic, "Why aren't we headed straight to Qui Nhon?"

"They want to carry your chopper back."

"Fuck that. My guys are worth more. Will they make it?"

The medic looked at both of them, "Only if the late JC will perform the operation. I've done as much as I can."

Cockpit noise was loud enough to require sign language, so I borrowed the crew chief's headset. I said to the two Warrants manning the pilot's station, "...appreciate ya' savin' our ass."

The aircraft commander smiled. "Nice landing."

"Need a favor."

"Go ahead."

"Both of my guys are critical. They're MACV SOG Team 2 Alpha. Got ambushed. Is the gunship still on station?"

"Yes, sir."

"And that's Qui Nhon ahead of us?"

"Yes, sir."

"You need to get us there. To the hospital. I'll bring the G2. This is important shit, guys. Wish I could tell you more." I looked directly into the eyes of the aircraft commander. "You understand?"

The A/C looked at his instrument panel. "Our orders were to extract the security force. They're not a recovery team but an infantry unit just in from the bush."

"Yeah. They looked like shit and smelled like a bar."

"What do we tell our ops officer?"

"Tell 'em G2 ordered ya' to bring in the two surviving members of the patrol... immediately. Reassure Ops the gun is still on station and your return ETA is quick."

Squinting like he had a bad case of constipation, the pilot said, "We should be back in about 20 minutes."

The headset blurted out, "Wildcat One, this is Gunslinger, over."

"Go ahead Gunslinger."

"Get your ass back down here."

The aircraft commander flashed the finger to the radio and pointed to Qui Nhon. On his other radio, he told the gunship and his ops center of his new mission.

"Hey Wildcat, this is Gunslinger. Where in the fuck you going?" Automatic weapons and explosions made his message nearly indiscernible.

The A/C transmitted. "We've been redirected to Qui Nhon immediately, our return ETA is in two zero minutes."

"Did that goddamn lieutenant feed you that bullshit? Tell that prick his ass is grass."

"Roger, wilco."

I said, "Ya' know, your aviator salute was as good as I'd ever seen."

The A/C smiled. "It works best when all other alternatives are eliminated. Its meaning is clear."

"Yeah, kinda like, fuck it...let's fly."

"Whatcha mean, a tank's coming?" Kaelyn slung the AK-47 over her shoulder.

Anh crossed herself and folded her hands in prayer, "They'll break through our blockade. They'll kill all of us. They have no mercy."

"So, you have nothing to lose." Kaelyn hugged Anh's tiny shoulders but looked at Minh, "What're you gonna do?"

He stroked his chin. "I hoped our blockade would hold until the Americans come."

"Well, maybe it will. In the meantime, take me to see it. I must understand so I can tell the world."

Minh said, "Of course, after I talk to the villagers." He turned to them, "My friends, all is not lost. We must keep the NVA away until the Americans come. Make more explosives. Assemble whatever we have materials for...it's our best chance. Phuong will direct you." Minh smiled at the villagers' new willingness to work as they ran toward the assembly tables.

Anh and Kaelyn followed Minh down a dingy tunnel. It smelled like mold, urine, and rat shit.

Kaelyn pointed to the bulbs on the wall. "Where's the power coming from?"

"I never thought about it. Probably one of those noisy machines."

"No shit, Einstein."

Anh said, "Did he have an excremental invention too?"

Kaelyn's stunned look gave way to a wide grin. "Not that I know of. If the machine's a generator, the lights are not a problem unless they stop. So, it must be on our side. But how much fuel to we have?"

Minh shrugged. "We have a generator near our assembly entrance. Near the guard station. Phuong can figure it out."

Kaelyn paused. "Who's he?"

"An unfortunate visitor to our hamlet on the day the Cong captured us. He must be some kind of a monk. He tolerates people and speaks with an educated tongue." With a slight bow, Anh left.

They descended a steeper grade amid giant boulders. Kaelyn perspired as she fought for solid footing. "This is the longest tunnel ever."

"Hon Heo Mountain is over six hundred meters high; this tunnel drops at least 350 meters from the work area to the sea. The NVA forced me to carry many loads to the shipping dock. In my boredom, I counted my steps." Minh's smile blossomed when he knew answers.

Kaelyn noticed many small hollows along the way. "Where do these go?"

"None go outside. Only the first one has lights. This is the fourth."

"What were they used for?"

Anh's smile disappeared, "The NVA used the Number One to interrogate, I mean *torture* the prisoners. The sounds of hell echoed endlessly. Number Two is the bomb shelter with a reinforced ceiling for our reptilian leader of this death camp. We slept in the Third and had a light—as long as we could pedal the bicycle generator. There are 40 rows of *cái vong* in there, stacked three high. We slept on hammocks. Fourth tunnel contains bodies of the villagers killed. I brought the dead in many times. No matter how I tried to mask it, the stench of death overwhelmed me."

"How many died?"

"More than 130. No wounded. They made sure of that."

Kaelyn studied the crude directions on the wall. "How many entrances are there?"

"You must be tiring—your questions are getting easier. The beach entrance is hidden by the tidal waters and a rock formation. Some of us played there as children, but few had the courage to wander this far into darkness. Too many ghost stories. The assembly area guarded a wide fissure used as an exit. It collapsed in the bombing."

"Did you dig all of these side tunnels and rooms?"

"Yes and no. The tunnels are new. Rooms were natural open spaces found by the diggers. Several as large as the assembly area. Many smaller ones." Minh stopped after a sharp turn in the tunnel.

A cordon of armed villagers aimed their weapons at Kaelyn. She stopped. "I hope they know I'm friendly? Or did they read one of my columns?"

Minh lifted his arms in a halt gesture. They lowered their weapons.

She sneezed. "Is it always this awful?"

"When we dug these tunnels, we lived in cloud of dust. Most of the time it was difficult. The rest...impossible."

"What made you blockade this space?"

Minh scratched his head. "Colonel Bobson wanted to destroy the hardest place of the tunnel to get through. This was the narrowest and steepest part. The NVA had been drinking all evening. Their noise coming up meant they were looking for our women. We stuck satchel charges into every crack we could find, lit them, and ran like hell."

Kaelyn inspected the rubble from the bottom of the pile to the top. "How could you possibly hear the tank through this?"

Minh signaled for silence.

Kaelyn held her breath but heard nothing.

The little runner spoke up, "Old pipe...carry sound."

"Pipe? Where?"

She pointed to a stub protruding from under a large rock. "I hear noises. Big motor sounds. Someone say tank."

Kaelyn knelt down to listen. Wrinkles clouded her face. She covered the pipe with her palm and motioned for Minh. "Listen. They talk too fast. I can't understand."

He stooped down to the pipe for several minutes and said, "Our commander from hell...will attack when fuel arrives...the tank will lead...a company of NVA...and walking-wounded from the hospital."

Kaelyn said, "What hospital?"

"There are two caverns below the blockade. One is the hospital, the other is storage."

"How large are they?"

"The hospital has 70 hammocks for wounded Cong and NVA only. Storage space about the same. Each larger than our assembly area."

Kaelyn leaned against the wall. "How much explosives have the villagers assembled?"

"Hard to say," Minh shook his head.

"I know." Anh appeared behind him with sweat dripping from her face. "They've assembled 20 satchel charges and eight grenades since we left."

"What about the generator?"

"Phuong told me there are two generators. One near the hospital and the second at the assembly entrance."

Minh spoke only to Kaelyn, "We could set up a line here and fight them as they come through."

"My daddy used to say, 'never lie to yourself'." Kaelyn gestured at the villagers. "These people are farmers. Not trained military. They'll run away from an approaching tank. I certainly would. You don't have to fight. All you have to do is keep 'em out. If they break through, plug up the hole. Explode satchel charges to collapse the tunnel again."

"What was your father, a general?"

"No, a politician."

"Ah...no wonder." Minh described the plan to the villagers. They brightened as they talked among themselves. He pointed the fastest runner to bring the explosives down.

Kaelyn continued, "Ventilation shafts are another problem. Assign someone to guard them...grenades would be the easiest to use."

Anh interrupted, "But if we run out of fuel, we're dead." An eerie look came over her face. She began her climb up the tunnel.

The young runner pushed her way through the villagers. "Come, listen."

Kaelyn ran to the pipe. Her face faded to a pasty white. "Oh, my god. The tank is running again."

General Danh kicked a clump of dirt. "Who's coming?"

The radio operator stood at attention. "Two aircraft from Hanoi. No envoy identification."

"Have a boat ready to meet them." General Danh watched his tank remove the debris from the cave. It ingested diesel as fast as the villagers could bring it up from the dock. Fortunately, its ability to move rock exceeded its appetite for fuel. The giant blade on the front of the tank acted like a hoe to pull debris back for the villagers to move away. Inefficient? Yes. Better than the peasants alone? Absolutely.

The driver's head protruded from the hatch of the Soviet T-54. As it clawed at the blockade, Lin Danh shouted over the roar of the engine, "Don't run over the pipe behind you." Lin circled back to the General. "Pipe is as difficult to get as the tank. Luckily, it survived the attack on the freighter."

Danh presented an audacious plan to the General's staff. His strategy to capture half of South Vietnam used armor as the equalizer to bring down helicopters faster than they could be replaced. Many of the officers laughed, all except General Giap, who applauded.

Slowly at first, then into a steady beat in unison with all at the conference table. This moment marked Danh's ascendancy.

The sweaty, radio operator shouted, "General, one plane arrived but departed immediately to wait in the Truong Sa Islands. Two men off loaded cases of supplies to our boat."

"The planes would dare to fly so close to the shipping lanes?"

Lin joined the General. "Vietnam's islands are a perfect place to hide in the open. With over 400 atolls, cays, and islands, it's the maze of the ocean."

General Danh stayed at the mouth of the tunnel while Lin walked to the boat dock. Both visitors wore simple black pajamas, sandals, and traditional *non la* hats. All hurried up the beach to the cave.

In front of the General, the tall thin man saluted. "Sir, Colonel Xuan Bay, Executive officer to General Giap. Reporting. My assistant is Sergeant Khan Pin, armor trainer." Xuan Bay's smile accentuated his clean-shaven face, while his bald head and straight, black eyebrows heightened his Machiavellian air of authority. "General Giap sends greetings."

"We are pleased you arrived safely." General Danh returned the salute. "I'm astonished you would risk the flight personally. In the daylight."

Xuan wrinkled his forehead. "Critical situations merit urgency. Your reported 'target of opportunity' helicopter did not get destroyed by the US fighters but was protected. Three unconscious survivors arrived at the hospital."

"Good information." Danh drew closer to Bay. "What are you not saying?"

Colonel Bay lowered his voice. "Before the pilot lost consciousness, he identified the wounded soldiers as leaders of Special Operations Group, or SOG Team Two. This hunter-killer squad had orders to disrupt the meeting of Boa Dai with the Binh Xuyen. Their initial report caused the First Cavalry Division to prepare a search-and-destroy operation on the entire Hon Heo range. In 24 hours. One of their objectives is to rescue the woman journalist, daughter of a US Senator. The second is to save the villagers held in captivity. A political windfall for them to validate their incursion on our soil."

General Danh shot back. "Are you sure?"

"Positive. From the highest level. Their warning of the B-52 bombing strike confirms their value. Our December campaign is too important to jeopardize."

"So, what does General Giap want me to do?"

"First, the village prisoners must disappear. We brought VX nerve gas. Second, destroy all entry ways to hide the location. And finally, evacuate the political personnel before the First Cavalry sweep."

General Danh reflected, "Le Van Vien received serious injuries during the raid, he's in our hospital. Doan Vien was to represent Bao Dai in the meetings. We have not heard from her since the bombing. Our lookout post saw some bodies this morning but could not identify anyone. The American reaction force would have reported a female survivor, but they did not."

Colonel Bay persisted. "What is your next step at the blockade?"

"The prisoners have small arms, satchel charges and grenades. We extracted about 20 meters of debris, but don't know how much farther. Our attack will lead with the tank, supplemented with the remnants of our infantry company plus some of the walking wounded. Nerve gas is a good option as soon as we get through the blockade."

"May I speak?"

"Go ahead," the General continued to face Bay. "You met my son, Lieutenant Lin Danh. He also serves as my *aide-de-camp*."

"Just before you landed, we verified our supply of ten-centimeter iron pipe and connections."

Colonel Bay looked at Lin with curiosity "Yes?"

"Our collapsed rubble is a mix of volcanic rock and sand. We could use the tank to ram the pipe forward and inject the gas. It will reduce casualties and expedite the shutdown of Hon Heo."

The Colonel turned to the armor trainer. "VX gas is pressurized. Can the tank handle the pipe?"

"Unfortunately, the appropriate ancillary equipment did not ship with this tank. It will *not* support such a ramming operation." Sergeant Khan Pin's smirk resembled the cat after eating the goldfish.

The General got nose-to-nose with him, "Don't care what shipped. We need to penetrate that blockade now. I only have one big bull. Find a way to use it."

Raw fright whitened the sergeant's face. "We may damage the breech block and firing pin of the gun. But there is a way."

"Well?"

"I'll cap the pipe before I ram it through the blockade. Shooting the stopper open will be no problem."

Colonel Bay wiped his bald head. "The gas will flood every passageway. But what if Doan Vien and the American journalist are there?"

General Danh looked toward the sea. "Doan is not a dependable link between Bao Dai and the Americans. And Kaelyn DeHaven is the journalist who has learned too much without handlers. Her friendly fire death is demanded. Indeed, both are regrettable costs of war. Along with deaths of the SOG team survivors and loss of their valuable intelligence. This mission will be another blemish on American history."

"You mentioned the deaths of the SOG team survivors. What do you have in mind?"

The General brightened. "We will extract them from the hospital. I want to smell their bodies burning."

THE LAST 100 meters to the top of the tunnel took away Anh's breath. She reached the assembly area to an upset Phuong, wiping tears from his eyes.

He said, "I removed the bayonet and a booby trap from my impaled friend. Just a simple fisherman, crippled, and a father of four. Totally apolitical. He died begging me to take care of his family. Why would they do that to him?"

Ahn hugged Phuong. "Such a waste. Soon we'll be free. Nothing at the university could have prepared me for this."

Phuong pointed toward his production line. "We now produce at three times the rate we did in bondage. Our people have longed for this chance."

"Yes, but now I need grenades."

"I'm sorry." Phuong bowed with reverence. "We only have a few. After the first run, I only produced satchel charges. Over two dozen complete."

"Are the guards posted?"

"One in the large ventilator shaft. And the other by the generator."

Phuong's powers of observation and communication were better than any monk Anh ever met. She picked up one of the grenades. "How do these things work?"

"Lay flat on the ground, hold the grenade in your throwing hand. Pull out the circular pin and let go of the handle as you throw. It explodes in four seconds. Has a killing radius of ten meters, give or take five."

Anh filled the first aid bag on her shoulder. "How long will the generator operate?"

"Three hours. They just emptied their last five-gallon can."

"We will need time. Select three villagers, each strong enough to carry two full cans of diesel. Have them meet me at the steps to the shaft."

In less than five minutes, two men and a woman reported. Anh's disappointment showed. The men were boys and the woman were beyond middle age.

"My name is Binh. I've carried water into the bunker from the beach since we've been here. I can carry more than they can." She displayed her shiny black, beetle-nut stained teeth in a forced smile.

Anh lined them against the wall. "Do any of you know how to use a pistol or grenade?" The woman nodded "yes" to the pistol and demonstrated loading and aiming. A grimace broke out on the face of the smaller boy as she explained how to use the explosive.

Their eyes darted from side to side. Anh said, "Don't worry. I'll lead you to the fuel storage to refill the cans for our generator. If we come under attack or I get hit, you must continue. Use my gun and grenades to stop them. Our village depends on us for light so we can wait for the Americans. And above all, don't let them find the vent."

With hands on their hearts, they bowed.

Anh led them up the steep ventilator chute. A frightened boy about 13, and no more than 80 pounds, stood guard. Heavy strands of bamboo woven into the grate covered the opening. She said, "Nien, have you seen anyone?" He shook his head.

"Have you opened the cover?" He uttered a meek, "No."

Anh handed the revolver to Binh, and a grenade to the small boy.

As she reached for the grate, the guard grabbed her arm. "Too dark to look outside. Hear patrol talk as they walk."

"What they say?"

The guard inhaled slowly. "They cursed America for collapsing cave."

"What else?"

"They pay double reward money for village prisoners, dead or alive."

"When did they pass?"

"Not long."

"Do you have weapon?"

"No." The boy had a vacant look.

Anh gave him a grenade and explained how to use it. She slowly opened the grate to a very dark outside. A fresh breeze poured in. Her heart sank as a distant light moved up the northern hill. She ducked back. "Soldiers are still searching the area. Find the bunker."

Binh moved close to her. "Use the trench to reach fuel, I walked it every day. I deliver water to bunker. Let me find." The woman squeezed past Anh to crawl outside the opening. She made no noise as she left or when she returned a few minutes later. "There are two dead men near the trench and many craters with much debris. I find way."

"Then lead." Anh reopened the grate.

One at a time, they squeezed through the opening. Anh crawled past the bodies of the crazy man and the dead Colonel. The trench curved around bushes, rocks, and trees. Bomb craters, as large as her hut in the village, smelled of burnt ash and garlic. To eliminate noise, each held the can with both hands, against their chest.

Near the bunker Binh whispered, "Smoke." She cocked her gun. "Come with me Anh. I know this bunker well. Boys, stay. Be silent."

Anh followed the woman in a low crouch around the side of the bunker and peeked in. Pungent tobacco fumes drifted out of the framed opening. They found a soldier snoring in a chair next to the radio, a cigarette smoldered on the ground. A lantern shared the table with small bottle of whiskey and an empty glass. Anh lingered a step behind, when Binh picked up the iron bar by the door and whimpered, "*mihn oi, mihn oi.*"

The soldier didn't jump at this strange voice calling him sweetheart but turned with an intoxicated smile. It quickly changed to total terror as the woman drove the pointed bar into his throat. His legs kicked the table and a sucking sound emerged as she pulled the bar out. He pointed at her as she buried it in his heart.

Binh hissed, "He raped me...so many times...in this cursed spot..." Tears streamed down her high cheeks.

Anh stood with her hands covering her mouth, while her whole body shook. Before she could settle down, a male voice outside slurred, "*Trung Wee, Trung Wee.*"

Binh signaled silence and drew her gun. She pointed Anh to the wall then pantomimed opening her blouse.

The voice cursed his sergeant and demanded more beer. "*Trung Wee...la vay...du mi ami.*" He burped like a bloated pig.

Binh teased him in a guttural tone, "*Dinky dau.*"

His red flashlight beam moved slowly down the wall until it found Anh with her breasts exposed. She held an NVA helmet covering a pistol.

The soldier whispered come to me, "...aah...*LAI DAI.*" Protruding young breasts mesmerized him. He missed movement of the rod. It plunged into his ear and stuck in the sandbag next to the door.

"He got me too. They took turns." This time the woman did not cry. "I called him needle-dick."

Twitching like in electric shock, his body flailed against his fate.

She pulled the bar out of his head and watched him slip to the ground. An eerie moan arose as his eyes bulged, until she kicked them shut.

Anh picked up Needle-Dick's flashlight and found the drums of fuel. "Bring in the boys."

When all cans were full, Binh and her parade disappeared like a slow breeze in the night.

Anh sat on a stool, leaned against the sandbags, and scanned the black nothingness of the valley. Her hands trembled so much she could barely see through the binoculars from the table. For 20 months this nightmare of slave labor, brainwashing, and abuse slowly killed every aspect of her humanity. By thugs who would make devils look angelic. The strong odor of urine on the sandbags made her loathe the images that surfaced in her mind. Silence settled on her like an anvil. And memories. And tears.

ANH HEARD the rumble of aircraft engines. Two strange helicopters flew irregular patterns in the valley below. Each had a transparent sphere mounted under the rotating blades, attached to an exposed frame. The first one moved close to the ground skipping over trees and splashing in the stream, while the second flew a lazy, circular pattern far above.

At the waterfall, the low one climbed through the mist straight up the hill. Anh refocused her binoculars ahead of it to the ridge outpost on top.

The radio on the table startled her when it blared. She inspected the little notes taped next to each gauge and switch. All functions were in Vietnamese except the little red light, which glowed during each transmission.

———

"Yellow bird, this is White. Somethin's ahead."

Click. Click.

As Yellow neared the top, machine gun fire ricocheted off his blades. The helicopter turned away at full speed and escaped downhill.

White raked the outpost with long bursts from both machine guns mounted to its skid gear. All fire from the ridge stopped. He descended to a hover over the well camouflaged bunker, dropped a grenade and banked away. Long, white plumes of flame exploded in the morning light.

"Yes, sir. Really love Wille Pete before breakfast." Yellow almost sang it in joy.

"Roger. Took a couple blade hits and I'm runnin' close on the sauce. Let's head back. Over."

Click. Click.

Both helicopters climbed in unison. White said, "Yellow, at two o'clock...another bunker. Think anyone's home? Over."

"Damn straight. Love them two-fers even better don't 'cha know."

▭

Anh tried to understand what they meant when she felt cold metal pressed on her neck. Her back stiffened.

"Don't move, you little bitch. If they shoot, I want you to take the hit. Where are my men? What did the American say?"

Anh rose with the sun behind her. This distracted the young soldier with leaves draped off his pith helmet, ammunition pouches hung on his chest. A sergeant's rank marked his uniform with creases still in his sleeves. His AK-47 remained leveled at her.

Pointing out the window, she said, "They coming to blow up this place. We must run away."

The sergeant pushed her aside and aimed at the approaching helicopter over open sights. He said, "Easy shot. I'll collect the reward. Watch this."

"You don't stand a chance. They'll squash you like a bug."

With the back of his hand, he knocked her to the floor. Yelling at his men, he pointed across the bunker. "Take cover and hold your fire." His breathing increased as the helicopter got closer and closer. "Come to me my little bumble bee."

Two soldiers with long rifles passed through the bunker and spit at Anh. One addressed the sergeant, "The whore killed our men. Their bodies are down the path."

Whirling blades got louder; the sergeant licked his lips then fired three quick bursts. He turned around, slid down the wall and laughed.

Anh cried on the ground, cupping her ears, cowering in a fetal position.

"Listen, cunt. We'll be back for you. My men will enjoy your tight little ass." The sergeant squirmed out the door to fire from the bushes. Empty cartridges ejected back into the bunker.

The helicopter responded with both of its machine guns. A solid stream of bullets split the wooden frame around the windows, doors, and shattered the blackboard. Punctured sandbags poured down grit.

"Shoot the bastard, shoot, shoot..." The sergeant screamed at his men as two deep-sounding, single shot rifles erased his words.

Anh picked up the first-aid bag with its two grenades. She caressed the perfect killing machine and moved near the door. Gunsmoke choked her as she pulled the pin, and counted one, two, then tossed it around the corner. A little *pling* sounded as the handle sprung off. Concussion from the explosion sucked the air out of the bunker. The hot blast riddled the back wall, not as a single line of bullets, but defacing the whole wall at one time. One instant of deafening destruction with a whooshing cloud of dust.

Moans and screams came from someone still thrashing around. Popping the pin on another grenade was simple. She covered her ears and leaned against the sandbag wall. The thump of the blast felt good.

When the helicopter stopped shooting, she peeked outside. Couldn't see or hear them. Another radio transmission came through, "White, what in the hell's that?

"Two explosions."

"Got any more Willie Pete?"

"Yep, only one and a grenade." White checked his instrument panel. "Dump 'em. Let's get the hell outta here. I'm on fumes, baby."

Anh's ringing ears didn't let the fuzzy message through. The lingering dust clogged her eyes. She couldn't understand how everything in her life went so wrong. Departure from the comfort of the academic world in Saigon allowed her to experience life in a farming village. Instead, she found hell in a re-education camp as slave labor and a sex servant for the last 20 months.

The noise of the helicopter battered her without warning. Its downdraft swirled dirt through the windows. A jar fell to the ground, breaking when it landed. The grenade inside released its handle and hissed. Another fell next to it.

The white phosphorous exploded and covered her and all the remaining fuel drums with the burning jelly. Shrapnel flew in all directions from other grenade, ripping open the drums of JP4 and stopped Anh's pain forever.

▭

After the massive ball of flame, black smoke billowed high into the sky. White said, "Got the jackpot. Don't know what it was, but there was a lot of it. Over."

You betcha Red Rider. Did ya' see all the other bodies?"

"Yup. Probably the Arc Light. But with my fuel condition, we gotta hook 'em. Put it in your BDA report. Over."

"Wilco. Out."

"*MIHN OI*, HOW ARE YOU?" General Danh called her sweetheart only on encrypted calls.

"*CONG BO*, I miss you." The sweet, syrupy voice called him Water Buffalo.

"A small problem has arisen. I need your assistance."

"Of course. Tell me what I can do."

"The helicopter pilot and two survivors from the SOG team are in the base hospital. They were unconscious. Can you make sure they do not revive?"

"Yes, dear."

"*GA MUG*." General Danh handed the microphone back to his radio man. "Get me the summit outpost." After several attempts, the General redirected the operator to the patrol on the meadow. He finally connected to a bewildered soldier, "Where's the squad leader?"

"Dead."

"What happened?"

"Attacked by helicopters."

"How many survived?"

"Only me."

"How?"

"I had severe diarrhea."

"And?"

"I squatted in the bamboo while the helicopters destroyed the bunker and the squad."

"Have the Americans departed?"

"Yes, sir. They flew directly over me. Very noisy."

"Did you find the ventilator to the tunnel?"

"No, sir."

"What can you see from your position?

"A lot, sir."

"God damn it. Exactly what?"

"The valley."

The General raised his voice, "Stay there. Do not engage anyone. Report every thirty minutes. Watch the sky and the ground. I'll send another squad."

He turned to the lieutenant. "Prepare another patrol. The squad must know the mountain and find the ventilation shaft. Kill all the prisoners you find and collapse the vent."

Lieutenant Danh smiled with a quick salute to his father. "Yes, sir."

Colonel Xuan Bay's arrogance irritated rather than facilitated. "General, my orders are to return with whomever I can. Please have Le Van Vien prepared for my departure."

"By all means, but not until dark. Your risk of being detected increases tenfold in the daylight. And if you are spotted, shot down, or captured, our chances of being discovered multiply geometrically. We have too much at stake."

"But General—"

"This is not a discussion. If that plane shows up early, I will shoot it down myself. Is that understood?"

"Yes, sir." Colonel Bay saluted and headed to the hospital.

A group of villagers sat in the shade and lowered their heads when the lieutenant approached. All except one, who removed his straw hat and smiled. Dahn said, "I need a volunteer to show me the quick way to the top of the mountain."

The smiling villager raised his hand. "I have been up there. I know the way."

"Perfect. Bring water and a blanket. What's your name?""

"Vuong."

"I'll wait here." Lieutenant Danh looked at the forbidding rock face of Thanh Ha. He knew this was not an easy climb but his golden opportunity.

Vuong ran to his hut. Inside he checked if he was followed before he lifted a plank in the floor. A fishing knife and a .38-caliber Smith & Wesson, snub-nose revolver awaited him. He vowed to kill this lieutenant devil, who shot his sweet wife because of her beautiful giggle. Her body lay next to the cave entrance for burial. He choked up and whispered into silence, "Lieutenant, I am ready for you."

On the beach, Vuong reported back to discuss the challenges of the climb. They would leave within the hour. His knife and pistol were hidden in the blanket strapped around his chest.

Colonel Bay said, "Lieutenant, what are you doing with my radio."

"Sorry sir, only one left in the staging area." Lin eyed the bandages on the old, wounded man who joined them. "Good afternoon, Mr. Van Vien." The ashen-faced man nodded.

Colonel Bay said, "Hand me the radio."

Danh stood up straight enough to be at attention. "Colonel, the General said not to depart before dark."

"I know what he said Lieutenant. But my intelligence showed US Navy patrol activity at least four times greater at night than during the day. Along this coast from Qui Nhon to Bon Song. It is not my place to argue with a senior officer, when my information is more current, and my superior is his superior."

Bay communicated by encrypted message to and from his

aircraft. He said, "The plane will land about 700 meters offshore in 20 minutes. I'll take my radio and your man with me to manage the boat."

The lieutenant said. "But the general wanted—"

Colonel Bay threw up his hands. "You can do what you want Lieutenant. I suggest you wait for your man to return then go to the mountain. Both your missions are critical."

Danh touched his holster and wondered if he should shoot him or bring him back?

Bay continued, "We both know your father's a ball-buster. If he found out you were complicit in ignoring his instructions, he'd have your ass. So, I'll do this at gunpoint." He pointed his pistol at Lin's face. "This'll provide both of you a plausible excuse."

Danh nodded weakly to Vuong and the four men moved down the beach. As they reached the mooring, Colonel Bay clipped the Lieutenant on the side of the head with his pistol. Lin fell to the planks and Bay secured him to the bollard. He said, "Enjoy your rest, Lieutenant."

▭

Inside the cavern, Sergeant Pin loaded the first five meters of pipe into the tank's barrel, over two meters drooped out of the muzzle. As his men held the pipe straight, Pin drove the tank forward, forcing the capped end into the sand. The tank groaned as its giant treads spun until they found traction and rammed three meters of steel into the debris. Pin reversed the tank to leave the pipe sticking out of the blockade. His men attached the second section and repeated the process twice. With fifteen meters of pipe in the pile, he hoped it penetrated the other side.

Amidst the deep layer of exhaust, General Danh stepped forward to listen for tampering. "Sounds quiet." He motioned for a soldier. "On your knees. Listen. Stay near the open pipe. If you hear the squeak of a cap turning, start firing. Keep them distracted."

"Yes, sir."

Another soldier brought nerve gas cylinders forward. Danh pointed at the listener, "If this man shoots, insert the nozzle into the pipe. Then turn it on."

Sergeant Pin said, "And watch the air, if they open the cap, it will suck the diesel fumes out of here."

The soldier on the pipe twisted around with the look of a rapist in a convent. "I hear tapping."

Behind the admissions desk at the Qui Nhon Airfield hospital, Sergeant Fatty looked at the wounded man on the gurney. "Do you remember this scruffy, bandana-head asshole?"

The MP straightened his patent leather holster. "Yea, wonder what the other guys look like."

Nurse Washington wheeled Z and Krotch into the same operating room, the attending surgeon surveyed the damage and winced. "A pulse?"

She said, 'Yep. And the big guy's still conscious."

Slobber dribbled down Krotch's chin. He barely held up the leather pouch, "For...hilot."

Nurse Washington bent closer to his swollen face, smashed like a meatball. "Pilot?"

Major Bromo said, "What pilot?"

"These two are the only survivors of a long-range patrol. I recognized the Ace of Spades tattoo on the big guy's forearm. He requested the MACV G2."

"What the hell is that?"

"The section of the general's staff for intelligence, which might be a contradiction in terms. You've heard of Westmoreland?"

"Very funny. Didn't he win the bushy, eyebrow contest?" He paused.

Carol Washington sighed. "Couple of nights ago, you released two pilots to take the patrol on a special mission. Only one of them made it back. I put him in Recovery. No apparent bleeding. Total exhaustion."

Major Bromo pulled on scrubs. "Yep. This falls into the category of fuckin' amazing. But these poor bastards'll run out of luck, if we can't stabilize them. Gotta sew the big chunks together. Let's prep 'em."

The nurse slipped the pouch into her purse and returned with a needle.

Krotch shook his head, the one good eye could hardly stay open. "Oh...leep...sleep."

She injected him. "Don't worry. I'll take it to the pilot." The sedative took effect like a blackjack.

Five hours later the medical team finished. Bromo said, "These guys'll make it if we can get them to Japan. If Fatty moves his big ass, he'll get 'em on the connecter flight to Vung Tau. But now I gotta sack out. You okay?"

She smiled. "I'm whipped. But I promised big boy I'd get this to the pilot." As she retrieved the pouch, a coin fell out, which she absentmindedly put in her pocket.

Bone-deep fatigue hit her on the way down the long, quiet hall. She took a shortcut through the waiting room. A Vietnamese man in civilian clothes stood with his arm in a sling. His starched shirt, well-groomed hair, and refined features did not mark him as a plebeian from the alleys. She demanded, "What are you doing here?"

Trinh Le looked for some sign of rank but only found blood stains on her scrubs. "My name is Trinh Le Danh, no relation to the famous General in the North. I'm a translator for MACV." He spoke without an accent and with the assured delivery of a professional. His nose twitched from the scents of mortality and humanity, sterile and the sick, the disinfected and the dead.

"I'm Major Carol Washington." Her twisted bun sagged to match the exhaustion on her face. Even without make-up, she got his attention.

"I understand two SOG team members and a pilot are in Emergency. How are they doing?"

"Doctor Bromo and I patched 'em up enough to travel. They'll make it if we can get 'em to Japan.

The windows shook and the blinds shuddered from a helicopter passing too close on approach to the heliport. She said, "Most of our staff is TDY at the First Cav. The Division is in what they called, a 'pitched engagement'. Now we're shorthanded. And they're gettin' their ass kicked. So, what do ya want?"

Trinh bowed slightly. "The pilot requested the G2. I am not exactly him, but I'm on his staff and available. What kind of intelligence do they have?"

"The guys we worked on are under sedation. Let's try the pilot. He only has bruises, bumps but no breaks or bullet holes."

Major Washington walked at almost a trot to the recovery ward. "This one has the wings. From his dog tags, he's Danny Hellberg."

Trinh recognized the name from the incident in his store. "My god, I know this guy. He saved my ass in Saigon."

Fatty and the MP bumped through the door and wheeled two more wounded soldiers to the other side of the room. "Major, these two are stable. But the three in the ER are really chewed up." Fatty looked at Trinh Le and back to Washington with a shrug.

She said, "He's from G2. For the pilot. Take Zmith and Krotch to the ambulance for their departure." Fatty and the MP unlocked their beds and pushed them into the corridor. Wheels of the gurney clattered down the hall.

Major Washington looked to Trinh. "How did you get in?"

"The side door. I've been here before."

"When you talk to the pilot, give him this pouch from his friend Krotch, the big guy." She undulated hypnotically toward the ER. Perspiration made her scrub pants stick in her crack. Her rhythm and his dreams were broken when the big, stainless steel, double doors flew open and banged against the wall.

A monster of a man barged in, with blackened NCO stripes, a cigar in his mouth, shirt open and grenades hanging everywhere. He shouted, "Where's that goddamned pilot?"

"Excuse me Sergeant, put out that cigar and shut your mouth. You're in a hospital."

"Well fuck you bitch. Where is that piece of shit pilot?"

"That's *Major* Bitch to you, asshole." She only came up to his nametag but looked him in the eye. "He's none of your fuckin' business. Now get out of here before I throw your ass in the stockade and cut your balls off for my purse."

The muted moment of confrontation between man-mountain and little, lethal lily astounded Trinh Le. Pollhill smoldered and disappeared through the swinging door. He echoed in the hall, "Goddamned bitch, I'm gonna rip 'er face off."

Major Washington continued undeterred to the ER.

A moan emanating from the corner refocused Trinh. He jiggled Danny's mattress to wake him. Nothing happened. He slapped it hard. Still no dice. Just short of kicking him out of the bed, Trinh used a command voice, "Get up. Ya' gotta fly."

Danny's body tensed and one eye opened with a dilated pupil. "Uh...where to?"

"Saigon. To that shop with the Madame Nhu poster in the window."

Cognition took some time to kick in. "Bullshit." He licked his lips while his eye closed. "There's gotta be some water around here."

Trinh looked around the room for the ubiquitous hospital pitcher. "I'll get some." After searching a couple of rooms, he found a water cooler and a stack of supplies. With a towel on his shoulder, glasses tucked in his sling, he balanced a full pitcher in the one hand.

Down the hall a solitary ARVN officer of some unknown rank, waited anxiously in front of Recovery. Hanging off his immaculately pressed uniform, a chrome-plated .45-caliber automatic protruded from a long holster. He differed from every ARVN officer Trinh had ever met. Most considered their dress code as a theoretical concept and validated the *loose-as-a-goose* descriptor of their unit. This guy filled the bill with sandals and unrecognizable rank, crooked on his epaulet. And his uptight was outta-sight.

Trinh said, "Can I help you?" And backed through the door.

"Yes, I am Lieutenant Teo Nguyen, MACV, looking for newly arrived soldiers from Hon Heo. Am I in correct ward?" His exaggerated posture arched like a new drill instructor. He pronounced words with a northern intonation, an accent converting the *d* sound to the English *z*.

Trinh said, "I don't know who you're talking about." He put the tray next to the snoring Danny.

Teo pointed his pistol at Trinh. "You pig. These are the vaginal scabs I'm looking for..." The silencer popped four times into sleeping soldiers. They convulsed from the bullet's impact. Blood spattered on the wall. Teo's gun swung toward Trinh as the door behind him crashed into his back. A solid whack of metal against a body obstructed the shot that followed, destroying the pitcher next to Danny. Water gushed onto his head.

Pollhill lunged for the killer's gun, which went off again into the cabinet. Monster man knocked the gun from Teo's little hand, but the ARVN twisted around to deflect Pollhill's body into the bed fame. Teo then kicked the big soldier in the side of his helmet and laughed, breathing heavily. He looked at Trinh like a dog that caught a chicken. "Well, Comrade?"

Trinh asked, "What do you want with me?"

"You sniveling snake." Teo reached for his weapon when Pollhill's boot jammed into his kidney.

Teo's legs collapsed. He fell forward with his jaw open in pain.

Pollhill crammed the barrel of his .45 into Teo's mouth. "Who sent ya' here?"

The little soldier gagged on broken teeth and said, "Fuc...yo...GI."

Pollhill flicked him with his pistol and knocked Teo out for the bout. Man-mountain grabbed the little soldier like a bag of dirty laundry. "I'll take him outside where we can communicate better. You can tell the MP what happened but not where I went."

Trinh Le stood speechless as Pollhill walked out of Recovery with the little lieutenant over his shoulder. Seconds later Nurse Carol rushed in the other door. "Oh, my god, what's happened?"

"An assassin. Shot both soldiers. Tried to get Danny and me. GI you threw out saved our asses." Trinh trembled against the wall.

"I'll call the MP. Dr. Bromo is at a critical point in a procedure. I have to get back. This coin is for Hellberg." She tossed it on the bed and left.

Trinh rubbed the grime off the coin until the luster of gold appeared. The dull black center square of dried mud fell out and emphasized the well-worn Vietnamese figures. Bao Dai coins had been removed from circulation in 1951, seen now only in the Saigon museum.

An MP busted into the room with his pistol drawn. "Is everyone okay?"

Trinh Le gave him the whole story and said, "Guard Danny, I'll ask the tower to issue a security alert to the C123." He took the pouch and headed up the hall.

In the front office, Trinh opened the pouch and found two tattered pages entitled, *US Imperialists Face Military Defeat in South*

Vietnam, by General Van T... Water obliterated the corner of the page and rest of his name. The second page listed the fresh victories against the American military and announced the Triumvirate for a United Vietnam. Emperor Bao Dai, Le Van Vien, and Ho Chi Minh were defined by position.

The MP touched the paper. "What do the Chinese characters say?"

"They requested the addition of two maps." Tears welled up in Trinh's eyes. "Their valiant effort for Vietnam's freedom wobbles in mortal danger. They now shape the tombstone for its grave. Where did the gold piece come from? What did it have to do with Hon Heo? Why the NVA assassin?"

Fatty finally caught up with Trinh squeezed into the chair next to him. "So, who the fuck are you anyway? One of them CIA pricks?" His bulbous cheeks quivered as he spoke.

"Nah, just a translator prick."

Fatty smirked, "Find whatcha looking for? No one gets into the tower."

"What makes you think I can tell you? Do you really want to serve the rest of your tour as a forward observer, directing air strikes over the jungle? Of course, in order to do that you'd have to lose a hundred pounds of fat with a tasteless diet, daily exercises, and long runs. Now, which is the shortest way to the tower?"

Fatty's bloated eyes widened. "I'll tell 'em you're coming."

A grizzled Warrant Officer guarding the Qui Nhon tower verified Trinh Le's identification through the Saigon office. He looked over his glasses. "What the hell does MACV want now?"

Trinh smiled, "I never fail to take advantage of fame or terror that precedes me. About 25 minutes ago, a C123 departed to Vung Tau. Two critically wounded SOG team members were put on board. I want the aircraft commander notified of the assassination attempt. More may be planned in Vung Tau. Any off-loading should be scheduled only in a secure hangar."

Old grizzly's pug ears were blown back. "Yes, sir, we can make that contact."

Trinh addressed the two air controllers on duty. "Who took the message from Serpent?"

"Which one sir?"

"How many did you receive?"

Tower controller said, "A simple position identification and arrival estimate. Rolling Thunder came in and Serpent never showed up."

"How about you, Ground? Did Serpent say anything before he went down?"

"I didn't speak to Serpent at all."

"Who'd you speak to?"

"To the F100s sent to shoot 'em down."

Tower looked at them like they just crawled off a spaceship. "Why?"

"They got word Serpent was gonna attack Qui Nhon with nerve gas."

"Why didn't they get him?"

"The fighters intercepted a pitiful, shot-up helicopter making a SOS signal in Morse Code with a flashlight saying, 'No fuel. Damaged. First Cav' or something like that. Only two of the crew moved, two others looked dead. Then it dropped out of the sky. The fighter tried to light its landing. Almost made it too. Until it splattered like cow shit on tarmac. That's when they asked for the ready-rat-fuck."

"Any more wild-ass calls, just contact us." Trinh Le flicked a John Wayne-type salute at them.

At the hospital office, he found Fatty dozing. Trinh said, "Who gave the order to shoot down the helicopter?"

Fatty launched his gelatinous girth hard enough to knock his Coke into the potato chips. "Probably ARVNs."

"But normally, those calls come through me, because the G2 jackleg doesn't speak English well enough or think at all. Only someone damn near the top could scramble that kind of metal. Can I call MACV from here? Is the line secure?"

"Yes, sir...No, sir." Fatty's perspiration dripped down his neck. "I'll place the call from the Security office."

"OK. Where's it at?"

Fatty locked the front door and moved like a big, fat cloud down the hall into a dark, dank, windowless office. He got through the imbecilic maze of the G2 staff and landed at the adjutant, an energetic Lieutenant Colonel. Trinh summarized the situation with all its curious issues. He said, "So if we could find out who scrambled those jets, we might plug the lethal leak."

"But the pilot's the real story. Can you get him to talk?"

"Only if I can wake him up."

"Wasn't that why we invented water?"

AFTER RUNNING to the assembly cavern, the young villager rested on the blockade. She pointed at the gleaming new pipe coming through the pile of rubble. "What is this?"

When it stopped, Kaelyn pushed volcanic rocks and black sand away from it. "Why would they push this pipe in?"

The runner explored it with her flashlight. "Villagers say a pipe is only inserted in a house, or wall or a rice paddy in order to deliver something."

"What'll it carry down here?" Kaelyn touched the pipe. She gasped with surprise at the loose cap.

"They say smoke is used to chase bees away from the hive, and rats away from the house." The girl's eyes got larger with each word.

Kaelyn cringed. "Surely they wouldn't gas us? Would they? Or are they trying to listen? If it delivers, it can receive." She asked Minh, "Can you put someone next to this pipe to make a continuous noise?"

Minh nodded to an old woman, who led the choir in the church of Phu Cat. She knelt down and produced a rosary and rustled her beads on the pipe. And smiled. "I'll ask Mother Mary to help us. Hail

Mary full of grace, the Lord be with you..." Her voice resonated in the cave.

Kaelyn stepped in front of Minh. "In college I discovered the martial art of Jujitsu. It taught me to use my opponent's force against him."

His face wrinkled in confusion. "So?"

"They sent in the pipe; we'll use it first."

"And what do we have to deliver?" He scratched his head. "We have no way to blow smoke back at them."

"But we have bullets. We can't expect to stop their plan, but we can be like cockroaches. It's not what they eat but what they get into and mess up."

The young girl translated to the villagers, they all smiled and nodded.

Minh scanned the crowd and selected a woman with gloves then pointed to the man holding a rifle. He said, "My little cockroaches. First unscrew the cap very quietly, then fire a full clip in four bursts into the pipe. And quickly reattach the cap."

His two volunteers bubbled with excitement. The woman turned the cap for what seemed an intolerably long time. When she removed it, the man banged the AK muzzle against the pipe as he inserted it. The sound pierced everyone's attention, like the dinner bell ringing in a prison. He fumbled with the safety and the recoil from the first blast nearly tore the weapon out of his grip.

After the third burst, a muffled scream trickled from the pipe. The startled gunner did not waver and squeezed off his last burst. Villagers laughed and clapped as the lady reattached the cap. An ominous sensation silenced everyone watching.

Kaelyn said, "Are the satchel charges in place?"

"They're connected. If the blockade falls, they'll ignite the fuses. If that doesn't stop them, they light the fuel."

"Wait...why waste all hundred liters of fuel when we need it for the generator? It'll give us more hours of light."

Minh turned to the young runner. "Leave only one twenty-liter container. Take the balance to Phuong."

Kaelyn said, "Who will be here to lead them?"

The lady with the rosary said, "God will of course."

Minh slapped his chest. "And if he doesn't show up, I will."

Kaelyn inspected the last satchel charge jammed in a crack. She didn't know "come here" from "go sic 'em" about explosives.

A woman approached wearing ragged, black clothes, breathing hard, with sweat on face. "My name Binh Sang. I bring fuel."

"Where's Anh?"

"With fuel. Americans blow up. She dead."

"What Americans?"

"Please forgive, I jump ahead. After bring fuel, Phuong want more. But nothing to carry in. So, search tunnels and find some trapped."

"How many?"

"Six cans. When reach vent, guard caution about noise. Strange helicopters fly by waterfall and to Hon Heo. Until get shot..."

"From whom?"

Binh's dazed look slowed her speech, "From ridge. One helicopter fly away, while other shot outpost. They dropped a bomb on it."

"Then what?"

Binh rubbed her high cheekbone and flat nose. "As helicopters leave valley, shots come from bunker. Very strange. Two explosions stopped the bunker guns, but the helicopters bombed it. All fuel explode. I feel heat on my face."

Kaelyn paused. "Is that all?"

"Then the helicopters went straight out valley. I came back to assembly room. Phuong try make radio work. Only bad sounds. Little conversation."

"What did they say?"

Binh pulled her hair back. "Voice on radio said couldn't find vent shaft...stop for diarrhea...saw helicopters destroy the bunker...wiped squad out."

Kaelyn asked, "Is that all?"

Binh worried. "I can't remember..."

Minh stood dumbstruck. "If it is not one set of bastards, it's another. I wish they'd all go away. Anh was wonderful." His eyes teared. "Anh was a visitor to our village. Only few spoke English. We had a special bond."

Kaelyn returned to reality. "We have fuel for 21 hours of light. Will the Americans be here?"

"Yes, but now we can't escape because of the NVA on top."

"No. We've stopped this threat for the time being. I'll go with Binh to the assembly area and see if we can contact an American unit on Phuong's radio."

Binh shook her head, "Madame Kaelyn. I remember the soldier's words."

"What are they?"

"He wait in bamboo. Above bunker. I take you there. In trench." Her black teeth, dark eyes, and full eyebrows made a sober impression.

Kaelyn mused, "Gotta find that radio. Without being seen. I'll call Danny. If he made it back? If there was ever a lucky penny, he was it."

Binh led the way. Kaelyn could barely keep up. Her jungle fatigues hung out over her belt; the pant legs were no longer bloused over her boots. She asked, "How did you find the trench?"

"Bring water to guards and workers." Binh did not slow her pace.

Kaelyn looked from side to side. "This is a steep climb."

"Yes, but climbing not worst part."

"What was?" Kaelyn wished she had a notebook.

"The guards. Raped me."

This image took the air out of Kaelyn's stream of questions.

Binh didn't blink. "In bunker. Every day. Every way. Every one."

Silence prevailed for the rest of the climb. As they entered the assembly area, Phuong approached Kaelyn. "Did sister tell you about the conversation we overheard?"

Kaelyn said, "Yes. We're ready to find that soldier and the radio. Do you have weapons?"

Phuong showed the assembly table. "Does a tiger have teeth?"

Both Kaelyn and Binh selected an AK47. As they climbed to the vent shaft, Kaelyn asked, "I didn't realize Phuong was your brother."

"Not related."

"Why did he call you sister?"

"My title in Order. Was Carmelite nun." Binh's voice choked up. Tears flooded her eyes.

Kaelyn embraced her. "That must have been hell."

Binh's whole body convulsed with each sob. She buried her head on Kaelyn's shoulder. "I hate my body. I hate the smell of them. On me. In me." She spoke in a hoarse whisper. "They turn me into animal. I kill like animal. Not sorry." She straightened up. "Thank you."

She crossed herself and chambered a round.

PART NINE_

IN THE AIR VENT SHAFT, Binh perched at the edge of a rock. She listened to an alert and nervous guard. He took serious pride with his report, for a twelve-years-old, at 80 pounds soaking wet.

She translated, "He heard a strange voice from the bamboo patch."

Kaelyn wondered aloud, "What'll hc do if thc NVA find this entrance?"

"I instructed him to move into his hiding hole and let them pass. Then he'll pull the pin on his grenade, toss it down the shaft and cover his ears."

Kaelyn grabbed her arm. "What happens if we want to come back? What's his name?"

"He's called Nien. The only thing he can say in English is, 'Ho Chi Minh is fuckin' asshole.'" Binh didn't smile. She opened the grate hidden between boulders and bushes.

Kaelyn blinked her eyes to adjust to the morning sunlight. She crawled past the bloated body of Colonel Bobson and fought the urge to throw up. Massive craters from the B-52 bombing were separated by body parts and uniform fragments: a scene from hell to make the reporter wish for a recorder.

Binh inspected every piece of debris she crawled over in the trench. Just short of the bunker ruins, the charred remains of a soldier laid clutching a burnt rifle and a headless body sprawled in a running position.

Near the top, Kaelyn heard a male voice sing a simple melody, crying each word. "Where is that coming from? What does it mean?"

Binh frowned. "He sing happy children's song but sound like funeral. He asks flock of white birds...flying in 'V'...to meet after school."

"If he's the radio operator, what do we do?"

Binh looked ahead. "All I know...we continue. When find him, figure out."

The trench flattened out with less rubble, more green bushes, and deep grass. A dense patch of ferns limited their view through the bamboo. No sign of the radio operator. Strong shore breezes changed to a westerly wind carrying the putrid smell of rotting flesh.

Someone vomited with intermittent moans. All of nature's pleasant sounds stopped. Binh pointed across the slope. They circled around the 15-meter crater gouged out of the earth. Shell casings and empty beer bottles blanketed the ground.

Kaelyn gagged at the stench of the bodies strewn inside. Their contorted faces showed life's last pain. All with hands tied behind and a bullet hole in the forehead. Dried blood and flies covered everything above the water.

Binh crossed herself. "These were my friends. They escaped after the US paratroopers killed the guards. The NVA waited until the Americans left and rounded up every runaway with lies about forgiveness. We hid below the grate and heard their screams. Shooting silenced everything."

The loud agony of dry heaves led them a soldier on his hands and knees. His rifle leaned against the radio. Binh kicked him in the head. He flopped over on his back, spread eagle. His cries were almost screams.

She slapped his face. "Remember, you told me—don't dare make a noise." Her Vietnamese no longer had the melodic, sing-song tone but the guttural, condescension of a victor over a hapless prey. Slobber slid on his sweaty chin. She jabbed him with the rifle barrel. "When will the patrol get here?"

"How should I know?" Heavy mucous congealed on his eyes.

Binh smashed the pointed edge of the rifle butt into his chest. "I don't believe you, little pig. When will they come?" His mouth stretched open with no sound. He shook his head. She rammed the muzzle into his chest deep enough to break bones and draw blood.

Kaelyn shuddered at the sight of him squirming in silent pain. She winced with each blow and froze when bones broke.

He spewed an acidic condemnation that Kaelyn did not understand. His laugh carried a haunting squeal until Binh drove the rifle butt into the bridge of his nose and then his testicles.

Kaelyn didn't move.

Neither did Little Piggy.

Binh gasped for breath. "They called him 'Little Pig.' Always the last one to get me and the most sadistic." Her sobs broke out while she translated his last words. "He said, 'They be here soon and fuck you again.'"

Kaelyn removed his pistol belt and ammo pouch. The Beretta had 'Delta 229' painted in blue on its holster. The radio blasted in Vietnamese faster than she could understand.

Binh held up her palm. In a weak voice she broadcasted, "I sick... dying." For a long time after, her finger held the frequency open with her heavy breathing.

The radio blared again, and she translated, "Little Pig. We'll be there soon. Hold on."

Kaelyn raised both hands. "I must contact the Americans." She searched the channels for twenty minutes with no response. "When I watched Z, he used frequencies out of the folder around his neck. I'll check the bag, you search Piggy."

Binh handled Piggy like a bag of manure. He moaned through

the blood bubbles in his mouth. She removed an oil cloth with a soiled sheet of hand-printed numbers.

Kaelyn inspected the list. "Only one from this bunch of acronyms sounds familiar. She dialed it, "App Con this is Kaelyn, can you hear me?"

A booming voice returned. "Go ahead Kaelyn, this is Qui Nhon Approach Control. I read you four by."

"What's that mean?"

"I hear you very clear. Who are you? Over."

"Oh, shit. Only one person knows who I am. A helicopter pilot. He should've got back last night or early this morning. His helicopter had its landing legs shot off. Did he make it?" She kept the transmit button down, discovered it and said, "Shit . . . over."

"Yep. You do and you'll have to clean it up. He ran out of fuel and crashed. Ready reaction force retrieved three."

"Pilot's name was Danny. Special ops types were Z and Krotch. Find them." She held the button too long again, "Goddamn it...over."

"Where ya' located?"

"He knows—with prisoners from the village. NVA's killed many...trackin' us down in the cave—"

Then the battery went dead.

"Sealord Two-Six this is Three. Say location, over."

"This is Two-Six. About two zero clicks west of target one. Over."

"First Flight reported an unidentified sea plane at 0910 hours docking in the target zone. Over."

"So?"

"Go sic 'em. Out."

The Swift Boat crew chief said, "What in the hell is Ops talking about?"

"We're playing some games because we think we got friends listening." Two-Six brought in max throttle. "I want everyone with a pot, vest, and their eyeballs peeled. Man the M60, MG Combo mount and the M79. Three of those little islands ten minutes ahead."

As the chief left the cabin, a young seaman bounced in, "Unidentified aircraft east bound, low level at 10 o'clock, sir."

"What do you mean, unidentified?"

"Profile unknown. No tail or wing number. But it got floats."

Two-Six grabbed the microphone. "Bogie at 10 o'clock, low level, east bound, 300 meters. Sixty, open up. Stand by Fifty. Eighty-one, gimme airbursts north of him."

Sixty led the aircraft a little too high on the first burst, way ahead on the second but nailed it on the third. The aircraft turned a hard left from the Swift but met the three airbursts to which it reacted with a sharp chandelle back at the boat.

"Everyone, open up, open up."

Coming at 100 feet over water, the bogie sent a line of machine gun fire splashing a path to the boat. Fifty responded with direct hits to the pontoons and wing structure. The second

burst struck the engine and blew off the right cowling. A hard left exposed the plane's tender underbelly to a free-for-all. Smoke streamed from the engine; one of the pontoons dangled from the strut. Every crew member shouted, hooted, and hollered.

Two-Six said, "Reload. Get ready for his buddy." The crew watched the wounded aircraft fly toward the little island, until a rocket exploded so close to the ship the water plume fell on the cabin. "Return fire. Goddamn it." Fifty kicked in as a second explosion came close enough to rip the bumper tire off the side and fling it up on the antenna stack behind the bridge. Through the falling water and bouncing tires, Fifty nailed the aircraft and exploded its rocket on launch. The aircraft limped toward the shore.

"Hold your fire. Reload. Find the first aircraft." Two-Six turned to Radio, "Call Three to intercept that straggler headed north."

The Swift approached the lonely little island and paralleled the shoreline. A long expanse of pristine white beach had a row of bright green vegetation and a line of anemic yellow bushes. The tallest point on the cay rose to no more than four meters high. Not even a bird flew near it.

"Chief, I want one set of eyes to our rear, one to check out the beach and another to focus on the vegetation. We'll circle the island." Two-Six goosed the river boat to a high gallop around the rocky point then slowed to a crawl. With his binoculars, he studied the landscape.

"Two-Six, somethin's weird here. That rocky point is where Swift 88 tied up when they fried their engine last month. Like a bunch of idiots, they reconnoitered this entire piece of dirt while they waited for us. The chief of 88 called it a desert island."

"You sure this is the place?"

"Damn right. Look at the big rock for the outline of a hand giving you the finger."

"Oh, yea, a regular Picasso. Okay, so how did all this vegetation grow so fast?"

"That's just it. Like sticking feathers in horseshit, man, it won't fly."

"Shit yeah. Make it burn." Two-Six put the coals to it and the boat nose rose above the water. Sound of a big diesel winding up and the outbound fire from the 81 made him feel good. Within three shots they hit the jack pot with several secondary explosions.

"Bingo. Something beautiful's there." Two-Six stretched his Boston accent so long it almost broke.

Chief shouted, "I saw the tail move."

"Great catch. Cease fire. Reload. Radio, ask Three for an air strike there. Tell 'em we're chasing a piece of tail." Two-Six pushed the throttle to the stops. He just loved the full blast of wind in his face, a clear day and a beautiful blue sea. "Chief, this is a duplicate picture. Constructed from the same plan. With the same dead bushes. If anybody sees anything, shoot it."

Two shots from the 81mm got the backbone, then five more hit pay dirt. Everyone shouted in triumph at the sight of flames blossoming underneath thick, black smoke. "Sixty, prep the rock area, too many straight lines there."

The first machinegun burst got one in return, only twice as long. Bullets riddled the bow of the Swift and the armor around the M60. "Fifty, return that fire. We're in range." Fifty silenced the annoyance before the shells hit the floor.

The Swift cruised around the corner for the first view of the seaplane. It floated on the water, trying to get flight RPM. Two-Six lathered with excitement at the sight, "Cease fire. Sixty, I want you to work the vegetation over to keep their heads down. Fifty, shoot the goddamn engines off. Either one of them, I don't care. Try not to kill 'em. I want 'em alive. That's the biggest damn float plane I ever saw."

Fifty's first burst showed tracers about three feet above the protruding nose cone of the

turboprop. The second burst knocked blades off both engines simultaneously.

"Damn, that is some kind of shootin'. Why'd ya' waste our taxpayer's money with the first four shitty shots?" Two-Six drew a single-fingered salute from Fifty with a grin.

The unmistakable screams of a rocket about to impact paralyzed Two-Six. It hit twenty yards away. A second explosion whipped the boat from four yards off the nose. "That water plume bastard's damn-near above us." Machine-gun fire splashed in front then ripped up the deck and cabin. Two-Six dove with his M16, landed on his back and emptied a full magazine at the diving plane. He rotated the three bundle. When a rocket landed directly into Sixty, the nose of the Swift blew up, Sixty's body parts skipped on the water. Debris landed everywhere.

Fifty laid face-down on the floor against the back rail. Two-Six shouted, "Radio, tell Three what happened. If you can't get through, do a May Day. Front superstructure should hold for a little, drive it onto that beach. I'm on the fifty."

He swung his attention back to the propeller-less monster off the beach, aimed the 81mm and pulled the lanyard, "Bye, bye asshole." The classic, hollow *thunk* sound of a mortar delivered a wicked hit to the front crew section. He delighted in the expansive ferocity of a high explosive shell. The front cabin windscreens blew forward followed by the yellow belch of flame, "You got to love this shit."

Two-Six watched the delicious destruction of the aircraft but came back to reality by their slow bumpy crawl onto the beach. "I don't know why we're still afloat. Looks like someone chewed the nose off this bitch. Aim for those shipping containers on the beach. With the First Cav horse blanket painted on the side. I'll be dipped in shit. What is this?"

Radio received a call then put down the receiver. "Three scrambled some Navy birds our way." The disabled Swift lurched to a stop.

Two-Six said, "Kill the engine, get low, be less of a target."

Camouflage netting festooned with plant branches, grass and leaves draped over endless rows. The shipping containers marked with US ARMY, NAVY, AIR FORCE and MARINE CORPS. Sizes ranged from the standard 24-feet long to the big boys he had only heard about. Many were open with everything imaginable exposed. Cooking pots, boxes of M60 ammunition, long wooden crates of rifles, cartons of jungle fatigues, canned peaches, cases of coffee, and a hospital gurney on top of C Rations. "This is a goddamn black-market depot. Tell Three."

With the engine off, Two-Six heard the sound of the waves of the South China Sea gently lapping against the hull and smelled the fishy beach. The land mass in front of him looked more menacing than it did from offshore. With all this material here, there has to be someone around to guard it. Not only from prying eyes and guns of US military, but also from thieving hands of the locals.

The boat had not yet sunk. "Let's get the hell out of here. Perils of the ocean are better than being overrun by gooks." Two-Six flicked the safety off and held the M16 ready. He walked backward to the bridge. "Start it up. Gently pull us off the beach. Hope we got an inflatable raft somewhere. I'll get on the fifty."

Radio moved it backward. "Hold it, listen. A turboprop. It's that goddamn Plume Devil again. Get us off the beach."

"Don't turn it around, there's less pressure on whatever is keeping us afloat." The whistling sound of a pair of rockets hit where they parked a half a minute ago. Mud, stones and seaweed splattered the deck. Two-Six found the amphibian bearing down on them. "The prick's coming right out of the sun." He held a steady stream of fire at a steep angle. The amphibian turned away again.

A hand fell on Two-Six's shoulder. Fifty said, "Let me shoot, damn it. Find something else to do." Fifty wobbled as he got on the seat. The Plume Devil strafed the ship and knocked the door off the cabin. With his dive lower than before, he exposed a wide profile out of the sun. "Perfect." He fired three bursts. "Yahoo, got a little piece that time." Plume Devil flew out of range again.

About forty yards back on shore, a lone soldier shot at the boat with a bolt-action rifle. He fired a second shot short and sprayed water on the hull. Two-Six fired a burst from his M16. Sand splattered up to the side of the shooter. He resolutely chambered another round, but nothing happened. He ejected that round and tried again with no result. He threw the rifle into the water and ran back to the safety of the containers.

Two-Six squeezed the trigger of the M16 only to hear the barren click of an empty chamber. "You lucky shit," and threw a half-assed salute to the soldier that just dodged death.

Lieutenant Lin laid on the dock, his head throbbed in rhythm with the waves breaking against the mooring. With great effort he staggered toward to the abandoned beach. He would never forgive Colonel Bay cold-cocking him and taking away his guide from the village.

Three wooden cases remained where they were off-loaded from the plane. One contained gas masks, next had bottles of bleach, and the third syringes with a small tube attached for self-inoculation of the VX antidote drug. Lin realized the possible danger overlooked: both the masks and antidote auto-injectors should have accompanied the gas cylinders in the tunnel. He grabbed two masks and a pocket full of injectors and ran to the cavern.

The masks in hand troubled him. Death followed a gas attack in minutes. His father's plan to wipe out the prisoners had critical strategic implications. No risk could be taken—he stopped to auto-inject himself through his pants into his calf. Then slipped on his mask.

Lin felt like the mask would drown him in perspiration by the time he caught up with his father in front of the tank.

With a look of profound disappointment, the General motioned

Lin to silence and to remove the mask. Lin tried in vain to loosen the straps holding the mask in place.

The *a cappella,* ritual Vietnamese chant of the rosary drifted from the pipe, like a siren's call to lonely sailors. The soldier at the opening said, "I can hear them wailing and tapping to a sad rhythm." He smiled. "Dumb bastards."

General Danh signaled for quiet to his men. "What do you mean tapping?" He pointed to the pipe rammed into the blockade. "Listen."

"They know the end is near, it's their processional dirge." The General's laugh echoed in the cave, while he blew smoke rings toward the pile. To his horror, the ring no longer stayed in the still of the cavern but got sucked into the pipe. He shouted, "Shoooot."

The soldier listening at the pipe turned his eyes to the General as the first burst of bullets blew through his nose, cheek, and head. His body flopped on the ground without a face. Blood splattered on the general, teeth bounced along the ground. Shooting stopped as fast as it started. Lin froze for a moment as the unbelievable happened in front of him. He turned and ran behind the tank.

"Return fire," the General pulled a scared shooter in front of the hole. As the rifleman stuck his muzzle of into the pipe, the second burst of fire knocked the rifle out of his hand and ripped through the bandolier across his chest. His body jerked back into the gas cylinders. More bullets from the pipe tore the pin off one of the stick grenades and ignited its fuse. Its explosion blew away the valves of the nerve gas. Upended canisters rocketed toward the rear of the tank, rebounded off its armor, and filled the tunnel with fumes.

General Danh, Lieutenant Pin and the shooter died from the first grenade. Behind the tank, the decimated remnants of the NVA 22nd Regiment waited stoically in reserve. The tank engine at maximum rpm muffled the detonation of the grenade. Both canisters of gas vented in seconds and sounded more like the whistle on a boiling teapot.

Lin left the mask on and ran to the rear as the odorless, tasteless liquid with the texture of motor oil turned into gas. It enveloped the crowded tunnel and caverns. Runny nose, nausea, vomiting, tightness of the chest and shortness of breath hit everyone at once. Loss of consciousness followed with contractions and a sustained paralysis of the diaphragm. Death came by asphyxiation.

The soldiers in formation behind the tank stood firm until their pupils pinpointed. Lin evaded the groping hands of the dying and ran to the water.

Trinh found the statuesque Carol Washington working in the recovery room. He repeated what he needed, "Danny is the only one who knows what happened on that damn mission. Wake him up."

Major Washington took a long look at Trinh and picked up the pitcher of water, poured about a half a glass. "The correct medical procedure is to make your trajectory enter his nasal passage with enough velocity to hit his sinuses." She flicked the water with at least ninety percent on target, the rest on Trinh.

"God damn it. What the hell you doing?" Danny propped himself on his elbows. He turned his head and stopped at Carol's cleavage.

"Up here lieutenant, I'm Major Washington."

"I don't give a shit who you are...ya' smell good. Wherever you are."

Trinh smiled like a snake. "How are you feeling?"

Danny's face showed the furrows of pain. "Head's killing me. Back hurts. Neck is stiff as my pecker. Yep, just peachy, ma'am." His glazed eyes looked around until he found Trinh. With an open-mouthed grin, he said, "Where do I know you from?"

"In Saigon. You and your buddies helped me escape from a

psycho in my store. I'm with MACV now, translating for the G2. But let's cut the bullshit. Tell me about your mission."

"What do you mean—where am I anyway?"

"Lieutenant," Major Washington softened her voice as she inspected his face. "You're in the Qui Nhon field hospital."

"Oh," Danny soured his face. "I'm in the hospital?"

"Forget the hospital, you're safe here. Talk about the mission."

Danny rubbed his cheek while he looked up. "When the Shit Hook got us out, they circled offshore. Waiting for the grunts on the beach...Z and Krotch dying...had to get 'em to the hospital...they all right?" He looked at the Major again. "Where are they? And, where am I?"

She said, "Right now they're headed to Japan. They're messed up, so we sewed up the empty spots, immobilized the rest. Got them juiced up so they wouldn't mind." She poured another glass of water.

Danny picked up his fist in self-defense. "I'm up already."

"Okay. This one's for me." She chugged the water. "You don't know how lucky you are." Carol stuck her finger in the bullet hole in the wall above his head. "This was for you."

Danny didn't move. "What do you mean?"

"After Z and Krotch were taken to their flight, Medivac brought a load of wounded from the ready reaction force. Three were critical and went directly to the OR, two others came in here to wait their turn. With that same load, an old friend of yours by the name of Poll-hill came in looking for you."

"He's a nutcase."

"Yeah, but this time he saved your ass."

Danny yawned again as his head drooped. "I'll bet he didn't plan it that way."

Trinh looked at Carol. "What's the matter with him. He acts completely different than the guy I met in Saigon. He fell asleep again."

"Look at those bags under his eyes, and his irritability, confusion, excessive yawning." She lifted his shaking hand. "And his tremors. Classic signs of sleep deprivation."

Trinh's voice grew louder, "Get him up. I have to talk, now."

"I'll try," she gently stroked his forehead and whispered into his ear, "Get up sweetheart. Please." She rolled him on his back.

"Okay. Okay. I'm up. Man o' man, you really smell good. Where's Pollhill?" Danny babbled with two-handed gestures.

Trinh grabbed Danny's neck. "He's outside the hospital somewhere helping the NVA to remember who sent him."

"Why did Krotch want you to have this?" Trinh put the pouch on the bed.

"What is it?" Danny's eyes were heavy, his speech slurred.

"It contained these gold coins. And pages about the political and military failure of the US in South Vietnam. He didn't say anything?"

"Man, no chit-chat..." Danny nodded.

Trinh went nose-to-nose. "Tell me anything you can about that mission."

Danny's eyes wandered. "After the mountain blew up, Kaelyn stayed on Hon Heo...for a damn story...villagers in a cave. Cong had helicopters...shot us up...we shot 'em down. Ha."

"Why did ya' go there? What happened to Doan Vien?"

"Big meeting...Doan's a traitor, got killed." Danny fell back to sleep.

Carol Washington put her arm in front of Trinh. "He's exhausted."

"Who in the goddamn hell is this Kaelyn?" Trinh grabbed Danny's shirt. "What does she have to do with anything?"

"Her daddy a sen..."

Carol loosened Trinh's grip and pushed him away. "Let him go. He gotta sleep."

"A sen? What the hell's a sen?"

Carol pulled the sheet up Danny's chest. "Her name rhymed. Kaelyn DeHaven. Her father's a US Senator. She's a newspaper reporter. Came to interview doctors, nurses, patients, anyone who would talk to her. Pushy as hell. Subtle as whooping cough."

Trinh scratched his impeccably groomed head, then patted it back. "I keep asking myself why did they go to Hon Heo? I remember the cave. Spooky as a graveyard. Doan a traitor? Can't believe it. Who scrambled the jets? Man, had to be way up at MACV."

"The top, *Kemosabe*." A low voice took the air out of the room. Trinh and Carol Washington almost jumped out or their skin. She sauntered to Pollhill in the doorway. Through clenched teeth she asked, "Oh god, you're back?"

"I came in at Hon Heo and the Cong helicopters, ma'am." Pollhill had his helmet under his arm this time.

"Where's the NVA?" Trinh watched Pollhill lean his M16 against the wall.

"He had a heart attack. Damnedest thing I ever saw. Shit happens." Pollhill swung his head from side to side in a shallow expression of fabricated grief.

"Died on the operating table, eh?" Major Washington glanced at Trinh, "Did he have any parting thoughts other than wondering when the lights would go out?"

"As a matter of fact, he mentioned a general by the name of Gwan or Dawn, famous sapper, who had a mistress in Saigon. She first worked for President Diem's brother and now is an assistant to an ARVN General. He has insatiable needs in addition to his principal duty as liaison to MACV."

"Sounds like General Danh, the commander of the First Sappers." Trinh shook his head. "I still don't see the connection."

The recovery doors flew open into Pollhill's back with a loud crack. He dove to the floor and he drew his pistol to a dead bead on the fat man in the doorway. Fatty farted. Pollhill murmured, "Ya' shoulda knocked."

"No, sir. Yes, sir. I mean..." He watched Pollhill holster his pistol. "App Con received another 'wild ass call' for the MACV gook, I mean for you sir." He blushed while Trinh bristled.

"Okay, where is the phone? Do we need a secure line again?"

"Yes, sir, right this way." Fatty led Trinh down the corridor to the secure office.

"Okay, App Con, this is your favorite MACV gook...what happened?"

After a gulp of breath, he said, "About 10 minutes ago, I got this strange call from some girl. American. Bad radio procedures. Over as quick as it started. Just another wild-ass call. So here I am."

Trinh pulled out his note paper and pen. "Now tell me every word you remember."

Another gulp. "Well sir. She identified herself as Kaelyn. Only the helicopter pilot named Danny would know her. Went with villagers in a cave. Hunted down by the NVA."

"Then what?"

"Then she said, 'oh, shit' and the transmission stopped. Couldn't bring her up after that."

"Thanks. Keep me posted." Trinh released the phone to Fatty. "Okay, get the G2 on the line again."

Connections this time didn't work well. Trinh's wounded shoulder burned with pain, exacerbated by another thirty minutes wasted.

The affable adjutant painted a different picture. "She actually is a person of tactical importance to us. If she got captured or killed, the shit would overwhelm the fan. The paper she represents is important nationally, and her father is the biggest hawk in Washington. Even MACV thinks it is important now."

Bingo, the dots connected for Trinh Le. "Goddamn."

The adjutant said, "Get him up again. If he was the last one to see her, he has a better chance of finding her than anyone else."

"But he's a basket case. He can't keep his mind on track. I'll check with the nurse."

"Fuck the nurse. When I rustle up a team to go in there, I'll be knocking on your door."

The nice-guy image of the adjutant morphed into the victory-at-all-costs, general-in-waiting mode. "Keep Danny Boy under guard. Stay with him at all times. They'll come back."

"Yes, sir, standing by."

"And if all goes down the tube, you gotta carry the ball." He laughed and hung up the phone.

"'Fuck the ball." Trinh held the phone next to his ear, while he considered what the adjutant said. Until he heard another solitary click on the line.

Vuong hated the sea. Waves were too rough for fishing. As a sleeper for the KGB, he enjoyed this tiny village on the South China Sea. In less than a year, he married Quy and worked for her father, who moved Viet Cong supplies along the coast. Both of his junks were sunk by American aircraft, killing the crews including her father. Then his beautiful Quy was killed by the devil, Lieutenant Lin Danh.

Colonel Bay steered the boat straight to the small island. He scanned the horizon with his binoculars for the requested docking instructions. Bay fired up the engine and ran the dingy onto the beach. "The aircraft will land in front of us, use this boat to board with Mr. Van Vien. Then bring it back to this beach. Our gun emplacement will shoot you if you get in the way of our departure."

Vuong bowed. The pitiful sand bar had dead elephant grass and palm branches entwined into the large rope nets. A simple camouflage over shipping containers, stretched as far as he could see. He played dumb. "What is this?"

Bay enjoyed the moment. "Might be the largest stockpile of US military equipment in Vietnam. Hid in the open, right under the nose of the American pigs."

The noise of the approaching amphibian obliterated conversation as the radio blared, "Bravo Echo 6...landing to the south." The huge, gull wing aircraft landed with an enormous splash. The wake almost rocked Vuong out of his boat.

Colonel Bay smiled at Le Van Vien. "The gigantic, twin oval tails resemble a monster coming home to its lair. Truly a Russian achievement. BE6, the attack amphibian." Bay glided the boat under the high wing and bounced against the airframe at an open door.

Vuong stabilized the connection while the old man and Colonel Bay climbed aboard. The Colonel pointed to the shore and dismissed Vuong.

Thunder belched from the monster aircraft as it left and the backdraft pushed the dingy right onto the beach. In a matter of seconds, the lumbering giant lifted out of the water in a gentle turn where it gained altitude like an obese, homesick angel.

Machine gun fire shredded the mystical feeling. BE6 fired its guns at a curious, squat military gunboat, which fired back. The amphibian broke away from the fight with smoke and fire billowing from one of its engines.

Out of nowhere, another amphibian dove into the action with rockets and machine guns against the little gunboat. The wounded aircraft circled back to shore. It taxied in the protection of the cay, fire from its engine dripped onto the water.

The stubby boat's machine gun and cannon raked the island causing several secondary explosions. With Colonel Bay's binoculars, Vuong saw a US flag flying as its shallow hull bounced off the waves like a river boat. He hid the dingy and watched. This little gun boat destroyed the attack amphibian like a wounded animal in a cage.

Vuong exchanged fire with the stubby boat and escaped in the opposite direction. His only desire was to kill Lieutenant Danh. But first he had to save him. Only a few clouds danced in the sky, while a brisk breeze on his back gave him an overwhelming desire to kill. The hour it took to find the village felt like five.

A very angry Lieutenant Danh stomped back and forth in front of his men. Vuong drove the hull onto the beach. With great patience, he told the Lieutenant all that happened. He presented him with Colonel Bay's binoculars, which acted like a soothing salve on a painful wound. The greedy bastard caressed its shiny leather case and wiped mist from the eyepiece.

Lin winced as he turned his swollen head. "Bay was an arrogant ass. He deserved it. My father warned him." Telling the catastrophe in the cave and his near-death experience invigorated Lin. "I ran straight into the water. I am now in charge. How long will it take us to get up the hill?"

Vuong lied, "Probably five hours."

"Let's go. I will lead. Tell me the shortest way."

"No disrespect intended, sir." He drew a deep breath and swallowed hard. "Villagers called this precipice the 'Rock Face of Dead Men' for good reason." Vuong recounted his last climb up. "The sergeant-in-charge slipped to his death with two of the village porters. Two other soldiers survived because they climbed only on natural footholds." He looked up. "If I don't lead, you'll die. There is no path. This is not a hill; this is a cliff. We climb; we don't walk."

Lieutenant Danh said, "Our search of the shoreline and the all-night vigil has left me famished, we must find food."

Vuong's opportunity glowed. "Please, come to my humble home away from the village." The soft white sand on the beach made the long trek from the water more difficult. As he drew closer to his hut, he heard noise through the cloth over the window. "Sir, no one should be inside."

Lieutenant Danh dispatched the two senior men with their guns drawn to investigate. They called out, "Who goes there?" and awaited the answer in defensive positions. After the third call, a weak voice said, "Something wrong here."

Danh stepped in front of his soldiers. "This is Lieutenant Danh, show yourselves."

The voice wheezed, "We can't move. The curse is real. Hon ma warned us."

"What curse?" Danh's condescending smile showed little concern.

"When we returned, the other soldiers were lying on the ground, shaking like a crushed dog and gasping for air. And not a shot was fired. Not one empty cartridge on the ground."

The realization came to Danh. "It's the gas." Then he spoke louder to the closed hut. "How did you survive?"

The winded, hoarse voice said, "In Hospital, sergeant ordered all those that could walk to follow the tank. Four of us were assigned to dispose of waste down the beach. When we returned, the sergeant lay on the ground with a terrible look on his face. Like he was possessed. He waved us away. All those who remained in the hospital died. In a very noisy place, it was deadly still."

"What about those in the cave?"

"At the mouth of the cavern, I heard the awful moans. Bodies moved like worms in a bucket. On the beach we rolled in the sand and crawled to the water. Then we vomited. Our eyes look strange. Tiny. Breathing is hard. We cannot stand. Our legs shake. Help us. Please."

"I will burn incense and recite the *cau chu* incantations to repel the evil spirits. Try to sleep. In the morning go back to the sea. You will stay alive."

"Pleeeaaase. Please help us...please." The voice faded.

Danh looked at Vuong. "Find another hut, keep the breeze in our face. By evening they will be dead."

Initially, Danh's sensitivity to his men's pain impressed Vuong, but then he realized it was only a meaningless appeasement. It steeled his resolve, he had to find a way to make him pay.

They walked into the wind where the palm trees grew close to the water, next to the big rock. The remnants of the burned helicopter lay broken in two, its big blades jutted out of the water, an acrid stench of bodies rotting in the sun pervaded the area.

Past the cove, farthest from the village, there was a single hut on stilts, with a long front porch. Its side walls were made from bamboo bundles, latched to heavier logs with a roof of thatched grass.

Vuong faced Danh. "Koon Sa lives here. He lays around and smokes whacky weed whenever he can find it. Without it, he is bad tempered, foul mouthed and violent. With the weed, he smiles all the time. He had a wonderful garden."

Danh motioned to his men to secure the hut. The more senior one climbed the high steps with caution. As his foot touched the porch, the front door exploded. Knocked him backward to the beach; death was instant. The body twitched as it lay, with parts of his uniform burning, his neck broken.

Vuong, Danh, and the three remaining soldiers flattened themselves on the beach and missed the explosion. "Enough, enough. We will not bother with any more of these huts." Danh brushed sand and door splinters from his clothes. "Go to his garden to find some food."

They settled behind the trees with coconuts for nourishment and drink. With the soldier's droopy eyelids and Danh's persistent yawn, Vuong hoped this might be his opportunity to kill them all. One after the other nodded off from total exhaustion, they slept like the drugged.

Unfortunately, so did Vuong.

MORE THAN AN HOUR elapsed before static crackled to wake Lieutenant Danh. "Get up. Get up. This mission is cursed. Vuong, carry the radio and show us the way."

Vuong led them behind the village of Thanh Ha, along a massive base pile of loose rock. Sheer limestone of the cliff stretched for hundred meters into the sky. He said, "Welcome to the Rock Face of Dead Men."

"I don't give a shit about dead men." Perspiration beaded on Danh's face as he looked up. "Where do we start?"

"You are standing in front of it, Lieutenant." Vuong pointed at the space between two giant slabs of rock. "We must follow these fissures to reach the first path. Then it gets a bit easier."

"You are out of your fuckin' mind. I'm *not* a mountain monkey."

"Fine sir. Then we must travel along the beach to the next village of Vinh Hoi then back up the mountain. We would be vulnerable for much of the way. If we walk fast, we'll be lucky to be there in twelve hours."

A blank look overwhelmed Lieutenant Danh's boyish features. With his new binoculars, he searched the cliffs toward Vinh Ha. "But there is nothing to grab onto for the climb. What do we do with our packs and weapons?"

Vuong studied the terrified expressions of the three men looking straight up. "The chute has notches to use as steps. Secure everything so you can use both hands. And don't look down."

Danh swallowed hard. "Let's go." Everyone cinched clothes, secured backpacks, strapped weapons, and double knotted boots. The Lieutenant stayed last in line.

Vuong planned to out-pace the soldiers and ambush them near the top. The width of the chute varied from three feet wide to a mere eighteen inches. Sun blistered the climbers, perspiration flowed. Irregularity of the rocks tested arm and leg muscles. The soldiers struggled to keep pace with their heavy packs. At the first change of direction, they called for help. He said, "Prop your feet against one side and your back against the other. Walk your shoulders up."

Near the top, Vuong climbed onto a wide ledge adjacent to the fissure. Several meters away, a big white bird sat on a branch watching his every move. A smelly nest occupied most of the space and made him gag. He pushed the loose branches aside and unfolded the scarf that held the .38 against his back. Its burnt grip filled his small hand.

In the chute below, the soldier looked feverishly for a foothold. Vuong held his breath to steady his shaking hand and squeezed the trigger. It sounded like the loudest click in the world. Like a hammer the size of Saigon crashing onto a giant drum of Vietnam. No one looked up to see the stupid, would-be killer who couldn't get the gun to shoot. He squeezed it three more times. Nothing. The soldier in the chute belly-ached at the unrelenting difficulty of the climb and ignored all noise.

Sweat dripped from Vuong's forehead, over his brows onto the barrel of the gun. His head sunk to the side in total despair. Failure accosted him from every side, first failing to protect his wife, now unable to kill her killers. A low, slow moan crept out of his lips. He heard the soldier's loud, almost out-of-control breathing. Everything below beaconed him: the tiny huts, beautiful white beach, and heavenly blue water of the South China Sea. How simple it would be to roll off this ledge and end all this pain.

A large, black spider with red stripes and thick furry legs moved toward him on the wall of the chute. Long sleek eyes bulged on a wedge-shaped head. Vuong pulled a stick from the nest. He gently poked, but it jumped directly at his face. His reflexes knocked it down the crevice.

"Aaaaah yaa. Spider." The first soldier lost footing as he tried to disentangle himself and slid down on top of the second soldier, who then catapulted away from the cliff. Lieutenant Danh flattened himself as both bodies fell screaming to the base. The Rock Face of Dead Men struck again.

Vuong could not believe his eyes. Both soldiers sprawled face down on the rocks below. Dead still. He leaned down as far he could, but the chute disappeared when it changed directions. "Lieutenant Danh, where are you?" Several times the call was made with no response. The revolver still felt good in his hand as it protruded over the edge. He spun the cylinder just to hear it turn.

Danh shouted. "What did you do to my men?"

"Spider scared them."

"The dumb shits. What are you doing with that gun?"

Vuong thought how foolish he was. "I found it on the ledge with the bird shit." He spit on the cylinder. "Do you want it?"

"Does it work?"

"I don't know."

"Just drop it over the edge."

"Okay." Vuong felt the pain of letting it fall. As he listened for the noise of the pistol hitting the rocks, another strange sound came from the sea. A high-pitched whir. Two strange helicopters followed the shoreline north. Each aircraft had a round bubble on a long metallic grid of a tail. They flew a little lower than his height over the village.

"Watch them. Don't move. Let 'em pass. If they come towards us, I'll have to shoot 'em down."

"Yes, sir. Yes, sir." Vuong tried to sound submissive. What could he do to get their attention? Would they shoot him? Could he point to Danh?

Vuong always wanted to ride in one. Untying the yellow scarf from his back, he attached it to the stick and waved toward the sea. Back and forth, up and down, the sea breeze kept the scarf extended. But the helicopters kept their solitary course away from the shore.

Suddenly another sound entered, a definite *whap, whap, whap.* "Another helicopter is coming." The lieutenant chambered a round.

Vuong waved more intensely. His yellow scarf streamed in circles. They saw him and stopped high above the water. His arms ached from this simple movement, but he enjoyed it. Like digging Danh's grave.

Then the little helicopters made a sharp turn toward them. Vuong dropped the scarf over the ledge but it snagged on the branch. He squeezed into the dried bird shit and pulled the nest on top of himself. Fortunately, his pants and shirt were black, his skin and hair dark. All he could do now was pray. And pray he did. "Oh God, I hope they kill his ass."

The lead helicopter banked down to the right. Its bubble looked like glass, on top of a metal frame and whirling blades. A soldier sat in the open side door.

Danh shot three bursts in a row, then switched clips. The door gunner immediately returned fire with solid tracers from the machine gun.

After the leader broke away, the second helicopter returned to hover close to the bodies on the rock spill and up to Danh's position hanging over the edge. As Vuong looked down, the rotating blades were like a big fan. The yellow streamer stretched toward it like a menacing hand. The door gunner motioned frantically and both helicopters flew back toward the sea.

Exhaustion and little food took its toll. Vuong fell asleep

watching the aircraft disappear. The big white bird woke him with the flush of its wings then glided majestically away. Vuong cried out, "Quy, my love, the monster Danh is dead."

Vuong removed the scarf from the branch and wrapped the knife in it. He rearranged it under the radio on his back to preserve the value of both. The last treacherous stretch of the climb made the base path look like a boulevard in Qui Nhon. It took an hour to make it to the top, he pulled himself over the edge and collapsed on a wide, flat rock. When he caught his breath, he struggled to his hands and knees. A drop of sweat fell next to his shadow. He shook his head like a dog and more drops flew on another head-shape shadow next to his. His eyes went from one to the other. "*Do Cho De.*"

The shadow voice commanded, "I'm not a son of a bitch. Lay down. Spread your arms. And your feet." He patted Vuong down everywhere except under the radio which he removed.

Vuong did not move. "Who are you?"

"Remember, I have the gun. Who are you?"

"Vuong from Thanh Ha."

"How did the helicopter miss you?"

"They shot at Lieutenant Danh..."

The shadow looked over the edge. "That worthless prick. Is he coming up?"

"It sounded like the helicopter killed him."

"That's good news. If the Americans did not get him, I would have. He was a fuckin' idiot. Way too big for his sandals."

The shadow removed the barrel from behind Vuong's ear. "Stand up. Slowly. Tell me, how did they miss you in that attack?" The shadow was an NVA sergeant with little vines and leaves stuck in the mesh on his helmet. Dirt on its red star. His shirt had grass under his epaulettes and in his pockets. His tired face had streaks of mud in its wrinkles. He said, "What did you do for him?"

"I guided him to the top."

"How did you survive that attack?"

Vuong said, "What do you mean?"

The sergeant's clear white eyes contrasted to his dark skin. "Those helicopters shot up our lookout post. They're killers, how *did* you escape?"

Vuong exhaled. "I led the climb. Both soldiers fell to their death about the time the helicopters appeared. Lieutenant shot at the helicopter, they shot back."

"Dumb as a stump."

"I called him several times. No answer. I didn't go down to look for him."

"Let the bastard rot. Why was he coming up here?"

"General Danh heard from the radio operator of the patrol. Piggy survived. I saw the whole thing."

"You saw what?"

"I led the squad to re-establish the outpost after the bombing. I split the squad and went to Vinh Hoi for more men while some of my advance climbed the face to man the outpost. When the helicopters attacked, they destroyed the fuel storage and wiped out the advance party. The same helicopters that attacked this face."

"How did you escape the attack?"

The shadow sergeant squinted with a nuance of a smile. "We made ourselves look like a stump."

"We?"

"My men and I."

"What men?" Vuong looked around.

"Squad. Stand." Five different looking bushes and grass clumps stood up at the same time. The sergeant smiled.

As the sun set over the mountain, Nien guarded the only entrance to the cavern. He heard his old friend humming as he climbed up the shaft. Hai said, "Phuong sent me to replace you."

Nien whispered, "Silence."

Hai put his hand over his mouth. "Oops. He is with the lady in the assembly area."

Nien moved down the steep crawl space at a break-neck stride. He interrupted Kaelyn and Phuong chatting in the big room. "I heard machine gun fire and a helicopter flying."

Kaelyn put away her note pad. "Could it be the patrol?"

Nien changed from eager and alert to confused. "No. No. This was the first anything I heard since yesterday."

"Got to be Danny. I just know he got my message. How much time do we have left on the generators?"

"There's no clock." Phuong turned to Nien, "Count the cans of fuel left." Nien disappeared.

Kaelyn fidgeted with the rifle slung on her back and the pistol belt on her hips. "I'm supposed to be a journalist. I look like a combatant. What the hell's the matter with me?"

Phuong said, "You know the atrocities we've suffered. You're helping us. Not just writing about it. But here, anyone with a rifle is fair game. Carry your pistol under your shirt, low on your back."

"This is the dream of every reporter. I don't want to screw it up, but..." Kaelyn wrapped the gun in her sash. "Have you heard from Minh?"

"Not directly but after they shot into the pipe, all noises stopped on the other side of the blockade. No tank. No tinkering. Total silence."

Nien returned breathing like a distance runner. "Four cans left. The operator just filled the tank."

"Only 20 gallons. That means around twelve hours left. Wow. We gotta make contact to see if they're coming. Or move out on our own. Can we borrow your radio?"

Phuong said, "No need. Just take the battery. It will fit the one on top."

Kaelyn slapped him on the back. "Good man. Binh and I will go up and try to get through to Qui Nhon. Then you figure how to move these people before the generator stops. If the lights go out, nobody will escape."

Binh moved in front of Phuong. "Show how to attach battery." Both women took turns installing the battery and turning knobs.

Kaelyn handed her AK-47 to Nien. "Come with us, in case we need to send word back."

He bowed his head toward her.

At the top they found Hai awake and vigilant. Binh whispered, "Remember, this exit disguised. If you hear NVA call out to you, never respond. Because if you do, you will sentence yourself and all villagers to death."

Nien and Hai absorbed each word and their lips puckered to a silent 'Oh'. In the deepest hush, Binh showed each one how to lock, load and aim the AK-47 again and again. When she chambered a round and put the safety on, she said. "Good luck. Do not talk, cough, sing, fart, or make any kind of noise. You're our last hope." Her years of teaching elementary school showed; she repeated instructions in four different ways.

When Binh lifted the grate, wood against wood made a soft squeak. It reminded her how she had to close the door each time she was raped. Her head always on the sand, looking up. She wanted to remember each man. Their little quirks, their ugly faces. Their tongues hanging out. Their slobber. She lost her ability to love.

Kaelyn said, "What's the matter?"

"Nothing." Binh whispered. "I go to ditch. I hear bird sing. No stinky NVA, tobacco smoke, or alcohol. Nothing but gentle, almost soft wind of Hon Heo."

Kaelyn smiled at the boys and mimed closing the grate. Outside the sky could not have been bluer, only a few, puffy white clouds of dusk lingered. In the deepest part of the ditch, she came to a decomposing body from the bombing. She gagged to the edge of vomit. Varmints had gnawed away prominent facial features and limbs.

"Someone's been here since we came through." Binh pointed at the piece of thin, frazzled yellow cloth. "Last time, the debris from the bombing covered the rocks and leaves. This fabric is clean. It was eerie, Let's change our route. It may be harder to travel but it'll be quicker."

"As long as you can find that radio."

"Oh no, almost forgot."

"What?"

Binh exhaled a long breath. "I left booby trap for patrol."

"Where?"

"Under Piggy. I pull pin from grenade, held handle down and lay him on top. If body is moved, grenade will blow."

—

The natural trail rose twice as steep as the ditch over big boulders, crevices, dead stumps, exposed roots and patches of gravel. At the top, they smelled the giant crater before they found it. Kaelyn felt sick again.

"We follow our nose. You alright?"

Sweat dripped from Kaelyn's nose. "Yes."

At the crater, Piggy and the radio hadn't been moved. Binh said, "Just don't touch his body."

"Oh, my gosh." Kaelyn peered over the crater edge at the remnants of a bloated body. An infant in the arms of a villager at the muddy bottom. "Their killers were inhuman."

In a matter of minutes, Binh secured the new battery and static filled the air. Kaelyn pressed the talk switch. "Qui Nhon, this is Kaelyn. Over."

More static . . . "Kaelyn, this is Approach Control, go ahead."

"Okay we're back. You guys coming?" She forgot to release the switch. "Shit, over."

"Okay, Shit. This is Approach. Someone's workin' on it. Don't know when. Over."

"Approach. Look at your watch, we only have until six tomorrow morning before the lights go out, then we're screwed."

"What's your location? Over."

Binh pointed at the trench. "Someone's coming."

"We're where they left us. Gotta go. Bye. Bye." Kaelyn removed the battery and ran into the deep bamboo. A hoard of flies scattered out of the crater.

Down the trail, Binh jumped from one boulder to the next, slid in gravel, and hopped over stumps. Kaelyn kept up but nearly out of control. Sunset passed them as light faded away. They stopped.

Kaelyn's heart pounded like she ran all the way up the mountain instead of down. She imagined movement, convoluted bushes into soldiers and morphed bird warbles into signals. Controlling her wild search for breath was useless. "Someone's looking at me. I feel it. Like I used to sense State Patrol on the highway."

Binh wrinkled her brow and shook her head.

Kaelyn's smile dissipated at a hissing sound and metal against a rock. A grenade rolled above her on the shoulder of the creek bed. Reflexively she tossed it up the hill and ducked. The explosion whipped them with debris. A short, painful scream echoed from a soldier camouflaged with branches and ferns. He squirmed in agony, his back arched, his hands tearing at the ground. Until it stopped.

She kept her head on the ground to regain control of her mind in this nightmare. Cold metal against her neck made her almost jump out of her skin.

"Now don't move. Four guns are fixed on you." A foot pushed her back down, her fatigue cap slipped off and her full head of hair cascaded over her shirt collar.

The shadow sergeant's voice resonated. "Well, well. We're lucky you got rid of that grenade. He should not have thrown it, but he was a new recruit. You've tripled our reward money. You must be the journalist. Say your name."

"Kaelyn DeHaven. Correspondent, *Cleveland Plain Dealer*." She steadied her breath. "And what is your name and rank sir?"

"Chien Phu, I am a senior Sergeant in the Army of North Vietnam. First Sapper Battalion. I dislike your attitude."

"And this is no way for me to conduct my first interview with a non-commissioned officer in the NVA. A soldier who can speak eloquent English. You are pure gold to me. May I stand up to address you properly? With my assistant. I'll need to take notes. Where did you learn to speak English so well?"

"Assistant? Carrying an AK-47? Ho, ha. You insult my intelligence."

"Not at all. With all due respect Sergeant, she has received some very bad treatment by your Viet Cong. Just because she was religious. That's why I insisted she protect herself. She didn't want to translate for me. She is terrified of guns. Come on." Binh raised her head without a smile.

"What are you doing?" The shadow's command voice climbed an octave in wonderment. "You are my prisoner."

"Please-a." She reeked of condescension. "I'm about to make you famous all around the world. Do you realize that every article I wrote from Vietnam has made the UPI Wire, and published in every major metropolitan area in the United States? The best thing North Vietnam could have now is good press. I am sure you understand that."

"But of course." He turned on his flashlight. "Now get on your knees. Both of you. Unbutton your blouses and let them fall. What weapons do you have?" Both women did as they were told.

His light focused on Binh. She exposed her small breasts, sagging on her lean brown chest. Ugly scars covered her bared body. A large scab replaced one of her nipples.

Kaelyn slowly unbuttoned her top. "Is this really necessary? Look at this poor woman. And how brave your Viet Cong were."

"Silence, woman. Take off your blouse."

The light illuminated Kaelyn as she undid her bra to let her breasts bounce together in the light. "See, nothing to hide." Her hands came together as in an offering. "May I dress now, Sergeant?"

"Yes, of course." His voice lowered although his eyes never moved. "Tell me about UPI. How many cities have received your articles?" Chien Phu stood taller than the average NVA soldier. His eyes the camouflage. A major Caucasian influence showed.

Kaelyn put her arms through the straps and caught her breasts in the bra cups. With the light still focused below her neck, her little distraction fed Sergeant Chien Phu's ego.

Enhancing his self-esteem was better than getting him sweaty.

She said, "UPI means *United Press International*. Receipt of the story doesn't count. Placement is everything. Over 6000 newspapers ran my last story, not counting their bureaus in more than 90 countries."

The numbers jolted the sergeant into regaining eye contact with Kaelyn. "Truly amazing."

PART TEN_

"I must tell Phuong." Through the grate, Nien watched the soldier hold the flashlight on both women. Binh took off her shirt and knelt half naked in front of him.

Hai said, "Don't go yet. Let's see what happens."

As Kaelyn's bra slipped down, her breasts swayed. Nien said, "Aaaaa...they really are formed, I mean, the leaders must be informed. You stay, I'll go." He took one more look and scurried down the tunnel like a man possessed.

At the assembly area, Phuong and Minh had just finished briefing the villagers on the plan of escape when Nien slid to a stop at their feet.

Minh helped him up. "What happened?"

Nien bent over to catch his breath. "They need help. When grenade explode, we scared. Almost threw up."

"Yes, go on." Minh patted his back.

"Soldiers had branches, grass and palm leaves on their uniforms. Pointed guns at women. Too far away. Couldn't hear. Lead soldier made them take off their shirts in the flashlight beam. American had very big breasts. She wore a special carrier for them."

"Then what?"

"I left. Can you help?"

"How many soldiers were there?"

"Hard to see in dark. Maybe four. Plus, leader. And one from village."

"Not a soldier?"

"When I deliver messages for NVA, I see him. One time he lean on boat, the other he dig."

"Now, go find out what happened to the women. Which direction did they go? Hurry back."

Minh gathered the villagers with military training. He said, "We know this mountain better than NVA. We need the journalist back. The Americans will return for her. She is our way home."

After a few moments he said, "If they walked direct to cliffs, they'd go down into Chanh My Valley, at least six hundred meters of steep terrain. A terrible route for women."

Nien returned from the top, panting. "Women went toward Thanh Ha cliff. Not bound. Walk with soldiers. Villager led way. And bad weather coming."

"How do you know?"

"Every time black clouds rush in from sea, strong winds and heavy rains follow. Earlier clear sky, now can't see moon."

"Certainly, he would not take them down the Face of Dead Men? He will go to Dong Luong." Minh looked confused. "Wetlands will make their march four times longer. But now they have a guide. Maybe he will change things."

His volunteers, all clad in black pajamas, straw hats, sandals had loaded ammunition belts and grenades.

Phuong said, "Go by west side of valley. I'll help the villagers. At first glimmer of sunrise, we move toward Phu Cat in shade of trees. The wind and rain will help our escape."

He assembled the villagers, his face beamed with confidence and affection. His smile radiated a quiet feeling of self-reliance.

Minh pointed up the natural chimney. "We climb to gap in rocks. Our path has roots, crannies, and some man-made footholds. A wooden flue is big enough to squeeze through to the tree. Crawl out vent hatch and down branches to ground."

Leaning on a primitive ladder, he said, "Remember. If one is killed, rest must continue until no one left. If we love our family, we must rescue those women."

Fatty ran down the corridor of the hospital like he was on the football team again. Since that was 150 pounds ago, he would be lucky not to fall flat. They called him "Skinny." He laughed.

"Where you goin' Fats?" Pollhill's chair leaned at an angle beside the lounge door, obscured from sight.

Startled from his mental merriment, Fatty fought to catch his breath. "I'm lookin'... Trinh Le...Danny."

"I moved 'em." Pollhill spoke with a deadpan face, M16 across his lap.

Fatty had never been in the Nurses Lounge before. A different world with curtains on the windows, sofas accompanied by end tables and a mannequin. But the ambience dissolved with the sight of straight-back steel chairs and government-issue tables. In the corner, Danny slept on a day bed, dead to the world, while Trinh Le cut z's next to him in a large, comfortable chair.

Fatty shook Trinh's arm. "Ya gotta come with me."

Trinh Le snapped his head up like a child found napping in class, "Yes. Okay. Why? What's up?"

"Another call from Approach Control for the MACV Gook." Fatty chuckled. "They have a new 'wild-ass' message for ya'."

Trinh jumped up like he had sat on hot poker. "When did it come in? What's happened?" He hurried up the corridor as fast as Fatty could go.

Back in the lounge, Pollhill slowly pulled the shades down. He knew the Cong would try to wipe these guys out Sapper style, with explosives. None of this shooting crap.

Maybe Pollhill's cynical nature over-reacted but a bad feeling lurked in the raw recess of his mind. Shit was going to hit his fan. He felt it. The same kind of miserable omen when the Shithook left him on the beach after he rescued Danny. He turned the steel tables on their side to face the door. Bent the bottom legs to slant the table surface. Pushed the sofas together for bulk. Dressed the mannequin with scrub pants, a fatigue shirt and hat from the clothes hook on the door. Finally, Pollhill put the sleeping Danny into the bathtub of the locker room. Pillow, pouch, and all. And placed an end table on the tub's rim to protect from falling debris.

Trinh Le and Fatty found the secure room in record time. On arrival, the big boy looked like a leaky bucket. With a simple connection to the secure line, Trinh greeted App Con, "This MACV Gook. You got a message for me?"

"Yes, sir. Kaelyn reported they had to be out by six. I asked where, she said 'where they left us.' And she hung up."

"Has the Bomb Damage Assessment launched yet?"

App Con laughed, "You shitting me? Looked outside lately? It's a frog strangler. Closest damn thing to a monsoon. Ain't nobody flying."

"Answer the question. Did J2 confirm the BDA?"

"Yes, Sir. Proceed with the mission."

"As soon as the weather breaks?"

"No, Sir."

"What am I missing?"

"Besides not having a BDA team, we're fresh out of helicopters."

"Very funny."

"Not very, sir. There's a lot goin' on."

"Yea, all tactical." Trinh remembered the late click on the phone after his last conversation with the J2. "I want the first one in."

"Helicopters are one thing, what about the team?"

"I'll take care of the team, just give me the flight leader." A massive explosion knocked the quiet out of the building, "What the hell—" Trinh hung up.

"Sounds like Pollhill got hit."

"And I left my pistol with Danny. Do you have a weapon?"

"Yes, Sir." Fatty strained to reach his ankle holster. "Use mine. It's the light weight .38."

Trinh held the weapon in his sling. "Call J2. Tell him I need the BDA team, *now*. We have an impossible deadline to meet. Or massive loads of excrement will make contact with the air distribution system. Send me SOG Team Delta if nothing else is available."

Gunfire erupted down the hall.

"Is there another way to get to Pollhill?"

"Yes, sir. The only stairwell complete lands next to the Nurses Lounge."

Upstairs Trinh found pallet after pallet of construction materials. He heard automatic weapon fire. Another smaller explosion went off. More smoke and dust billowed up the stairs.

When the air cleared, Trinh peered down at two Viet Cong on the steps. "Come out," one shouted in barely understandable English.

"*DU, DU, DU*." Pollhill shouted back, "fuck off" in his best, Sunday-go-to-meeting Vietnamese.

Trinh laughed, took the gun from his sling, carefully aimed at the back of their heads. He squeezed twice. Earsplitting sound in the small space hurt like an ice pick in the ear. The soldiers fell like balloons without air.

Pollhill shouted, "Who goes there?"

"The MACV Gook."

"Well, damn, am I glad to hear you. Come on down."

When Trinh reached the lounge, the windows blown out, the mannequin shot in two, the sofas tore up, four Cong and two MPs dead on the floor. Every wall had bullet holes or chunks of plaster board hanging out.

"Where's Danny?"

Pollhill opened the restroom door. Danny curled in a fetal position in the tub. Pouch and pillow on his chest. "What in goddamn hell do we do with him?"

"Excuse me, sir." Fatty picked his way over the dead bodies and debris. "SOG Team Delta Niner is due in ten minutes. A ready-reaction flight of two slicks and a gun are on final approach to the airfield. Both slicks with wounded on board."

The thunderous approach of helicopters stalled at a constant, deafening level. Pollhill looked at Fatty. "What the hell?"

Trinh said, "Probably the weather, they're hovering to the pad. That nurse seemed pretty good at waking Danny. Get her in. We need him now. I'll find the helicopters."

Fatty moved toward the patients and Trinh went for the chopper. Pollhill checked for any signs of life or papers on the Cong bodies.

Rain dumped by the bucket as eight wounded soldiers were removed by gurney to the only surgeon in the hospital. Trinh introduced himself to the flight leader, Colonel Exton Givens, as they both watched the crew chief try to clean the cabin floor. He used a paperback book to shove blood out the door. It clung to the belly of the helicopter like glue. And then to the ground. A puddle of death.

The Colonel tossed his cigar. "What a fucking waste. Dying in this shithole."

"That's what I want to discuss with you Colonel. On behalf of J2, we need your help in a mission of vital, strategic importance." Trinh Le gave his best one-minute recap.

The Colonel leaned against the door, unwrapped another cigar, "Shit. I didn't realize Vietnam had a goddamn Emperor. Ya' want us as a Bomb Damage Assessment team? And find a bunch of villagers? And look for a journalist?" His crow's feet crinkled around his eyes. "Who the hell is he anyway?"

"He's a *she*. Kaelyn DeHaven, daughter of Orville DeHaven, Senator from Texas."

"Now the light burns with clarity." The Colonel grimaced. "I know one of those bodies carried off. My pilot took bullets through the calf, thigh, and butt. He now has a shitty attitude and won't be able to fly."

"Colonel, no sweat. We got one."

"With a shitty attitude?"

"Nah, just unconscious."

"Fuckin' wonderful, it's getting better and better."

Beau entered the room with his chicken plate on, a wet cigarette hanging from his lip and a dripping ball cap squeezed on his head.

The Colonel said, "Trinh, meet our Ops officer, Lieutenant Beau Buncher. He's my wingman since we're plum out of pilots."

Beau extended his hand. "Man, you look familiar."

"In Saigon, you and your friend rescued me from a drunken, mad man. Trinh smiled, "He's here, too."

"Who? The mad man?"

"No. The redhead."

Colonel chimed in. "Ox?"

"He's the one who knows where Kaelyn is."

"What's the matter with him?"

"Nothing. But the nurse called it extreme sleep deprivation. Two hours of sleep last three days or so. They're trying to wake him."

The door opened as three, strange-looking soldiers entered like a slow, cold breeze. With full camouflage paint, steel pots, ill-fitting LRRP fatigues, pistols, and Bowie knifes. The tallest one carried a

M63 machine gun, shortest one had a M14 rifle with a scope, while the left-over had a M16 with two magazines taped together. Everything they wore came right out of the box. Fold marks still evident, boots clean and polished. No rank showed.

Colonel stood in front of them. "I'm Colonel Exton Givens, A Company, 229 Aviation Battalion."

The smallest member put his sniper rifle down and assumed the 'at ease' position. "We're SOG Team Delta Niner. I'm Captain Wysoc, this is Supply, and that's Radio. Normally we're base operations for all SOG teams in II Corp. today we're your BDA Team. We may look like a bunch of candy-ass, strap-hangers. We're *not*. J2 briefed us."

"You're gonna do a BDA with three men?" Trinh raised one eyebrow, "You'll do a quickie out of the chopper."

"Yes, sir." The three soldiers stood motionless.

All heads turned to Nurse Washington. Colonel Givens said, "How's Ox?"

"Actually, the doctor's concerned about his concentration and judgment issues. He needs a couple more hours of sleep."

"No sweat, GI." Beau unstrapped his chicken plate. "The tower said nothing's flying within a hundred miles and won't be for the next eight to ten hours. We got sixty to eighty knot winds comin'. Plus, sixteen more inches of rain by morning."

"Okay. Might as well get some sack time. We'll launch early, wake at 0400. Those people will spill out at dawn. Gotta be there by then. Figure it out. Nurse Washington, you get Danny up. Beau, handle the ship crews. Wysoc, get your poop grouped. I'll do breakfast." The Colonel looked at everyone. "Any questions?"

Silence occupied the room. Wind howled outside.

16 MAY 1966, 0430 HOURS_

Approach Control lost patience, "I know ya' got less than two hours left Colonel but look out the window. It's damn-near zero-zero. Clouds are sitting right on top of the hangars and visibility is no more than one helicopter length ahead. Weather says this storm's not going anywhere."

"Roger, I'll get back to you." Colonel Givens hung up and surveyed a sea of dejected faces. His plastic-covered aeronautical chart sprawled over the conference table.

I tapped his fingers methodically on the map until I stopped mid-beat. "I think we can get there from here."

"No shit, Sherlock." Beau put down his coffee cup. "*When* is the real question."

"Right now. If we have a 40-foot ceiling, we can get real close. Lookie here," I pointed to Qui Nhon. "We can go right off end of the airfield and hover along the shoreline of the bay to the northern-most inlet. Then turn north into the Chang My Valley. Top of the hill in the meadow is about where I left Kaelyn. Trinh, you familiar with it?"

"With my family, I spent several summers on Hon Heo." He moved his finger up the map. "There are six villages along the west side of the bay, none are directly on the water. This has been a major point of entry for the NVA. Chang My Creek will be swollen now. If you miss it and go to Dong Luong, you'll probably get shot at for sure. The Cong have owned that village for a long time."

Givens crowded into the circle. "What happens at the end of the valley?"

"A waterfall. Very pretty, used to swim at the bottom."

The Colonel moved closer. "You let Kaelyn off on top of that hill?"

"Don't know if that's the exact spot. There was supposed to be a meadow up there and a hospital with a munitions factory."

"Supposed to be?"

"Yes sir. Remember I landed there at night hoping not to crash and departed sometime later in a cloud bank hoping to fly. An Arc Light bombing in between. No telling what it looks like in daylight."

Colonel Givens stood up. "Gentlemen, we have to get there before the villagers lose their light in the cavern. Only got two hours. This plan makes as much sense as anything. All three aircraft have been re-fueled, we'll crank in fifteen minutes." He turned to the SOG Team. "Captain, put a man in each Slick. The crew chief'll fix you up with a headset so you can be in our loop. Trinh, you're gonna stay."

Outside, the rain came at us like a firehose, sideways. Serpent Six's aircraft had a big snake entwined within the blue triangle painted on both front doors. A large OD tank sat in the cargo area with "50 gallon, JP4, US" stenciled in white. I'd never seen a ferry tank before. The Colonel nodded me into the right-hand seat. Rain buffeted the front windshield. Wind gusts rocked the helicopter. It smelled like a beach, but it wasn't.

I shouted above the storm, "Not very encouraging."

"Listen Ox, this is your big fuckin' idea. Crank this mother." Givens smiled as he put on his helmet. "Not to worry, beats walking."

On the instrument panel, every switch worked, all gauges read correctly. I pulled the starter ignition and the turbine whine made me feel like I was home again.

Givens said, "You fly first. I'll navigate."

"Okay. Ya' know they put a cork in my sucking chest wound, most of my big gouges have scabbed over, and my vision is down to double. I'm good to go."

"Keep the twirling side up, and the dirty skids down, son. And don't hit anything you can't knock over."

Despite the deluge, I hovered over the perimeter fences and lost sight of the ground every time I got higher than twenty feet. The city crowded the water's edge. My path inched over piers, around buildings, across chunks of beach, through bunches of small boats and large junks with scary masts.

Yellow Two followed me, as did Delta behind him. Every time I went beyond a crawl, I would tell Yellow Two. Every time I did a quick stop, I'd call it out. His objective was to not eat my tail rotor. Mine was not to do something stupid. Colonel kept squeezing his arm rests, flinching for the cyclic, slapping his knees when I missed something big.

I drug my skids through two palm trees, side-swiped a boat mast and snapped one telephone wire. Everything I hit scared the hell out of everyone. Especially me. They hurled scurrilous condemnations of my talent, lineage, and IQ. But gave me a real epiphany: you can't go faster than you can see.

Perspiration dripped from my chin to the chicken plate. Gale force rain leaked through the window on my door, and I held a 45-degree crab to follow the beach line. Heavy waves crashed against the white sands; those trees that didn't break bowed deeply with the wind. A small rowboat flipped out of the water twice before the wind pinned it high in a palm tree.

I drifted into the middle of a village completely inundated with water. No palm trees. No streets visible. Just water through every door and window of the first level of everything standing. People clung to the remnants of clay tile and thatched roofs as we passed. I inadvertently drug my skids through a gable causing the villagers, their dogs, and ducks to jump for safety into the water.

When we reached the Chang My River, it looked like a fast-moving lake with trees submerged in water up to their palms. For the next ten minutes the other side of the river never appeared. The first totally visible palm tree drew cheers from inside our helicopter and on the radio from those behind us.

Dawn broke as a lush, green valley appeared, capped off by a solid cloud layer. I flew at a cautious 40 knots.

Givens transmitted, "Yellow flight, our only chance is to hover up the side of the mountain, through the clouds. If we run into any problems, we can always climb out and get a GCA back to Qui Nhon. Yellow Two, Delta, stay down in the valley. When I get to the top, I'll call. Out."

Givens saw the expression on my face, as if I was taped to a rocket while he played with matches. "You ready?"

"Yes, sir."

The thought of hovering up the side of a mountain exceeded all the terrorizing tales they scared us with in flight school.

Givens got on the controls. "I got it. Let me play for a while."

I sat back. My heart thumped so fast for so long, it felt strange just to sit and look. Motionless as wallpaper, our grunts with "significant field experience" gave new meaning to the idea of "scared shitless." The end of the valley had a beautiful waterfall, or at least what we could see of it. We burned almost half our fuel load, so the Colonel established an easy 50 foot per minute climb rate up the mountain side into the clouds.

He kept our rotor disk right next to all the green shit. All these trees, so close-up, slowly passing by our windshield, spooked me. I have no idea what kind they were, other than what our instructor pilots called *genus greenest, hardest, tallest*. We avoided fighting trees if we could because they won every time.

Givens focused through the glass above his windshield. He said, "It'll get lighter as we ascend. Keep your eyeballs peeled, this place crawled with Cong before the Arc Light."

Outside my window a continuous wall of green and gray with

chunks of black took forever to pass by, so I cross-checked the instruments. "700 feet indicated, sir. We should pop into meadow around 1000." The separation from the green started to fluctuate uncomfortably and erratically. After he clipped branches with our rotor blades I said, "You all right?"

"Yeah...sure." The Colonel's normal cool, in-command voice came back in cryptic, staccato. The aircraft nose pulled away from the trees far enough to let a cloud in between.

I grabbed the cyclic and the collective. "I got it." But the Colonel pulled the stick backward to the stop and his feet locked on the pedals. "Get off the fucking controls." I whacked him on the shoulder.

He raised his hands as in an arrest. "You got it." His shoulders turned to pull the armor shield back. He stuck his head out the window. A pilot's remedy for all things vertigo.

The helicopter's steep climb turned us to the left. I straightened the nose and a great glob of green slapped the entire windshield. My rotor tips chewed up leaves. I pulled back immediately, dragging some branches with the front of the skids. My angle of climb stabilized, and the mountain stayed away.

Altimeter pointed to 950 feet. The cockpit got brighter and lighter. Colonel slid his armor shield back in place. I leveled off. And resumed breathing.

An ugly, new sound reverberated when a crisp, single hole blew through the windshield and knocked the wiper blade into the rotor. I broke right. My skids and tail absorbed more hits.

Givens stomped the floor mike button. "Yellow flight. Don't come up, it's hot."

Yellow Two screamed back, "Goddamn it, move right, we're behind ya'." Yellow Two took a solid stream of fire as they tried to hide from the Cong.

The gunship broke through the cloud bank firing rockets to vaporize the offenders. "Yellow One, Delta's here to save your ass. Again." He transmitted from a high hover in front of the line of smoldering dead soldiers. His helicopter's nose dipped down in a bow like a matador to his fans.

From my position north of him, a line of giant craters from the Arc Light spread across the meadow. A soldier camouflaged as a bush popped up with an RPG tube. Fire and smoke launched the rocket at Delta, exploding aft of the cabin and below the exhaust. It severed the empennage, which flew backward like a disemboweled bird. The body of the helicopter spun in the opposite direction of the rotor before it screwed itself into the hillside. Big slabs of mud soared into the air. Though mortally wounded, it did not stop. After the blade's final jab, its momentum lifted the mutilated cadaver and rolled it down the hill. Two bodies tumbled out as it came to a stop.

Yellow Two moved closer to Delta's ugly dance of death. The sapper reemerged and shot again. Two's right skid exploded and ripped his cargo door off. I put the nose down and got the hell out.

Wysoc yelled, "Level out. I kin get him." The husky boom of an M-14 reverberated behind my seat. Of course, our naked cabin could make the muzzle concussion of a .22-caliber pistol sound like a damn cannon. A two-shot cluster knocked the first bush shooter on his ass.

Givens slapped his hands above his helmet like a Spanish dancer. "Not bad from a moving platform at 300 yards."

The chief said, "Yellow Two's burning. He fell straight down, knocked one rotor off."

Another bullet went through the pillar behind Givens, hit his armor shield with a splat and ricocheted into his panel.

"Yellow One, I can't see shit. Our nose's in the bushes. Got flames from engine compartment. Crew chief and my pilot are dead. The SOGs are out. I gotta un-ass this buggy."

"Roger. Pop smoke when you're ready for pick up. Out." Givens took control of the helicopter. "Chief, you okay?"

"The shot hit my chicken plate and buggered my arm up. Pollhill wrapped it. I'm Okay."

"We have a variable ceiling to 50 feet, maybe more. Gunner,

when I pop up over the ridge, lay fire to keep the Cong away from Yellow Two."

The clouds moved in a state of agitation, eating one another, slipping underneath or leapfrogging above. Our visibility swirled down the toilet. Givens gained speed and climbed above the hill.

"Hold it. Hold your fire," Wysoc screamed as he looked through his scope. All shooting stopped. "They're holding guns to the heads of both women."

Bullets pulverized the helicopter's exposed side, knocked out the bottom quarter of the left front windshield, splintered the left door panels, missed the armored seat to go through Givens calf, and fell spent into my lap. A gush of his blood hit my face.

I grabbed the controls and dropped below the crest but didn't escape hits to my rotor mast. The big ugly chip detector light ignited to a bright red. I was about to die if I didn't land.

Givens flicked his hand. "Fuck it. Get to the bare spot, they popped smoke."

The rain intensified again. A cross between a deluge of Biblical proportions and a sacred cow pissing on a church step. At the landing zone, the red smoke didn't float but curdled down the steep side of the hill toward the burning Yellow Two.

Pollhill pulled our gunner's body to the cabin floor. He cleared the gun.

I hovered below the ridgeline. "Something's moving out there."

Pollhill said, "Just below the crater, a little guy in black pajamas, waving yellow cloth like in semaphore...."

Givens held up his hand. "Wysoc, scope him."

"No weapons visible. Scared as hell. His shirt's open."

"Go grab him and see what he knows."

Wysoc inserted a fresh magazine in his rifle and rattled in a monotone. "You bet your ass."

I LANDED the helicopter and kept it light on its skids. Wysoc ducked under the rotor path with his M16 leveled at the man in black pajamas. He pressed the rifle barrel hard enough against the little guy's head and pushed him sideways. They talked for a long time before he lowered the rifle and ran to the helicopter.

Wysoc said, "Little guy says there were at least six sappers. Very tough guys."

Colonel Givens said, "Trust him?"

"Worth the gamble. Vuong is his name. He knows about the captured villagers and all three exits in the prison cavern. Plus, a stockpile of supplies on a deserted island. And how he'll die if any thing's wrong."

"What about the women? That's why we're here."

"One sounds like the journalist, the other's a nun."

"Ah, shit. Ox, hover to Yellow Two. Get the crew out and destroy the ship."

I said, "What? It's still burnin'."

"Yeah, but it's too slow. Can't defend it and the weather won't let anyone sling it out. If the Cong get the machine guns, ammunition, and radios, it'll be a field day for them."

I made it slowly to the cliff's edge. Smoke from the Huey smelled like diesel and rubber burning. Givens held a handkerchief on his calf wound, blood seeped between his fingers. I said, "Chief, get something for the Colonel. He's bleedin' all over the place."

Givens turned around, "We gotta get the journalist. No time to play fuck-around."

"And you won't be worth shit if you lose consciousness."

He paused and almost smiled. "So now you're Ox-the-Fox. Just keep flying."

Wysoc leaned over the pedestal holding the first aid kit. "Pollhill, Radio, and Vuong will attach the demolition charges. Then go after the Cong."

As I approached Yellow Two, Beau Buncher and a gunner limped out of the brush toward us. They helped Colonel Givens out of the cockpit into a cargo seat. Beau climbed in, looked at the bloody floor and plugged in his helmet. "You boys sure run a messy ship." Big smile, little wink.

"Don't get your dress caught on the jagged edges before you put your sorry ass in. Sweetheart. Sorry about your gunner and pilot."

"Couldn't outrun the RPG."

Givens shouted from the cargo area, "Quit fuckin' around. Get 'outta here!"

Beau said, "If we weren't trapped by the Cong, impossible weather, and impassable mountain jungle, I'd say you had a great fuckin' idea for this mission. What the hell we gonna do now?"

I said, "We still got one flyable ship. Kaelyn's still in the game. I'm gonna keep bobbin' and weavin' until we leave or crash."

A dark line of roiling clouds and churning winds set the stage for a lightning strike so close it felt like hell spurted out. Thunder boomed louder than the roar of the helicopter.

The radio kicked in with static, "Ox, this is Pappy, I'm at the spot."

Another dead Cong in complete camouflage lay on the flat spot ahead. I landed right next to the body and Pollhill ran out of the bush and jumped on board. He pounded the back of my seat. "Get the fuck out of here."

I drifted down the hill as Yellow Two exploded. Three separate charges went off a fraction of a second apart. I beat out the debris field for a change, but the low fuel warning lit up. "Okay chief, how accurate's the light?"

"Right on the nut, Sir. With our ferry tank, we have fifty-four minutes of flying time left."

"That means only fifteen minutes to find Kaelyn. Great, switch it over."

Givens passed a headset to Pollhill. "So, what happened?"

"Soon as you split, a sapper ran out of the bamboo. Vuong spotted him and I took him out."

"So?" Givens snorted.

"So according to our count, there's only four sappers left."

Givens said, "Radio and Vuong are in position. We need to distract the sappers."

I said, "Remember, this chopper ain't invisible, quiet, or bulletproof."

Did these bozos think we could sneak up on them?

Heavy static from the FM intruded again. "Helicopter, this is Minh. Can you hear?"

Givens turned to Pollhill. "He'll do better in Vietnamese. Do you speak?"

"No sir, but Supply does." Pollhill passed his headset.

Supply and Minh spoke for almost a minute, as I hovered downhill. I felt like a fish in a bowl waiting for food. Or to be food. Or to be in the big flush.

Supply put on the headset. "As the leader of the village Minh and three others tried to save the journalist and the nun. Two of his men got killed. He found this radio in the remnants of a bombed-out bunker."

"How about the women?"

"They moved 'em downhill."

"Ox, take us back to the ridge." Givens leaned forward to look at the disturbed line of clouds. "We gotta distract 'em."

Supply said, "I got a M79 but I'm not good at long shots."

Crew chief said, "I am."

Givens repositioned everyone. "Ox, give 'em a clear shot from the left side."

I crested the hill at a 15-foot hover and held my breath.

Supply focused his binoculars. "One's draggin' the white girl to the tree line. The other one has his sword out."

The hollow *thonk* of the M79 sounded and a beautiful explosion with white tentacles of fire splashed downhill from them.

Supply's tension was evident, "The white skinned woman disappeared. Other one's on her knees...shit...he chopped off her head."

Two more sappers surfaced firing their rifles.

Wysoc blasted four times.

The concussion felt like a hammer to my brain. Reflexively, I climbed higher until my rotor blades churned the cloud cover.

"Wait. Wait." Supply roared, "Both shooters down, the blade man's gone. I'll be damned. Snipe, ya haven't lost your touch."

"What now?"

Supply said, "That's why I brought the rope. If you hover uphill from where the sapper took her, I'll rappel down and block 'em. When I drop, launch Radio as intercept."

Colonel said, "Ox, you need ten seconds for him to reach the ground through the canopy. Get after it."

Supply secured the end of our coil to the bulkhead next to Beau's seat. I looked through my chin bubble at the swirling tree tops. And swallowed hard.

Minh's slow staccato severed the static. "Helicopter, there is one more bush shooter here."

Givens kicked the pedestal. "Goddamn it! Shoot da bastard!"

"Sorry, cannot."

"Why not?"

"Can't find him."

"Why the hell did ya' kill Binh?" Kaelyn's voice cracked, "She's damn nun, for Christ's sake. Doesn't make sense. Ya' had two women to hide behind. Oh, mighty warrior."

I can't lose my cool.

Chien Phu didn't flinch at the zinger as he searched for a way down the hill. "They were trying to kill me. I showed you what I would do. She bought me time."

"So, why was your team on the meadow?"

"We lost contact with the villagers working for us. Both the seaside and the meadow entrances caved in from the bombing."

Kaelyn nearly choked, "You mean you were huntin' the villagers who escaped from your prison? What changed your plans?"

He said, "Two mistakes. I thought my men could take down the helicopter. And I didn't plan for a sniper."

She stopped when he caught his breath. Her nose itched. She couldn't scratch it with her arms bound behind her at the elbows and wrists.

Every question she put to him, he answered with no effort to obfuscate any of the evidence or excuse himself. Was he traumatized by the slaughter of his whole squad? Did the potential loss of the reward for prisoners disrupt him?

Kaelyn said, "What're you gonna do now?"

"Take you back to battalion headquarters." He pulled her along by her belt. The slope of Chang My valley was steep and muddy. She slipped on loose stones and slid on her back until she wedged onto a tree.

"Why the hell are we goin' downhill? I'm gettin' all bruised up. Pictures of me in that condition won't play well in Peoria."

"What is Peoria?" An honest question sounded weird from Chien.

"It's a town in America. A standard gauge for the country's attitudes. If something isn't accepted there, there's a good chance no one in America will buy it." She pushed away from the tree. "Untie my hands already. And gimme my blouse back."

Chien Phu mumbled, "Fuck Peoria. But—" The sound of the helicopter filtered into the area. He searched for a break in the tree cover. The ominous beat of the rotor blades got louder and louder.

Kaelyn shouted, "You really think your headquarters is still operational?"

The light of comprehension blossomed on Chien's face. "Stand up, turn around."

Her bare arms, breasts, and back were caked with mud as she resolutely dug her boots into the hill. She did not want him to notice the gun in her sash. She feigned a slip to thrust her breasts against his leg and looked up. "Oops, here, just cut it off." She twisted her body away demurely and extended her wrists as far as she could. "The tape...on my wrists."

Chien slit the tape. "This conflict is such a bother."

Kaelyn whined, "How about my blouse?"

He dropped it into her muddy hands.

"My bra?"

"Nah, be glad you got the shirt."

She stuck her tongue between her lips and blew him a raspberry, "pfft".

Chien wrinkled his face in confusion. A series of rifle shots at the helicopter. It responded immediately with machine gun bursts.

"Move now. Keep close." He checked his AK for a round in the chamber.

Kaelyn buttoned her blouse as they set off through the dense vegetation. A green sea of flora spread in all directions. Several times she called his name when he moved out of sight and sound.

He reappeared as silently as he left. "Do not touch anything I don't touch. Beware of snakes. Walk exactly where I walk. Hurry."

No wonder. No leash on. No place to run.

Another exchange of gunfire sent bullets over her head. Death streaming by excited her. On the other hand, changes of the massive rotor rhythm while thrashing through trees sickened her. The bone-chilling crash ushered in a numbing silence. Like a car accident but much larger, louder, and lonely.

Kaelyn's mind raced. Different levels of trees co-existed. Every bush, vine, stump, rotten log, and man-sized fern got in her way. Not an easy place to step.

Chien plunged through foliage that looked impenetrable. "Stop!" His harsh whisper blasted like a shotgun. He crouched below a big green leaf and directed Kaelyn to the ground.

Something moved ahead.

Chien looked like a hawk searching for its prey. A predator, feasting on the unprepared. An expert in death. The moving sound turned to crunching. If it was an animal, it was big, dumb, and clumsy.

The time to whip out the little gun and blast him? That goddamn sash.

Chien pointed his rifle where he looked. He whispered, "Be very quiet. If they start shooting, you could get hurt. Americans waste bullets. So, lay on the ground."

A bullet from a distant rifle ricocheted off the tree above them. Footsteps ran briefly then slowed to a noisy walk.

Kaelyn knelt on a large leaf and fiddled with the sash. Her blouse hung loose but two hands behind her back would be a dead giveaway. She picked at it with one hand and finally touched the smooth metal surface of the Beretta. Should she shoot him now? Or interview him first? What a story he could tell. She could almost smell the Pulitzer.

More gunfire. Single shots. She couldn't tell which direction. "Who's shooting?"

He surveyed the area. "One of my men was an outlier. After I withdrew, he forced the helicopter down. Now he is tracking the scout."

She realized the problem. They isolated the American. Chien wanted to get in the fight. What would he do with her? She had slowed him down. He would tie her to a tree, probably gag her this time. And what happens if he gets killed? And the American can't find her? Or they both get killed? Be hooked to the tree forever. Shit outta luck.

"You gonna help him?" She recoiled when she realized her suggestion.

"No. I do not know where he is. But he knows where the American is. Regardless, I will greet the victor. "Do not worry, I will get you out." He carried his rifle casually and moved through the plant life.

Chien slowed his pace. Everything was more deliberate. He no longer paralleled the top tree line but angled up the hill. On a very steep hill. A wall of vegetation.

Kaelyn's thighs throbbed. She felt lucky to be shrouded in a cloud layer or she would be blistered. Every leaf splashed her. The smells changed in intensity from plant to plant. From crisp freshness after a rain to mildew. Or sweet flowers to rotting leaves.

Chien regularly drained a leaf of water into his mouth. She did the same.

As he checked a captured US map, she said, "Is the mighty warrior lost?"

He eyed her sharply when a metallic clank echoed in the trees. He lunged at Kaelyn and covered her mouth. On the ground, he straddled her waist.

Kaelyn's eyes widened when she felt his heavy breathing on her face.

He whispered, "We are near the helicopter. I would not hesitate to use you as my shield." His lips drew across her cheek. "Don't make any noise, don't want to break any of those perfect teeth." He kissed her ear. "I'll be back." His hands cupped her breasts and gently kneaded them.

At that moment, he was a dead man. A lifeless piece of meat. She wanted to look captured by terror, paralyzed by fright, but enjoying his massage. One opportunity is all she needed. Her gun was ready.

A hatch slammed. "Goddamn it." An American's frustration soared through the trees. Chien reached for his tape.

CHIEN PHU SLAPPED tape over Kaelyn's mouth. He froze in the middle of clamping her wrists together by the sound of *chec, chec...
chec, chec,* the identification of deep cover. He repeated it exactly since contact was safe.

The outlier whispered, "Chien Phu?"

Chien aimed his rifle at the sound. "Advance."

A bush stood up next to a tree. The outlier's total camouflage was broken only by a large, ceremonial sword at his side. "Seven are down."

"More than I expected. I heard only a few shots. What happened?"

"The sniper set up his position about 100 meters in front of me. By the time I got him, he killed five of our men. I cut his head off." He caressed his bloody sword like it was gold.

Chien despised drama. "Go on."

"After you disappeared with the girl, I moved to the opposite ridge. Two villagers couldn't control the squelch on their transmitter. It sounded like English. I dispatched both to their ancestors. Here is their radio."

Underneath the dense camouflage, the outlier's face barely resembled a human. He said, "Then the helicopter stopped above the trees, at an easy distance. I shot a machine gunner inside and one soldier rappelling to the ground. The helicopter remained motionless, so I put one bullet into middle of the windshield and another into the engine inlet. Smoke poured out its exhaust. It flew backward up the hill to escape. Backward!"

"Well done. Who ran down the path?"

"A villager. I didn't shoot because it would ruin my cover. But later I got him." The outlier looked at Kaelyn on the ground. "That the journalist?"

"Yes. Still unconscious. Deal with the helicopter. Strike before the weather breaks and the extraction force arrives. The Americans always search for their downed aircraft. I'll listen if they're transmitting."

"Didn't know you knew English."

"Been very helpful. Find out how many are in helicopter."

The outlier blended into the green without a sound.

Time dragged by as Chien clicked one frequency after another until he heard, "Bronco 36, this is Serpent 6, I repeat. We are down..." Static reigned supreme until Chien twisted the squelch knob to, "Contact the 229th Assault Helicopter Battalion. Over." Followed by, "Bronco 36. Wilco. Out."

"Aaahaa." A worried Chien Phu said, "How many are there?"

Breathing heavy, the outlier reported, "The helicopter crashed into a crater. I counted one sitting up in the helicopter. One pilot inside and a new soldier with shiny brass in front of the helicopter. Three regular soldiers formed a perimeter about fifteen meters from the aircraft."

Heavy rain chased hazy clouds away with gray sheets of water.

"There are six?"

"Yes, Sergeant."

"Too many to capture. Get the most valuable. Kill the rest."

She lurched up, "You son-of-a-bitch—"

His elbow caught Kaelyn's temple. Her head twisted into the tree. Consciousness escaped.

Hovering above the trees I said, "How the hell'd he lose 'em?"

Colonel Givens transmitted, "Minh, where'd ya' see 'em last. Over."

Painful empty static answered.

Supply wrapped the end of the rope around a case of C Rations so it would lower straight through the trees. He moved outside the helicopter to the skids shouting, "This is it."

He jumped. I could tell when he broke his fall because the aircraft pulled to the right.

A heavy thud impacted behind me. Pollhill shouted, "We're taking fire. Chief's hit." He fired his M16. Shell casings rattled on the cargo deck. Sounded like a hailstorm.

A second thump landed between me and Beau. The radio compartment door in the nose ripped open then slammed back down. But the most sickening sound banged behind my head in the engine. I heard and felt it at the same time.

Beau slapped the instrument panel. "It's lighting up like a Christmas tree. Oil pressure. Chip detector. Fuel pump. It's all shutting down. Got a minute if we're lucky."

The Colonel crowded the pedestal. "Back up the way you came.

I'll guide ya'. Pollhill. Gunner. Cover us." They laid a solid stream of machine gun fire from both sides of the aircraft.

I said, "You gotta be shittin' me."

He shouted, "Now!"

Flying backward required counter intuitive movements. I drew the cyclic to me rather than pushing it forward. Looked through the chin bubble for ground reference rather than up-the-nose'n-go.

Givens played conductor. "Go to your right...up, up, up...damn it, doooown." I felt like a monkey on a basketball.

Beau tapped the fluctuating RPM gauge. "Need to put this baby down."

"Bullshit." The read-out varied from what meant "fly" to "no-fly" several times in a row. "Colonel. If I dump it, what's it look like?"

"It's all canopy. But we're near the top."

"Okay, hold on. If I crash, I wanna see it." I kicked it around. The spastic RPM didn't give me much. "I'm gonna fly this mother forward until it chokes".

And it did.

A loud *kawoump*. Deafening silence made my heart go into overdrive. Seventy feet to the ground and damn-little speed made playtime no fun. A big, bad old tree popped up as the first thing I couldn't miss. My skids made lot of noise smackin' and whackin' through all kinds of green. Branches caught my side window scattering little bits of sticks. But I was still moving, kind of flying, almost in control, but lurching toward the dirt nose first. All I could do was stop forward movement and drop like a rock. We had enough RPM to cushion our belly flop in the deep water of the bomb crater. Our splash would have made a whale proud.

The jolt on the bottom jerked my seat harness tighter than a fat lady's corset. Water rushed into the cargo area, to the bottom of my seat and over the pod-mounted machine gun. Everyone hung on until the rotor got stuck in the mud.

"One hell of a landing." The chief coughed up blood.

Colonel's voice lacked emotion. "Damn straight. And we're above ground. But we gotta secure our position. I'll call for anyone. Ox, stay with me. Sarge, set up a perimeter."

Pollhill detached the machine gun, grabbed the ammunition box, and jumped out. He directed the bandaged chief and the bleeding gunner to points around the helicopter. "Lieutenant Buncher. Get behind the stump ahead of the nose."

Beau shed his flight helmet and climbed over the pedestal. The clouds opened up again with a torrent of rain and reduced our visibility almost across the crater. "Now I understood what Noah felt like."

"How long can a radio work if the battery's drowning?"

Colonel sat on the rear web seat with his feet in water. "Hope I don't find out."

Thunder rolled. A lightning bolt lit up the zero-zero visibility, simply to convince us how little we could see. I changed frequencies while the Colonel transmitted to any unit listening.

One heard him.

"Serpent Six, this is Bronco 36. I remember you. You brought us to this pile of shit. But it ain't May Day baby. What the hell you been smoking? Over."

Serpent kicked at the water flooding in the door. "Bronco. We crashed this fuckin' bird. Got wounded. We're at Chang My meadow across from Hon Heo Mountain. Hill 2018. I repeat, Hill 2018. North of Qui Nhon. Relay this message to 229th Assault Helicopter Battalion. Over."

"This is Bronco. Wilco. Out."

I said, "I barely see Beau and he's at the tip of our rotor."

The Colonel shook his head. "What's good is, we're not flying. What's bad is...no one else is either."

PART ELEVEN_

WATER RUSHING up Kaelyn's nose choked her back to consciousness. The roaring rain wiped out all other sound. Her eye sockets puddled while the back of her head stuck in the mud.

The urge to kill Chien enveloped her.

She wondered where the scuzzy creep went and what he did to her. Blood tasted metallic in her mouth and only one nostril worked.

Chien had fastened her wrists and boots together with Army-green tape. It took several painful minutes to loosen the shoestrings with only two free fingers. The heavy tape, wrapped three times around her wrists, had to be pulled with her teeth. Her jaw muscles ached; her lips throbbed. As the last inch tore free, she felt the gun. She almost smiled.

A nice little Beretta.

Rain cascaded off her forehead like a faucet. Broken fern and crushed stems gave her the only hint of Chien's direction. Thunder drowned the rain sound and lightning fried her eyes.

Was this déjà vu? Kaelyn remembered hunting in the numbing December rain of Texas. She'd gut-shot a buck and followed its trail through the netherworld of her family's largest pasture. After a two-hour trek, she found the twelve-pointer in the underbrush. No one would believe her if she didn't drag it back.

Maybe just cut off an ear? After his interview.

The fern trail disappeared into a fast-moving, run-off stream. Weary to the bone, she tilted her head back to capture some water in her mouth. She couldn't even remember when she ate last. Chewing on a grassy, bitter fern helped, but didn't take the place of meat. Thoughts of Daddy's chef cooking venison on a campfire made her salivate.

Weapons fire destroyed the delicious dream. The first shots came from a pistol, an automatic rifle answered. Bullets ricocheted through the trees. She hugged the ground, gritting her teeth so she couldn't scream.

Kaelyn wondered who won.

Torrents of rain obscured all traces of the trail and muffled her slog up the creek. The current grew stronger, her boots heavier. Visibility diminished from fuck'n lousy to nonexistent.

Two more shots cracked over her head. She crawled on her belly below the ferns.

Just like hunting that buck, must look and not be seen.

At top of the hill, she rested behind a big tree. Her heart pounded.

Another shot sounded close enough to be too close.

Was that a muzzle flash or delirium?

The rain stopped. Chien's voice filled the void. "...if you try anything, I'll shoot you too."

A slight breeze improved visibility, like a curtain going up at the beginning of the show. Kaelyn grabbed a handful of ferns. The ranch foreman once told her to disguise an arrival with something familiar. From a kneeling position, she held the ferns outside the tree line, peeking between the fronds.

Three bodies squirmed on the ground near the helicopter, bloody, but alive. Their wrists and ankles taped. Behind them a heavily camouflaged soldier held a rifle and a roll of tape.

Danny, Beau, and the Colonel lay face-down, taped at the wrists. She recognized the other pilot from the Officers' Club in Saigon. "Gentlemen, this is why you must obey me." He nodded to the guard. Three rifle shots echoed and the wounded Pollhill, gunner, and crew chief convulsed for the last time.

Kaelyn dropped the fern because her hand shook so much. If she could only steady herself, she'd kill 'em without an interview.

Chien said, "And this is how you must obey me. Take off all your clothes except dog-tags, shoes, and stockings. We must travel very fast. Carry your clothes. If you move too slow, you will be eaten by mosquitoes and your blood sucked by the leeches. And if you don't obey, we will stake you to an ant hill."

The Colonel lifted his head. "Sergeant Major. Do you realize how wealthy you would be if you came back with us? I am not speaking about the ARVN Chieu Hoi Program. But amnesty that a leader of your rank and cultural background could appreciate. Our program includes a generous pension for life in the Philippines or Hawaii. And a mentor to ease your transition."

Chien nodded without expression, then kicked him. The impact of the boot to his head flipped the Colonel on his back. "How naïve do you think I am? *You* are my retirement." Chien laughed, "This pig tried to seduce me with a shitty American amnesty program. Strip him naked and tape him to the other two." The outlier laid his weapon down.

"Say your name and rank." Chien kicked Beau in the ribs.

"Goddamn. Why didn't ya' gimme a second to answer?"

The power of the next kick turned him over. "Only your name and rank!"

No answer. The soldier said, "He is unconscious."

Chien said, "Next. "

Danny did not move a muscle. "Second Lieutenant Hellberg."

"And your partner?"

"Second Lieutenant Buncher."

Chien nudged the Colonel but got no response. He wiped mud

off Given's rank and wings. "A colonel and master aviator, excellent. Retirement just got better."

Kaelyn extended the fern beyond the line of the tree. *Concentrate: steady...steady.* With her elbows on the ground, she laid the peep sight on the guard in front of Chien and squeezed the trigger. The bullet hit low into his neck and caused him to spin around. He fell backward.

Chien dove to the ground. He shot his pistol three times without a target.

Kaelyn aimed at the center of his head. "Bye, bye asshole." She pressed the trigger and heard the miserable slap of the hammer on a dead cartridge. Two more quick attempts got nothing. She slithered behind the tree. "Goddammit..."

"Hee, hee. That scrawny tree does not hide all of you. You'll be dead if I you don't drop your weapon and come out." He spoke as if she was an errant child but walked toward her with two hands on his pistol.

Kaelyn let pistol fall to the ground. "Okay, I'm coming out. Remember, you'll get three times the reward if I'm alive." She stepped out.

"My dear, soooo good to see you again. This is truly my lucky day, hee, hee. How do you get three times the price? I understood it's only double."

Kaelyn leaned against the tree. "My newspaper loves me. They'll up the ante."

"What is 'up the ante?'"

Danny rose to a football stance and launched his 190 pounds into Chien's back. As they hit the mud, his gun fired and knocked Kaelyn off her feet.

With his wrists taped together, Danny struggled to lift her up. Her head flopped like it wasn't attached. Blood gushed from her head.

He said, "Shit."

I smiled when Kaelyn opened her eyes. "Nice move. Nothing like a permanent part in your hair...in your head, babe."

Kaelyn touched the side of her head. "Ooowww. I hope you got that prick."

"I mashed him down. I don't know—"

"No, he didn't." The monster materialized from the mud with his pistol aimed at us. "The Chien prick lives. Ha haaaa. Miss DeHaven, please. Turn face down." He aimed the gun at me. "You too, face down. If you do anything stupid, I'll shoot you."

I laid like a log while he taped her eyes closed and her wrists to a sapling.

"And now you." He stepped on my head jamming my face deep in the mud. "How does it feel, Lieutenant?" He kicked me in the thigh. "Like a knife in your leg, isn't it lieutenant?" He stomped my back with his heel. "When you piss, it will burn, lieutenant." He screamed while he kicked my ribs. I lost count after six. "Breathe now, lieutenant."

When I blew the mud out of my nose, I could breathe again. As long as it wasn't deep. My leg and back went numb beyond the high side of pain, while he dragged me to the stinger. It protruded from the tail boom normally about six feet high, but because the nose sank in the hole, I had to stretch past seven. He placed my wrists over it and taped my forearms together.

Chien strutted back like a happy rooster. "Don't try to move, my dear Kaelyn. We'll be leaving soon." A *chec-chec* signal stopped him in his tracks. He repeated the all-clear response and looked around like someone stole his chickens.

A voice in Vietnamese emerged from the deepest bush, "Sergeant, maybe I can help."

The voice became more matter of fact. "We met when I posed as a villager from Thanh Ha. I guided the patrol up the Rock Face of Dead Men. You were waiting for me on top."

"Ah, your name is Vuong. Stand and be recognized."

Ninety degrees from where Chien aimed his pistol, Vuong stood. "I am standing."

The only thing I recognized in the Vietnamese was the name Vuong. When he stood, I couldn't believe it. Only cats had nine lives.

Chien's lips bunched in anger. "Who assigned you to deep cover?"

"General Giap's staff. I arrived last week from Hanoi with my wife. We lived here many years ago. Our mission was surveillance of the summit meeting."

"What's in your hand?"

Vuong held up a grenade. "The pin is pulled. If I die, we all die."

"You were shot by mistake of the man lying in front of you. If you are going to lead us to the beach, I'll have to stop your bleeding, or you'll never make it." Chien unbuckled a small First Aid pouch and applied an adhesive compress to Vuong's side.

The radio blared, "Serpent Six, Bronco Three-Six. Over."

Chien pushed the dead outlier off the PRC 25 radio and whispered to the microphone, "Roger Bronco, this is Serpent Six. Over."

"Man, I can hardly hear you. Are you still at Chang My meadow?"

"Negative. We moved down the valley to Vinh Hoi. Are you coming?"

"Soon as they find a couple of choppers. Over."

"Roger, I'll stand by. Out."

Chien motioned to Vuong, "Strap this radio on and get a weapon. Put your grenade under the Colonel and turn him into a trap." Chien laughed. "And they'll get more than they expect at Vinh Hoi. When they don't find the survivors, they will widen their effort. The higher the rank, the greater the search. We must reach the beach by sundown. Line up the prisoners."

Hanging from the stinger was no picnic. Every part of my body hurt like I fell out of a speeding Jeep. I moaned and Chien turned to me quick as a snake. "Remember the rules. Total silence. If I hear you again, I'll show you the real meaning of pain. One...ball...at...a...time."

The radio blared, "Bronco Three-Six. Who you calling a dumb-shit straphanger?"

"Well Pumpkin, if the fuckin' slipper fits, wear it. We gotta chopper down. What's left of the crew is on the run. I gave you that two hours ago. And you're still fiddle-fuckin' around waitin' for an aircraft. These sons of bitches risk their asses for us every day. Least we can do is pull 'em out when they're down. Over." Bronco slapped his hand on the table.

Silence.

"Nothin' I can do, Man. I'm stuck in this tower."

"Roger that. How about G2?"

Silence.

"Are you there?"

"Yes, sir...No, sir...Shit...Don't know who to call."

"Well goddamn, just make a guess."

Explosions and gunfire drowned Bronco out. "Gotta go Joe. I'll be back. Out."

The Qui Nhon Approach Controller turned to his supervisor, "What'll we do?"

"How 'bout the MACV gook? I'll bet he can find someone. Where's he?"

"With Fatty at the hospital..."

"Get him on the horn."

Fatty picked up on the fourth ring, between slurps from his big cup of chocolate marshmallow milk shake. "You bet, Trinh Le's sacked out in the secure room. I'll let you know." For a big man, Fatty made it to the back of the hospital in record time. Through the secure room door, he heard a conversation in Vietnamese. He rapped. It stopped.

"Come in."

"This is Fatty, it's locked."

The door opened slowly. "What's happening?"

"Need your help." Fatty brought Trinh up to speed. "You've gotta find a chopper. Can ya call G2?"

"No, Joint Command will be our best bet. I know the Hon Heo area. Especially the village of Vinh Hoi."

Fatty yawned. "Let me know so I can pass it to App Con. A grunt lieutenant out there has threatened to come in and kick his ass if something doesn't happen soon."

"Will do," Trinh dialed and waited. Twenty-five minutes later, "*MIHN OI*, how are you?"

The syrupy female voice loved to be called sweetheart. "Yes, what is the emergency?"

"I need a helicopter to pick me up at the Qui Nhon tower. The chopper should show no markings and be capable of carrying from four to eight. Top it off for maximum range. When they're 20 minutes out, have the Tower get me."

"Yes dear. I'll contact First Flight."

"*GA MUG.*" Trinh choked up.

The voice understood. "And thank you. It has been a long time since you have seen your family. Your father is the unchallengeable force in the reconciliation of Bao Dai, as the Emperor of all Vietnam.

The time is right. Only Bao Dai can act now. But the mystery is still Ho Chi Minh."

"No, not at all. My father understands Ho Chi Minh's infirmity, his minions of clueless Viet Cong." Trinh formed a small paper airplane.

The heavy rap on the door brought him back to the planet. "Trinh Le."

"Yes, yes." He opened the door to find Fatty, who was now sweaty.

"A helicopter is ten minutes out. What's going on? Who's the First Flight Detachment?" Fatty wiped his face with an olive-drab towel.

"You wanted me to find a helicopter, I did. You can call them the SOG ready-reaction force; if a team's in trouble, you push their button."

"Then help me out. When I approached the Air Force, they switched me to MACV. I ran into a brick wall there. They couldn't even verify you as one of the staff. What's the deal?"

"Who'd you speak to?"

"Colonel Thaxton, or somethin' like that."

"He's new on the post. Lucky to find his desk every day." Trinh posed like the smiling Buddha.

"That's strange...'cause my Air Force contact knew him. Said Thaxton held the post since the last Westmoreland visit." A rare shadow of doubt troubled Fatty. "Anyway, this inbound has orders to pick you up at the tower pad. Can ya' get there in time?"

"Sure, help me find my briefcase."

Fatty came in, his eyes scanned the empty Jack Daniels bottle, the open cabinet drawers, and files on the floor. His incredulous look grew but he couldn't duck the bottle that crashed on his head. Fatty's body splattered on the floor with a squishy thud.

Trinh Le pulled a can of solvent out of his bag and splashed it over the radio, telephone, and the files. At the door he lit the small paper airplane. It burned slowly in flight right into the middle of the desk. Ignition sounded flat like a puddle of gas popping, and the flame illuminated the room.

Trinh pushed the interior lock button and closed the door.

I REMOVED my clothes as fast as I could until I stood in the mud, stripped down to my boots. Vuong knotted Kaelyn's rope around my neck and shoved me in front of her. Helpless and endangered were feelings never felt before. I whispered to Kaelyn, "Once I worried I wouldn't have a war to go to."

She winked then shouted at Chien, "What the hell ya mean, 'your turn?' I'm a respected journalist, for a national newswire and a major daily newspaper. And you're gonna drag me around the countryside bare ass naked? Do ya' realize the gravity of your fuck-up?"

He snarled. "Miss DeHaven, you assassinated one of my men and tried to kill me. How do Americans say it...you shit in your mess kit. Penalty is loss of your non-combatant status. Now a common war criminal. Take off your clothes, or I will rip them off, along with your shoes, and leave them here to burn with the ship. Make your choice. You have three seconds."

Kaelyn looked dumbfounded. "Okay, Okay. But, I'm still your major opportunity to reach the American public. If you wanna see my ass, stick around." She unbuttoned her blouse and exposed the conditioned shoulders of an athlete. Next her zipper sounded like a tiny chainsaw in the dead silence. She dropped her pants to uncover legs and hips of a dancer. Her hands taped together made it impossible to remove her bra.

"Danny, give me a hand," she said.

Chien shouted, "Vuong! Cut 'em off."

Kaelyn looked at Vuong with a dare under her stare, "The straps that is."

He immediately drew his knife to cut the straps on each shoulder then freed the hook and eye closure.

Her breasts swayed as she folded everything to a neat bundle on her shirt, tied by the sleeves. She winked, stepped out of her panties, and bent over and gave them a beautiful moon.

Cursing the limitation of what I couldn't see, I'd bet there were no areas to mar her tan.

Vuong explained we had to move in unison or the rope would tighten. He said, "Chien Phu, may I suggest our route?"

"That's why you're here."

In a melodic, nasal tone, Vuong continued, "Considering the value of your prisoners, we should go north to the village of Chanh Thang. The beach means better range for the radio and an easy pickup from your boat."

Chien nodded in agreement. "Let's go."

Vuong adjusted the radio on his back. "We can't leave the Colonel; he is too valuable."

"He'll slow us down."

"Not if Danny and Beau carry him on a stretcher. I saw one in the helicopter."

"Absolutely not. He's only a Colonel. She's a US Senator's daughter." Chien finished arming himself with an M16 and several magazines. "She is our path to the Americans. Our priority."

"Yes, Sergeant." Vuong took a white phosphorous grenade from his belt.

"Do not torch the ship. Let them look for it. Just lead us to the beach. *Di. Di. Mau.*"

Vuong led us down the mountain path, a very generous description for a cliff-like trail of torment. We jumped over rocks, balanced on dead logs, waded through dense fields of green with thorny leaves as big as my chest.

"Stop." Vuong raised his hand. We halted a common body frozen in time.

"What is it?" Chien aimed his rifle where he looked.

"A helicopter."

"Where?"

Vuong pointed at the dense canopy and we heard something with two blades but smaller than a Huey. Until the sound disappeared.

Chien shouted, "Move your lazy ass." He swatted Beau across his back with a bamboo limb. It sounded like a hand clap hard enough to draw blood. Beau contorted in pain but swallowed the agony in silence.

Vuong moved from side to side down the trail to make detection from the air difficult. Following him on the ground with my hands tied was borderline impossible. For Kaelyn to keep in lock step, she bumped my heels, rammed my ankles, and kicked my calves. I feared a freaky pile-up where we would all slide to a stop, on top of our bundled clothing. So, I made my track predictable.

The rest of the hill took forever. At the bottom I caught my breath. I dripped from every pore. Nakedness liberated me despite the penalty of scratches up past my hips on every inch of skin.

"Vuong." Chien's stress level became more evident.

I turned toward him but got stuck on Kaelyn. Giant drops of perspiration dangled from her nipples. It had to be against the Geneva Convention to distract a hardened warrior, from the business of escaping, with a flagrant sexist ploy.

Chien pointed up the hill and commanded Vuong, "Go back, get the Colonel or kill him."

Kaelyn murmured, "Understood only 'kill' and 'Colonel.'"

Vuong said, "But Sergeant...can you handle all three by yourself?"

"Don't be impertinent. I must reach Chanh Thang by dusk."

Without another word, Vuong slipped off the radio and disappeared back up the trail. Chien picked it up and dialed across the frequencies, listening for anything. He couldn't find the repeater station and cursed each blast of static received. His numbed scowls showed frustration.

All through his misery, I stood motionless. Disconcerted as a lamb going to slaughter. We had numerical superiority, but Chien had nasty old guns, knives, grenades, and wore clothes. And he could use both hands.

All I need is a moment and I'd get him.

"Hellberg, put on this radio."

"Yes, Sergeant. But how can I do it with my hands tied?" My soul laughed at him. He couldn't catch Vuong with us tagging along. Nor could he leave us or signal with his rifle.

It hurt me not to smile. Chien's eyes drilled a chill into my bones. "You won't laugh when I get you to the village." He handled the radio like he wanted to punish it too. While strapping the rope around my neck, a whirring sound of blades interrupted Chien tying the last knot.

At almost 25 pounds, the PRC 25 radio was heavy as a half-case of bottled beer and just as clumsy. Chien wrapped its most sensitive part in an oil cloth.

"*Di. Di Mau.*" Chien, looking like a pooped explorer, pointed up the path.

"Come on, what's that?" Kaelyn loved to bait him.

"Certainly, you must know it means to move quickly."

We followed the stream's edge, amazed at the sheer volume and speed of the water. The clouds gave way to sunshine on the high, steep cliffs around us. Treacherous seemed inadequate as a description of the canyon. Clear sunshine came in at a broil, I felt freckles frying on my white skin. Mud and grass changed to rock and bushes.

The incline became precipitous. Scratches and puncture wounds gave way to screaming aches from every imaginable muscle. I panted, each gulp of air demanding another, bigger than the last. Kaelyn peppered her march, with a single description, hissed through her clenched teeth, "Hate that needle-dick, bug-fucker."

As fast as Chien went, I followed. I vowed never to let the rope get taut in front of my nose. The knot loosened.

Chien sweated through his precious, tailored uniform. The antenna magnified the clumsiness of the radio. Technically, its length was "just too damn long." When the trail narrowed down to a width requiring us to balance on every step, the weight of the radio made him wobble like a drunk.

The path twisted into a ledge and the incline increased to damn near vertical. Mist from the roaring eight-foot-wide runoff slicked the rocks.

Chien wheezed and slowed down. His skinny butt got wider when I got too close. He tried to move faster and slipped on a stone. His arm stretched out for balance. I bumped his steady foot and the weight of the radio sucked him backward into the torrential water. To stop his fall, he pulled my rope and the second knot unfolded like it was made of silk.

Outrage twisted his face like it was on fire. He screamed at me, "Bastard . . ." His legs flailed in search of traction as the run-off rolled him over and over like a beer barrel. The microphone, clutched in his hand above the water, bobbed down the rapids.

Kaelyn rejoiced, "I hope he goes straight to hell."

"If he survives, we got a problem. We gotta get outta of here."

"Get me out of these ropes." Kaelyn wiggled her neck back and forth, which gave her torso counter movement, her breasts slapped wildly from side to side.

Mesmerized, I said, "No."

Beau struggled to his feet, "If he lives, he'll hunt us down. We're his retirement and road to glory. And if he buys the farm, Vuong will come after us."

"That helicopter was an H-13. Couldn't see any markings. Assume it was friendly."

Beau looked around. "Man, how could you tell?"

"I saw a little bit of the open frame. Maybe the gooks have more helicopters from where they got the last bunch."

"We got attacked by a couple of H-34's."

"You what?" Beau's face showed the same disbelief Kaelyn's did.

"No time. We got to move."

Kaelyn yelled, "What if the helicopter returns?"

I pointed down the valley at the two H-13's flying away. Nothing disheartened me like the two little dots dissolving into a grey horizon.

Qui Nhon tower searched for the aircraft reporting, "Foxtrot, where the hell are you?"

"Foxtrot over Xuam Quang. Is passenger at pad?"

The tower operator shrugged, "Man, his accent's too thick. Ain't Vietnamese." With field glasses, the supervisor helped find the helicopter in a cloudy sky. "Foxtrot. Passenger's here. You're cleared to land."

"Qui Nhon. Where is pad?"

"Land on the east side of the tower." The operator turned to the supervisor. "Where the hell's that MACV gook, anyway?"

The supervisor dialed Fatty's desk. A low, slow, southern drawl answered, "Front desk, Specialist Bowman speakin'."

The Super heard an alarm in the background. "This is tower. Did Fatty find the gook?" "Damned if I know. When he got your call, he ran down the hall.""Go find him. Chopper's here."

On cue, the helicopter landed, but too close to the building. The tower operator and the supervisor jumped back from the vibrating windows. Deafening noise flooded the control room.

Super shouted, "Tell that dumb sombitch to back off."

Completely oblivious, Bowman continued, "Well, as soon as Fatty left, this damn fire alarm started screaming. Don't know how to shut it off. This is a goddamn zoo."

Super looked around, "Well, get your ass out of that chair and send the gook to me. Then look for smoke."

"Yes, sir. Wait—"

Fatty suddenly appeared and grabbed the phone from Bowman. "Stop da fuckin' gook. He tried to kill me and burn down the joint."

"Why'd ya' piss 'em off?" The Super's smile changed to surprise as he looked down from the tower. Trinh Le walked on the pad with a briefcase, the other arm in the sling.

The big cargo door of the H-34 slid open. A crew member jumped out in a bright green flight suit and helmet. He helped Trinh Le board while the rotor blades stayed at flight RPM.

Fatty panted into the phone. "I shit ya' not. Don't let him go."

"Okay, I'll get down there." The Super chambered a cartridge in his carbine and hurried down the stairs.

The operator shouted into the phone, "Super's down there. Got the crew chief and gook at gunpoint. They jumped 'em, knocked him to the ground..."

Leaning out the cargo door, Trinh Le gestured at the Tower to come down to the pad.

The operator shot him the finger and called Fatty, "The gook's coming for me; I'm bolting myself in."

Trinh ran up the tower stairs and shot the handle off the control room door. He kicked it several times, but the slide-bolt held.

On the concrete, Super raised up on his elbow and fired a long series. Bullet holes slowly walked up the side of the helicopter and knocked out the right-side cockpit window. The co-pilot ducked out of sight.

Back at ground level, Trinh Le maneuvered behind the Super and shot him in the head. Reloading as he moved out of the rotor path, Trinh fired four times into the window of the tower.

Reinforced Plexiglas shattered and the operator hid under his desk. Without a weapon to stop this bird, he heaved his wooden folding chair out the window opening. The chair smashing against the rotor blades sounded like sonic boom and blew wooden splinters everywhere. Like a case of toothpicks exploding.

I WHISTLED three times in my best ear-piercing style. The two H-13's kept flying away in the valley. I said, "The chopper's leaving. Didn't see us."

Kaelyn grappled with the trail. "Well, they sure as hell couldn't hear us either."

The near vertical incline of the trail and slick rocks made the short distance to the crest miserable. We collapsed at the top in the shade of a tree and caught our breath. Exhaustion, depression, bewilderment crashed down on my head. My parched throat barely moaned. The tape across my hands felt like a band of razors. I couldn't suck water from my palm. Didn't care if it was a pure mountain run-off or seepage from a hospital cemetery. I plunged my face into the stream. Cool and musty smelling, its wetness satisfied my aching soul.

When I laid my head back to the comfort of a rock, I fell asleep. More like passed out into oblivion. I dreamed about the summers worked at Calvary Cemetery. There my headrest was a tombstone.

"Danny, get up," Kaelyn kicked my legs. "A helicopter's comin'."

My heart rate went from barely tickin' to peggin' the gauge. "What? Where?"

She shrugged. "Don't know. But it's gettin' louder."

The sound wasn't a cute little H-13 poking around, but a denser, multi-blade rotor whine with the baritone roar of a big, reciprocating engine. "Take cover in that clump of bamboo."

"But it could be our guys."

"What if it ain't?"

We moved like a single, naked body to the deep shade. Tangled bamboo stuck, cut and ripped us with thorns strong enough to slice tanned leather, much less naked skin. Echoes in the canyon amplified the sound of the rotors until the helicopter hovered at the crest of the hill. Both cargo doors slammed open, as the H-34 did a slow 360-degree pedal turn over the tree. Crew members in bright green flight suits manned the pod-mounted, machine guns on both sides.

"Are they the bad guys? There's no markings on it." Kaelyn peeked through the leaves.

"Last time I saw a helicopter like that, it tried to shoot me." The helicopter followed the trail for another fifty yards and flew off in a slow, climbing turn out of the valley.

She whined, "Can we please put on our clothes?"

"No time." I scanned the empty horizon, but I couldn't take eyes off her. Perspiration and mist made her glisten. It ran off between her breasts to her belly button then bunched up in her pubic hair. What a lovely trip. I said, "Don't know where we're going, but we have to hurry up and get there."

"Brilliant. Getting clothes on won't take five minutes."

Beau said, "And how do we get out of this tape? Chew 'em off? Danny's right, let's go."

I crept into the sunlight. A partial overcast drifted in to ease our trot down the scrawny path. The torrential stream widened its swift flow.

Compared to our trek up hill, we covered a lot of ground. I felt exhilarated from our run. I panted, "Our boots help. Best thing ol' Chien did."

Beau gasped, "Get real. He was only making sure our guys wouldn't find us."

The valley transformed into a canyon. A gentle sloping hillside turned into the bottom of a rocky cliff. We ran out of trail into a mega rock at least thirty feet high. It jutted into the current like a baseball backstop. Water curved into a ninety degree turn and disappeared under a log. I asked, "How good can you swim with your arms tied?"

Kaelyn stared at me like a deer in the beam of a head light.

It didn't faze Beau, "Like a fish, man. Why not use the log? It's wide enough."

"No." Kaelyn covered her mouth and shook her head. "No. Won't work." She squeezed her clothing bundle with her arm.

I said, "We got nothing but canyon wall here and more places to hide on the other side."

"You don't understand. In college, my sorority sisters pushed me into a pool. Hands tied behind my back. Scared me so much I didn't swim again until graduation."

Beau raised his thick eyebrows at her. "Did ya write a story about them?"

"It was the initiation ritual."

"Look at us." Beau inspected the rope. "We're tied together with our boots on. But without our hands, they'll be like cinder blocks on our feet. It's loose braided twine. We can smash it apart, one strand at a time." He placed the leader on the boulder and smashed it with a jagged rock. It didn't cut all the way through, but one braid freed up.

We all pounded on our ropes until we were free. Then pulled each other's tape off. Clapped our hands. Flexed our fingers. What a difference.

Kaelyn said, "Listen! Hear that?"

"What?"

"The same rotor noise."

I backed away from the boulder and searched the sky. "Yeah. Get outta here."

Beau said, "Cinch your clothes tight with your belt and throw them to the other bank." We did.

I stood on the log, "Here goes." And three baby steps later I paused, "C'mon Kaelyn."

"Goddamn it, I'm comin', I'm comin'." She gave a huge sigh and tried to find her balance.

Beau stopped her sway and she got up. The log shifted. "She-itt."

The reverberation was like a hiccup, I stuck my newly freed hands out front for stability. We moved in the cadence of a zombie for an interminable session of walk-the-plank, on a log sagging in the middle, that moved a lot. After I passed the rock, the water flow got louder and farther below us. "Damn. Damn."

"What's the matter?" Kaelyn's voice had a strange, melodic, maternal softness. It could have passed for empathy.

I said, "I looked down. Don't. Keep your focus straight ahead. Don't let anything in on it."

Beau shouted, "On the other side. Think how flat, wide and solid it is."

Kaelyn replaced the sing-song softness with a precise, coach-like dictum. "Nothing can keep me from it."

The roar got louder. I peeked anyway. "It's a waterfall..." My words dissolved into the sound of whirling rotors and the raucous of a mighty, radial engine spooling up from an autorotation.

I looked up at the belly of an H-34 in a full flare ahead of us. Felt the wind of the blades. Like a flying tank. I lost my focus...my balance... and my log. My body followed.

Everything blurred. I hit the deep, swift water face first. When I surfaced, the downwash of the helicopter pushed Kaelyn back into Beau. They bounced off the log and fell through the air at me.

VUONG RAN like a hungry fox to get away from Chien Phu. When he reached bottom of the hill, fatigue, and loss of blood from his seeping chest wound devastated his body and impaired his brain. He had made some mistakes, and in this game, any slip could be fatal.

Heart pounding, he lowered himself to the ground. Meditation had always been an effective tool for Vuong. It revived body and mental functions. Cross legged, he focused on rejuvenation but passed out against a coconut tree.

Movement in his lap awoke him. His heartbeat spiked. A green bamboo viper, longer than both of his feet, slithered over his motionless legs. Its diamond-shaped head angled up with fiery red eyes and a flickering purple tongue.

Vuong resented the time lost maneuvering on this edge of death. He yearned to avenge his precious wife, little Quy. Chien will deserve to die for his country, she didn't. But Vuong needed to keep him alive until he found the gold.

Le Van Vien said the North was just as corrupt and stupid as the South. Only the Binh Xuyen could control these people. They proved it to the French, while policing Saigon in return for a monopoly on gambling, opium, and prostitution. No politics, just peace. A piece of everything.

During the rendezvous with the giant, amphibian evacuation aircraft, Vuong did not recognize Le Van Vien when he carried him aboard. Vien's bandages obscured his name tag with dried blood and a clump of shit. He did not survive the aircraft crash, but the organization he led, the Binh Xuyen, has withstood has every political change it ever faced.

In the meantime, the North would pay Vuong handsomely for the American colonel. But he had to find him soon: A live colonel is worth three times more than a dead one.

His preoccupation with the reward evaporated with the muffled sound of helicopter rotor blades. He carefully scanned the small patches of open sky. Seconds later the helicopter drug its skids through the top palms of his tree and knocked coconuts to the ground. The snake slithered from Vuong's lap into the brush.

After knocking off more palms, the helicopter dove low enough to splash water in the rice paddy with its skids. He saluted the helicopter, opened a broken coconut, drank the milk, and savored the meat.

Markings left as a trail made the return trip easier. About thirty meters from the wrecked helicopter, Vuong crawled through the undergrowth as quiet as a gentle breeze. The helicopter stuck nose-first into the crater with its tail high in the air. Surrounding the ship, bodies on perimeter all died execution-style. Head shots painted an ugly scene. He pried a .45-automatic from the hand of one of the soldiers.

Even though he planted a live grenade under the Colonel's neck, Vuong sweated disarming it. Just reinserting the pin.

Watching intently with his weak, irregular pulse and blood caked forehead, the Colonel slurred, "Who're you?"

"Vuong is my name."

The Colonel's eyes blinked rapidly. "I'm tired. My head's gonna burst...ringing in my ears."

"Colonel, can you walk?"

"Where to? What's your name again?"

"Vuong. Vuong."

"Who's wrong? I didn't say you're wrong." He got nose to nose with Vuong. "I'm always right. Now what's your goddamn name?"

Vuong grinned. "Just call me Charlie."

"Like that name." The Colonel laid down again.

"Can you walk?"

He attempted to stand but fell over like a drunk and laughed. "Oopsie."

Vuong helped him up. "Put your arm around my neck."

The Colonel's hand felt like old cold mud. His weight almost buckled Vuong. "What did you say your name was?"

"Charlie...Charlie." The first few steps with him reminded Vuong of his job in Qui Nhon. He hauled drunken GIs out of titty bars and learned all about their units.

This would be easier.

Strange intestinal rumbling came from the Colonel. "Charlie, Charlie." They stopped and he vomited on Vuong's sandaled feet.

Rotor blades of the H-34 traveled at two hundred twenty revolutions per minute and turned the wooden chair into mulch. "Damn... Keep going!" Trinh Le flinched as debris bounced off his windshield but did not balk when he tossed a grenade into the tower. The explosion splattered the operator all over the landing pad.

Trinh Le directed the aircraft commander, "Fly north. Stay low level." The big helicopter lumbered across the active runway, over the hangar and to the bay. Blood from the co-pilot's wound made a puddle on the pedestal panel as he labored to pull himself out of the cockpit.

Trinh Le climbed into his seat. "Been a long time since flight school." Checking his gauges, he said, "If they scramble the gunships, we're screwed." Trinh scanned the radio frequencies for advisories. "That's why I wiped out the tower. Needed a head start."

Vietnamese spoken by the Chinese pilot carried a thick accent. "Get on controls."

"This sling is for real. Took a ricochet in Qui Nhon. Here only to navigate." Trinh Le pointed his sling away from the shoreline.

The pilot lifted his visor to expose a strong, round Chinese face with a high forehead. "I am Captain Ren. Excuse my poor Vietnamese. Receive message from reconnaissance patrol. Only survivor is Chien Phu. Lost three captives of major importance. He in flood plain, Chang My Valley. With radio. Must reach Chanh Thien before dusk."

Trinh motioned, "I've been there. What call sign?"

"Chien." The Chinese pronunciation distorted the word completely. Ren shouted louder, "Chi-en."

"I don't understand." Trinh Le gasped. "Change course to 330 degrees."

Ren alerted the crew, "I receive report on American activity from outpost in Vinh Hoi."

"I did not know radio outpost." Trinh flushed with embarrassment.

Captain said, "Many American aircraft. We have many villages. They shoot up everything. We shoot them. Because we track them."

A female voice interrupted, "This is Vinh. Two helicopters west of me."

"Have you contacted other units?"

"Not since attack. Our scout see freighter sink, lose several boat and something terrible at cave. He very sick. Died before he tell more." A child wailed in the background.

Trinh said, "Where is patrol leader from Hon Heo?"

The woman keyed the microphone with the baby screaming louder. "He say 'rapids.' Not know which one. Sorry. Over." More static.

"Advise Chien we come in H-34."

"Must leave frequency for that. What is H-34? Over."

Ren snapped, "Check damn chart. Medium helicopter."

"Yes, sir. I sorry. Normally husband do this. Over."

"Where the hell is he?"

"Dead. He scout."

Silence weighted heavy. "Roger. Out."

Trinh Le said, "But how can you transmit without detection?"

Below the Captain's visor, a smile appeared. "For last thousand years, Vietnamese avoid war with superior forces. They use land where no enemy. Stole equipment where no guard. Now, they transmit on band width where no enemy."

The crew chief reported, "I've bandaged co-pilot's arm. I'll help him."

Trinh lowered his binoculars. "This is where I spent my youth. Normally, this fast-moving river is only a stream. Always floods."

The chief swung his machine gun forward of the aircraft. "Left side. Body in tree."

"Fox, this is Vinh. Over."

"Go ahead."

"I talked to Chien. He hang on log, jam against tree. Over."

"Roger. Out." Trinh steadied himself against the door and scanned the flooded plain. All the rice paddies disappeared into moving, muddy water. A few treetops stood out, collecting elephant grass, palms, stumps, and vines.

Sound of an automatic rifle penetrated the noise of the helicopter. The door gunner pointed. "Behind the bush." He opened up with his machine gun and the water danced around the target.

Trinh lunged at him and butted shots wide of target. "Stop. That's him! That's him!

PART TWELVE_

CHIEN FLOATED on the river's strong current with a death grip on a palm tree.

Trinh Le watched him from the cargo bay. "Chief, do you have a snare on board?"

The crew chief had Chien in the sights of his machine gun. "These helicopters are stripped to the bone. Fuel. Ammunition. Hardly anything else."

"Put your wheels in the water and lift him to the other side of the river." Trinh Le leaned toward the pilot.

"Too tricky." Captain Ren's head never flinched from watching the river's flow. "They order me to minimize risk, only have few helicopters."

"Fuck 'em. We can always steal more. Only one chance to save him. I'll take responsibility."

"General Danh piss fire when I crash. Promise to shoot me if I do again."

Trinh Le tapped Ren's helmet with his pistol. He pointed the barrel down between the pilot's legs and cocked the hammer. "And you'll have a messy accident, if you don't pick 'em up."

Ren let the helicopter settle on top of the water up to the fuselage. Chien grabbed the wheel strut like a long-lost friend. The wake from the tire swamped him. Floating roots of a rotten stump entangled his feet. Chien's weight had doubled with wet camouflage, ammunition belts, weapons, and a radio. The diminutive crew chief, spread eagle on the cargo floor shouted, "I can't pull him in, but I can hold him."

A watery mist swirling from the rotors, obscured visibility. Trinh Le snarled into his mike. "Don't let him fall."

The chopper lifted Chien from the water. Dangling underneath the wheels, he smashed into a small tree and a stand of bamboo until he slipped out of chief's hand. Shallow water cushioned his landing. He tried to stand but collapsed like a broken palm.

After removing his radio, both the chief and gunner strained with his weight before getting him on board. On the floor Chien puked out the muddy river. Reddish-black leeches stuck to his neck like a slimy necklace. He opened his eyes to cough, spit and mumble a curse.

Trinh interrupted and put a headset on him, "Sergeant Chien Phu?"

A snarling hesitation replaced Chien's brief inspection. He waited, "And you are?"

"I'm Trinh Le. I'll help track down your prisoners."

Chien slowed his heavy breathing. "Go upriver to saddle in valley. Several flows meet. Only escape follows north."

"Why?"

"Canyon walls too steep. And my man was coming with prisoner."

"Who?"

"An Army colonel."

Trinh tapped Ren, "Any questions?" Smiling, he flew from the riverbank toward the mountain.

Chien stunk like a latrine. He couldn't sit up. His arms, back, head and chest were battered and bleeding. The bloated river shrunk back from the ferocity that nearly killed him. He chuckled at all he had been through to capture the American aircraft...then to almost die because of one distraction. It had been difficult not to watch her every move. He had not been with a woman in a very long time.

"Sergeant. About a hundred meters ahead. Two villagers. Walking slowly. The second with a bale on his back. No weapons visible. Instructions."

Trinh Le passed his binoculars to Chien. "See anyone you know?"

Chien perked up. "That's Vuong, the second must be the colonel. Look at his size. Can you land on the bank?"

Ren set up an approach with the big chopper but noticed metal rods about fifteen feet high over the landing spot. "It's a trap." Ren banked away.

Trinh Le pointed. "Hover over the stream. Chien will signal them from the door."

Vuong understood the gesture through the dense mist kicked up by rotors. He agreed to meet up the trail.

The helicopter climbed straight to the saddle and hovered slowly over the tree. Chien removed the last leech from his neck. "They're here somewhere. All three are still naked, except for their boots."

Trinh looked at Ren. "Will this thing climb above the ridge?"

"Like a sick vulture, but it will make it."

Chien searched with his binoculars. "There they are! At the waterfall. Get 'em."

Ren laughed. "You fool with me. This is helicopter. Quiet as grenade exploding. As soon as hear us they run back to bush."

Trinh Le said, "Not exactly. We'll autorotate to the pasture at the neck of the canyon. I slept there under the stars when I was young."

"Will it be silent?" Chien gaped outside.

"The engine will be at a much lower RPM, like idling in a car."

Chien shook his head, "I still don't understand."

Trinh gestured with both hands. "We'll climb high enough so they can't hear us. Then we'll throttle-back and coast all the way down. They won't know we're coming until the last 50 feet. About ten seconds before we land."

White Bird gritted his teeth, "Yellow. So ya' want a good time. Huh?"

"Fuckin' A. Why do you ask, oh, noble leader?"

"Listen man. I know you'll do what you have to. Even sacrificing an aircraft to get it done. But testing fate, twice in a row, is dumbass. Over."

Yellow laughed, "What ya' mean? Just havin' a little fun."

"Bullshit. You dragged your skids through a tree to knock off coconuts at 60 knots then belly-flopped in a rice paddy to make a splash. You're either stupid or stoned—now knock it off. Meet me over the ridge, south bound. Out."

"Break. White this is Bird Three. Over."

"Roger, go ahead."

"A rogue H-34 wiped out the Qui Nhon airfield tower. Departed north bound. Twenty minutes ago. Battalion says we gotta find those bastards. Over."

"What about our search for the Serpent flight?"

Bird Three quelled his anger. "Find 'em both. The 34 has no markings."

"But he travels faster than we do."

"So just shoot the sombitch."

"Roger, wilco. Yellow, ya' copy?"

"Sure did partner. Wish we had a bigger posse."

"I hate to split up, but we gotta cover a lot of landscape. Cut north in this valley. I'll check the west side of the mountain and meet ya' over the canyon."

"Roger, dodger." Yellow descended to 500 feet, turned up the valley and wished for his on-board observer. He would've shot the coconuts off that tree.

The sun climbed high in the sky and the bubble tested every sweat gland in his body. Yellow dug through a box of C rations for some smokes. He held the cyclic between his knees and lit the cigarette with his Zippo. Wind turned his lighter into a blowtorch and singed his mustache.

Movement of two people on the trail got his attention. The gook in front dressed in black pajamas but no hat. Very strange. Following closely, a second person carried a bale of sticks and wore Army fatigue pants with bloused boots. More strange.

Yellow transmitted, "Hold on Kemosabe. I'm lookin' at a gook with a GI in tow. North of Vinh Hoi, followin' the stream. Need some cover, babe." He armed his guns and dropped down to a hundred feet for a better look.

"Roger, wilco."

Yellow stood the nose of the aircraft straight up and dropped to 35 feet off the ground. His mounted machine guns pointed tight at the twosome. "White, don't know if I can wait. Got 'em pinned."

Squinting through the downwash, the gook extended both hands like a crossing-guard at a grade school corner. The bale hauler plowed into him and dropped his load into the stream.

Yellow recognized his flight school Commander. "I'll be damned. Found ol' Colonel Givens. Under escort."

"I didn't know Goddam Givens was lost. What the hell does escort mean?"

"The Colonel has no visible weapon, no helmet, and he's carrying the load." Yellow hovered to a different angle. "Correction, there is a rope from the gook to the Colonel. Pajama-man has his hands up. Colonel looks confused."

White laughed. "Givens, confused? I thought God never got puzzled. Aha, just crestin' the hill, gotcha covered."

Yellow said, "What ya' want me to do?"

"Get the Colonel. Take him back to Qui Nhon."

"And go by myself? Ya' got to be shittin' me."

"Nope. That 34 needs to be found."

Yellow flicked his cigarette at the stream. "That doesn't mean you can fly off with an unknown gook. A heartbeat away. Sounds like you got the bad case of dumb fuck. Over."

"Okay. It must be catchy. So, you get the Colonel and I'll take the gook, we'll both go north."

"Roger, wilco." Yellow hovered under the edge of the trees and landed on the bank. Kinda like nickel tryin' ta fit in a dime slot. The Vietnamese came right up to him pulling the Colonel.

Yellow drew his pistol but didn't believe his eyes. The Colonel stood docile as a puppy, with a blank stare.

Yellow figured this was just another rough cut, ignorant peasant. "Speak English?"

"Yes, sir." Simple, loud enough to be heard, but not too close. His smile showed bad teeth.

"What's wrong with the Colonel?"

"Probable concussion. He was kicked in the head by an NVA."

Yellow could've been blown away by a butterfly. Where'd this guy come from? Yellow pointed, "Sit the Colonel next to me."

The gook led the Colonel around the front of the bubble. Made sure he didn't trip over the skids or guns. Helped him into the passenger seat, like a nurse with his favorite patient. He buckled him in and took off the rope.

Yellow motioned him back. "The other helicopter will land as soon as I lift. You'll fly with him. What's your name and unit?"

"My name is Vuong. I work for the CIA as an agent within the North Vietnamese Army and the Binh Xuyen. DO NOT broadcast my name or affiliation over the air. I'll share that info with your wing man when I board." He pulled a small dental appliance out of his mouth and smiled over perfect, bright white teeth. "Tell him I'll wait here."

"White. Pajama-man awaits." Yellow backed out of the area and circled as cover. He tapped the Colonel on his shoulder. "Good to see you. It's been forever since flight school."

The Colonel sat with one hand on his leg and the other under his chin, like the statue of *The Thinker*. He ignored the remark, lowered his head, and threw a wild punch. Yellow deflected it to his chest protector. Givens screamed in pain and cocked his other fist.

Yellow unleashed a powerful right jab to his jaw. Spit splashed on the bubble and the lights went out for Goddamn Givens. Years of Golden Glove boxing built a powerful protective mechanism deep in Yellow's psyche.

"Yellow, I got the hot skinny here. Over."

"And you ain't gonna believe this shit either, big boy. Go." Yellow was not the most powerful gun in the rack, but he worked well with White. Even if he was a college boy.

White's enthusiasm flowed. "I didn't know how special the Serpent flight was. They carried a journalist whose daddy is a US Senator. Over."

"Well la-de-fuckin'da."

"They're prisoners. Being' hauled to Hanoi today. We gotta find them before 1600 hours."

"Not great. What about the special ops team?"

"The entire SOG patrol and the gunship crew were killed."

Yellow lit another cigarette. "What about this rogue helicopter?"

"Not a coincidence. The prisoners escaped up the road and the H-34 is on their tail. So, tell me, what shit am I not gonna believe?"

"I just coldcocked Goddam Givens. Out."

Is there enough pasture to land?"

Trinh recoiled with indignation. "Only if you know what the fuck you're doing."

AFTER MY FACE slammed the water, Kaelyn fell on me. She latched onto my back. We sank to the bottom of the stream. I pulled her in front of me. With her eyes closed and body rigid, the water moved against us. My boots felt like wooden shoes. They stabilized me against the current, but they weren't much for swimming.

I couldn't see Beau but found a tree root along the bank. It gave me a handhold against the power of the water. Holding Kaelyn at her waist, she kicked her feet then wiggled around in my arms. The struggle turned into an embrace with our arms around each other. She clung to me like water on a frog until we surfaced. Air never smelled sweeter. Engine noise never louder. Waterfall never closer.

Breathing hard while pulling us out, Beau said, "Come on guys, no time for this."

I had plenty of time. It was just too hard to stop.

We collapsed against the steep incline of the bank. Trinh Le startled us when we discovered him perched on the log. Doing nothing but watching with his arm in a sling. He smirked. "Enjoy the water?"

My dry heaves blocked my response and didn't make sense after nearly drowning.

"Sure as hell did." Kaelyn opened her eyes and removed wet grass from her breasts. "What're you doing here? Where's our clothes?"

Trinh stared at Kaelyn's wet body. "Fortunately, your clothes were blown away by the down draft." He snapped an order to his crew in Vietnamese, "Move these round-eye devils next to the helicopter." Kaelyn whispered the translation through teeth.

The crew chief smelled like dead fish. He concentrated on her so intently I could have been a burning bush and he wouldn't notice. Maybe that's why he made us lay face down in the mud, not quite next to the 34. I could care less. Good old dirt. Sweet smell of grass. Warmth of the sun. I couldn't bitch through my incessant gagging.

Wow, this war-crap's really for the birds.

Vibrations felt strange when they were in sync with the slow beat of the giant engine. I had never been this close to an H-34. It sounded like a tractor compared to the sweet whine of the Huey. The blades revolved slowly, and their gentle breeze patted me with each pass. My earthworm perspective made the aircraft look as big as a barn. At 12 feet above the ground, the pilots sat over big ol' wheels at the end of long struts.

"Impressive isn't it?" Trinh understood my amazement. After all, we both went to the same flight school.

A big Chinese guy in a green flight suit ran from the cockpit. He shouted over the rumble of the engine, "Goddamn you Trinh. Landing area not big enough for helicopter."

"Ren. Ren. It's big enough, if you knew how to fly the fuckin' thing."

The Chinaman grabbed Trinh's shirt. "You sniveling shit."

Kaelyn kept translating.

"So what if you clipped a few branches. Not going to stop our mission." Trinh's smirk turned into a smile when he pushed aside the big Chinaman's hands.

Ren poked him in the chest with one finger. "I fly hundred hours in this. Rotor imbalance and strut damage invitation to disaster."

"Fuck off you stupid fool."

The pilot drew his revolver. "Hanoi seaplane evacuate prisoners 1600 hours." He cocked the hammer of his gun, "You not MACV operator. You under arrest."

Trinh nodded as he looked Ren in the eye. "Not a problem." He fired through his sling. Three quick shots in the middle of Ren's chest pitched his body backward. Bits of smoking gauze floated away in the down draft.

Kaelyn moved away but kept translating.

Chien Phu shouted, "Helicopter coming."

Trinh pointed to the cockpit. "Make sure the other pilot can fly."

I peeked through the grass at Chien. "Holy shit, that ol' boy's beaten death again. Sure looks different."

Beau said, "He's not wearing camo."

A shot rang out from the cockpit. Blood splattered against the side co-pilot window. Trinh Le motioned the crew chief to the mounted machine gun. "As soon as that chopper comes into range, shoot it down."

Chien signaled Trinh to board "You must fly. Pilot's dead.".

The chief fired short bursts at the approaching H-13 until blue smoke trailed from its exhaust. On the way down, the chopper released two rockets. At us. Ear-breaking explosions sent shrapnel screaming by and showered us with more mud. The 34 idled untouched.

Chien raised his hands in victory. He shouted, "Yes!" as bullets ricocheted over his head. He jumped into the ship for cover. "Where's it coming from?"

The chief pointed across the valley. "Another helicopter. I can't shoot at it. It'll hit our blades."

"Make this thing fly." Chien screamed into the cockpit. He moved with his AK to the other side of the tail boom. Heavy smoke belched from the exhaust when the engine increased to flight RPM.

I pointed to a trail for Kaelyn. "We gotta get the hell out of here."

"I'll get Ren's gun." She crawled on her hands and knees in front of me. Muscles in her naked butt tightened with each leg movement.

My eyes couldn't move off her until the big helicopter started rocking, like an outhouse in an earthquake. She squirmed back carrying the pistol. Wouldn't it make a lovely picture? A nationally known peace demonstrator and anti-gun activist.

Just the naked truth.

Leaning against the swaying tail section, Chien emptied a 30-round magazine at the approaching bird. Bullets danced off its bubble until it veered away.

Kaelyn shouted, "What's happening?"

I squinted through the swirling debris of the rotor wash. "It's thrashing itself to bits."

The 34's tail flexed violently, up and down. A cargo door sprung loose to the ground. Chien jumped on board and was bucked out. If noise was power, this bird would be over the ridge. Vibrations stopped the moment the aircraft bounded into a high hover.

About 50 meters away, the second H-13 rose in the air. It fired two pair of rockets into the wobbling giant next to us. Four explosions severed the pilots' compartment from the fuselage. The cockpit wedged itself between two trees. Rotor blades flew off like a scythe, chopping brush and limbs. Unattached, the tail rotor zipped into obscurity. A ball of fire enveloped the mid-section. Waves of scorching heat blew over us. Boxes of ammunition cooked off with military precision.

"Holy shit, beautiful." The burning rubble cast a glow on Beau's face.

The H-13 came forward from its firing position and hovered directly over the crash. I jumped up with both of my hands in the air, in what I hoped was the universal sign of help. The helicopter pointed machine guns at me and blew the smoldering stench of destruction over us. I wagged my head and screamed, "Noooo."

Kaelyn laid down her pistol and jumped with me. The incredible image drew the small chopper closer. Its rotor and engine whispered compared to the 34. Colonel Givens leaned forward, motionless, as the pilot gave us thumbs-up.

Shots rang out. Lying on his back, Chien fired into the belly of the bird only 15 feet above him. A shriek of mortal agony came from the helicopter as it tore itself apart. Clanking, squealing, ripping metal. Yet it clung to the air. Chien switched magazines. A solid stream of his bullets severed the tail rotor like a cleaver through a chicken's neck.

The bubble then turned in the direction opposite of the rotor. As a whirling cluster of burning metal, shiny plastic, and a desperate pilot, it screwed itself into the earth and flipped over. Both blades took turns beating the ground, throwing huge clusters of dirt at us. The last stub of the rotor pried the cabin up and slammed it down to punish it one more time. Raw av gas fumes mixed with the smell of hemorrhaging exhaust and oil.

All noise stopped. We rose to our feet. From deafening destruction to screaming silence. The dumbfounding quiet vanished with the sound of a receiver, locking a shell in its chamber. Chien staggered through the smoke of the burning hull with his AK pointed at us. The indestructible image of evil incarnate said, "I'm glad you made it."

Beau opened his hand to the ship. "Let me pull the pilot out."

Chien laughed as he shot the pilot through the bubble. "We can't take anyone else."

I couldn't stop staring at the hole in the pilot's head. One eye remained open.

"Lieutenant, Lieutenant what is the problem?" Chien lowered his rifle.

Kaelyn screamed right on cue. "My god, I can't stand this." She crumpled on the grass and cried hysterically. Her hair draped over Ren's pistol.

Ammunition from the burning H-34 exploded behind Chien. He recoiled.

From her kneeling position, Kaelyn cocked the hammer and aimed at him. Her hands shook.

"Come now, Miss DeHaven."

She jerked the trigger and shot over his head. Chien flinched then kicked the gun from her hands. He slapped her face, hard enough to knock her backwards and bring blood to her lip. She staggered but did not fall. Straightening her shoulders, she walked slowly toward him.

Chien's crooked smile widened. "You're remarkable," and drove the stock of the AK into her belly. She folded to the ground. Kaelyn laid in the mud, mouth wide open, trying to suck air in tiny gulps.

He aimed his rifle at her. "Now get up and move."

She took time to kneel and wipe mud off her breasts and stomach. But did not stand.

Chien shot one round over Kaelyn's head, then over Beau and me. The blast buffeted my face with a *boom crack whizz*.

"I'm worth more alive than dead." Her hands opened as a flower in bloom. "And Daddy will help."

An incredible iron tit response.

Something energized Chien, his eyes darted around, like he heard intruders. "Okay, lieutenant," he pointed with the rifle. "Go to the gorge. No more bullshit."

We moved amid chunks of the H-34 still smoldering. Beau identified each, "...avionics door, FM antenna, seat harness, headset..." If we weren't prisoners walking naked through the mountains, I'd say Beau was having a hell of a big time. He said, "Kaelyn, does Daddy like you to play in the mud naked."

She dead panned him, "Depends who's with me."

Chien paused at the solitary clank of metal-against-metal. "Shut up. No more talking. Go toward the sound." We walked across a new path where the solid undergrowth of bamboo and vines were cut. The culprit rotor blades lay mangled against a tree.

The bulbous nose and cockpit, minus its windshields, laid on its side. "Father." The weak voice was familiar, but the language disguised it.

"Yes. Are you alright?"

"Just trapped."

Kaelyn listened to the rest of the conversations in Vietnamese, but they spoke too fast for her to follow.

Chien tied us to a piece of the cargo compartment. In a few minutes, he cut Trinh loose and they stood side-by-side. Their striking resemblance explained a lot.

"Amazing." Kaelyn cocked her bruised face. "Do you want to tell us the rest of the story of this father and son team? Start with the North sending a seaplane. Flying into a war zone full of American aircraft is an extraordinary risk. We must have strategic importance. They're protecting their ass...or their assets. Which is it Trinh?"

A toothy smile brightened his face. "Yes."

SMOKE POURED out of White's helicopter as it crashed into the bamboo thicket. The blades

jerked to a stop while he shut everything down except radios. Vuong didn't move.

White transmitted, "Mayday, mayday, this is White Bird. Over."

"Roger. This is Bird Three. Say location."

"I'm between Hill 449 and Hon Heo Peak. Yellow Bird got hammered after he cooked the gook. Over."

"Say again all after Hon Heo..." Bird Three dissolved into nothing but weak static.

White turned to Vuong, "Don't know if the US Army would buy your story. Your chances are better if you had a score to settle with Chien. If you hear this chopper explode, a rescue is coming. Good luck."

As White watched him disappear in the bamboo, a new radio voice blasted, "Bird Three, this is Spark Gap Two-Zero, flight of two. Understand two birds down. Can we help, sir? Over."

"You bet your ass, where y' at?"

Spark Gap answered, "A click east of Hon Heo. Over the drink."

"And you understand the mess were we're in?"

"Affirmative. Lo-o-ve those little toys. We'll stay as long as we can play." Eight minutes later, the ARA flight found the valley. "White, this is Gap. Where y'at?"

"About 200 meters north of the saddle. Damn good to hear you. Over."

Two-Zero held a pattern above the ridge, "Stand by for recon. Break. Two-Two. Copy?"

"On the way. Wait." Two-Two started a steep descent. The distinctive *whop, whop, whop* sound of the Huey echoed in the valley. He flew over the crash site. A solitary plume of smoke climbed to the sky from the charred ruins of the 34. "Two bodies in the 13. One's alive."

"Zero this is Two."

"Go ahead."

"I betcha I could pick up those guys if you'd keep the shooters duckin'."

"Hey man. You don't get paid for that. We land only to rearm, refuel or pick up a partner."

"I don't give a happy damn. It could be me out there. If search isn't mounted up already, they're shit-outta-luck."

"Roger. You got room?"

"Affirmative."

"I betcha I can put some lead over their head. Break. How about it, White? Can you make it to the LZ?"

"Damn straight. Let me torch this honey first." White ripped the microphone out of the panel and grabbed his M16. He looked for Vuong in the bamboo but saw only green and more green. Tossing a grenade next to the fuel tanks, he said. "Duck, man."

Spark Gap leader prepped his wingman's approach with a run at probable targets around the LZ. Two-Two landed next to the burning carcass of the big helicopter. Not large enough to land on, and round on top, forced the pilot to keep full power at ground level. His tail boom hung over the stream.

White saw the problem and sprinted down the hill with his flight helmet on. He didn't slow down over the log. At the remnants of the 13, he cursed the bullet holes in the bubble. Tears ran down his face. White struggled to remove Yellow's remains to the ARA ship. "Why the hell did you get yourself killed. I promised Susan I'd protect ya'... sorry. She's the best thing you ever did. I'm gonna miss ya'."

The crew chief dislodged a groggy Colonel Givens and helped him board.

Zero flew low and slow to rake every possible target with more suppressive fire. He transmitted, "So ya' had room, did ya'?"

Two-Two stopped laughing when he couldn't hover. "This baby's gotta fly." He slid the ship through the hot debris like a snowplow, gained speed downhill, bounced off the bank, and got in the air.

Two's pilot called, "This is O'Shit. AC's dead. Got drilled as soon as he made it fly. My main rotor is doin' funny. Engine RPM goin' nuts. Over-grossed, the ship couldn't go high enough, quick enough so I waded through the treetops. Lucked out with no hidden stumps in the leaves."

Zero said, "Well... I'll be dipped in shit; 'twas bum-fuck ugly, but you're still flying."

AT 50 METERS below the landing zone, we couldn't see the sky through the triple canopy. But I heard the helicopter approach. "We need to get away from here." A fraction of a second later, explosions ripped the hill behind Chien. He hit the ground before we did. An inbound rocket sounded meaner than a mortar shell. It was a tube of death usually with a name on it rather than "to whom it may concern."

Chien rose with leaves and dirt on his clothes. "Put your hands behind you." He loved that ol' rope trick so much, he tied our hands again then lengthened the rope to Kaelyn. "I won't lose you this time. We have only two hours to make the rendezvous."

Trinh said, "I remember a quick way to the valley. Let me look." Even with his arm in a sling, Trinh climbed up the leaning tree then across the trail, sure-footed as a monkey. Dense brushwood covered every inch of the hill. Like magic, he vanished into the vines then reappeared. "This is it."

Mist from the waterfall cooled us but it made every surface slippery. The leaves smelled sour, the bark rotten. Our disastrous walk over the stream made me pay attention this time. No distractions. If the water stung from five feet, how would a belly flop feel to the dirt at ten?

Why couldn't I just fly instead of this ground-pounding bullshit?

Chien pushed me forward. "If you can fly a helicopter, surely you can climb a simple tree."

"But he's a fuckin' monkey with at least an arm and a half to balance with." The leaning tree made the log over the stream look like a highway. I gulped hard and climbed to the cross branch over the trail.

I'd rather die quickly than worry myself to death.

What started as a little rumble over the hill turned into a valley filled with the sound of two helicopters. Again. One stopped over our heads and shot in all directions except straight down. Shell casings fell through the trees like rain. Then it disappeared.

Kaelyn and Beau struggled to join me at the cross branch. She shouted at Chien over the noise, "Why don't you remove these ropes?"

Beau stifled a laugh, "Because you hide too much with your hands."

Chien looked at Trinh, "Be careful of the bitch. She is a viper waiting to kill you." Then he slipped on the shell casings and fell hard.

In the middle of our heroic effort to walk the plank, Beau laughed at Chien's fall and fell right on him.

Trinh bolted forward and stopped. "Father."

Chien's eyes blazed. He tried hard to catch his breath, "I'm alright."

Beau laid motionless on the muddy trail. Chien stood and kicked him in the ribs. "Okay, jackass, get up." Only silence. He kicked him harder. "How about something funny?"

Beau leaned up on his elbow. "Father? That's a knee-slapper alright."

"We don't have time for this." Chien leveled his rifle and fired into Beau's ear. Blood and brains splattered on Trinh's leg.

He shoved the warm muzzle high up Kaelyn's thigh, "Get into the cave."

She lurched sideways and almost screamed. "Okay."

Kaelyn walked deftly as a cat, I followed closely, imagining Chien in a coffin.

What a bastard.

Trinh Le came after us into the cave. Light shown through the vines like a grotesque mosaic. His disposition and voice changed. "Stop. Wait for Chien."

Branches broke as the skids dragged through the top of the trees. The helicopter finally returned. Its turbine whined as it clawed to hover above the canopy. Through the vines, Chien followed the sound overhead with his rifle. He squeezed off three bursts. The sound ripped at our ears. Echoes bounced forever. The helicopter limped away without killing our bad guys.

With a sadistic smile Chien said, "They'll shoot-up this place then get condemned for killing one of their own. Ha, ha. I love friendly fire."

Vuong squatted to study the landing zone after the rescue heli-copter limped erratically toward the sea. He listened to the valley and soft sounds of nature without man. Nothing stirred except the stream beneath the log and the smoke from the ruins of the three crashes. Like a fish on a stick, a wheel still smoldered on a strut. Stench of scorched rubber contaminated the mountain breeze. The overturned little chopper with both blades broken off looked like a pile of sad trash.

In the middle of the landing zone, the Chinese pilot lay in a blood soaked, bright green, flight suit. His bulging pockets begged to be examined. Vuong ate all the candy and nuts while he pocketed a flashlight and the aeronautical map of the Central Highlands.

Broken trees, burnt branches, ferns uprooted, and vestiges of the helicopters obscured the trail. Vuong felt like a forester until he found the dead prisoner. His naked body spoke silently of a painful journey, with bruised wrists, bloody knees, skinned thighs, and one bullet through his head.

Mist from the waterfall dampened the smoldering rocket damage of the trees. A column of smoke curved over the trail, disappearing into the hill of dense undergrowth. The leaves resembled the ferns but had the furtive look of a hiding place. Muddy footprints on the leaning limbs showed him the way.

Vuong climbed as fast as his pain would allow until he parted the vines into the caves' darkness. He waited for his eyes, ears, and nose to adjust to the stillness. Deep inhales and slow exhales cleared his mind. The smoke dissipated into mushy mildew, accentuated by bat guano. A flutter of tiny wings opened his ears for anything human. It arrived as a Vietnamese voice down deep below him saying "This is too steep, too slow...at 1600 hours."

Echoes of a second person responded in fragments, "...too dark...gold?"

Vuong recognized Chien but not the other. The path resembled a cliff rather than a cave. He scanned with the red beam for safe footing and called, *chec, chec, chec.*

Chien said from a pile of rocks, "How did you get here?"

"Escaped."

"Are you armed?"

"Yes. With a flashlight, map, and grenade."

"Your tricks are the same. Switch on your light. Come forward."

Vuong climbed down to Chien. He recognized the two prisoners standing naked with tape over their mouths and their hands tied behind them. "Who were you talking with before?"

"My son."

Trinh Le stepped out of the darkness. "We cannot waste any more time. Lead the way with your light."

Vuong concentrated on what he could see. The cave twisted from left to right, wide to narrow. Mostly a stubborn steepness cascaded over ragged chunks of clinkers, pea gravel, long stones, and boulders. "Where are we going?"

Trinh said, "To the beach. We have less than two hours to get there."

"Near the tunnel?"

"What tunnel?" The air left the conversation. Chien's irritation replaced it. "Bullshit, I would have known."

"Maps were verified; I walked in it." Vuong said with strength in his voice.

"So, what does that mean? How far is it to the beach?"

"I was never in *this* cave. The new tunnel connected several old caverns from Chanh Thang to the beach village. About four kilometers."

Trinh laughed. "This cave was blocked for years. It was used as the escape route from the ancestral beach estate of his third wife. Bao Dai loved the peacefulness of the valley and nearness of the sea."

"But there were so many stories."

"Of what?"

"People disappearing." Vuong shined his red beam ahead. "Gone without a trace."

"No trace in a cave? Come on."

"The mystery worsened with the story of Bao Dai's bullion. Villagers who tried to find it never returned."

Vuong said, "Feel that? The air is like a breeze. My light can't reach the walls. Wait." He clapped his hands. Echoes reverberated with an evil tenacity.

Chien slammed his rifle butt into the ground. "Quit fucking around. We have a schedule to keep."

"I can't."

"What do you mean you can't?"

"Can't see."

Chien stepped forward. "Get rid of the red lens."

Vuong switched to the white light. It stung his eyes.

"Huge." Trinh watched the beam expose the length and width of the opening.

"There has to be a way across, or down." Chien dropped a stone the size of an orange into the darkness. In a couple of seconds, rocks clattered.

Vuong gagged. "I can't see the bottom, but I can smell it."

Moaning through her taped mouth, Kaelyn nudged Danny. She maneuvered so he could pull the tape loose over her mouth, with his hands behind his back. "Damn it to hell." She shook her head, "Take these ropes off me. I'm not going anyplace. Shoot me if you have to, but why the hell don't you look up?"

Sᴘᴀʀᴋ Gᴀᴘ Tᴡᴏ-Zᴇʀᴏ released six rockets to the departure path of his wingman from the LZ. "If that gook is still shooting, get his autograph."

"He got us good on the way down." O'Shit checked the instruments.

"Yea. You're trailing smoke. Got too much lead in your sled, don't cha? Can you make it to the beach?"

"Beats the hell out 'a me. My panel warning lights could pass for a Christmas tree in here...daaamn."

"But you're still in the air. Not a hard call. It's fly or die."

White Bird grunted as he pulled the dead aircraft commander out of the front seat. He took his place and lit a cigarette. "It's been a while since I've flown a Huey. They stuck my ass in that 13 ever since I've been in country. Man, this feels like a bus compared to my little hot rod."

"I'm Fred Oszewski. Call me O'Shit."

White extended his hand. "Chuck—" Bullets shredded the control panel and switches. The ash tray bounced to the floor. "Hot damn. Way too close."

The crew chief stomped his feet and yelled, "One o'clock, tree line." Bullets pinged off their rotor, the crew chief returned fire with his M16. Spent casings bounced on Givens and the two dead pilots.

O'Shit transmitted, "Two-Zero, they're kickin' our ass from east side of the village. Over."

"Roger, I'll cook off a couple of my finest and see if we can't blow their mind." Four rockets screamed out of their pods. White poked at the windscreen with his gloved fingers, "Two o'clock, machine gun."

O'Shit banked to a direct line at the target. "This'll lighten our load." Two rockets sailed like they were on a string. His well-placed shot made him smile until the ship jolted from impact. A warning screeched in his ears, the chip light blossomed, and the transmission squealed loud enough to drown out the gun firing. He transmitted, "Goin' down."

Small arms fire pelted the helicopter like June bugs as he stretched his descent. Overcompensating for the beach, O'Shit flared too high and missed the target berm. His down draft created a swirling zero-zero sandstorm. Shit landed hard. The front skids rose in the air as the stinger jammed in the sand. A fragment of the Mayday call came in, "...I said Spark Gap Two-Two is down. Half a click south of a village...on the beach." The call faded.

O'Shit yelled, "Everyone out. Get the Colonel to cover." The blizzard of sand receded to a panoramic view of tall palm trees and a crystal whiter-than-white beach. Straight ahead, NVA soldiers streamed from their bunker, like rats out of a sinking ship. The crew chief and the gunner dumped Givens in a crater. He slid face-first to the bottom.

White tapped the engine gauge. "RPM's comin' back."

Spark Gap Two-Zero broke out of a dive above them. After releasing three pair of big ones into the palm trees, two secondary explosions choked the rat hole. "What the hell you guys doing? Un-ass that ship."

"I gonna fly." O'Shit bent closer to the gauges.

"Listen to that baby whine. It wants to go." White pounded on the glare shield like an excited drummer. "I'll get the crew back," he turned in his seat to look for them. "Goddamn…"

About 100 meters up the beach, three NVA knelt with RPG grenade launchers on their shoulders. They fired 40mm rockets simultaneously.

The first explosion landed on the rim of the crater. It blew the gunner and crew chief airborne, their bodies flopped in the sand. Two meters short of the helicopter, the second exploded. Shrapnel tore apart the left front door. White Bird's helmet blew off with the top of his head. Number three rocket exploded in front of the cockpit, unhinged the helicopter from the berm and tipped it over. Waves of sand churned from the blades and pinned O'Shit into his seat.

Fred was lucky. The top of the cabin hadn't crushed in, the blade didn't cut through the cockpit, and his head was still attached. Although hanging upside down made peeing a real bitch.

Two-Zero attacked the charging NVA with relentless precision. Some soldiers blew down into stillness on the sand. Others flew forward or backwards in a sea of torment. Guns, hats, and body parts spewed in the air. Concussion mixed with agonizing shrieks. Only the dust and the dead remained.

In the bottom of the crater, Colonel Givens stirred when the severed hand of the crew chief fell on him. He couldn't see the slaughter because he faced down in the hole. An odor like ammonia over rotten meat turned his stomach.

A Huey's rotor sound made him look up to three faint trails of smoke in the sky. Two shots hopelessly underestimated how to lead the helicopter. The third rocket collided with the top of the fuselage and blew the main rotor off. This guillotine slice sent Two-Zero into a death dive like a hurled spear. On impact, the rocket pod explosions showered the beach with secondary blasts, larger than the first. Detached blades rotated like a runaway pinwheel. They screwed into the beach with a giant splash of silent sand.

Givens saw the explosions. The aircraft crash was like a thousand fingernails scratching a blackboard, but more gut-wrenching. He hated the cold tentacles of death toying with his soul. His forehead sank back into the sand.

Jubilant Vietnamese voices rang out in child-like delight on the rim of his crater. They raised their RPGs in triumph, slapping them with their hands. The ammo bearer wearing a bulging backpack, waved his rifle back and forth, then drove his bayonet into the gunner's forehead. One NVA urinated on the crew chief. They all laughed.

O'Shit couldn't see anything but knees, boots, and urine falling less than five yards away. He slipped the .38 Special out of his shoulder holster, loaded with five, shiny tracer bullets.

Givens tightened his double hand grip on the .45 and clicked off the safety. The pistol sounded like a baby cannon and kicked like a mule. Four times. Two shooters arched their backs and lurched forward. While still urinating, the third turned halfway to receive the huge impact of the .45 slug in his gut. He spun sideways like a wet top. The ammo bearer couldn't remove the bayonet from the gunner. When the next bullet tore into the remaining rocket, the explosion kicked him onto the carcass of the chopper.

It looked like Givens got a bang out of that.

THE LIGHT BEAM passed over deeply striated rock. I said, "It's a goddamn hole."

Kaelyn touched the rope burn on her wrists. "About 20 feet wide or better."

Chien mumbled, "Vuong, give me your phosphorous grenade."

"Why is that sir?"

"I must see into the cavern." Exasperated, Chien pointed his AK. "I'll shoot you if you don't."

Vuong pulled the pin with a flourish. "Shoot only if you want to dance with the flames." His thumb held down the handle. "I've helped you twice, yet you still don't believe me."

"Nobody volunteers without a reason. You're anything but a simple peasant."

"And you are much more than a non-commissioned officer."

"Who am I then?" Chien's lips tightened.

Vuong's casual smile penetrated. "Your allegiance is to Bao Dai. Your son's loyalty is to you. You both lit up when I mentioned his name."

Chien's eyebrows raised, "And who do you serve?"

Vuong backed away. "I serve no one."

Chien cocked his head, "You sound like the CIA. You're conniving enough to be with Binh Xuen. Too smart to be an ARVN. Why don't you join us for Bao Dai?"

"Naah. I just look dumb."

Trinh leapt for Vuong's grenade and knocked it over the edge.

Kaelyn sprung forward to block Chien but only bumped his rifle loose. Shock contorted his face as he slammed into Vuong and Trinh. All three toppled into the hole. A blinding flash from the white phosphorous ignited their screams.

She stared at them. Boulders, bodies, and boxes burned on the bottom. What didn't sizzle, screamed. An eerie, flickering radiance danced above us on the rocks.

Kaelyn turned to me, stunned. "The nightmare that wouldn't end, finally did." She buried her face in my neck. "Danny." Her body writhed with deep sobs. Tears dripped on my chest.

Her exquisite softness pressed against me. Thigh to thigh, belly to belly, her breast to my chest. I found the small of her back. Rope once connected our necks, now tried to stop us. I pushed her away. "We gotta get out of here."

She wiggled back into my arms. "Nooo. Just hold me."

"Listen. You've had iron panties so far, this ain't the time to lose 'em. They gotta be lookin' for us. We have to hear 'em. See 'em." The flashlight still blazed into the black beyond.

Dazed, she shook her head. "Okay." A bashful smile crested her lips. Her eyes could've drowned me.

From the hole, an explosion shook the cave, shrapnel ricocheted, rocks fell from above. Secondary detonations made their way up the cavern like a mad dog, hungry for meat. A rocket shrieked past us to be a giant fireball. Ear numbing noise and debris scattered around the dome. We shielded our heads and ran.

"Get this rope off me!" She shouted, oblivious to bursts around her.

I pulled her along. "Screw the rope." Two more rockets created a double concussion. Like worlds colliding. A wave of dust chased us.

Bombs burned our butts, making us run up the cave until our lungs gave out. Kaelyn pulled me to a stop by my neck rope. She crumbled to her knees, blood on her lips.

I sat on a big cinder which was no fun with a bare ass, but less painful than pebbles or the sticky stones. "I gotta take my boot off."

"This coin in some paper is the problem. I got it in the hospital." I rubbed the mud off the title, *The U.S. Imperialists Are Facing Military Defeat and Political Failure in South Vietnam*. Kaelyn held the flashlight. The first six entries of the Contents were illegible. I read the last two:

VII The power of the United Vietnam with Emperor Bao Dai, Le Van Vien and Ho Chi Minh.

VIII Our allies in the US Press.

Kaelyn reached for the page. "This is a lethal combination of loyalists, organized crime and Communists. Where'd you get it?"

"From Anh, after the Arc Light bombing. I asked her to search the bodies. She found it on Doan Vien."

Kaelyn held the page next to her heart. "Anh took me to meet her villagers. A sweet person. I'd give anything to see that document." The hard-driving journalist reappeared. "Could this be why she wanted to get to the meeting so badly?"

"What meeting?"

"When we first entered the cave, Chien was unhappy and Trinh Le soothed him."

"So?"

"They spoke Vietnamese so quickly I didn't understand all of it. Something about Bao Dai's gold." Kaelyn paused. "And the beach at 1600 hours. We gotta get there."

"Screw the beach. Our chances are better in the valley."

On the verge of crying, she balled up her fists. "Fuck the valley. We gotta find that meeting."

"Have you noticed that we're not exactly in control?"

She straightened up while her nipples seemed to come to attention. "I know, I know. Something's wrong. Pushing Chien to his death didn't bother me."

"Because you knew what a swell guy he was. Don't forget, you tried to kill him twice."

She had that little girl-with-the-rosebud look.

I said, "It doesn't matter. We're trying to survive. You want to write about it—and I want to fly away from it."

"No, not just write. I gotta do something about it. Maybe this meeting is destiny. Maybe it's up to Bao Dai."

She paused for a moment. "Do you remember the canoe? It feels like a thousand years ago. You had a cramp, I massaged it away and remembered my daddy's words, 'If you find the right spot, you can make things happen.'"

THE AMMO BEARER blew apart in front of O'Shit's eyes. Body pieces bounced off the wind shield and chin bubble; only bloody smears remained. Someone once told him prayer might help so he said, "Holy Shit."

With one arm hanging dead at his side, the second RPG shooter crawled back to the top of the berm. Ten feet away, O'Shit hung upside-down in the pilot's seat, aiming his pistol. When he squeezed the trigger, the sound in the cockpit drove sharp pain to each ear, like nails into his brain. His tracer bullet burned through the shooter's torso and spun him around. Sand stuck to the NVA's pleading smile. Thick, black eyebrows glistened like tar in a puddle of piss.

O'Shit yelled, "Did you shoot the one in the air or on the ground?" When the dumbass gook nodded yes, O'Shit shot again.

For a few moments, O'Shit looked at a wisp of smoke crawling out of the barrel. A slight breeze blew away the smell he'd always liked. Not as good as muffins in the morning, but just like home on the shooting range. His first eyeball-to-eyeball kill didn't provide the orgasmic high his drill instructor promised. It was brutal as smashing a face with a rock lacking only the splatter of blood. But that's what he was here to do, kill or be killed.

———

Two dead NVA lay on the berm, another on the back slope with holes in his chest still smoking. In the silence following the carnage, a muffled radio call from the headset surprised O'Shit. He forgot to shut off the battery switch. "Gap Six this is O'Shit, over."

"Where you at, big boy?"

"On the beach, stuck in this goddamn helicopter."

"Come on man. We gotta lotta beach to work with. Where?"

"I'm north of Hon Heo. That's the best I can do."Givens opened his eyes. With his wounded leg, he struggled to crawl toward another headset. "Gap Six, this is Serpent Six, over."

O'Shit almost broke his neck trying to figure out where Givens was.

"Good to hear you Serpent. We thought you bought the farm."

"I damn near did and still might. Right now, we are about three clicks south of Chanh Thien. Gap Two Zero's been shot down. O'Shit and I are the only ones left. Over."

"Roger. Estimate one-five minutes to your location. Serpent Eight One Zero is flying chase. Will contact you one minute out. You have smoke? Over."

O'Shit answered, "Man, I'd love one."

Givens looked at the NVA soldiers pouring out of the tree line and transmitted, "Shii-it."

"Yes, sir?"

"Come on what's your real name?"

"Friedrich Oszewski."

A hard-to-achieve silence plopped in until Givens said, "Okay, Shit. Two-Zero didn't get 'em all. They're coming."

"I got a problem."

"What?"

"I'm pinned in this goddamn seat. Upside down. Get me out of here."

"No. Hang on. You still have almost a full load of rockets. They scare the hell out of most gooks, even if you don't hit 'em. Is your system working?"

"Can't tell for sure."

Sand splattered on Givens as he heard the report of several rifles. "Let's find out." Another shot ricocheted off the skids. "Fire right."

Two rockets flew over the tops of the trees to the left.

Givens waited for the blizzard from the blast to settle. He spit out the sand. "Goddamn, now try your other right."

O'Shit corrected and blew up the trees. "Alignment's Okay. Drop down a piece." Another puff of sand and several pings off the blades.

With the helicopter cabin balancing on the sandy berm, the tail boom hung 14 feet in the air. Upside down, it was three feet off the sand. Givens shouted, "I'll rock the ship. When it gets where you want it, rip one off. First left and then right." Forty-four feet of leverage allowed him to dip the nose low enough so Fred could get a good line. "Keep firing. Ya' got thirty loaded and twelve minutes to make them last. Alternate sides. Keep 'em guessing." The pain from Givens's leg impaired his concentration. Rocking the boat took more brawn than brains.

O'Shit shot six in a row. "Range correct, got their breeding hole on the right."

Moving the tail laterally required punishing a whole new set of muscles. Givens strained them three times before he got it right. Each step felt like a knife penetrating the bone.

The first mortar round kicked up a sandstorm to their left. O'Shit shouted, "Can you see the emplacement?"

"Fuck no. Fire faster." Another explosion on the right. Givens yelled, "Call Gap—they're on us."

"Gap Six this is Two-Two. We're in deep shit. And I can't swim." The third mortar landed a few yards in front of his windshield with a monstrous roar.

Givens hung on the stinger for one more frantic pull, "Shoot 'em all. Now!"

O'Shit squeezed the trigger as the nose rose. All the remaining rockets ignited in a giant flurry of fire. They raked the approaching soldiers in a straight line to the trees.

A fourth mortar hit the aft radio compartment, severed the tail, and killed Givens. Blast impact spun the cabin while the fifth explosion flipped his body from the aircraft. He lay spread eagle with his face buried in sand.

The last salvo eradicated the front line in the charge and reduced the second to half strength. These NVA remnants seemed unstoppable running at the last hated rocket ship, blowing whistles, whooping, hollering, and hacking the bodies of the crew.

O'Shit tried to relieve the pressure on his suspended body. He caught the dim glow of the indicator light. His eyes were blurry. A rocket hung in a tube. Couldn't tell how many. Didn't remember which way to clear it. Needed to pee but didn't want the shower. And now the little cockroaches were coming for him. In his anger he squeezed both triggers and pressed every goddamn button he could reach. Wishing for the wonderful *whoosh* of the rockets' red glare, while he shot into the line of NVA.

O'Shit watched bullets perforate the remaining Plexiglas of the chin bubble. "Gap Two-Two, this is Six..." The radio stopped but the punctures continued into O'Shit's unprotected stomach, above his chicken plate and through his sun visor.

▭

At 40 seconds out without response to his repeated calls, Gap Six transmitted, "Serpent, I got an active battery at nine o'clock and gooks running away from two burning aircraft at 12. I will engage. Stay at altitude unless we get whacked. Over."

Click. Click.

Gap Six took out the mortar emplacement with the first pair of rockets. Then stopped while Serpent followed with machine gun fire. Gap said, "Which part of 'stay' did you not understand?"

Serpent's voice crackled, "Goddamn near all of it...that was my

Six down there..." He held the transmit button down for air noise to hide his choke. "You said something about getting whacked. I thought you were offerin' me some weed. Sir. Over."

Gap Six flicked his cigarette outside. "Serpent and I go way back. To the same basic flight training class at Wolters. Now drop down and do the final check. Do not shut down. Just look for the living. We will circle with our finger on the trigger. Over."

"Wilco, Out." Serpent descended to a high hover, upwind from both of the burning ARA ships. He said. "Nothing left. Da god damned gooks smoked 'em. Counted nine bodies in the flames."

Gap Six made a low pass. "Okay. Follow me in trail. A scout identified NVA's with POW's going north along the stream below Hon Heo. Could be the missing journalist and pilots. Over."

Click. Click.

"And remember the rules of engagement."

"So, when do we fire?"

"You don't...until I tell ya'."

Click. Click.

The silence worried Gap Six. "Serpent, don't give me any of the *click-click* shit. Did you understand? Over."

"Roger. More or less...sir. Out."

ON HANDS AND KNEES, Kaelyn and I made it back to the entry of the cave. The air felt moist, sweet, and heavenly.

Kaelyn's body glistened with sweat. Only her face and breasts stuck out of the vines covering the cave's entry. She checked both ways like a kid at a school crossing. "What time is it?"

Her pose distracted me. "Time to get the hell outta here. Best guess, around 1500."

"Where's the beach?"

"About five clicks east."

"Can we make it in time?"

"You got to be shittin' me. We're on the deep jungle side of this mountain—" The faint sound of a Huey rotor popped into our conversation.

Her head jerked up. "Chopper?"

"Sure sounds like it."

"How can we signal 'em?"

"Don't know. I'm fresh out of napalm."

She almost growled, "Screw you."

"Yep, that's what I wanted. But right now, we gotta go to the crash site where the helicopter'll focus."

She bitched all the way up the hill. The boulders grew bigger, the hill got steeper, even ferns chewed us up. Everything glistened like the sweat pouring off our bodies. When the ARA ship and our slick popped over ridge, echoes bounced off the canyon walls. A symphony orchestra couldn't sound better. My heart did a backflip.

"Son of a bitch. This oughta get their attention." Kaelyn shouldered the AK.

I pulled the muzzle down. "What are you gonna do, shoot 'em? Don't be an idiot."

She stuck out her tongue, crossed her eyes and squeezed her cheeks for a funny noise.

Two shots from the other side of LZ made us duck behind a boulder. We peeked out at two gooks with light-colored conical hats moving next to the wreck of the H13. "I'll bet they were scrounging through the rubble."

Flying in trail, the helicopters paralleled the ridge line. The VC's long rifles followed them.

"Goddamn. The choppers are coming low enough to knock 'em down with a rock."

Kaelyn brought her weapon to position, "Those bastards ain't gonna stop me." She let off a long burst and the first shooter crumpled to the ground. The second gook fired shot after shot from a clumsy bolt-action rifle. Clueless to our location, he screamed, *"Dung Lai!"*

She whispered, "The dipshit wants us to stop." Her next burst blew off his hat and some of his head. Bullets impacting another human had a brutal finality. Hard to mistake. Or forget.

"Should've never let ya' carry that damn gun."

Kaelyn slammed in a full magazine. "Fuck 'em."

I said, "Just shootin' ain't gonna hack it."

She blinked like she finally understood the universe. "Then I'll give 'em something to look at." Handing me the rifle, she ran to the widest spot between the upside down 13, the burnt-out 34, and the dead gooks. Kaelyn chose a simple jumping-jack exercise to magnify her movements, allowing her goodies to bounce freely in a spell-binding rhythm.

The helicopters damn-near came to a halt. Even I rose to the occasion.

Ya' gotta love animal magnetism.

I scanned the surrounding area for leering looks and listened for any out-of-control slobber. Both helicopters turned our way. She kept on jumping, they kept coming. Until the slick was on short final, the bushes provided a decent cover. Then I wondered if anyone could mistake a bare-ass, red-headed, white boy for a Cong?

I hoped not.

The number 810 showed on the nose of the helicopter and the blue triangle covered the door. Made me feel like I was among friends. A lot of ash and trash blew away when the Huey came to a hover.

Another straw hat popped up, out of view of the door gunner, below the tail, and beyond the downdraft. The Cong pulled out a grenade, went into a straight arm pose like in World War Two movies. I squeezed the trigger three times. Didn't know how many times I hit him, but he fell on the grenade. A muffled explosion tossed the body up into the air like a feed bag. On the ground, shoulder length, black hair unfurled on the body of a skinny woman. Remnants of her clothes smoldered.

Glad I didn't know he was a her before I pulled the trigger.

Kaelyn ran to the ship. The smiling gunner jumped outside to help her in. Crew chief laid covering fire as I sprinted to get onboard. As soon as my sweaty butt landed on the cold cargo deck, the Huey climbed straight up. The ARA ship covered us by ripping up the perimeter of the LZ with machine gun fire.

Sweat in the tropics turned cooler at a thousand feet. Black bars were sewn on the starched collar of the aircraft commander. I shouted, "Captain, thanks a bunch. Can we get something to wear? At least a shirt. And headsets would help."

He asked reluctantly, "Gunner, chief: You wearin' tee shirts?"

"No sir. Only od sleeveless."

"That'll have to do. Take 'em off." The captain turned around for one last look.

While we waited for our shirts, Kaelyn leaned on the captain's seat. "Thanks Captain. What time is it?"

"1538 or—"

"I know what that means." Just fly me direct to Chang Thien."

"And where in the hell is that?"

I handed him the map. "A heading of six-zero will get you there."

"Now just a goddamn minute. Who says we're going anywhere but Qui Nhon?"

"I did. I'm Kaelyn De Haven, AP Correspondent. My columns are syndicated in over 90 cities in the US. My father is Orville DeHaven, Defense Appropriations Committee Chairman, Senator from Texas. He'll make sure you get a paycheck and a promotion."

"So? We're in a fuckin' war, babe. We're gonna do what'll save your ass because our orders are to bring you back. I could give-a-shit-less about this ass-kissin' Army. I'm out-a-here when my tour's up."

"Okay so my heart bleeds for ya', but here's the deal. At 1600 hours, the strategic players against the US will be in Chang Thien. I wanna to be at that meeting."

"Oh, is that all?"

"No. As committee chairman, Daddy can put you in front of recruiters and hiring committees, before you can say good-bye to all your asshole buddies."

"Are you done yet?"

"Not exactly. I don't want you and your other ship to be seen. Don't wanna scare 'em away."

"Being loud and slow, we're hard to hide. Where's the meeting?"

"Don't know for sure. Near the water."

The Captain signaled a gentle bank to the pilot and transmitted her demands to the ARA ship.

Gap Six resigned himself with a grunt. "We got twelve minutes to go. I'll circle at altitude. You cruise up the valley. Pop over the ridge at 1600."

"Roger. You're as fucked up as she is."

"Done dumber stuff. If we don't and she takes it to the press or daddy—you can pick your poison. Or prison."

"Roger. Out." The captain turned this time to look in her eyes. "Miss De Haven. So why the hell haven't we heard about this? I'm tight with the G2 and this didn't appear on any of his intel boards."

"Between no information and crap that's wrong, you guys operate without a clue."

"No shit. So, what are we gonna do when they see us?"

She smiled in her sweaty undershirt with the rope still around her neck. "I'm gonna interview them."

"Really?" The captain tilted his head. "How do we do that?"

"That's up to you."

"Gap. It's 1559." The captain did a quick stop behind the ridge. "Man, oh, man, look at that." A large amphibian plane touched down on the water about a hundred meters offshore. It floated high to a group of eight junks in a u-formation.

"Serpent, turn around immediately, get high behind him."

The pilot did a 180-degree pedal turn that made Kaelyn scream. She lurched at the pilot's seat while a breast slipped out of her roomy shirt. A quick hip and shoulder move brought the flopping boob behind the sweaty green.

Gap transmitted, "Miss D. Are you sure you want that interview?"

She stomped the floor so hard, I thought we got hit with a fifty. "Goddamn right I am."

Kaelyn leaned out of the open door of Serpent 810 and screamed at the amphibian, like it could hear her, "I don't know who you are, but your story is mine."

The radio blared over our headsets, "Serpent, this is Gap Six. I'll contact them on guard channel."

"And what're ya' gonna say?"

"I'll tell them who you got and what we want."

"Big fuckin' deal. They gonna blow your ass right out of the sky."

"Not if I can get above his take-off path at two thousand feet. Beyond the junk's range—I hope."

"Roger. What's your offer?"

"She interviews the commander on the beach for twenty minutes. While we circle."

"Brilliant. Brilliant." Kaelyn clapped her hands in glee then stopped cold. "Why only twenty minutes?"

I pointed at the fuel gauge. "Gap won't be able to make it back if he doesn't leave then. Neither will we."

The captain transmitted, "Six, it's your show. Time is 1601. At two thousand feet, the only thing that could reach us is a 20mm or a

51." His grave digger laugh sent a chill up my stinky shirt. The gunner must have slept in snake shit before he gave it to me.

Radio blurted through the static, "Serpent. The deal is on! We get a free pass during the meeting and they get a free exit for the amphibian. I'll contact Navy. Put Miss DeHaven down as quick as you can. On the widest chunk of beach. Did you get her some clothes?"

The captain started his descent with a smile. "Reluctantly."

We dropped at over 3000 feet per minute, straight down. "Pucker up. We're going into the mouth of the tiger." The chopper landed about five meters from the water and kicked up a cloud of sand.

When the cloud blew away, Kaelyn unbuckled her seat belt.

I couldn't resist patting her ass. "Good luck, babe."

Kaelyn returned an impish smile with wide, clear eyes. "I couldn't have done this without you." She caressed my face and kissed my lips. Not long or passionate but simply warm with genuine feeling. Then she slapped me hard enough to make my eyes water.

I'd seen her polar opposites before, but never felt them.

Kaelyn jumped to the beach, ducked beneath the rotors, and gave a thumb's up to the pilot. She stood in her combat boots with tearing eyes and muddy hair. With two fingers extended in a victory sign, she pointed at me until the downdraft forced her to shield her face. Her sleeveless top inflated past her arm pits for one last, good look.

We flew over the water close enough to see fish and pass the amphibian at cockpit level. A rocket pod and two machine guns hung under each wing. A flotilla of Cong junks formed a menacing perimeter more than 50 meters wide. I laughed. "I can feel their eyes drilling holes in us. Ships are low in the water. Carrying something big."

Our slow climb turned discomfort into agony. The captain watched over his armor shield with binoculars. He said, "Yeah, looks like an artillery piece under that canvas. A small motorboat is leaving the plane. Goddamn, an ARVN's at the wheel...drivin' it right up on shore. He's bowing to her, she's backing away."

Our helicopter climbed into orbit; the captain wiped the perspiration from his face. "This is nuts, man. If she doesn't get back, we're fried. If those junks open up, we're toast. Lovely, just fuckin' lovely."

Gap called, "G2's having a shit-fit 'cause the Navy doesn't want to fly."

"Keep your tubes loaded. We're in for the whole ride." The captain's head quickly turned from side to side. "Holy shit. The amphibian's crankin' both engines." A thick, bluish-gray cloud of smoke belched from each engine of the big plane.

Gap broke through the static again, "Serpent! Serpent! She asked to go to Hanoi with them. Got 'em in my glass. She isn't restrained."

I tapped the captain. "Get me an angle so I can see their faces." With his binoculars, I found Kaelyn sitting next to the ARVN, who had one arm in a green sling. "Well, I'll be dipped...it's Trinh Le...but it can't be. I saw him die."

"What do you mean?"

"He helped his father capture us. Both died in the cave."

"You sure?"

"I'm not sure of anything. But a 40-meter fall into a pit, closely followed by white phosphorus explosion...that'd slow down Superman."

The captain fidgeted in his seat like his pants were on fire. "Are you done yet? I want some distance from these turkeys."

"Wait, wait they're boarding..." I laughed. "Ah, come on."

"Now what?"

"She raised her arm and slapped the inside of her elbow. Then boarded"

"So?"

"In Cleveland, that's an Italian hand-sign for fuck you." I laughed. "Man, she's something else. No hammer is big enough."

The captain banked hard out of the target zone. "So, why'd she flip you the bird?"

I rubbed my cheek. "It's her departing wish. She's such a romantic."

Almost mechanically, the protective line of junks opened a departure path. The gray silhouette of the amphibian contrasted the bright, royal blue of the water. Its wake went wide until lift off when it banked smoothly to gain altitude.

"Serpent, this is Gap Six. Navy's bitchin' about the free travel. That goddamn strap-hanger won't turn 'em loose."

Captain tapped the airspeed indicator. "With this head wind, just dump it." The pilot traded altitude for air speed until streaks of red terror glowed by us on both sides.

I almost forgot how much I hated tracers.

An airburst went off about ten seconds in front of us. We flew through its smoke and felt a bump.

The pilot missed another explosion with a 60 degree turn but ran into tracers. A bullet went through the door post and knocked out a hole the size of my fist. The second one ripped off the movable armor shield from the pilot's seat, tore open his right arm and knocked his helmet off.

"Get those fuckin' junks!" The captain rescued the controls. "Danny, get up here."

I unbuckled the wounded pilot and pulled him back to the gunner. His blood-soaked seat didn't feel right on my bare ass. But neither did my missing side armor and chicken plate.

The captain made another steep bank while Gap Six dueled with two of the junks.

"Lookie here now. Navy jets." They impressed me even more when they fired at the bad asses that just ate our lunch. It took a little longer than a blink to blow by. I got on the controls again and they felt good. Muzzle flashes from the junks were big as flame throwers. Three mid-air explosions greeted the lead jet. It was like the movies of the flack against the bombers over Germany.

The captain said, "Goddamned flechette round."

Smoke streamed from the lead jet as it released the napalm. Two shiny canisters flipped slowly to land midway on the first junk. Fire engulfed it and the next two ships. Secondary explosions spread the burn to the fourth ship. Flames gushed from the jet as it turned hard to the east and gained altitude. Both the pilot and weapons officer bailed while it arched like a flaming arrow into the pond.

The captain pointed to an intercept point. "Gap, we'll follow 'em down." Two parachutes floated toward the shore. As they descended, a junk separate from the rest, opened up with machine guns. Tracers crisscrossed the chutes. "Return that fire."

Crew chief laid an entire box into the junk. All tracers. Within the first ten seconds, the junk stopped shooting. With the rest of the box, he nailed the ship until a blast at dead center sent bright orange streaks into the sky. He never let go of the trigger until the gun stopped, red hot.

As soon as the jet jock splashed down, he swam to his motionless partner. A sheen of blood covered his floatation gear. I hovered with my skids in the water so our crew could drag 'em in.

The captain transmitted, "We're low on fuel. Headin' to the barn. Where's the other jet?"

Gap blasted back, "Don't know. Navy said the amphibian was not NVA, Cong, or ARVN."

"How the hell would they know?"

"They have a lock on what's leaving the North and South."

"Ah, bullshit. Did he even see the amphibian?"

"The jock chased it up the coast past Bong Song. Then ran into a curtain of fire. The F-4 got roughed up. Barely made it back to the carrier."

"It can't just disappear. Not with the girl onboard."

Gap said, "Oh yeah? She might be in deep shit with that interview, but she's standing on our head."

"Bullshit. If you haven't been there and done that, you wouldn't understand. That story is hers. Out."

Jerome Gladysz served in Vietnam as a helicopter pilot in the First Cavalry Division (Airmobile). For his service he was awarded the Distinguished Flying Cross, Bronze Star, and Air Medal with 24 oak leaf clusters. He also holds a Bachelor of Business Administration from John Carroll University, and an Executive Master of Business Administration from Texas Christian University. After almost 40 years in marketing, Jerome is tolerating retirement. He'd much rather be in the middle of the action – whatever and wherever it is.